GENESEE FEVER

To

Lola and Whit
with love

Carl

Carl Carmer
Christmas, 1941

Books by Carl Carmer

DEEP SOUTH

STARS FELL ON ALABAMA

LISTEN FOR A LONESOME DRUM

THE HURRICANE'S CHILDREN

THE HUDSON

GENESEE FEVER

GENESEE FEVER

BY CARL CARMER

FARRAR & RINEHART, INC.

NEW YORK   TORONTO

To Three Brothers

MYRON *and* WILLIS *and* HERMAN

and their Sisters, Wives, and Children

I write these sentences to readers who, like me, want to know the relative proportion of fact and fiction in what they read. All the chief events of this tale (dinners, launchings, fights, shows, celebrations, and so on) are matters of historical record. With the exceptions of Nathan Hart, Whirling Gragg, Eleanor FitzHugh, and Catherine O'Bail, all of the characters were actual residents of the Genesee Country. I have given them qualities and abilities ascribed to them by their contemporaries, and on many occasions have let them speak in words authentically set down as their own.

Many people have given me friendly aid in obtaining the materials out of which this book has been made. Though I cannot name them all, I would seem ungrateful indeed if I did not express my sincere thanks for the assistance of Arthur C. Parker, Director of the Rochester Municipal Museum; Arnold Potter and Mrs. Walter A. Henricks of Penn Yan, New York; Miss Content Peckham of New York City; and Professor Ernest Bernbaum of the University of Illinois.

CARL CARMER.

1793

"May we cultivate the vine and sheaf
In this new world and furnish the old with bread."

(Familiar Toast of the 1790's)

I

"*I fit in the Revolution,*" said a voice just below Nathan Hart's ear, "an' when we got the peace in eighty-three I never thought I'd live to see the day when we'd be fightin' each other. Ten years, an' here's you an' me bein' marched through Philadelphy like dancin' bears."

The chatter of the fat little man, almost running to keep up with his long strides, began to bring to Nathan some sort of consciousness of the picture of which he was a part. Ahead of him lay a long narrow street lined with brick houses. He and his short companion were marching at the rear of a long double file of shambling, haggard, muddy men. Blue-uniformed soldiers marched beside them. Their muskets slanted over their shoulders in stiff parallel lines. Hundreds of people stood at the curb, and the open windows of the houses were filled with faces. There was a great gay sound in the raw, sun-brightened March air. A snatch of song rang out above it:

"I am a law-abidin' drinker
So I'll not buy from Tom the Tinker!"

Nathan looked down on his mud-stained tow shirt, his damp breeches of wrinkled homespun, his boots, stiff and water-soaked. He looked upon the dangling rectangle that hung across his chest and for the first time since his great rage had come over him he saw it as wood and paint. He was surprised that so many of the letters were easily recognizable. The W looked like an M, but the H, I, and S were the same upside down. The K and E, though turned about, were obviously K and E, but the Y looked like a flagstaff on a mountain peak.

"I couldn't read mine if it was right side up," said the voice of the little man. "Know what it says just the same—'Whiskey

3

Rebel,' that's what it says—an' you'll excuse me for laffin' at a schoolmaster wearin' a badge so unfittin'.' "

"Schoolmaster," said Nathan bitterly, and then the blackness out of which his mind had just come swept over it again.

The man laughed and buttoned his brown butternut coat into a series of wrinkles across his ridiculously round paunch. "Guess you're right," he said. "You ain't no schoolmaster—not now!"

Once more light entered the whirling darkness. While Nathan's body kept up its rhythmic swinging down the cobbled pavement a glowing beam was traveling back through a tunnel of years to himself—a boy—waked in the attic of his father's York valley cabin by the ripping of shingles from the roof above his head. Wind, tearing down from the Laurel Mountains, was rushing round and round the bowl of the valley. He had seen a bobcat run in such circles once, when his father had tempted it with raw meat into an empty cabin and shut the door. Every time it loped by the barred window through which Nathan looked it had whined in a despairing agony.

Nathan knew now—as the sound of the little man's voice gradually brought back awareness—that, like the wind, like the cat, his mind had been racing about within inexorable walls, frantic with the necessity of escape. And he felt that as the slow rhythm of dawn had brought rest and clean, bitter light into the wind-swept valley, as the sure timing of death had brought stillness to the thrashing animal, the inevitable rhythm of going on had begun its healing in himself.

A blare of brass sounded ahead of him. He ran a hand through his unkempt sandy hair and took a deep breath. His fists clenched. His eyes sought first one side of the street, then the other. He must get away. It would be better to die than go on.

"Nice place, Philadelphy," said the little man casually. "Ain't seen this part before. Never got higher up than the taverns an' whorehouses down by the river. They was fixed up pretty nice back in seventy-nine jest after the British skedaddled. Know the town well?" His small blue eyes looked up with sincere questioning.

Nathan laughed shortly. He wondered if the man was trying to be kind.

"Yes. Been coming back every so often since I left school here."

"Ye have, eh? Sounds like a woman to me. Should've stuck to her an' left makin' liquor alone. Ye could make a livin' all right without bein' a Tom the Tinker. Women, bein' already distilled so to speak, ain't subject to tax."

Nathan had known that he would see her again ever since that night when he had heard the knock and opened the door and they had been standing there in the moonlight—two uniformed men with muskets raised and a captain in braided regimentals. The officer had been brusque.

"The house is surrounded. You are under arrest by national authority for violation of the liquor-excise law."

"I don't make liquor. I'm a schoolteacher."

"You know why we're here. You have counseled and aided these people in armed rebellion against proper authority."

"Because I say a man ought to be allowed to take the juice of his grain to market in place of the grain itself? The Constitution says I can say that. Are we run by the Constitution or that monarchist foreign bastard, Hamilton?"

"I don't argue laws. I enforce 'em."

Nathan looked at him contemptuously. "It's hardly ten years since we got rid of George the Third and already you Federalists have set up another tyranny."

"Take him," said the captain, and that had been the moment Nathan had felt the sureness of seeing her—before the long march across the mountains and down the old Philadelphia road, before the nights in the lousy jails, the wading of icy streams, the starvation meals, the bayonet pricking his belly while the captain dropped the derisive wooden label about his neck.

Now it was happening. She was standing on a second-story balcony to his right and she was laughing as he had somehow known she would be. He could see her throw back her head in the gesture he loved and he knew the tricks that lights were playing in her hazel-brown eyes. He saw the swing of her dress as her sturdy figure bent backward in merriment. Then he was looking upward into her face as she turned and leaned over the balcony rail. Once more he was seeing her straight, full-lipped mouth, her strong nose, the curve of her brown hair about her cheeks, above her wide brow. Her hand dropped to the rail, closed on it hard. Her eyes were on him but the muscles of her face did not move. It seemed to Nathan that the shock of seeing him with the wooden sign about his neck had stunned her. He turned his head to keep her in his sight as he marched on and saw a man clasp her arm and point down to his companion. He heard the man's laughter first, then her own—the laugh he had listened to more often than counting would tell him. Nathan turned his head and tramped on. It seemed that he was still hearing her when the marching stopped before the door of a stone building. The captain who had arrested him climbed the stone steps and opened an official-looking paper as though to read it.

Nathan wondered afterward why he chose that moment to run. It seemed to him, looking back, that he had put aside the idea after the long march when with every step he had thought of escape. It seemed that his action was instinctive rather than planned. He was thinking of her laughter, yet his legs leaped to the side and his arms tore off the painted board at the same time. He did not remember that he heard the order "Ground arms!" before he leaped, but consciously or unconsciously he had chosen the second when the command was in execution. The butt of every gun in the detachment was on its way to the pavement. The soldier nearest Nathan, catching a flicker of movement out of the corner of his eye, tried frantically to seize his musket and use it as a club, but as he raised it Nathan's board cracked down upon his skull. There was a sound of splintering wood and Nathan was racing back between the lines of spectators. If he could reach the corner thirty yards away before they recovered from their surprise and surged forward he might plunge into a quiet side street. He had gone ten paces before the roar of the crowd told him that they knew what was happening. He heard sharp commands and looking back saw a soldier kneel to fire, then lower his musket as two small boys rushed into the street and started the chase. Ahead of him at his right two men were running toward him. He slanted toward the left corner and realized that he would not reach it before they caught him. He stuck out his right hand, palm open, into the nearest runner's face and drove forward with his legs. The man lost his balance and fell heavily against his companion. A woman screamed and fell in a heap on the pavement as Nathan reached the corner. A fat Negress bent over her, blocking off his nearest pursuer. He was in the side street and running with exaltation. . . .

II

"*Don't go in,*" said Nathan.

She turned with her right hand at her throat. In the dusk he could see it stroking the little V of flesh above the line of her dress. "You shouldn't have hidden by this house," she said. "They might look for you here."

"And that would humiliate you, wouldn't it?"

"Don't be silly," she said, and he wondered if his imagining had created the note of impatience in her voice or if it were really there. "I just mustn't see you."

"Why not?"

"You know how my mother feels. It was bad enough for you to talk the way you did. Now—"

"Now that I'm a jailbird—"

"It isn't that. Of course people may differ. Why, Uncle John agrees with you—in principle. But—"

"But what?"

"I hate to think of your being a part of the crew they're marching to the prison. They're not people like you. That gross little man beside you—bowing and waving his placard at everybody as if it were something to be proud of. If you want to fight his battles why not do it legally, get Uncle John to help you?"

"To hell with Uncle John!"

She stepped forward quickly and put a hand on his arm. He looked into her eyes and saw there the old look that had captured him—a look both serious and quizzical as if she were almost ready to laugh at her own sincerity.

"Now I've made you angry. I didn't mean to. But I'm worried. You've sacrificed your career. It might have been distinguished. What will you do now?"

8

"I don't know," he said, looking down at his shrunk and muddied clothes.

"Mother says that a man who breaks his life in the middle never amounts to anything afterward."

"So you've talked this over with your mother?"

"I couldn't help it. She was home this afternoon when I came in after—after—"

"Do you love me?" said Nathan roughly.

"You've had proof of that."

He looked at her grimly, remembering the sweetness of her lips, the firm smoothness of her flesh, the stout clinging of her body.

"Come with me, then."

"Where?"

"Anywhere. Go in that house and pack your clothes."

"But Mother would forbid it."

"Do it anyway."

"I couldn't hurt her that much."

"Don't tell her. I'll meet you at the back door in ten minutes."

"I couldn't deceive her. I want to be honest with her."

"Listen to me. I don't want to hurt your feelings but I don't give a continental damn about your mother. Come with me now or I'll know this is the end."

"Don't say that," she said slowly, and in the dusk her eyes seemed brighter. "This isn't the right time for me to see you. You've broken the law and escaped from arrest. Get out of trouble. Uncle John will help you. Then start again. Perhaps you could read law with Uncle John. After a while perhaps you could teach again—in another state. And after you are established—if we still love each other—"

"Is that your idea or your mother's?" he said fiercely. Her hand was again at her throat. The hand and throat were an indistinct glimmer, a little blurred white cloud in the darkness.

"Why, both," she said.

Nathan turned on his heel and walked away.

III

*The square stone house was solid on the hillside. Isolated tri-*angular patches of snow lay on the slopes above it, remnants of the scattered army encamped about the upper reaches of the bowl-like valley. Water took the light here and there beneath the nap of greening grasses in the yard. Far below, Codonus Creek lay in shining curves at the bottom of York valley. A lank, white-haired old man sat on the sunlit wooden steps outside the front door with his son.

"Nate," he said, crossing his right leg over his left knee, "we didn't expect this kind of trouble from you. You've always been sort of hasty—but you've been smart, too. We've been mighty proud of your schoolin' and all. And you've certainly helped your folks. Remember when this house here was nothin' but a one-room cabin and you slept in the attic?"

"Yes, Pa."

"Couldn't a-built this place if 'twasn't fer you. Well, after it was built and you finished school and went to teachin' we thought maybe you'd get married and settle down over the mountain there. Heard you was ridin' to Philadelphy regular. Then this come—" The old man stopped. After a moment he went on reflectively.

"Seein' things different must of come from yer ma. I always done what I thought was right, but seems like I was always on the side of the most folks. Yer ma ain't like that. She does sorta unexpected things every now and then—like namin' that long-shanked mare I give her Charlotte Corday. Reckon ye got your ideas from her along with your brown eyes an' that snubbed nose. None of the Harts ever had no snubbed nose."

The gay eyes under his thick snowy eyebrows looked on Nathan quizzically.

"I 'member ye was about the gangliest colt in these parts. Hair was a sight redder'n it is now. Always makin' up yer mind first an' bein' sorry after. Drilled yerself with my old musket down thar in the lower forty hollerin' commands like ye was G. Washington himself. Goin' t' kill all the redcoats from York to Kingdom Come, ye was. But when I took ye to Philadelphy to see Burgoyne's Hessians on their way south to prison ye wanted to let 'em all loose."

"They weren't to blame," said Nathan.

"That's always been the trouble with ye," said the old man impatiently, "tryin' to figger out who's to blame an' all that. When ye git it worked out, like as not ye're wrong. Now take this liquor business. Ye wasn't makin' it yerself. Ye could a kep' on teachin' school and mindin' yer own business. But jest because some farmers couldn't git their wagons over the mountains when they was loaded with heavy grain an' took to haulin' a few illegal distilled kegs instead, ye join up with 'em an' holler about unjust taxes on distilled sperits."

"They were right," said Nathan hotly. "You can haul a load to market and they can't. The only way they can lighten their loads is to distill the grain. Just because they're across the mountains—should they have to pay high taxes on their crops when you don't have to?"

"I don't know what it's all about," said the father wearily. "All I know is the best way to git along is not to have no trouble with the law."

"That's the kind of talk that makes me and all the rest into Tom the Tinker," said Nathan. "Mr. Hamilton and Mr. Adams sit up there at the capitol, not knowing wheat from barley, and get the Congress to tax the only distilled liquors that poor folks can afford. I've heard tell they've persuaded even Mr. Washington that they're right. The only one that takes up for ordinary folks is Mr. Jefferson, and they say he's going to be put out of the Cabinet for talking against aristocrats and a hifalutin' government."

"Here, here now," said the old man sharply. "I don't keer how much ye carry on, but ye leave George Washington out of it. I won't hear no talk agin him."

"Pa," said Nathan. "We better stop talking. You know what's on my mind. I've got to get going."

"I been thinkin'," said the old man, and his voice had gentled and held almost a pleading note, "that mebbe if ye laid low fer a little while until things blowed over ye could come back here and work this farm. I could work this land on shares with ye and it'd give up a real comfortable livin'; yes sir, a mighty comfortable livin'—enough fer all of us and a few more—a wife fer ye an' a grandson or two fer me. I been thinkin' about settin' out that lower forty in Injun corn an'—"

"Pa," said Nathan, "if they didn't come for me right away, I'd think they'd be coming some time. I've got to go. I think I know where I'm going. It's not so far I can't get back once in a while. I'm going, Pa."

"Well, boy," said the old man, stretching his long legs in their worn yarn stockings and homespun breeches. "I knowed ye was goin' all along. Just wanted to bid ye welcome to stay. Ye better lay that on thick with your ma—about yer comin' back often. She'll want to be thinkin' of that. But it don't fool me none. I've seen ye go away before. This time I won't expect ye back no more."

"I'll be coming before you know it, Pa."

"Way I figure it is this. If I was to die I wouldn't be seein' ye any more anyway, now would I? An' at my age that's somethin' ye got to expect pretty soon. When ye go and I say good-bye it'll be a kind of special way of dyin' as fer as ye're consarned—standin' up with some guts in me and my land under my boots."

"Forget it, Pa. You won't be dying for a long time yet. I'll be bringing you those grandsons."

"Well, either way's all right with me, boy. There's plenty of folks to look after us. But ye better cheer up yer mother. I'll go in now and start gettin' her ready for the idee." He rose and went heavily up the steps. At the door he stopped, looking back. "Ye can have yer ma's mare, Charlotte Corday. I call her Lottie when yer ma ain't around. We won't be needin' her. I've got the oxen fer plowin' an' the colt. Ye need money?"

Nathan shook his head.

"Got most of a half-year's pay."

"What was ye plannin' on bein' whe nye get where ye're goin'?"

"I don't know, Pa. Might go back to painting wagons—

like I did when I was getting my schooling. Think I could do
tavern signs, too."

"Better stick to yer wagon boxes. Ye ain't no pitcher
painter."

"One time I did General Washington on one side of a
blue Conestoga and Mount Vernon on the other. The owner
liked 'em."

The old man chuckled.

"They sure won't be lookin' for a Whiskey Boy in a
pitcher painter. Bound for the Genesee Country, ain't ye?"

"How did you figure it, Pa?"

"To hear 'em talk there's a good livin' up there an' no
questions asked."

"That's where I'm going, Pa. And I'm taking my old paints
with me."

The door closed behind the old man, and for a while
Nathan sat and looked out over the sunlit valley. Then he stood
up and followed his father.

IV

"I got to thinking that most every woman goes through something like this sometime," said Nathan's tall mother. She ladled corn mush out of the kettle hanging in the fireplace until the bowl in her left hand was full and then placed it before her son.

"Think of Joseph's mother, I said to myself. She lost her youngest and had to live with sons that were really bad. I've got one son and he's a good boy and I know where he's going. Then I turned over and said to myself, now you can go to sleep."

"I didn't heer no talkin'," said her husband from his chair by the window. Light had begun to fill the sky above the valley and to settle on the pines that lined its high edges. It sifted through the window and made clear his quizzical, affectionate smile.

"Oh, you go on," said his wife. "You know what I mean. But I couldn't get to sleep even then. Seems as though everything Nate ever did kept coming back to me—the time when he was four and went out to weed the garden like his pa and pulled up all the corn sprouts—"

"An' ye wouldn't let me whale 'im."

"He didn't know any better. He was tryin' t'help."

"He'd a knowed better if I'd fetched him a couple licks on his seat."

"Are you going to start that again?" said Nathan, grinning. "Anybody'd think you spoiled me forever by one act of mercy."

His mother looked at him keenly and then at her husband.

"You two don't need to keep up this play acting," she said severely. "I'm not going to get myself upset about Nate's going. That's what I been trying to tell you. Nate's a man now and I've decided that whatever he does suits me."

"Well," said Nathan, swallowing a spoonful of hot mush hastily, "it's about time."

"It was different when your pa let you march off with the militia to fight the Britishers and Indians when you were only fourteen. 'You can't take my baby,' I said—"

"Ye said more'n that," the old man grinned. "I'd ruther faced a chance o' Injuns—but that youngster would a gone off by hisself if I hadn't took him with me."

"If you'd found that raiding party I'd never have forgiven you."

"Ye took on most as much when he went off to Pittsburgh to paint wagons."

"I never minded his going off to school," she said, "but Pittsburgh was a low, immoral town an' no place fer a young lad. He got a lot of ideas there I don't approve of to this day. They tell me painters are never strict about women—"

Nathan laughed.

"Wagon painters are different."

"You're no more a wagon painter than I am, Nathan Hart, and you know it. That man should have been ashamed to pay you so little to put those pretty pictures on wagon boards. Every one ought to be on a canvas."

"All right," said Nathan, "I'm a sinful canvas splasher instead of a pious decorator of Conestogas."

"Well, I should think so."

"I thought he done mighty good," said the old man, "earnin' money enough to go t'school in Philadelphy. The thing I don't like come later when he got to teachin'. He didn't have no call to get mixed up with them liquor makers from the west o' the state."

"You leave him alone," said Nathan's mother fiercely. "He did what he thought he ought to. No woman likes to see her son get in trouble and have to go away, but I'm satisfied he did what he thought was right and I want him to get out of here before anybody comes after him."

"Going right now, Ma," said Nathan cheerfully.

"I put some boiled ham and wheat bread in your saddlebags and I've got something for you."

"What is it, Ma?"

"I thought of it and made your pa cut it out for you this morning before you were up."

She went into the front room and came back immediately holding her right hand behind her. Standing before Nathan she suddenly brought forth a wide, thin slab of white pine in which at one corner a round hole had been carved.

"A new palette," said Nathan. "It's a beauty."

"It's cleaner than the old one," said his mother defensively, "and you better keep it that way so that you make a good impression where you're going."

"I will, Ma. Thanks. It's a fine present."

"Better go now, son," said the old man. "I don't want to have to hold 'em off with my gun."

"They won't be here for a while, Pa, but I'm going."

He went to the door and opened it. Charlotte Corday, hitched to the post outside, whickered and turned her head, regarding him with big reproachful eyes. She was a long-legged, long-bodied chestnut with a big barrel-like nose. In the center of her forehead, below her pert ears, was a shapeless haphazard splotch of white.

"Good-bye, Ma!" He threw both arms around his mother and held her close.

"Good-bye, Nate," she said cheerfully. "You'll be coming back to us before very long."

"Yes." He shook hands with his father.

He untied the bridle and swung up into the saddle. His mother put a hand on the soft nose of the horse.

"Good-bye, Charlotte," she said. "Don't shy at any more butterflies."

The mare trotted down the familiar path. Her gait was awkward but she covered ground swiftly. When Nathan was about fifty yards away he turned about.

His mother's head was on his father's shoulder and she was sobbing convulsively.

V

Nathan rode east and north along Codonus Creek until the brown waters of the wide Susquehanna gleamed through the trees ahead. Then he turned upstream. During the day he chose to ride close to the river, sometimes in it when the bottom was gravelly and the water not too deep. For two days' ride he could depend upon recognizable landmarks to guide him. He forded the little Conewago in the late morning and in midafternoon the rippling waters of Yellow Breeches. That night he tethered Lottie on the banks of the Conodoguinet not more than a quarter mile from the west end of Harris's Ferry and, when the lights in the cabins below had gone out, he hobbled her and let her graze a few hours in the high brown grass while he slept. His rest was fitful. His mind was still striving to realize the new condition of his life. Sometimes when he dozed he would waken with a start, reaching for his gun—certain that pursuers had come upon him.

In the morning, after he had bathed his face and hands in the stream and eaten sparingly of the boiled ham and wheat bread which his mother had placed in his saddlebags, he faced northward again. And as he rode he felt despair settle upon him, despair and shame and a heavy, spiritless lassitude. His stomach sank within him and his mind was one dull ache. He tried to imagine a life ahead for himself, wondering where he would first dare to join other men again. What would he say when they asked him of his past? Would they believe he was a painter? Perhaps he would have done better to give himself up. In jail there would be a bed and three meals a day. After he was let out he could go back to painting wagons.

Then he thought of his arrest and the long march into Philadelphia and his quarrel with the mother-ridden, mewling girl on the steps of her home; and he urged his horse forward.

17

He heard voices ahead of him when the sun was high and spurred Lottie away from the river, making for Paul Reider's ferry across the Juniata. The raft ferry lay on the south side of the river as he rode up and he saw Reider seated on a chair at the far end holding a fishing pole. He stood up as Nathan led Lottie aboard.

"Don't need no ferry with that horse," he said lazily. "Jest drive her into the river and walk across on her backbone." He was so silent and so impassive of countenance as he poled his craft across the swirling water that Nathan suspected him of knowing his passenger to be a fugitive. He was the more certain of this when Reider, having run the ferry on the shelving north bank, said suddenly:

"Mahantango's mighty riled. Better keep straight north from here if ye want to cross her. Ye kin meet up with the west branch o' the Susquehanna later if ye folly Penn's Crick down towards Northumberland."

Nathan did not reach the banks of Penn's Creek until the next morning. He bore eastward farther than he had intended and unexpectedly came upon the Susquehanna below the creek's entrance at a spot where bladelike rocks, just below the surface, drew a thin white line across the dark water. There, lulled by the chatter of the riffle, he slept.

He spent the third day on a slanting ride up the sides of the Laurel Mountains. Often he had to leave the river and try to find an inland passage that would bring him back to it at some less impassable point. More than once he was forced to retrace his steps and try again. There was snow on the crests of the Laurels and Lottie picked her way delicately and slowly. In the afternoon came a slow, drizzling rain. A steep cliff towering over roiling deep water once more turned him away from the river. When he came upon it again he could see by the vague glimmer in the west that the stream now flowed from that direction and he knew then that he must go on to the north without its friendly guidance. He found a shallow riffle, crossed to the north bank, and plunged into the forest.

He rode steadily through the continuous rain-whisper of the woods and at last the night was black around him. Realizing then that he could no longer stay on his course he looked for shelter. Complete darkness had come so quickly that he

could not find even an overhanging ledge to keep off the rain.
He tied his mare to a pine. She looked at him inquiringly.
"Good night, Lottie," he said. "I'll do better by you after this.
There'll be butterflies to shy at soon." He slapped her steaming
flank assuringly and lay down a few yards away. He stayed
awake, shivering, for a long time, while his mind went back
to the old circling of the wall of events that had hedged him
in. Grayness had begun to sift among the trunks of the trees
before he slept.

When he awakened the ground was mottled with shadows,
and rays of light had found small openings through the high
foliage. He discovered a pool of rain water and drank deeply.
Then, munching on his wheat bread, he rode north.

The sun was directly above him before he saw river water
again. He was puzzled at first because the stream on his left
was flowing north, but, after calculating as best he could the
number of miles he had ridden since he left the Susquehanna,
he reckoned that he was on the banks of the Tioga and rode
downstream.

The river was smaller and seemed more friendly. The sun
was bright and warm and there was a smell of coming buds in
the air. From each patch of snow along the banks tiny drip-
pings trickled into the smooth stream. The trees stood wider
apart here. The tamaracks and hickories had been dark and
close upon the mountains, but beside the chuckling water now
the willows and the beeches made creamy patterns against the
sky. Just at sunset he came to a cabin clearing. He would have
circled it if a little girl had not appeared in the path just in
front of him and said, in a language he identified as French,
something he did not understand.

At the sound of the girl's voice her mother rushed from
the cabin and ran to her baby. She was a thickset, dark woman
with a mobile face and large brown eyes. A coarse, loose dress,
caught in at the waist by a leather belt, hung down to her bare
ankles. She wore no shoes. She smiled at seeing Nathan and
said "Bonjour, monsieur." She motioned to him to tie the mare
and follow her to the cabin. As he did so her husband, dressed
in tow frock and trousers, strolled out, his gun under his arm.

Then by alternate gestures and shouting in French they
bade Nathan welcome. The woman at once set to work cooking

supper in the cabin fireplace. Nathan saw her make a paste out of corn flour and water, roll it into little balls, and place them on an iron skillet which she had greased with a piece of salt pork. Into her coffee pot she dumped water and a handful of burned corn kernels. The cakes were soggy and unsalted, the coffee was a muddy, weak mixture, and Nathan was glad when supper was over. He felt safe with these people, but he was embarrassed at his ignorance of their language and his dislike of their food. The woman chattered steadily—as if by very rush of words she could make him understand a portion of her meaning. The little girl flirtatiously offered him portions of her cakes and giggled delightedly when he took them.

After dinner the man motioned his guest to the only bed in the cabin—a wide board structure over which lay two dirty woolen blankets. When Nathan asked awkwardly by signs and grimaces where the family was to sleep the woman pointed to herself, her husband, and her child, and then out of the door to a covered shed which sheltered a small stack of hay. Nathan pointed to it and then to himself and nodded vigorously. The outside couch was far more inviting to him than the bed. The woman seemed relieved. The haycock would obviously accommodate one sleeper far more easily than three.

This settled, the Frenchman and his wife both shook hands cordially with their guest and the little girl put up her cheek for a kiss. Immediately the man took off his pants, and the wife loosened her belt and fingered the button at the top of her one-piece dress. Nathan left the cabin and walked out to the shed. The hay needed leveling off if he was to sleep upon it. He lifted his right foot and kicked the pinnacle of the stack.

A rumble that came from nowhere filled the night and the stack suddenly came alive. There was a cascade of hay and out of its stringy veil something white arose. For a moment it was impossible for Nathan to connect all the elements of the picture in front of him into a unified whole. Apparently a ghost had materialized from the dry grass, and gradually it was taking the shape of a tall man, clad in the pure garments of sainthood. Now, out of a bushy beard, jet black against his white robe, poured roar upon roar of outrage. Stunned with astonishment and fright Nathan looked on, motionless.

"I—I didn't know you were there," he said lamely.

"By the Eternal," shouted the bearded one, "the prophets have ever been persecuted, but they have sometimes retaliated. Remember the bears who ate the children! Remember—"

"Sorry I kicked you," said Nathan, "but who are you and what are you doing here?"

The bearded one rose on tiptoe and lifted a bare arm toward the sky.

"I am Elijah," he said, "habitant of the body of the late James Parker of Rhode Island. I cry aloud in the wilderness where there are none to hear."

The door of the cabin opened and the Frenchman stood naked in the starlight—his woods rifle aimed at the bearded head.

"Don't shoot," shouted Elijah, "*C'est moi, le Prophète.*"

"*C'est ça,*" said the Frenchman with a sigh and closed the door.

"You may share my couch," said the Prophet abruptly and he began spreading the hay about with vigor. Suddenly he stopped and glared at Nathan and shouted, "Unless you follow The Friend."

"What?" said Nathan.

"No," said Elijah. "A young man, strong and right-minded, a young man, long-legged and lusty, would not be deceived by that profane blasphemer, that female deceiver of the weak, that Pretendress to Divinity."

He switched his white robe about and scratched his thigh.

"Perhaps you are a raven," he said mildly.

"I don't understand you," said Nathan.

"A raven. A raven. 'And the ravens brought him bread and flesh in the morning and bread and flesh in the evening.'"

"I have boiled ham and wheat bread in my saddlebags."

"Then you are a raven," said Elijah and he shook hands solemnly.

After the food had been fetched the Prophet munched contentedly and talked less formally. The Genesee Country, he said, was but a day's ride northward. There was plenty of work there. There were houses to be built and seeds to be sown. The soil was rich and it could be bought cheap. In some sections there were many trees, and clearing the land was hard.

But the great flats along the river and beside some of the smaller streams were almost treeless and there the grasses grew to a height far above a man's head. Dangerous animals—bears, wolves, and wildcats—had begun to disappear, though a trader could still make a good living from the furs of minks and foxes and muskrats. Flocks of wild pigeons darkened the skies above the river every spring. There were fish in the waters to be had for the taking. Indians were growing a hundred bushels of corn to the acre in their flatlands. Settlers were beginning to plant hemp and flax and tobacco, and all were doing well.

"Why don't you live there yourself," said Nathan, "if it's the heaven you say?"

"I do," roared Elijah, "and it was heaven until the Vale of Kedron was rent in twain. Until the Universal Friend betrayed herself and me, we dwelt beside still waters in a land of milk and honey." He went on for a moment matter-of-factly. "I've been in New Town buying seeds and now I'm going home. As soon as my spring sowing is done," his voice rose again, "my cry shall be heard through all the land proclaiming that sin has seized upon The Friend."

"Who is The Friend?"

"The Spirit of Life from God before she assumed the power of the Almighty. I came with her to the Vale—I and Rachel Malin who is the prophet Daniel operating in these latter days in the female line—and together we counseled the faithful and our words were good."

"But what happened? Why are you angry with her?"

"She cast me out because of a little child. For years she preached at me—a seventh child—that all must love God more than earthly pleasure. Time and again she told me I must leave my wife and live as celibate as she. And when my seventh child was born she took my mantle from me before all the faithful and proclaimed I was no more Elijah." The prophet's voice rose sharply to a sudden sob. He turned and lay face downward in the hay. The shed was silent, then, all night.

VI

The little French girl awakened them. Nathan and Elijah fed and watered their horses. Smoke rose from the cabin chimney and the woman came to the door to beckon them inside. Breakfast was the same as the last night's supper and Nathan saw that the Prophet found the foragings of these ravens distasteful. He noted, too, that the Prophet's robe, a long white gown with voluminous flowing sleeves, though creased from the night in the hay, was clean and that he had an air of authority. He kept up a constant flow of remarks to his hosts in their own language, and when he had finished he put a hand beneath his robe disclosing a wide white girdle about his waist. From underneath this he took a fat purse and offered to pay for his meal. Nathan immediately reached for his own purse but the French couple with profuse gestures refused recompense.

As Elijah returned his money to its accustomed place Nathan saw him fumble at the wide belt for a moment. Then he went on drinking his corn coffee. A minute later the Frenchman leaped to his feet and crossed himself. At the same moment his wife's eyes seemed to project from their sockets in horror, and in a second she was on her knees and bending her head while unintelligible prayers came from her lips. The little girl had begun to cry piteously. Alarmed, Nathan turned to Elijah and doubted his senses—for the Prophet had begun to swell. From his chest to his waist he was popping out like a blown-up pig bladder. Greater and greater he grew while his four companions looked on in stunned wonder. Suddenly then, when it seemed that he must burst if his upper belly extended any farther, he spoke:

"I am Elijah," he said, "and I am filled with the wind of prophecy; I look into the future and I see this home blessed with other offspring as few homes are blessed. I see ten children more to honor this union and I see wide lands tilled and great harvests reaped. I see my young friend beside me here the lord of acres by a long blue lake—a husband and a father. And I see her—The Publick Universal Friend—no longer immortal, forsaking Time. And behind her I see her people—like a flight of steps supported by a single beam—breaking down as their main support is destroyed. All, all will come to nothing. I have spoken."

During this whole speech the wind of prophecy had been obviously seeping out of Elijah. When he had finished he was of the same size he had been before he began to swell. Then, as if he had been a mere auditor of his own words, he translated them to the French couple, and the woman giggled and ran out of the cabin. But when Nathan and Elijah had mounted their horses and were ready to take the north road she came back. Nathan told them the name of his mare and they roared with laughter, making swift remarks to each other which he could not understand. Then all three waved and smiled until their guests had ridden out of sight.

Feeling sure that he was beyond pursuit Nathan decided to accept Elijah's pressing invitations and ride with him into the Genesee Country. He felt a little uncertain however when, after fording the river to the north bank and covering only a mile, they came upon a wide clearing containing a half-dozen log cabins centered around a tall wooden pole, carved into fantastic figures and painted in many colors.

"Painted Post," said Elijah briefly. "Now we ride the Williamsburg road." Over a cabin door just opposite the variegated column the words PEOPLE'S STORE had been lettered in white and with little regard for spacing. Under a wide elm beside the cabin squatted two Indian men, wrapped in identical blankets of red and yellow and blue. While one looked on in rapt admiration the other was earnestly playing a jew's-harp. A lanky white man lounged out of the store.

"Good morning, Mr. Parker," he said, "an' did ye get your seed at New Town?"

"I did, Bill Harris," said Elijah, "and by this time next year I hope you'll be keeping seed yourself, instead of beads and tobacco and scalping knives and the Devil's other inventions."

Harris laughed.

"I buy what I can sell," he said. "Except whiskey. Ye'd rather have Nellie Fuller pour that fer ye."

"A clever woman," said the Prophet. "But I must go back to my farm and my wife and my new seventh child. Besides it's too early for whiskey."

The jew's-harp was still droning as Nathan and Elijah left the clearing. Neither Indian had looked up from his fascinating pastime. Before the riders lay a wagon-wide road through the forest. The stumps of trees rose in countless projections from its bed, though some were hidden in the jungle of alder bushes that had risen after the road builders had passed. Off to their left the waters of the little river were one bright gleam save where the shadows of bare limbs fell across them. Here and there sycamores had sent out great leprous roots that dipped gnarled white fingers into the stream.

Nathan had discovered by now that his new friend spoke with shrewdness and common sense as long as his mind was not on his former leader. He told of his farm near Crooked Lake and its stand of hard maples, even now yielding gallons of sap to be boiled into sugar. He said that he sometimes wondered if plowing was necessary on his acres—for an Indian family nearby had simply stuck their seeds in the earth and had obtained a full harvest. Wheat had brought a dollar a bushel last year and he expected to plant ten acres more of it this season.

"And now, young man," said the Prophet unexpectedly, "why did you come here? To join the Captain or are you an honest citizen?"

"I do not know the Captain," said Nathan slowly, and the old sick feeling of being a fugitive overwhelmed him for a moment.

"That recommends you," said Elijah, "but how will you earn your keep?"

"I am a painter," said Nathan uncertainly.

"A painter! You mean a picture painter—a man who can make colored likenesses of places and people?"

"I do general painting," said Nathan weakly, "wagons and tavern signs and such."

Elijah's blue eyes glistened and his beard seemed to tremble with eagerness.

"And you could paint a picture of the prophet Elijah crying aloud in the wilderness?"

"I could try."

"A painter came to Geneva a year ago," said Elijah, bouncing eagerly up and down in his stirrups, "but he had all of his paintings already done except the face. They were from the belly up and the men wore coats and the females wore neckcloths and breastpins. He would paint your face in and give you the whole thing for four dollars. Could you paint me from the feet up and get my robe and beard in?"

"Yes," said Nathan.

"I shall be standing like this," said Elijah, raising an arm in a prophetic gesture and beginning to shout, "and The Universal Friend shall look upon it and repent. She shall stand before it and know the true prophet."

"It won't be good enough for that," said Nathan.

"I will inspire it," said Elijah.

VII

The two men had ridden steadily all of the forenoon when Elijah, telling Nathan to follow, turned his horse from the road and urged it up a steep incline. For twenty minutes or so the horses climbed on, coming out suddenly upon an open plateau.

"Look down," said Elijah, "and mark the line between the Dark Country and the Genesee Country. Look south, and as far as you can see the pines and hemlocks are almost black. Below us are the flats of the Conhocton covered with grass and scattered oaks and poplars." The measured sound of an ax biting into wood came up to them from far below. "Down there," said Elijah, "the Captain is building a dwelling for the ungodly, a Sodom of corruption—"

"Who is this Captain?" said Nathan.

"Charles Williamson, Charles the Great, Baron of the Backwoods, Warden of the Wilderness, King of the Conhocton, Agent of the Devil.

"He has been sent to the Genesee Country by its British owners who call themselves the London Associates. They bought a tract of nearly two million acres from the American Robert Morris, who had it in his turn from the partners, Phelps and Gorham. Now they have organized the North American Land Company and hired this Beelzebub to sell it for them at a road agent's prices. He wants only sinners and revelers about him—that they may lure other sinners and revelers to his lands."

Elijah stopped speaking as if overcome by his own vehemence. Then he went on casually, "Beyond that blue gorge that breaks the hills is Crooked Lake. We'll soon be home."

Three hours later the two men rode into a wide clearing almost filled with cabins and sheds. It stood on a small hill and each building was at a different level, the largest one, obviously

27

the dwelling, being lowest of all. Hardly fifty yards down the slope from it a narrow blue lake lay still in the cold night of late March. Nathan could see that a high green point divided its waters only a few miles away, making them lie in an irregular Y shape.

"Home," said Elijah, and he uttered a long whoop which brought buxom, smiling Mrs. Parker to the door of the dwelling, seventh child on one arm, sixth at her side. An avalanche of children followed, all bent on being the first to greet their father. Nathan, standing aside and smiling, saw that this mouther of wild words was a man of property and loved by his family.

When Elijah had explained Nathan's presence he said, "The young man will live with us until I can spare him time to paint my picture. And when it is done," he turned to Nathan, "I'll pay you eight dollars for it, and perhaps then you'll paint the Captain or go to Big Tree to paint old Bill Wadsworth and his brother. But mine will be the first—the Prophet Elijah crying out."

Eagerly the older children—a boy of about twelve and two girls somewhat younger—aided the travelers in removing their saddlebags and harness and tethering the horses. Then there was a fire blazing in the fireplace as the air grew cool and sundown was near. When there were only hot coals left a smell permeated the whole cabin, and it was so compelling it brought Nathan close to the fire. There his hostess told him with a serious smile that though her husband had been known at The Friend's Settlement for years as the Prophet Elijah, she had always been known as Mrs. Parker. She gave him a pan of frying pickerel to hold, while she tended to the roasting wild turkey in the oven and the kettle of boiling yellow ears of Indian corn. Nathan told her of his meal the night before and of how her husband and he had found their breakfast hardly to be eaten. At that she shook her head in sympathy with the poor French family, but she hurried the supper and before long all but the baby were listening to the loud roaring of Elijah's grace before meat. Then all ate until there was almost nothing left and Elijah remembered only once during the meal that he was a prophet crying out. When they left the supper table the children washed the plates and the knives and forks, while Nathan and Elijah and Mrs. Parker sat before the fire. After they had finished their work the boys and girls stretched out on the bearskin rug before their elders and asked Nathan questions about the Laurel Mountains and his home in the valley. And Nathan said nothing about being a teacher or a rebel against liquor taxes and he did not speak once of Philadelphia.

The next morning after breakfast Elijah brought up the subject of the painting. Life-size, he said, was the smallest he'd consider, and he wanted a fancy frame around it. Hastily Nathan raised an objection. He had expected when he set out from Pennsylvania to paint only wagons and tavern signs. He had brought no canvas with him.

"Take your time," said Elijah. "I'll ask the Captain to order some from the first post that rides to Northumberland. You can get your paints and palette out of your saddlebags and start practicing up. Young Barnaby here can fit you a couple of boards so you can't tell where they're joined. I'll be busy logging today anyway. Sam Cobwell and Solomon Bull are coming to help."

"Then I'll help, too," said Nathan.

"No, no," said the Prophet. "You'll paint and Barnaby will help. He's been running wild since he left the school at The Friend's Settlement."

VIII

An hour later Barnaby, with two smooth boards skillfully joined on an underframe, presented himself before Nathan. Carrying the improvised canvas he led the way up a trail beside the lake. Twice Nathan suggested that they stop and consider the view as matter for a picture, but the boy protested earnestly and led on. They had walked perhaps two miles with the lake constantly in sight when Barnaby stopped on a little rise of the shoreline and let Nathan come up with him.

"There," he said pointing ahead. "It lies right to the morning sun."

Below them lay a little semicircular green cove. At its deepest indentation a full brook splashed into the lake. The curving, shining channel led back and up to a large white frame house shaped like an L with the long side facing the wide water. It stood in dazzling brightness and its reflecting white sides gave it so clean and luminous a quality that sight of it seemed almost unbearable in the intense clarity. The effect was the stronger for the softness of the atmosphere that lay upon the lake. Out there was blueness and a misty blending of light and air. Here the sun seemed to have sent a straight shaft down to illumine the objects within a sharply defined circle. In the center stood the tall white house, and on the edges but still within the light squatted weathered gray log cabins. Beyond the circle other cabins, many of them, were indistinct in the blurred distance. Where the upward slope of the shore ended on a high plateau a grove of towering hickories dispelled the light and seemed to keep it from spilling outside the circle.

"It's the Vale of Kedron," said Barnaby, "where The Great Friend lives. We lived there once and sometimes I wish we'd go back—only I'm afraid of her."

"It's beautiful," said Nathan, and as they stood looking

they heard sounds coming from the white house—syllables as clear as the light in which it stood, voices as sure in tone as bells, girls' voices in swift risings and fallings.

"She lives with seven handmaidens," said Barnaby eagerly, "and they wash her feet and dry them with their hair. I would like to see them wash her feet, but my mother says The Great Friend doesn't like little boys and girls. Shall we paint the picture here?"

So Nathan found a sapling and trimmed it with his knife until only a few twigs remained, and they held the board surface Barnaby had made as well as any easel. Then, while the boy watched, he mixed his paints on the white-pine palette his mother had given him and tried to paint what he could see. He was ashamed that he had said he was a painter, but where the lake showed blue he spread blue on the board, and he made a frame of budding limbs that dipped into the gray of the cabins which seemed to kneel around the edges of the scene. In the center he painted, stiff and awkward and straight-lined, the shiny white house, with its big windows divided by small white threads into tiny squares of glass. He had never tried to paint glass before, and he tried again and again to get the glimmer of it and to catch the color that lay in and behind it. He was trying so hard that he had forgotten Barnaby and the passage of time; he had even let slip from him for a moment the bitter consciousness of all that had happened to him in the last few days. And so when he heard a voice it seemed to come from far away although it was not far.

"Barnaby, Barnaby Parker. You are wrong to come here, you know The Friend will not—"

Turning from the picture Nathan saw her standing there in her gray dress and with the rim of her gray bonnet not quite shading the deep blue of her eyes. She had stopped speaking in her surprise at seeing a stranger, but there was no hint of embarrassment or of fear in her face. Though she had been moving as she spoke to Barnaby, her body, stopping short, was as lithe and as balanced as a hickory on the slope beyond her. Her face beneath the straight lines of her strictly confined, dark-brown hair was fair and tinged with rosy color underneath the skin, her nose was straight and small, and her mouth was wide and curving slightly upward at each side. And though the gray dress fell full from the trim white collar of her neck, its folds lay like stripes of shadow on the deep curving of her breasts.

"I'm sorry, sir," she said. "I did not know that Barnaby was with a companion."

"I hope that we do not trespass," said Nathan.

The girl seemed to hesitate. A troubled look came into the big blue eyes.

"I do not know," she said. "The Great Friend has forbidden his father and his father's family—"

"I'm going back home anyway," said Barnaby agreeably. "I'm tired of watching him paint. I'm going hunting when I get home."

"I'll go too," said Nathan quickly, wondering whether loyalty to Elijah forbade him to stay with the girl. But Barnaby was already trotting along the homeward path, and as Nathan started to lift his wet picture from the sapling he stopped at her sudden exclamation. He looked at her and he thought that never in his life had he seen such delight in a human face. The blue eyes seemed to darken and fill with light, the lips of the broad mouth parted, showing strong white teeth, though she was not quite smiling; a quick intake of breath lifted the folds lying on her breasts.

"It is very beautiful," she said.

Nathan knew it was not beautiful. His ignorance of painting and his inability to draw were too apparent. And yet the girl seemed honest in her delight and a warming glow spread within him.

"The scene itself is better," he said.

"It is my home," she said and added, rather hastily it seemed to Nathan, "it is the home The Publick Universal Friend inhabits with some of those who love her. They will want to see the picture. Would you come with me into the house and show it to them?"

Nathan felt as if he were walking in a dream as they approached the white house and the clear sounds of the voices inside grew louder and louder. It was not until he and the girl were climbing the three steps which led to the fine, fluted doorway that he felt silly and helpless.

"Come," said the girl and, as if she understood his hesitancy, she took from him the painted board and went into the house. They entered a large, bare, high-ceilinged room. Along the walls on either side stood many sturdy wooden chairs—perhaps fifty of them—and at the end was a small platform surmounted by a graceful pulpit of carved wood. Nathan saw six girls, all in gray dresses like that of his companion but without the white collar at the neck, busily cleaning the floor, the windows, the chairs, and it seemed to him that they all uttered one startled squeak of surprise as they saw him.

"See what the young man has painted," said the girl beside him, holding the boards out in front of her and looking very flushed and eager. Instantly the picture was the center of the group as the girls converged excitedly upon it, exclaiming as they came. Nathan stood self-consciously outside the circle, wishing himself anywhere but where he was—save for the fact that all these girls were young and pretty, though none so lovely as the one who held the painting. Excitedly the latter moved about, pointing here and there to familiar objects reproduced on the board, and the others responded with soft ohs and ahs, cooing over them like a bevy of sleek gray doves.

But all noise stopped at one moment. Nathan in his embarrassment was looking out of one of the tall windows toward the lake, and yet it seemed to him that he felt a powerful influence before the absoluteness of the silence told him of another presence in the room. When he turned his head a figure stood on the rostrum in front of the pulpit. At first glimpse Nathan thought it a man, for the face was strong and masculine and beneath it, around the neck, was wound a white silk cravat bordered with fine lace, its ends tucked under a man's waistcoat of the same color. But the jet-black hair, tumbling in curls to an open purple gown which hung from the shoulders to the ankles, gave evidence that this was a woman. Like deep-set, shining coals, her eyes seemed to be lighted not by reflection of other light but by some intense blaze within. The silence was long before she spoke. Her voice was sure and calm.

"Rachel Malin," she said. "Explain what I see."

The girl who held the picture out before her dropped it to her side.

"I thought it beautiful," she said, and her voice was strained and high, "and I wanted all to see it."

"Have I not told you," the calm voice went on in measured rhythm, "to shun at all times the company and conversation of the wicked world. O disobedient and rebellious children who turn again into Egypt, who will not strive to overcome your wills and be contented as were the Apostles. Beware lest I seek to take a parting hand with you."

The girls stood huddled together, silent and with bowed heads, until, as the voice said "a parting hand," a little moan escaped them.

"I do not forget faithful souls." The words rolled out inexorably. "I bear them in my arms continually. But rebels and traitors and whatsoever maketh a lie I cannot abide."

There was a pause. Then the voice went on—but it had changed its texture. It held the quick, sharp tone of a practical and competent housewife:

"Bathsheba Cahoon, Abigail Condol, Desire Brown—to the churns for a week; Candace Kinney, Orpha Scott, Tamar Stone will clean the springhouse, taking out and replacing all cheeses and hanging meats. Go at once."

Tiptoeing, the six girls picked up their mops and brooms and cleaning rags and left the room.

"Rachel Malin," said The Universal Friend. "Bring me that idolatrous work of the Devil."

Nathan saw Rachel's blue eyes fill, saw her clutch the side of the painting with nervous fingers and start forward down the long room. In six paces he had caught her and snatched the picture from her hand. Then he faced The Friend.

"The Devil will keep his work to himself, madam," he said fiercely.

"Young man," said The Friend agreeably, clasping with firm fingers the edge of her purple robe where it lay above her bosom, "I would like to see that picture."

"You'll see it in hell," said Nathan, and he strode from the room.

IX

When Nathan returned to Elijah's home he did not speak of his adventure with The Great Friend. Barnaby, he discovered, had been so roundly scolded for going near her dwelling that he had not mentioned the meeting with Rachel Malin, and Nathan kept the boy's secret. Mrs. Parker admired the painting extravagantly and stood before it a long time, exclaiming over each recognizable bit. But when Elijah had come in from his logging there was a scene.

"Ye paint the tents of the wicked," he shouted, "and ignore the dwellings of the godly. I hire ye to paint Elijah and ye forsake him for the priests of Baal."

"I was practicing as you told me," said Nathan.

"That's enough practice," said Elijah shortly. "Sam Cobwell says the Captain is in Canandaigua with Thomas Morris. I should wait until he comes to Bath, but I'll not wait! Maybe Tom Morris can order your canvas from Albany and it can be brought along the Mohawk. We ride to Canandaigua in the morning."

Late on the next day, while he ambled with Elijah through the woods beside Canandaigua Lake, Nathan had his first sight of Charles Williamson. As the shadows lengthened he could see ahead between the trunks of the trees a small cluster of low gray cabins, and two tall white frame houses. The blue water beside the town had just begun to burn with the red-gold of sunset. It seemed to him that the horsemen who suddenly intercepted the long level rays from the west had been riding silently, for they were within a few rods before he was aware of them. They appeared at first as silhouettes against the waning light—three riders galloping. One rode in advance on a clean-limbed, long-bodied horse and swung his tricorn hat in his right hand. He sat easy in the saddle, his long, booted legs relaxed

35

in the stirrups, his white-wigged head erect. A fluttering cape, caught together across his chest, swung out behind him in the wind of his passing. About thirty paces to the rear, two other riders spurred their horses, galloping heavily.

"It's the Captain," shouted Elijah excitedly, and standing in his stirrups he raised a long halloo. At once the swift horse wheeled and bore down upon them, and Nathan heard the Captain's voice for the first time.

"Well, if it isn't my friend Elijah," it said, and Nathan was drawn to its rich male timbre and sympathetic friendliness.

The Captain brought his horse to a halt as Nathan and Elijah reined up. The other two horsemen stopped and waited at a distance. Nathan could see now that they carried baskets and he guessed that they were servants. The voice went on:

"Have you decided to let me stand on the lake of glass with the chosen or am I to be scolded again?"

"Ye are a wicked man, Captain Williamson," said Elijah directly and sincerely. "Ye dance and ye race horses and ye'd build a devilish theater. I want no intercourse with ye except to ask ye a favor."

The Captain's long narrow face did not alter. Beneath his high forehead his blue eyes looked placidly upon Elijah. His small mouth beneath his long aquiline nose twitched into a wry, half smile.

"I'll grant it if I can."

"My tall young friend here is a painter," said Elijah, "and he needs a canvas to paint a portrait."

The blue eyes, in sockets slightly tilted toward the big nose, rested upon Nathan with warm friendliness. There was respect in the inclination of the long head, and a desire to please.

"I am Captain Charles Williamson, Agent of the North American Land Company."

"I am Nathan Hart, Captain."

"Welcome to the Genesee Country. It is young yet for your profession. A year, perhaps two, and you can depend upon being always busy. Still we must find you commissions—perhaps Colonel Wadsworth at Big Tree, perhaps, if Elijah does not object, The Friend."

"Never!" thundered Elijah. "The Friend shall leave Time and there shall be no trace to mislead the innocent."

"As you prefer," said the Captain quietly. "And now I have thought of a possible place to find a canvas. I believe Mr. Berezy, the leader of the German settlers at Williamsburg, was once a picture peddler. His wife and his baggage have recently been sent up from Northumberland. It may be that he has canvases he would part with. I am for Williamsburg tomorrow and would be pleased if you gentlemen would go with me."

"I must go back to my sugaring," said Elijah shortly, "but Nathan Hart may be willing—"

"I will go," said Nathan.

"We will be leaving from Mr. Morris's house at seven in the morning," said the Captain, "and Mr. Morris and Mr. Cuyler ride with us."

Nathan enjoyed the ride to Williamsburg. Thomas Morris, whose fine white house had sheltered the Captain overnight, was a pleasant, bland young man, too conscious of his father's eminence as a financier of the Revolution. Richard Cuyler was an earnest, silent, scholarly sort of fellow. He carried before him a hamper from which Morris assured them refreshment would come at midday. No sooner had Nathan joined the group than the Captain had engulfed all three in the charm of his personality and they rode happily together. Williamson was bubbling with enthusiasm for his project on the Conhocton, and Nathan remembered that Elijah had pointed out the site to him from the high hill above it.

"I named Williamsburg for Sir William Pultney, chief of my employers," he said, "and the new venture after his daughter, the Countess of Bath. I tell you, gentlemen, the Pultneys will be glorified, for on these two sites will grow the greatest cities of the Western Lands. The waters that flow by their walls will carry grain and lumber, furs and ore to the oceans of the world. Each one of you will own many acres then and have a sturdy prosperous tenantry to reap the harvests."

"Like Berezy's Germans?" said Thomas Morris with a sly smile.

Williamson's laughter was so infectious that Nathan grinned, not knowing the joke.

"That dour countryman of mine, Johnson, is in a panic," said the Captain. "I laugh every time I think of that Scot bargaining with the scum of the Continent. A Swedish pastry cook, a Russian pickpocket, a Norwegian sailor, a Hessian gambler."

"Don't forget the opera singer," said Morris sweetly and the Captain's laugh rang out again.

"You see," said Morris, "Sir William recently met—God knows how—this Berezy, a vagabond picture peddler, and the fellow so enchanted him and his London partners that they sent him to Hamburg to recruit a hardy Saxon peasantry for the Genesee lands. When next heard from he had landed in Philadelphia at the head of a band of sturdy farmers—or so he said. My father received them and sent them to us here—little knowing they were as fine a lot of city-bred rogues as the gutters of Hamburg could supply."

"You are too harsh," said Williamson smiling. "Sir William and his partners, Mr. Hornby and Mr. Colquhoun, were deceived, I fear, by Berezy. But these followers of his, whom you say he found in the Old-World gutters, might yet become respectable burghers if they could be withdrawn from his influence."

"What sort of fellow is he?" said Nathan. "Why is his influence so strong over them?"

"Indescribable," said Morris shrugging his shoulders.

Williamson laughed. "Perhaps you're right," he said. "I have not yet been able to make up my mind. Sometimes I think him a charlatan, and sometimes I think he believes himself chosen of God to lead these motley hellions to their new Canaan. Mr. Hart will have to judge for himself when he meets him."

Short shadows indicated that noon had passed, as the little group, after six hours of riding west, turned southward. Williamson urged them on for another half hour, leading the way on his fast-stepping chestnut. He was a hundred yards or more in advance when he turned from the road, dashed up a little incline into a grove of basswoods, and waited.

"I chose this spot to stop and eat," he said jovially, "because I wanted to be the first to show our painter friend the Genesee. Ride up, Mr. Hart."

Nathan wheeled his mare to stand beside the Captain's and looked out. To the southwest lay a long shallow valley. Its interior was a flat plain and its edges rose gently to the horizon.

It was not a bowl like his home valley in Pennsylvania. It was more like a plate. On the sides were scattered woodlands, but the wide center was treeless save for here and there a solitary elm spreading broad into the sunlight. Over the whole vast area stood grass so high that it dwarfed a man. It spread on and on, mile after mile of unbroken greening tangle, a jungle of tough waving fiber, concealing all things but itself and the lonely elms.

"That's it," said the Captain, "the richest land in America. There's eighteen feet of loam in those bottom lands. Hundreds of wild horses live in the grass the year round, completely hidden from man."

"But where is the river?" said Nathan. The Captain smiled.

"Lost in the grass," he said. "South of us it builds steep walls and rushes about, and to the north there are high falls before it empties into Ontario."

Cuyler had emptied the hamper of its contents and they lay on a white cloth upon the ground.

"The wine is still cool," he said.

"It is from my father's cellar," said Morris.

"An excellent Madeira," said Captain Williamson, lifting his glass. "Enjoy it, for tonight we shall be obliged to be sociable and drink the dollar-a-gallon whiskey that Tom the Tinker sends up from Pennsylvania."

All the muscles of Nathan's body went taut. He feared for a moment that, like the movements of his escape in Philadelphia, his next gestures would be involuntary. As the Captain spoke the name that symbolized the liquor-excise dissenters he felt that he might leap upon him and strangle him. With an effort that left him trembling he looked at each of his companions. Morris and Cuyler were innocently bending over to pick up their glasses. Only the Captain, glass in hand, gazed speculatively at him, his blue eyes wide and knowing. Blindly Nathan reached for his glass. As he raised it Williamson's voice was offering a familiar toast. He had heard it last on a Fourth of July in Philadelphia.

"May we cultivate the vine and sheaf in this new world and furnish the old with bread."

X

The four men had slept an hour or so after their meal, for the wine had made them drowsy. The sun was far down toward the horizon before they set out to cover the few miles of the remainder of their journey. An evening wind had begun to blow and the blending odors of the grasses were very sweet. Dusk had come before they saw the yellow lights of Williamsburg. It was a small town of about twenty cabins set in regular array on a slanting hillside and facing to the west. They could hear shouting and singing as they approached and they could see a big outdoor fire. When they rode into its light the noise was almost deafening. Nathan guessed that there were more than a hundred people gathered about the blaze and, never in his life, not even when as a boy he had watched a part of Burgoyne's captured Hessians marching south under guard, had he seen such faces and clothes. A grossly fat, black-bearded man with a tremendous baritone voice was stepping girlishly about before the others and bellowing a song. He wore short crimson breeches that were much too tight, and a stained purple jacket covered with tarnished gilt embroidery, and Nathan knew, though he had never heard an opera, that this must be the singer at whom his companions had laughed. The crowd was roaring at him, shouting directions, making motions as if to conduct his singing, and he postured and cavorted in high good humor. The slattern women, mostly blonde, Nathan noticed, were laughing hysterically, their heads thrown back, their mouths open, showing stained decaying teeth. Some of them wore caps, shawls, ribbons—bits of their costumes in the homeland—but these made cruel contrast with their shapeless baglike dresses of torn tow or dirty pressed wool. Most of the men wore woolen shirts and short homespun breeches. Few of them had stockings and many were barefoot.

The appearance of the four horsemen surprised the singer and his audience. There was a moment of no sound—and then a murmur, deep and menacing, began to grow. "Veeliamson!" screamed a woman, and the grim muttering grew almost to a roar. Then an erect compact man stepped forward to stand before the Captain. As he lifted his face Nathan saw that it was nearly square and that the hair above it was oiled and combed in a long swirl about his head. His eyes were large and of a strange glass-green, and his mouth was small and smiling. He wore a dark-green coat, of military cut though it bore no insignia, and black breeches that ended just above the tops of his newly greased boots.

"Good evening, Mr. Berezy," said the Captain.

"Your servant, Mr. Williamson."

"Will you be kind enough to ask the people to stay assembled here? As soon as we have dismounted I wish to speak to them."

The greenish eyes blinked. Berezy wheeled about as though on parade and held up a hand. There was an instant hush. He began speaking loudly in German. Williamson moved on, leading his companions to a long cabin bearing the sign "Store." A stout, red-haired, freckled man who looked to be about forty rushed out to grasp the Captain's hand.

"Thank God ye've come, sir," he said, and Nathan knew he meant it.

"Is it as bad as that, Johnson?" said Williamson, smiling as he dismounted.

"Gentlemen," said Johnson dramatically and speaking in a thick Scottish dialect, "will ye come into the store where I may speak with you before your supper?"

He hurried inside and the others tethered their horses and followed. He stood by a barrel on which a candle guttered.

"Berezy has stated that his power comes from Pultney. He has made fifteen of the men his personal servants and they wait on him at all times. Instead of settling each family on fifty acres as ye ordered he is building a big town with one acre to a house. It will give him control of all the rest—more than three thousand acres."

Nathan saw Williamson's eyes narrow, and the flickering candlelight seemed reflected in them as a steady fierce blaze.

"I'll attend to him," he said coldly.

"I beg ye not to lose your temper with him, sir," said Johnson desperately. "He has told these people he is their sole director. He has squandered money on them—buying from Mr. Wadsworth and charging to the association—and he has made them believe he is their savior from a thousand dangers. They'd hang us all if ye harmed him."

"I am sure that will not be necessary," said an even voice in clipped syllables that held a slight trace of a French accent. Berezy stood in the doorway—a dark, stocky figure.

"Berezy," said Captain Williamson advancing toward him, "as Sir William's sole agent in America I revoke the powers he gave you."

"You have not the authority," said Berezy, "and you had better not assume it. My people are tired of your promises. From now on they will obey me, and work under my leadership."

"William Berezy, alias La Motte," said the Captain contemptuously, "you may lead those 'good moral religious peasants' of yours to hell where they belong."

"We'll stay in the Genesee Country," said Berezy, "and live out the destiny that was promised us. We are not slaves but founders of a great city where each shall own property and employ others to work for him."

"I'll tell 'em their destiny," said the Captain grimly. "Come along, Morris, and translate for me. I can't speak the beastly language."

"As you please," said Berezy calmly, standing aside as the two men walked out. He followed on their heels, and Nathan fell in behind leaving Cuyler and Johnson inside.

Though the Captain had been in a rage when he left the store Nathan noted with admiration that as he approached the crowd seated around the big fire he was smiling. He strode swiftly, his blue cape drifting from his tall, lean figure. Again the menacing growl of the mob arose, but it subsided as the two men faced their audience. Nathan could see from the edge of the crowd where he halted that Morris was pale and distrait, but Williamson lounged easily against the tree by which they stood.

"Tell 'em," he said, tapping his right boot with a willow twig he had plucked on his ride, "that I have provided them

with more luxuries than any other settlers' camp has ever had
and that I'm glad to see that they enjoy 'em."

As Morris began his halting translation Nathan felt a hand
on his arm. Berezy stood beside him.

"May I ask," he said with a polite little bow, "if you are
in the employ of the association?"

"No," said Nathan. "I am here because Captain Williamson thought you might have a few picture canvases which I
might buy cheaply."

"You wish to buy pictures?"

"I am a painter and I need canvas."

"A painter!" exclaimed Berezy enthusiastically. "But I
should have known. You have the broad forehead, the keen
eye, the long hand of the true artist. I have had in the past the
opportunity to be helpful to a number of painters, and now I
shall help you. In my baggage but just come from Northumberland are a number of pictures, poor daubs I could not sell when
I dealt in paintings. You shall have them."

"I fear I could not afford them."

"But they are yours. I am happy to be once more a patron.
My servant shall bring them to you in the morning."

"I prefer to pay for them," said Nathan bluntly.

Berezy shrugged his shoulders. "They are worthless to me.
Send me what you like."

"Tell 'em," the Captain was saying, still switching his boot,
"that now they are so well established they no longer need a
superintendent and I am therefore abolishing that office."

Again came Morris's strained uncertain German, but this
time a fierce howl from the crowd silenced the trembling translator. Men rose and shook their fists and moved toward the
speakers. Nathan started forward but Berezy was ahead of him.

"*Achtung!*" he shouted, moving to Morris's side. "*Schwei-
gen Sie!*" He paused and Nathan was amazed at the sudden
silence. It was as though the man led a skilled orchestra, so
perfect was his control of this snarling group. "If you have anything to say at this time let it be from a spokesman—I suggest
your beloved Pastor Liebich."

Like an automaton, a robust, bleary-eyed fellow in a long
coat appeared with lifted hands before the crowd. He bowed
his head and offered a moment's prayer in German. Then he

took from an inner pocket a long roll of paper and began to read from it in labored English. It was obvious, Nathan noted, that Berezy had foreseen every event of the evening and had prepared a definite program. Though he must have known that Captain Williamson would understand this at once he had preferred to give each step the impression of spontaneity. The Captain was smiling now and Morris was looking relieved. Nathan was uneasy, feeling a sinister and ominous threat in the smoothness with which the picture peddler had managed everything. The preacher droned on and on, bringing countless accusations against the association and against Williamson, and praising the thoughtfulness, courage, and honesty of the superintendent.

"By our arrival it existed no tools at all at Williamsburg," he read. "At Bath, however, where Captain Williamson lives and where it exists a very small settlement he has begun and finishes a sawmill this spring." He spoke of delay in obtaining spinning wheels from The Friend's Settlement, of failure to obtain hemp and flax for thread, of wormy meat, of detained baggage, of a church unfinished, of high prices "at Captain Williamson's store who forces us to pay every article immensely dear."

As the list of complaints continued Nathan found himself wondering if there were truth in them. The motley group around the preacher nodded their heads as each point was made. "*Ja*," they said, "*Jawohl*." Suddenly the preacher stopped reading, dropped his papers to the ground, and obviously prepared for a final verbal assault.

"Captain Williamson has hindered Mr. Berezy to provide all the unavoidables of our necessaries," he shouted. "Should this be the free commonwealth to which he promised to bring us? Should this be the land where according to his assertions law alone commands, where oppression of the weak never is?"

Again, the well-drilled mob were on their feet, howling curses and advancing upon the quiet figure leaning against the tree. Morris looked for a way of escape; Nathan hesitated. It isn't my fight, he thought. Perhaps these devils are right. But as the leaders closed in and Morris backed slowly away, and as Williamson abandoned the support of the tree to stand erect, he felt ashamed. He realized as he plowed his way through the angry men that he was going to the Captain's aid because he trusted him—and mistrusted Berezy. The Captain might be wrong but he was honestly wrong. Berezy might be right but never honestly right. Someone struck Nathan a heavy blow between the shoulders and, almost falling on his face, he pitched forward into the little open space in which Williamson stood. Fists clenched, he came erect. A heavy-set, pig-eyed fellow lifted a gnarled thorn stick and brought it down. Nathan leaped for it, caught it just short of Williamson's head, twisted it from the wielder's hand, and struck him smartly with it across his protruding abdomen. The man roared and charged.

"Nein," said a calm voice. "Nein, Nein, meine Kinder."

Once more the glass-green eyes were exerting their power; once more the crowd, including Nathan's opponent, stood silent and obedient.

"We must not be so impatient," said the sure voice of Berezy, and Nathan realized that he spoke in English for the benefit of Williamson. His own people would do as he wished without questioning.

"I am very grateful to all my good friends for this hearty recommendation," he went on, "but Captain Williamson and I can come to an agreement, I am sure, without violence."

"I do not choose to agree," said the Captain doggedly, "and you have no further business here since you are not in the association's employ."

"I am glad that my friends do not understand you," said Berezy coolly, "for if they did I fear I could no longer control them. Perhaps you will wish to reconsider your effort to deprive me of my rights. I will try to influence my people toward moderation until you have had more time for thought."

"I do not need it."

"You had better take it," said Berezy. "Tomorrow being Sunday, I suppose you will not care to discuss our affairs, but on Monday morning I shall come to your desk at Miller's cabin for my answer."

"You already have it," said the Captain.

"For the sake of your friends and yourself I hope that you will change your mind. I trust you are not planning to leave Williamsburg before Monday."

"I am not."

"I am glad, because my friends here would not like to see you leave before agreements are made."

"You dare not keep us prisoners," said Thomas Morris, summoning courage to speak. "My father shall hear of this."

"I am planning to inform him myself by Tuesday's post. And now, gentlemen, I hope you will rest comfortable at Miller's. I regret that Mr. Miller has gone to Northumberland and cannot himself entertain you. And if you have no objections to receiving them on the Sabbath, Mr. Hart, your canvases will be at your doorstep in the morning. I still hope you will let me present them to you."

He turned and spoke a few German words to the crowd. At once they drifted back toward the cabins. "Liebich," he called, and that dissolute-looking cleric stood at his side. Together, arm in arm, they walked off into the shadows.

XI

Fog was rising from the grass flats by the river as the three men
turned away from the dying fire and walked up the slope. Soft
gray fingers stretched out after them, reached beyond them
here and there to make indistinct the outlines of their long
shadows. James Miller's cabin was dark, and Williamson, leading the way, stumbled here and there and turned to warn those
behind him of obstacles in their path. Slowly they coaxed from
the black embers in the fireplace a tiny flame. By the dim light
of the fire they silently drank the rest of Morris's Madeira and
ate the remaining food that had been in Cuyler's hamper. Then
they climbed the ladder to the upper chamber and there, after
their eyes had become accustomed to the darkness, they saw
Cuyler sleeping on a mattress on the floor. Beside him they
could see other mattresses and they were soon stretched out
upon them. Nathan, lying nervously awake, could hear Morris
tossing restlessly, but no sound came from the Captain. He
wondered if the tall man lay hot-eyed and troubled, going over
and over again the events of the past evening and considering
the present danger, just as he himself had done on the nights
after his escape. Those hours of torment seemed now much
farther in the past than they actually were. He wondered, too,
if Berezy had posted guards around the cabin to make sure Williamson did not try to evade the issue he would have to face
on Monday. Twice Nathan thought he heard footsteps nearby
before he dropped off to sleep.

The climbing mist had evidently presaged rain, for in the
morning when he awoke there was a continuous rattling roar
upon the roof and a steady splashing on the ground beneath
the eaves. Someone was walking about down below and there
was a smell of hot coffee. This seemed to awaken Morris and
Williamson at the same instant, and all three were merry as

they dressed and hurried down the ladder. Johnson, still looking darkly troubled, had already fried a mountain of eggs and salt pork and there was little talk for a long time. Though all thought of nothing else, no one seemed to wish to bring up the subject of the night before. Finally Captain Williamson spoke:

"The gutters of Hamburg must have been full the night Berezy cleaned them. Did you ever see such a set of villains? These are the sturdy Saxon peasants with which he promised Sir William he would establish this country's yeomanry."

Morris laughed.

"My father told me he had encouraged our art-merchant friend to sell the association's acres to German noblemen. Perhaps these are dukes and barons."

"That will come later," said Williamson quickly, as though the young man's remarks had entailed a criticism. "Once The Friend has lost her hold upon the hundreds she has sworn to poverty in her settlement, the great estates will come—and we must have hardy peasants to serve them. Berezy fooled us with his promises of settling honest German farmers on this land if we would pay him for it. But settling near two million acres is the work of a lifetime." He paused for a moment and then went on eagerly. "And what a lifetime! To see a glorious country spring into being, to see men grow rich upon their acres and enjoy the fruits of riches. This shall be a land of such wealth that even the poorest shall live in plenty." A fanatic light shone in the blue eyes. The rich, deep voice filled the cabin with sound. He's really not concerned, thought Nathan, with today's danger. With him the important things are all in the future. Berezy may really turn his jackals loose on us at any moment. Yet he goes on planning for what may not happen for decades to come.

There was a quick rap on the door. Johnson opened it and Berezy stood on the threshold. He wore a black greatcoat ornamented across the chest with green braid. Beside him stood a frightened-looking young man in gray woolen shirt and homespun pants. Disheveled blond hair fell in loose strands from under a cap that had evidently once been both smartly military and bright red. In his arms he held two pictures in ornately carved wooden frames.

"You see that I keep my word, Mr. Hart," said Berezy, "and if you still insist on paying for these canvases, I have thought of an easy method. When I am less busy, if you will be so kind as to paint so bad a subject, I will sit for my portrait."

"This is an impertinence," shouted Williamson, and Nathan was surprised to see that for the first time since he had met him the Captain was showing an undisciplined emotion.

"I was speaking to Mr. Hart," said Berezy. "I hope he will forgive the unpleasantness which circumstance has created and I want to assure him that I bear him no ill will for the company he keeps." He bowed and then spoke sharply in German to the young man beside him. At once the latter piled the two pictures against the cabin wall, saluted Berezy smartly, and stalked out. Berezy closed the door behind them both.

There was a silence after the latch had rattled into place. Nathan was embarrassed. He had been so surprised by Berezy's sudden appearance and strange request that he had stood awkwardly, mutely by, and let compliance with it be assumed. Berezy had made it clear, moreover, that he looked upon him as completely outside the present controversy. Nathan wondered if his companions so considered him—or were they depending on a loyalty they had little reason to expect? Williamson interrupted his thinking:

"Mr. Hart," he said, "since your errand is done, perhaps you would prefer returning to Friend's Mill in the rain to later discomfort here. If so my companions and I would understand."

"Naturally," said Morris, and Cuyler looked at Nathan but did not speak. Johnson rose from his chair to put more wood on the fire.

"I'll wait until the weather is better," said Nathan and wondered whether he was making a decision or postponing the making of one.

His remark, he realized, did little to lessen the tension which Berezy's presence had created. As time wore on he knew that this was a day he would not soon forget. The constant pounding of the rain gave him a sense of ominous isolation and he wondered if the others were feeling it. Secret things were happening, he knew. Men whom he did not understand— so many that all the lives in the cabin were in their power—were planning evilly against his companions and possibly against himself. He wondered what they were saying to each other just then in their strange guttural language. Williamson went to the door and opened it. He stood, holding it, looking out through the steady downpour for a long time.

"Berezy and the minister are going from house to house," he said finally, "holding a powwow in each one."

"Do you think," said Morris, "that we should try to ride off and come back with the sheriff?"

"Berezy would claim there was no disturbance and we would be laughed at from here to Boston," said the Captain angrily. "It would ruin our reputations and the prestige of the association. We can't afford to send for help unless we need it."

No one said anything for a long time. The snapping of the burning logs before them sounded as futile as their own mouthings in the face of the collective strength in the cabins of the town. Finally Captain Williamson began to talk, and at first it seemed that he was talking to keep up their courage; but as he continued the listeners knew that he had forgotten everything except the dream that possessed him. He said that he was sorry that Sir William and his partners had been so deceived by Berezy as to allow him to bring this ragged lot of ruffians to America. He was sorry, too, that The Universal Friend had already established her people in the Genesee Country. But these, he said, were not unconquerable difficulties. Berezy was but a buzzing fly, a minor opposition soon overcome. As for The Friend, though her settlement vastly outnumbered his own, it would be engulfed in the vast tide of immigration soon to set in. He had made plans to attract to this little town and to Bath, which was even smaller, great crowds of the sort of people that should inhabit this land. Before the first snow in the autumn he would bring thousands of prosperous, hearty, high-living people from all the states to the great Williamsburg Fair and Genesee Races. From Maine, yes, even from Canada to the north, from Virginia, nay, South Carolina to the south would come men of property who loved horseflesh and gaming and the theater. They need but see this grassy Eden to covet it—a land where hemp grew like young willows, rampant and strong, where sugar sap ran golden from the maples, where wheat sprang from the mellow mold so fast you could almost see it grow.

"From this very spot," cried the Captain, bringing an emphatic hand down on the surface of a desk at his side, "it is but a few miles by wagon to the navigable waters of the Canisteo. The time will come, sirs, when the waters of that little river will bear countless tons of freight through the Conhocton, down the Susquehanna to the Chesapeake. There'll be a day when the grain we grow beside the Genesee will empty in a golden flood upon the wharves of China."

"By gad, you make me regret that father sold the tract," said Thomas Morris, laughing a little ruefully.

"But it is not the association that will profit most greatly," said the Captain, and again Nathan thought he noticed a defensive note in his voice. "It offers the lands most cheaply at two to four dollars an acre. The people who will come next year to Bath to see my theater and the finest racecourse in the world, who will come to Geneva upon the American Lake Leman to visit the finest hostelry on this side of the Atlantic—with new American foods cooked by the best of English chefs—it is they who will buy my lands and reap the richest harvest."

Stimulated by his own prophecies the Captain suggested that they adjourn to Johnson's store to go over his accounts and make notes of necessities to be ordered. Nathan excused himself as he was obviously expected to do and remained in Miller's cabin. He went back up the ladder to the chamber above and lay long on his mattress, puzzling over the part he should play in the strange melodrama going on around him. And as his mind went back over the events of the past few days it came to rest with delight on a lithe, deep-breasted figure in a gray dress with a white collar, a blue-eyed girl with a fresh, eager voice who loved a picture he had made of a white house standing beside a blue lake. He wondered if she were thinking of him. He wondered, too, if that strange, strong woman whom she served would forbid her ever to speak again to the impertinent fellow who had insulted her. Then he dropped off to sleep.

It was late afternoon and still raining when he awakened. He could hear men's voices below and he rose and climbed down the ladder. Johnson had milked one of the cows browsing in the clearing and was boiling corn-meal mush. All four seemed determinedly cheerful. They ate and joked heartily, but

Nathan could see that worry over the next morning had wrapped them about as in a dark mist.

Since they spoke mostly of the technicalities of carrying on the business of the settlement he did not join in the conversation. He ate his supper and listened as the others talked afterward of tools and seeds and provisions. They spoke of going to bed early, and it was evident that they wished the morning would soon come that it might be over with. Williamson said he would work at his desk a while before going up. Then Cuyler said modestly that he had a suggestion to make.

"If there should be trouble tomorrow, they would drive off our horses. If we were to lead them into the back room of Johnson's store they might be safe there until we need them."

"It will not be necessary," said Williamson impatiently.

"Perhaps Cuyler's right," said Morris. "No harm in it, anyway. What about your mare, Mr. Hart?"

Nathan felt the necessity of decision suddenly inevitable. For a long moment he sought some way of postponing an answer. He looked about him at the four men.

"We'll lead her inside with the rest," he said, and his companions smiled gratefully.

The candle on Captain Williamson's desk cast little tongues of light through the cracks in the floor of the upper chamber. Nathan saw them advance and retreat again and again as the minutes of the night crawled on. He had lost all measure of time when he heard the big man down below move from his desk. The tongues of light were lost in blackness. Then he heard the Captain climb slowly up the ladder. There was silence for a moment, then the sound of a body lying down heavily upon a bed. Nathan heard no more.

XII

By morning the persistent hammering of the rain had stopped. When Nathan looked out, a leaf-thin layer of white mist lay above the wide savannah of tall grass, shaming the gray monotone of the sky.

Johnson had locked the store and joined them before they had wakened. His breakfast coffee was strong and hot and the five men, feeling its genial stimulation, talked eagerly. Later Nathan could recall the nose of the big coffee pot pushing in here and there around the table to emit dark gleaming fluid, but he could not remember what was said. Captain Williamson had propped the door open with a chair so that they could more easily see the movements of the men in the cabins up the slope. It was nearly noon before he spoke:

"He's on his way."

The sturdy erect figure of Berezy was marching toward them through the heavy air. The green military jacket hung rigid as a coat of armor as he halted in the doorway.

"Captain Williamson, I have come for my answer."

"There is no question," said the Captain. "You were discharged as superintendent of this settlement two days ago."

There was a long pause. Then Berezy said thoughtfully:

"I will do what I can, gentlemen, to prevent my people from acting in a hostile manner toward you when they hear of this. I may not succeed entirely. I know you will agree that Mr. Hart, being an artist very welcome to the Genesee Country, is entirely outside our disagreement and should retire."

"He may do so," said Williamson.

"They'll not break the law," said Nathan bluntly, "unless you command it. I wouldn't do that if I were you." Blandly, Berezy fixed the stare of his green cat-eyes on the ceiling.

"I am surprised," he said, "that a lone vagabond from Pennsylvania should be so solicitous about the law."

Nathan's voice choked in his throat as he leaped from his chair. He hurled himself forward, but Morris, nearer to the door than he, intercepted him. There was a moment of struggle and Nathan flung Morris off. But in that moment Berezy had wheeled and stalked from the cabin and Williamson had closed the door behind him. Nathan jumped for the latch, but as he reached it Cuyler dropped the solid bar into place.

"Let me at him, damn you," said Nathan furiously. He was white with anger at Berezy and sick within himself because the words had some basis in truth.

"You'll have your chance," said Williamson from beside the window. "They're swarming like wild bees."

At the two front windows the five men watched the settlers gather. There was a great shouting and running about, and they saw with relief that many of the women attempted to dissuade their men from joining the band of attackers which was gradually forming. Some succeeded, but Nathan reckoned there were between thirty and forty in the mob which now began to advance down the slope. He looked for Berezy, but that stocky, easily recognizable figure was not among them. The men of the crowd moved in a close formation. On the slope above, they seemed to be part of one strange creature, a large beetle with many legs. As they came closer Nathan and his companions could see that they carried a stout log, obviously to be used to batter down the door.

They halted within about thirty paces of the cabin. The big, pig-eyed fellow whom Nathan had struck across the belly the night before stepped out in front of them.

"Herr Veeliamson," he said mockingly, "we haf der tree chosen to hang you alreaddy, if Herr Berezy no longer *unser Führer ist*. Vat you say, Herr Veeliamson?"

"Don't answer," said Williamson softly. The silence of the cabin seemed to frighten a few of the mob. They loosed their hold on the log and tried to sneak away but they were dragged back by the others.

"If we had only brought guns," wailed Morris, nervously striding up and down the cabin.

"One shot might mean death for all of us," said Williamson, "and they could claim they killed us in self-defense. Berezy is clever; they haven't a gun in the lot. What happens in a scuffle is more easily explained to an inquiring sheriff than murder by gunfire. Here they come!"

Like a sudden clap of thunder the noise of the striking log ram seemed to shake the room.

"The door won't last long," said Richard Cuyler quietly. "We must use other defenses too," Nathan looked at the little, pink-cheeked, black-bearded fellow curiously. On the long ride over he had seemed a subservient, quiet, scholarly dullard, almost a caricature of a clerk. Yet when practical suggestions were needed he made them.

While the log ram beat its slow, deafening tattoo, the five men, shoving with desperate strength, moved the two heavy desks in the room into a V-shaped bulwark.

"When the door breaks, if Captain Williamson will move into the space between the desks," said Cuyler, "we can try to defend them. We can't hold out long, I suppose, and so if things go badly I will try to run to Johnson's store and ride for help. When you see me run, try to make some sort of diversion to keep them from suspecting my plan."

The door was splintering now and Captain Williamson took his place between the desks. Nathan was surprised to see that he looked more annoyed than frightened or angry. His courage was inspiring in a way, Nathan thought, and yet somehow he hated it. They will be coming through the doorway in a few moments, he thought. Last month I was fighting for people like these. Why am I fighting against them now?

Then they came through. The bar broke and the log and its holders shot into the room. Three of the eight men who had arrived so unexpectedly loosed their holds and fled. The others dropped the log and turned about. As they did so, Johnson kicked hard into the buttocks of one and he fell forward on the floor. Nathan struck viciously at the chin of the fat, pig-eyed man and missed. The next instant, badly stunned, he was lying in a corner of the room. As he rose to his knees he saw Cuyler shove the lightest of their opponents over the body of the man Johnson had kicked. Morris was having a stout tussle with a dark fellow about his own weight.

The big man who had hurled Nathan to the floor had

advanced to the desks and was reaching for Williamson. Nathan took a running start and threw his body across the back of the fellow's knees. The knees buckled and their owner dropped forward to the floor. His chin caught on a corner of the desk as he fell and his head snapped back. Nathan was up on his knees just in time to put all the strength he could muster into a blow that caught his opponent full in the nose. Blood spouted as the dazed man groped for his enemy to crush him. At that moment the foot of the ubiquitous Cuyler landed in his groin. With a shriek of agony the man crawled toward the door, urged mightily from behind by Cuyler's renewed foot attack. Nathan rose. Two men had grabbed Williamson's arms and were trying to pull him over the top of the desks. Inch by inch, despite all the big Captain could do, they were succeeding. Nathan's stout torso struck the backs of their knees and they came down in a heap upon him. Their fists beat on him unmercifully as he tried to rise. Then suddenly there was little Cuyler with his right foot flashing like the lightning, and Nathan was up and hitting out again. Johnson had meanwhile devoted his time to slamming his first victim back on the floor every time he tried to join the fray until the fellow lay still. Then he had given help to Morris.

As suddenly as the attack had begun it ceased. In a fraction of a moment all their attackers had run away except the prone object of Johnson's fury. Johnson grabbed the seat of the fellow's pants, dragged him like a bag of meal to the door, and dumped him outside. The five defenders of the cabin looked at each other and grinned. Then Captain Williamson spoke:

"We can send for help now. Berezy won't dare attack again if one of us can get away."

"I can manage it," said Cuyler, "if they don't chase me into the store."

"I think I know how to fool them," said Nathan doubtfully. "If we put Captain Williamson in our midst and sally out as if to try to fight our way through they won't notice Cuyler."

"Quickly, then," said the Captain, "before they try again."

"Bear to the left after you leave the door," said Cuyler, "to give me a free field."

Shouts of astonishment and rage greeted the four men as

they walked quickly out of the door and bore to the left away from the town. Then the mob broke ranks and ran to cut them off.

"Don't look around," said Nathan.

"I hope he times it right," said Morris.

A wall of men confronted them—at a distance of ten feet. Nathan smiled. The lesson given the fat, pig-eyed man had not gone unobserved.

"Play for time," he said. "Let them start it. Retreat to the cabin if you can." The crowd moved forward screaming at them. The front line was being pushed along by those behind.

"Back slow," said Nathan, and they retreated foot by foot.

Suddenly, as if out of the low gray clouds, came a long high tenor cry. On the top of the ridge above the town sat Cuyler on the Captain's horse. Even as their eyes flashed to the point where he stood the chestnut was away in a swift gallop. With a cry of anger the mob was once more upon them. The four fought desperately, futilely, for they were borne down by sheer weight and numbers. In a minute they were all helpless, held motionless by their captors.

"Hang him!" cried the crowd, circling about the tall Captain. "Hang him!"

Then there was silence, for strolling down the slope came Berezy. Nathan saw that his hands were clenched, his nostrils quivering. He's lost, thought Nathan. He doesn't dare go through with it now that Cuyler's spreading the news.

Berezy stood before Williamson. He barked a sharp command and his men loosed their holds on their captives.

"I am sorry, Captain Williamson, that my people are so quick-tempered. Sometimes they get out of control."

"You don't deceive me," said Williamson without any evidence of feeling. "Mr. Morris and the association shall hear of this."

"I have decided to go to Philadelphia myself," said Berezy, "to tell Mr. Morris how the loyalty of these poor faithful people led them to unconsidered action. I am advising as many of them as can do so to go with me that we may together explain the justice of our case to the association."

"You're running," said Nathan, "because you know you and your men will be under arrest before another day."

"Mr. Hart," said Berezy. "You will think better of me in time. I wish you joy of your painting." He turned away and his men followed him up the hill. Bruised and exhausted, Nathan and his three companions returned to the cabin they had defended.

XIII

The four men had hardly reached their doorless shelter than
Berezy rode down the sloping middle street and turned into the
Bath road. Nathan, watching the straight figure bob away among
the trees, knew his companions must share his sudden feeling
of helplessness. This man for purposes of his own had saved
their lives more than once in the past two days and now he
would no longer intervene. As if to confirm their fears came a
series of wild yells from the town. Once more the mob was
moving down the slope but not as it had done before. Each
man was in a helter-skelter race with his neighbor. As the four
looked on, too weary and frightened to prepare another defense,
the whole group swept by.

"It's the store," said Johnson in anguish. "Cuyler un-
locked it."

Standing just outside Miller's cabin Nathan and his friends
watched the looting of Johnson's stock. Barrel after barrel came
rolling out, was seized and carried up the hill by the triumphant
settlers.

"My pork, my flour, my sides of beef," moaned Johnson.
The three horses were led out, but so great was the greed for
food that those who led them rushed back into the store, leaving the animals to wander off toward the high grass bottoms.

The fat, pig-eyed man was standing on a barrel and
shouting.

"Give me the names of that man and those around him,"
said Williamson crisply. "Morris, go to the desk and write them
down. Sheriff Colt'll have work to do when he gets here."

"Buckendahl," said Johnson, "Bauer, Shutte, Spanouse,
Capnian, Wagner—"

He stopped, for the group had suddenly dispersed again
and were running along the lower row of cabins. Before one of

these they paused, and Buckendahl, lifting an ax, beat upon the door with powerful blows.

"Starr's place," said Johnson. "They're after whiskey."

As the door broke and the looters with wild yells burst in, five men came running up from the grass pastures, stoning an ox and three cows before them.

"Cart oxen," groaned Johnson, "breeding cattle."

The men rolling whiskey barrels from Starr's tavern greeted this sight with whoops of delight. Buckendahl ran to one of the cows and, lifting his ax high, brought it down with terrific force on the animal's skull. It fell heavily. The butcher turned to the ox.

"We had better join Morris inside," said Williamson, "and decide what to do."

"If we try to catch our horses in daylight," he said a moment later, "the settlers will see us and drive them away. After it is dark we can't catch them. Our best chance is to try early in the morning while the men are sleeping."

"If they don't attack us in the meantime," said Morris.

"They'll be too drunk, but if they do we can run for the grass and hide until help comes."

A bright tongue of flame leaped in the soft grayness of the afternoon. The settlers had dragged their booty to the place of the last night's merrymaking and had started another fire. Women were running from the cabins to join them and the air was alive with shrill chattering. A feeling of security enveloped the four in Miller's cabin. Johnson set to work preparing a meal while the others sat watching the revels of their recent attackers.

"I need not tell you, Mr. Hart," said Captain Williamson, "how grateful I am to you for your assistance. If you had not aided my friends here I should have been torn to pieces."

"You're welcome," said Nathan, wondering why these short words were the best he could muster.

"I could think of nothing that could equal my situation but some of the Parisian scenes," said the Captain.

Nathan did not answer. The words had set his mind once more on its speculative circling. The knowledge that the Captain pictured himself in his moment of danger as an aristocrat about to be rent apart by an enraged populace startled him.

Was it hardly a week ago that the shabby prisoners of a Federalist government were plodding through the streets of Philadelphia? Had he risked his life in the attempt to escape, only to find himself risking it again to defend a monarchist? Long after the supper that Johnson had prepared had been eaten he was still puzzling over his past and its relation to his future. His companions made few attempts to interrupt his revery. Ruefully they sat surveying the debauchery around the fire. Snatches of singing drifted down the slope. Male whoops and the soprano squealing of drunken women rode above the snapping of the flames.

Nathan did not know how long it was before the change. He had become so accustomed to the sounds of revelry that they seemed a natural accompaniment of his thinking. Yet, though he was deep in contemplation, he was as quick as his companions to notice the difference. First came the long high scream of a woman, then the affrighted shouts of men. Beside the fire there was a wild scrambling and the settlers began running about in many directions, some of them aimlessly. Indians, thought Nathan, in cold apprehension.

"It can't be Cuyler yet," said Williamson. "Judah Colt couldn't get a posse here until tomorrow evening at the earliest."

Then suddenly they saw the reason for the alarm. A small black cloud was moving from deep shadow into the light. It was breaking up into dark figures, eight of them, close together. Then the light seemed to leap to their faces and Nathan felt stunned. For into the bright focus trotted a horse so black that he seemed a curving piece of the night, and on his back sat a woman wearing a broad-brimmed, light-brown beaver hat, tied with silk ribbons under her chin. Her full-flowing silk skirt of the same color covered the horse's flank, and above her loose waistcoat a white stock fitted snuggly. One look, as the flames suddenly lighted the face beneath the hat, and Nathan was aware that a new enemy was near.

"It is The Friend," said the Captain, and while he said it Nathan's eyes, looking frantically about, stopped on the figure of a girl in a long gray cloak, a bareheaded girl whose shining, dark-brown hair fell about her rounded shoulders in a curling voluptuous tangle.

"We must warn them," he said and started for the door.

Williamson laughed.

"No need," he said. "The Friend has housed and fed half of their women for months. She has cared for the sick and fed their hungry. They'll not touch her. Listen to her."

The Universal Friend lifted a hand above her head. The black horse was motionless. The settlers who had scattered in alarm drifted back and stood looking. Rachel Malin reined her dappled gray to a stand behind and to the right of her mistress. Farther back the other six riders, four men and two women in somber clothes, sat rigid in their saddles.

"Unregenerate children," said The Friend, and her voice, though it was not loud, carried far out through the heavy air. "I came to this country that I might spend what few remaining days in Time are left to me in peace. I am for peace, yet all of you declare for war."

She jerked at the bow of ribbon at her throat and swept the big beaver hat from her head, loosing a cascade of curls. The big eyes sparkled and the firm chin lifted.

"The Great Friend had a vision," she said simply, "and in it she beheld an island populated by a thousand souls and they were standing together cursing the Lamb of God. And even as The All-Friend gazed upon them the earth yawned and swallowed up the island. God swept sinning humans from the face of the earth."

She paused, and when she spoke again Nathan thought that never in his life had he heard a sound so struck through with the quality of doom. Nothing of her person was in her message. The words were coming through an inanimate image, an idol speaking objectively in the language of a god but with an idol's voice.

"Beware lest the arrow of death should strike you also."

The settlers groaned. Some fell on their knees. Few had been able to understand her, but all felt the woman's power and were afraid. Selecting Buckendahl as their leader apparently by intuition The Friend urged her horse forward and, looking down with fierce intensity, demanded:

"Where is Captain Williamson?"

The fat man blinked his little slant eyes and pointed down the slope.

"Come," said Williamson, "we'll go to meet her."

The Friend had started to ride down to the cabin but reined in as she saw its occupants walking up the slope with Williamson at their head.

"The Lord has been good to you, Captain," she said, when the advancing men had entered the fire-lit circle. "Repent, that it may ever be so."

"You have been good to me, madam," said Williamson with a courtly bow. Nathan admired the easy tact with which the Captain turned away her thrust, and noted with surprise the quick gentling of her face, the sudden softening of her eyes.

"I am but a humble worker in His garden. We were returning from a visit to the Indian village at Squawkie Hill when we were overtaken by Richard Cuyler who told us of your danger."

Lights beginning to shine through the greased-paper panes of the cabin windows betrayed the fact that the settlers were drifting away. Nathan looked about. Only a few women were left beside the fire. He grinned. The men would be jailbirds in another week. Suddenly he felt hot pity for them. He had been in a jail himself ten days ago. The Captain's voice was saying something:

"My young artist friend, Nathan Hart."

Once more the strange eyes of The All-Friend seemed to burn through him.

"Mr. Hart," she said, without a trace of feeling in her voice, "you painted a picture of the dwelling which I inhabit. I still wish to see it."

"You can have it," said Nathan, and Williamson and Morris laughed.

A look as of some secret triumph came into The All-Friend's eyes.

"The Lord hath need of it," she said. "He will repay."

Nathan turned from The Friend to the gray-cloaked girl on the dappled horse. She was looking at him and quickly dropped her gaze. Then she lifted her head and the blue eyes looked steadily into his own.

XIV

On the next morning most of the men of Williamsburg had disappeared. Save for a few houses where meek males greeted him respectfully, sullen women answered as Johnson made a quick canvass of the village. Three settlers appeared from the direction of the Bath road and said that they had just come back from four days of fruitless hunting. Captain Williamson accepted their story good-naturedly, though he and Nathan agreed that they had seen them among the rioters the night before. It was obvious, Nathan thought, that he wished all the deserters to return. As the morning went on the Captain became nervous and irritable. After the horses had been driven out of the grass by Johnson and a settler, Williamson mounted and rode down the Bath road for a few miles looking for returning penitents. He returned discouraged. Morris tried to assure him that his father would not be deceived by Berezy.

"Not by him alone but by him and his confederates," said the Captain bitterly. "We must catch them before they get to Philadelphia. Why doesn't Judah Colt come?"

Colt trotted in at about eleven, a tall, solemn, slow-speaking man. He said that Cuyler had ridden on toward Albany with the intention of persuading Governor George Clinton to order aid. He would not be heard from in many days. In the meantime, he said, there were not enough men available to form a posse and pursue the fugitives.

"We'll find enough in Bath," said Williamson impatiently. "I have a crew of carpenters working there. We must start at once."

Since he had arisen Nathan had been gazing up the slope every few moments, hoping that Rachel Malin would come out of the cabin in which she and The Friend had spent the night. Once his heart had quickened as the door swung slowly back, but only a little girl had appeared. Now it opened quickly and The Friend and Rachel walked briskly into the street. At once the rest of the followers surrounded them. The Friend spoke earnestly for a moment, and then all went to their horses.

"If you are riding with us, Mr. Hart," said Captain Williamson, "perhaps you will collect your canvases and saddle your mare."

Berezy's framed pictures had, to Nathan's surprise, survived the fight in the cabin. One was a panorama of a big barnyard with many little human figures, clad mostly in red, doing the chores. Another was a portrait of a ruddy-faced old gentleman in severe coat and simple white neckcloth. They're better than I can do, thought Nathan, but I'll have to paint over them to earn food and lodging. The pictures were heavy, and as Williamson's party dashed from the town clearing and headed down the Bath road he realized that he would have trouble keeping up with the sheriff and the Captain. They had not ridden a half hour before his arms were weary and aching. He tried resting the frames on the fore part of his saddle, but this interfered with his control of the mare and slowed her progress. In an hour's time the rest of his party were out of sight and he was beginning to hear sounds of The Friend's group behind him. He turned to look and saw The Friend riding easily and lightly on the back of her curvetting black gelding. The broad-brimmed beaver was again on her head and the wide light-brown silk skirt fluttered out behind her, unveiling stirrups studded with silver. She rode perhaps thirty paces ahead of Rachel, whose gray cloak so nearly matched the color of her horse that she seemed an animated stone statue, all of one piece. At a respectful distance to her rear the rest of the followers trotted sedately.

As Nathan gazed The Friend cantered to his side.

"There is more room on my saddle than on yours," she said. "Shall I carry your pictures for you?"

Nathan was startled by the offer. He looked into the brown eyes and saw no warmth within them. This is her philosophy, he thought, and she acts on it. She is The Universal Friend. She is not actually playing a part. She is carrying out a program based on convictions that are separate from her as a person.

"I thank you," he said. "But they do not trouble me."

Her full mouth closed grimly into a straight line. The muscles of her jaw tightened as if she were grating her teeth in vexation. The florid face which he had previously thought youthful showed fine lines in the forehead and deeper furrows which slanted from her nostrils toward the corners of her mouth.

"Mr. Hart," she said, and he was aware as she went on that she was forcing herself to speak the words though she had great distaste for them, "the Heavenly Father has appeared to me in a vision saying that the wickedness of this world is so great that He would soon ask me to leave Time temporarily and return later to carry out His unfinished business; I have told my people of this and they are so distressed as to be almost beside themselves. It has therefore occurred to me that if I could leave behind me during my sojurn outside of Time some likeness which might console them and aid them until I return. . . ."

She paused as if she expected Nathan to answer, but he was not ready. She wants a portrait, he thought, because she's afraid she's going to die. I'd like to do it for her because it would give me a chance to see Rachel Malin. But Elijah isn't going to like this a bit!

"I'm afraid I'm not sufficiently skillful," he said.

"That is why I asked to look at the picture of the house I inhabit," she said calmly, "but I am satisfied with the reports my young friends gave me."

"I will try," said Nathan.

"My people will be willing to pay you twelve dollars for it," said The Friend. Nathan noted that she did not mean to pay for the picture herself, but that she seemed to know to the penny the amount her followers would pay.

"When will you be ready to begin?" she asked.

"As soon as I have made arrangements for lodging and eating."

"In three days' time?" She's in a hurry, thought Nathan. She must expect to die soon.

"I will come to your house on Thursday morning ready to begin."

She kicked a heel into the side of the black gelding, and the horse, rearing, plunged forward down the road. Nathan knew she did not expect him to follow and he was glad. He slowed his mare until he was riding beside Rachel Malin. The blue eyes looked straight ahead and the strong, full-curving face showed no emotion.

"I hope you have not forgotten me," said Nathan.

"I would be happy if I could forget all sin," said the girl.

Nathan laughed. "How much of me would be left if you could do that?"

"You blasphemed in the presence of The All-Friend. You spoke in anger to the Lord's agent in this sinful world."

"I'm really sorry," said Nathan contritely, "and you must forgive me—as she has."

"What?" said Rachel. "She did not rebuke you?"

"She has given me work. I am to make a likeness of her—so that you may look at it after she has 'left Time' and be consoled."

Rachel did not answer, and Nathan looking quickly over at her saw that the blue eyes were full of tears. Slowly they welled out and rolled down her cheeks.

"I didn't mean to make you weep," he said helplessly. Suddenly a torrent of words burst from the trembling lips of the girl.

"She is the Christ in female form as many of us have said. She has never denied it. And now because of wickedness like yours and Captain Williamson's and all his settlers' she must return to her heavenly home and wait for a more favorable time to save the world. I can't bear it, I can't bear it—she must take me with her." Rachel was weeping openly now and Nathan was miserable. He shifted his pictures from one side to the other, and as he did so he caught sight, out of the corner of an eye, of The Friend's followers riding behind—six black crows perched on ambling horses.

"She said she wouldn't be gone long," he lied, and even in his misery he was amused by the sound of the words, "and she may not leave soon. She won't go until after I've painted the likeness."

"She is so kind to have thought of that," blubbered Rachel. "It will help us to be brave."

Hot anger took hold of Nathan. "Who is she?" he said roughly, "and what is she to you?"

"She is the Spirit of Life from God," said Rachel simply.

"She inhabits the body of Jemima Wilkinson, a girl who died long years ago in Cumberland, Rhode Island. The Spirit entered that body and rose from Jemima's deathbed to speak for our Lord. Now she is the leader of hundreds who recognize her divine power. When I first heard her I knew her to be my savior and my friend. I am the first of her handmaidens, the prophet Daniel operating in the female line."

A set, faraway look was in the blue eyes and a dreamy quality in the fresh voice. The tears were gone though their wet paths still gleamed upon her cheeks.

"I have been told," said Nathan recklessly, "that The Friend is opposed to children."

Rachel turned quickly in her saddle. "You heard that from Eli—James Parker," she said, and her voice rose in exasperation. "The Friend loves all souls alike but she cannot abide fleshly sin."

"The world must go on," said Nathan.

"Not if the Kingdom of Heaven is at hand."

He saw the quick rise and fall of her full, rounded breasts beneath the gray gown, looked up to the red curve of her broad mouth and up again to the earnest eyes. For a period he could not measure he was lost in fathomless depths of blueness. And then, to his delight, she turned her gaze away. She's no impersonal prophetess, he thought. The body she inhabits is her own and deserving of a better fate than to win heaven for her soul by continence. She responds as any human woman responds to the purposes of man.

"Perhaps we define our heavens differently," he said, and as he spoke the black gelding bearing The Friend flashed toward him through the trees.

"Rachel Malin," said The Friend, "have I not told you to shun at all times the company of the wicked world?"

"I was but pleading for the good of his soul," said Rachel, flushing.

"Remember to keep watch and pray for assistance when the wicked are before you lest you lose your own," said The Friend coldly. Then, using the familiar gentle language of her faith she added kindly: "Come, The Friend hath need of thee."

Forlornly Nathan watched the two women ride away from

him down the stump-crowded muddy road. The pictures in his arms were heavier than ever and he was more conscious than before of the grim half-dozen behind him. He halted Lottie and waited while they passed him—silently and in single file.

XV

When Nathan rode into Bath in late afternoon he knew that here was what he wanted, a new and busy world in which to make his way. He remembered he had heard a single ax when he rode past this spot with Elijah. Now he heard many hammers and the shouts of men. The road led him by two log cabins into a big square. It had been cleared so carefully that the stumps of the cut-down trees were no higher than the sedge grass about them. A score of log dwellings bordered the clearing in a double line. One, much larger than the rest, was made up of several cabins joined in a sprawling irregular pattern. Before it stood a single tall pine that had been trimmed of all its branches save for a single nodding tuft at its peak. A liberty Pole, thought Nathan, and his mind warmed to memory of a like shaft in the valley that was his home. His father had helped to trim it in the days when to be a Liberty Boy was to risk a flogging in the jail yard while Tories and British officers jeered.

The noises he had heard rose from the north side of the square where a crowd of perhaps thirty young men were raising the framework of a new cabin. There was a great heaving and groaning and a laughter that was like shouting. As he dismounted and tethered the mare to a bar beside the Liberty Pole, Captain Williamson hurried from the big house.

"Ah, Mr. Hart," he said smiling. "I feared that by now you would have become a follower of The Friend."

Nathan grinned.

"I could easily follow her handmaiden."

The Captain laughed.

"You may put your canvases in my office," he said, waving a hand toward the front room of the big house, "and you can find lodging of a sort at John Metcalf's. I am hoping we can

persuade you to join the posse that is forming to try to catch
Buckendahl and his confederates."

"That's hardly a painter's province, is it, Captain?"

"It's the province of all citizens to enforce the laws of this
country," said the Captain seriously. "Once a man has decided
where he wants to live he should do his best to make living
there happy for himself and his neighbors. But that's not all.
You would, of course, be a paid deputy under Sheriff Colt—at
a dollar a day. When you return you will be able to make a first
payment on a house I shall have raised for you."

"I can't afford a house, Captain."

"Pay for it when you please. We need men like you, Mr.
Hart. A house and, shall we say, a hundred acres of land. That's
fifty more than I gave each of the damned runaway Germans."

There was a sudden blast of a horn and both men turned
to look down a wooded slope to the south. Another longer
blast and wild shouts followed. The men working on the cabin
in the square shouted in answer and, leaving their work, ran
down the slope.

"It's my boat from Northumberland," said the Captain
triumphantly. "Now I can have a posse without stopping work
on the town." He turned and strode rapidly in the direction of
the sounds, then stopped and bowed to Nathan.

"Forgive my eagerness," he said. "I did not mean to leave
you so abruptly. Won't you join me?"

Nathan would have gladly run with the rest of the men.
He found walking with the Captain difficult, for the long legs
ate up distance without seeming to and he had to exert himself
to keep up. Soon the narrow Conhocton River glimmered
through the trees, and in another minute they had joined the
yelling crowd milling about a makeshift log wharf.

About a rod from shore a twenty-foot flat-bottomed barge
slowly moved over the river, poled by a dozen men. The men
whooped and pranced about as they set the ends of their poles in
the river's bed and walked the boat toward land. In their excitement two of them crossed poles and the whole lot fell over each
other in a tangle of arms and legs. One, rising from the melee,
took a running start and, using his pole to vault with, leaped
from the gunwale toward the shore. His stocky body started out
in a graceful parabola, but the end of the pole slipped on the

mud bottom and he fell flatly with a loud smack into the shallow water at the stream's edge. Eager hands reached for him and dragged him ashore. A companion on the barge lifted a long curved wooden horn to his lips and blew blast after blast in derision.

Nathan, guffawing beside Captain Williamson, felt as if a sudden blow had knocked all breath from his body. For from the water, glistening like a wet pumpkin, emerged a bald poll that brought a rush of memory. The butternut suit was dark with water as the crowd lifted him up, but the round paunch and the small blue eyes looked the same as on the day of the march through Philadelphia.

"God-a-mighty," shouted the little man above the roaring of the laughter, "but ye make a touse over a man's takin' the name o' your town serious." He struck his chest a resounding thump and drops of water leaped from his clothes.

"I'm as clean and white as hickory ash," he yelled, "a fitten man to meet your womenfolks an' segashiate accordin'ly. I ain't no sweatin' stinker or polecat rafter like ye behold afore ye. I'm a—well, I'm a gilded whangdoodle!"

The crowd would never know what he had meant to dub himself when he began the sentence, for at the instant of declaration his eye had fallen on Nathan, standing rigid on the bank and hardly believing his eyes. For a moment that seemed far too long to Nathan the two men looked at each other. Then the little fellow turned and silently helped moor the barge while the crowd closed in to help.

"Mr. Hart," said Captain Williamson smiling, "did you happen to recognize that comical fellow. It seemed to me that he was a little abashed at seeing you."

"He looked familiar to me, Captain," said Nathan, hoping that his voice was not trembling. "I may have seen him in a tavern when I was painting a sign."

Again Nathan thought he saw the candid, open-eyed, wise look on the Captain's face. I wonder if I'm fooling anybody, he thought. I don't believe the Captain would be against me if I told him the whole story. Neither would anyone else here, except maybe Thomas Morris. But I wouldn't admit being a fugitive if I knew that they all knew it. I want to fool myself more than anybody else. I won't admit that anybody has power over me.

The Captain had stepped down the bank and now called out for attention.

"Men," he said, "somewhere south of us are a number of the Williamsburg Germans. In spite of every effort made by me to satisfy them they revolted yesterday, nearly murdered me and my party, and have now fled toward Philadelphia. Sheriff Colt here is on their trail but he has insufficient men for a posse."

"Let 'em go," came a voice from the crowd. "They ain't worth the powder we'd spend on 'em."

"The reason we want them back," said the Captain, smiling pleasantly, "is that the association has invested a lot of money in them, paid their way across the Atlantic, built them houses, fed and clothed them. We don't want any powder spent on them. We just want them back to work out what they owe us. They've done the same thing as steal our money."

"What'll we do with 'em if we catch 'em?"

"Bring them back here. They'll be sent to Canandaigua for the next session of court. If they can't pay their fines they can work them out for you fellows at cheap wages."

There was a roar from the crowd. A voice shouted, "Cap'n, they wouldn't be worth a damn, but if you say you want 'em we'll get 'em."

"I want 'em," said Williamson, and his hearers roared again. Nathan saw that these rough men admired the Captain with a kind of jovial fanaticism. Suddenly wet brown homespun was beside him.

"Schoolmaster," said the little fat man softly, "maybe we better jine up for this job. Put a lot o' folk off our track if we was deputies."

"I've been on the other end of it and so have you," said Nathan. "I'm not arresting anybody."

"I didn't say we had to ketch 'em, did I? But we don't want to give anybody the idee we ain't on the side o' law an' order."

Nathan saw the Captain turn about as men pressed around him to enlist as deputies. Tall, self-possessed, he looked over the heads of those nearest him to where Nathan stood, and there was an amused whimsical smile on his face, a quizzical look in his eyes.

"Listen," said Nathan quickly to the little man. "I've told

it around here I'm a painter—I am one, after a fashion. The Captain already suspects I know you. Tell him you were working in a tavern where I was painting a sign."

"Tapster at the George Washington Arms in Pittsburgh," said the little man calmly. "Used to be bar boy there when it was the George the Third. That'll fix it. What's your name?"

"Nathan Hart."

"Mine's Gragg, Whirling Gragg. Folks call me Whirl. Some on 'em think it's unfitten."

"Let's go tell the Captain."

"I've got an idee. I'll speak first."

They walked down the slope and stood in line, waiting while Sheriff Colt and the Captain accepted other volunteers.

"Cap'n," said Gragg, "me and my friend here—we got an idee."

"So you do know each other," said Williamson.

"Cap'n, ef'n y'ever need as fine a picter as you'd want to see o' Mount Vernon, home o' the father o' his country, in four colors an' with plenty o' foliage around, jest ask Nathan Hart to do it fer ye. Done a job at the George Washington Arms in Pittsburgh that'd make ye think ye was lookin' at the real thing. Had an arrangement with him—one cup o' rum fer every pillar—I was tapster there. Yes, sir, he'd go out an' paint one white pillar an' come in an' say 'Where's my rum?' Last couple o' pillars looked sort o' wavylike, but he straightened 'em the next day."

"Yes, yes," said the Captain smiling. Nathan saw his fingers twitch impatiently. "Get on with your idea."

"Them critters can't travel much in the dark. If Nate and I was to git a log raft and pole it downstream all night we'd be below 'em in the morning. Then if we was comin' up the trail, a few shots ahead of 'em might slow 'em up considerable so's the sheriff could catch 'em."

"I'll have these carpenters make the raft," said the Captain promptly. "You'll need guns." He reached to his belt under the blue cloak and drew out two long gleaming pistols. "These are easy to keep dry," he smiled, "and be sure to return them. Mr. Robert Morris gave them to me."

He's always clever, Nathan thought. He knows that if I'm not going to come back I won't take this pistol.

"They have excellent balance," said the Captain quickly, as Nathan held the pistol in his hand hesitantly, "and don't forget, gentlemen, you can buy land and lodging with a six-year credit when you return." He turned to the crowd. "Boys," he said, and Nathan noted how eagerly they responded to the gay note of comradery in his voice, "Let's have a raft for two voyageurs."

XVI

Sunset was a golden fan on the horizon when the raft was done. The sheriff had already been gone nearly two hours and he had taken most of the men of the town in his posse. Left behind to complete the lashing of the logs four carpenters stood on the bank of the little river as Whirling Gragg poled the primitive craft into midstream. The rain of the past few days had swollen the Conhocton and it bore its new burden lightly and swiftly. In a few moments Nathan and his companion had rounded a bend in the stream and the cabins of Bath were out of sight. Ahead of them the brown water was a narrow avenue overhung with drooping willows and with birches, silver white in the dusk.

"Now," said Nathan, and, as if he had been awaiting the signal, Gragg began to talk.

"Them two soldiers beside us," he said, skillfully poling the raft away from an outjutting rocky point and beginning the narrative as if it had been interrupted only a few moments before, "was skeercely able to think o' one thing at a time, so natchully they couldn't carry two. When they got down on one knee to aim at ye I stepped to one side to give 'em a more complete view. If them fellers can see what they're shootin' at they can't hit it, but they're always makin' a mess accidental. About that time the board I was wearin' round my neck got sort o' up-ended under my coat. I takes another step to the side an' says to a stout old fellow standin' in line on the curbin', I says, 'Seems to be trouble here o' some kind. What's it about?'

" 'I hope they ketch him,' he says, growlin'; 'that last keg I got'd burn the guts out'n a brass eagle.'

" 'It's terrible,' I says, slippin' round behind his belly, 'the way them divils pours unslaked lye in their grain juice. It fair gives me indigestion,' I says, backin' away from him into the

76

crowd. Then I run like the devil was after me. When I sorta come to I was lost. They was a lot o' big houses around and a fancy-dressed lady was comin' out o' one of 'em. I walks up to her an' says polite, 'Madam, can you direct me to the banks o' the Schuylkill?' She looks at me an' screams from here to Pittsburgh. I looks down, an' by God that signboard had come outside my coat agin an' was tellin' her all about me. Well, I takes it off and throws it away and I runs some more. Pretty soon I'm outside o' Philadelphy an' I climbs a little hill and sees the river. So then I says to myself—if a feller wanted to git ahead without sayin' what he'd got behind, where'd he go? The Genesee Country, I says, like it come straight from the catechism—an' so I come."

"I'm glad you did," said Nathan laughing. The companionship of a man who had had a similar experience filled him with grateful warmth. Moreover the casualness of Gragg's attitude toward the adventure gave him the feeling that his constant sense of being pursued would eventually be gone.

"Do you think they'll send officers after us?" said Nathan. "Maybe they can figure out where to go as easily as we did."

"They c'n find trouble closeter to hum," said Gragg. "Now you tell me what you done. Last time I seen ye, ye was rapidly disappearin' beyond the rear fortifications of a stooped-over black wench."

Nathan told his story haltingly. He hated to force his mind back across the memories of his humiliation. Yet he discovered that, as the narrative unfolded, events seemed to assume a less troubled perspective. The torment of his mind abated and he began to speak more objectively than he would have thought possible. Occasionally he was obliged to stop to allow the little man to howl his glee into the darkening aisle of the river. And when Elijah made his unexpected entrance into the drama Whirling Gragg's guffaws bent him so nearly double that he did not see a big sycamore root ahead and the raft was suddenly spun with sickening speed across the dark surface. Standing with feet spread wide apart Gragg used the long pole to balance the craft with all the ease of a tightrope walker. Darkness suddenly poured through the open spaces in the foliage above and filled the shallow ravine. A moon was somewhere in the sky, for tiny patches of white light gleamed on the black ripples.

"I ain't got it figgered out to a dead standstill," said Gragg, "but them fellers that are runnin' away can't git further'n a coon c'n spit on a night like this. By tomorrow noon we'd ought to be below 'em."

"And what then?" said Nathan bitterly. "We're fugitives ourselves. Are we going to capture other runaways and surrender them?"

"It ain't quite the same," said Whirling Gragg reasonably. "We was fightin' fer the principle that a feller who sold his grain wet shuldn't pay more tax'n a feller that sold it dry. Now these fellers, accordin' to what I been told, had their keep fer months an' now they won't work it out. That's stealin', I figger."

"They didn't mean to steal," said Nathan. "If anybody's wrong it's their leaders who tell them what to do. But the whole lot of them, leaders and all, are here because they wanted to move on from wherever they were to some better, safer place. They're just like us."

"Not jest," said Gragg imperturbably. "Do ye like them fellers?"

"I don't know about most of them," said Nathan, "but I suspect Berezy and Buckendahl. I'm not sure that has anything to do with it."

"It has a lot," said Gragg. "Now I'm like a dog I knew once. Never wasted no time smellin' round another dog's behind. That dog jest knew right off if he was all right or not. If'n he wasn't he took hold an' shook the daylights out of 'm. It give him an advantage."

"But they're in the same kind of trouble we're in," persisted Nathan.

"Hardest thing to learn," said Gragg. "A son of a bitch c'n be on your own side."

Nathan laughed.

"Better ketch some rest," said Gragg, lazily. "I'll call ye if I need ye."

Nathan stretched himself full length on the raft. Through the holes in the foliage above he could see that the sky was a blue bowl of moonlight. He could hear the rippling of the water against the raft and the breathing of Gragg as he swung the pole in slow regular arcs. While he listened the sounds seemed farther and farther away, then ceased.

When he awoke there were no trees above him. High grass grew down to the water's edge and light was flooding across its waving tips. Gragg sat cross-legged, looking off down-river and occasionally shoving half-heartedly against the turf of the nearer bank.

"You should have waked me," Nathan said.

"Twan't necessary. We come out in these flats after ye was asleep. Ain't done a lick since."

Nathan rose. The grass was too high for him to see what lay beyond it. They were floating down a narrow water lane through walls of fresh spring green. The sun, not yet visible, had stained a little cloud to the color of pear blossoms and the gleaming river gave back a fluffy pink image. They slid around a point made white with bending birches and saw ahead of them a widening of the waters. The right bank bent in a long grassy arc so deep they could not see its center. They seemed to be sliding into a landlocked lake, and when they had gone a little farther and were about to enter it Nathan was aware that there was something familiar about the scene. He looked to the left ahead and there, lifting above the shore grass in grotesque dignity against the early morning sky, stood the carved colored pole he and Elijah had beheld only a few days before.

"Painted Post," he said, proud of his discovery. "Over to the right there the Tioga comes down from the Laurel Mountains."

"So 'tis, so 'tis," said Gragg. "Musta brought that barge by here in the night. Think them critters'd be fools enough to foller uphill water to Pennsylvany?"

"It's the way they came," said Nathan.

Now they could see the gray cabins of the settlement. The light of the sunrise glinted dully on the greased-paper panes of their windows. The chimneys of two of them had set up a furious smoking in the clear air.

"Nothin' in our orders about starvin', was they?" said Gragg. "They's real coffee in them provisions they give us. Better land afore we start cookin' an' set the river afire."

"I know a cabin near here," said Nathan, remembering

gratefully the French family that had sheltered him. "There's a fire already burning there and I'd like to give the folks that live there part of our breakfast."

"Why didn't ye say so?" said Gragg. "The night wasn't too sociable with you asleep. I like company."

"Pull up to the right bank. It's not more than a half mile from here."

The walk to the Frenchman's cabin took them longer than Nathan expected. They sighted a small grove which he thought near their goal, but when they entered the high grass the green world that surrounded them was confusing. It cut off all sight of the forest beyond and they had to proceed by memory and such direction as they could reckon from the glow of the curtained sun. The ground was miry beneath them and the smell of the grass seemed almost overpoweringly sweet. As they tramped heavily on, parting the tall fibers, startled bobolinks flirted out of their low nests and shot upward. A red-winged blackbird, perched on greening cattail stalks in a marshy hollow, whistled discordantly. Despite the cool of early morning the two men were hot and sweating when they came out of the grass and looked about them. The grove toward which they had started was almost a quarter of a mile to the south. Nathan's eyes followed along the willow-lined bank of the Tioga. There was a break in the foliage only a few rods away. Luck had brought them close to the cabin.

Later, neither Nathan nor Whirling Gragg was quite sure which was the first to feel that something was wrong. From the moment they could see the cabin they agreed they had sensed that behind its closed doors and untransparent windows all was not well. They felt it, they said, even before they heard the crying of the little girl and knew by its strange, horror-struck note that they must hurry to prevent mysterious disaster.

"Give me one o' them pistols," said Gragg, as they moved across the clearing. "I don't like the look or the sound o' this."

Nathan dropped the provisions he was carrying, drew both guns from his belt, and handed one to his companion. As he did so a roaring, threatening voice drowned the little girl's high screaming. It was not that of the Frenchman, he knew, and he wondered why he knew it. Suddenly he realized that it was because the voice was shouting words heavy with the gutturals of German.

"Go slow," said Gragg, and Nathan sensed by the deliberation of his utterance the excitement that lay beneath it.

"There's a window behind," said Nathan. "I'll go poke a hole in it and look in."

"I'll be behind this here stump if ye want me," said Gragg. "Drive 'em out o' there an' I'll take keer of 'em if they ain't too big." Nathan smiled as he ran. Gragg tries to conceal his courage, he thought, for fear somebody might think he's asserting it.

The window at the back of the cabin was a single small pane of greased paper. It was already cracked across, and Nathan was able to pull the sides of the crack apart. He was puzzled at first because he saw nothing but what appeared to be a brown wall. Then it moved and he realized on closer scrutiny that he had been looking at the broad back of a man who was clad in a shirt of dark-dyed tow. Above the shirt a short bull neck wrinkled in heavy folds. Suddenly the shape of the head and the color of the hair startled Nathan into recognition. The man was the pig-eyed Buckendahl. Nathan widened the crack in the paper. On the floor, trussed with a heavy rope, lay his former host. In a corner vainly trying to soothe her screaming child cowered the mother. And standing before the fireplace was a young woman. She was short and slim and her thick black hair hung in two neat heavy braids almost to her waist. Nathan could not see her face distinctly, but against a background of leaping flame her eyes shone like black coals. She wore over her thin shoulders a full-length red cloak of a kind that Nathan had often seen on women of society in Philadelphia. But under it was a shirt of brighter red, a knee-length skirt obviously made of a many-colored Indian blanket, and deerskin leggings that were laced above beaded moccasins.

"*Noch einmal,*" roared Buckendahl, and Nathan saw him raise a pine-knot club in his hairy right hand. "*Geben Sie mir das Geld.*"

"*Il dit,*" said the girl slowly and uncertainly, "*Donnez-moi l'argent.*"

The man on the floor groaned. "*Je ne peux pas,*" he said. "*Je n' en ai pas.*"

The girl's eyes blazed at the German. "*Er hat keines Geld,*" she said quickly.

For answer Buckendahl advanced and grabbed her by the arm, holding her tightly with his left hand while he stuck the pine knot into the fire. It burst into a quick crackling blaze.

"*Nun,*" he shouted, "*Geben Sie—*"

Nathan stuck the pistol through the pane. The greased paper crackled and Buckendahl whirled about. The barrel was scarcely six feet from his ponderous belly. He gazed at it for a moment, his beady slanting eyes sick with fear. Then he tossed the blazing torch into the fire, grinning weakly.

"Whirl," shouted Nathan. "Go in the door."

He thought it a long time before there was a sound. The surprise of the occupants of the cabin was so great that none of them seemed able to move. All stood as in a tableau, waiting for a curtain to be drawn. Then Whirl was shaking the door and Nathan saw that it was bolted. The girl in the cloak leaped across the room and lifted the bar, and Whirl came in warily, pistol in hand. He saw the direction of Nathan's aim and took up a position in front of Buckendahl.

"Hold him there. I'm coming inside," said Nathan, and he ran around to the door. When he entered the girl had picked up a heavy knife from the utensils lying beside the hearth and was advancing on Buckendahl who seemed petrified with fright.

"Now," said the girl, speaking with an accent Nathan could not recognize, "God damn you, it's my turn."

The knife glittered above her head, and as he caught her arm and held it Nathan had the desire to shake her fiercely, not for her action but for her cursing. In his home valley women-folks had been too God-fearing to swear. In Philadelphia the wish to be considered ladylike had exercised an even stricter ban. But this girl was profane as naturally as Whirl Gragg. She strained against him now, trying with fierce effort that Nathan found hard to resist to bring the knife down on Buck-endahl. He looked at her and their eyes met. Suddenly her arm was limp and she was laughing. Peals of husky mirth came from her open mouth. Nathan grinned.

"It's the Indian cussedness in me," she said. "I get as mad as tinder." She knelt to untie the Frenchman's bonds, and Nathan noticed that her body flowed into position without effort, every muscle seeming infinitely more powerful than necessary for the work she called on it to do. Her face intent above the thick ropes was suddenly as compassionate as it had been fierce a moment before. Whirling Gragg had marched Buckendahl off into a corner and he stood there with his face to the wall, a sagging, bulky figure. The French mother rushed to her husband and knelt, waiting for the young woman's fingers to release him. The little girl grabbed Nathan about the knees and clung to them desperately.

Now the man on the floor was free and he and his wife were voluble in gratitude. The woman seized Nathan's hand and covered it with kisses. As he drew it away in acute embarrassment he saw the girl grinning. The red cape had fallen from her shoulders to the floor as she rose and stood looking at him.

She had said that there was Indian in her, but she was a lighter shade than any savage he had seen. In her lean cheeks a touch of red was overlaid by a surface sheen of yellowish bronze, producing such a color as he had always imagined a fine Chinese lady might be. Above her straight nose her hair invaded her broad forehead, forming a shallow black V. Deep-set and slanted, her eyes were so black that they seemed to reflect every ray of light that entered the room. Her mouth was curved and strangely full above a small and childlike chin. The long black braids down her back seemed out of keeping with her straight short figure and gave her the appearance of a fourteen-year-old boy masquerading as a girl. There could be no question of her being of mixed bloods, and Nathan was a little shocked at the idea, for in Pennsylvania he had been taught to believe that the offspring of Indian-white unions inherited the bad characteristics of both races.

"I am Catherine O'Bail," she said, and the black eyes told him she knew all he had been thinking, "and is it the Seneca in me you don't like or the Irish?"

Nathan flushed. She had not only read his thoughts but she was laughing at them.

"You don't look Indian," he said and wished he had said nothing.

There was a note in her laughter this time that he had not noticed before. It sounded like contempt.

"I don't look white," she said shortly. "I'm an Irish-Indian."

"No sich thing," said Whirling Gragg, tying Buckendahl's hands firmly behind his back. "Name's O'Bail, ain't it? You're an Injun-Irishman."

The girl laughed again and Whirl guffawed. Nathan saw that these two seemed to understand and appreciate each other at once, and he felt shut out of a relationship that was warm and enjoyable.

"My teachers made me take my grandfather's name when I went to the Friends' School in Philadelphia," she said. "They called it my Christian name. Now our enemies insult my father with it. My father is The Cornplanter."

She spoke the word simply and Nathan knew that she accepted being the daughter of a famous chief as a matter of course. He tried to remember what he had heard of The Cornplanter. Some one of his father's cronies who had marched with Sullivan through this country ten years ago had come back to the valley with tales of the burning of Seneca villages, the destruction of granaries, and the humiliation of great chiefs, smart, fine-speaking men like Red Jacket and Farmer's Brother and The Cornplanter.

"You learned to speak French and German at school?" he asked.

The lights in the black eyes mocked him.

"You heard almost all the words I know in both languages," she said smiling. "Yes, I learned them in Philadelphia."

"How did you happen to be here when this fellow arrived?"

"I wasn't. Bill Harris asked me to walk over here from Painted Post and tell these people in French that he had a new supply of powder. The door was open and I walked in just as the big man finished tying up the Frenchie. I tried to run but he caught me and barred the door."

"Here's a bundle for delivery," said Whirl tying the last knot firmly, and he kicked Buckendahl expertly in his fat buttocks. The German howled and Whirl, with the light of innocent enjoyment in his mild blue eyes, once more landed his right foot unerringly. Buckendahl fell to his knees beseeching mercy in a torrent of language.

"What about breakfast?" said Whirl.

Eagerly Nathan sought the provisions he had dropped when

he had heard the child crying and had felt that there was danger. A half hour later coffee was boiling on the hearth, pork frying in the pan, and all save the lonely Buckendahl in the corner sat before the fire awaiting their portions. Whirl and Catherine O'Bail were laughing together like old friends. Occasionally the girl interrupted the conversation to attempt a translation of one of Whirl's remarks into her labored French. Her hosts listened intently and went into hysterical shrieks of mirth, more often apparently at the translator's errors than at her humor. Nathan wondered why he was himself so incapable of light-hearted acceptance of people. Here sat persons of strangely varied bloods and experiences frankly enjoying each other at their first meeting. What lay back of his own silence, his uncomfortable uncertainty? His companions seemed to accept him with both joy and respect. Why couldn't he be as free and easy as they?

"Listen," said Whirl, abruptly breaking his reverie.

From the direction of Painted Post came a dull faraway thudding.

"Gunfire," said Whirl, pulling the Captain's pistol from his belt. From the same direction, drifting across the grass down by the river, came another sound—long and wailing. It was repeated and one like it, but on a higher note, broke in.

"Horns," said Whirl, returning the gun to his waist. "The Cap'n's reached the Post. We better be takin' his present over to him."

Nathan wondered how the Captain would receive the strange group that set out from the cabin a few moments later, and he was disturbed with himself for wondering. It was the girl who made the difference, he thought. Williamson might reasonably expect to see him and, of course, Buckendahl and Whirl. But this boyish part-Indian whose fashionable cloak covered the clothes of a savage hoyden would need explaining. Why? he asked himself. There is no relationship between the rest of us and her. She is with us by accident. Still he could imagine Williamson's understanding tolerant smile at meeting her and he was annoyed. He was the more exasperated when he saw Whirl cut for her a stout hickory pole and realized that she intended to help propel the raft. After they had set the repulsively grinning Buckendahl in the center of their improvised vessel Nathan tried to take the pole from her, but she refused to let it go. She loved making the raft skip across the rippling water and, although they were moving athwart the current and somewhat upstream, she made Whirl hustle to keep his side moving evenly with hers.

After they had landed Nathan saw a crowd of men gathered about the entrance to Bill Harris's store. Towering in their midst he recognized the cloaked figure of the Captain. It was obvious in a few moments that he had seen them. He pushed his way out of the group beside the carved pole.

"This is good news," he said smiling and apparently without surprise at beholding the prisoner. "Sheriff Colt will be glad to see this fellow." Then the very look that Nathan had anticipated came over his face as his eyes fell on Catherine O'Bail. "I am honored," he said, with a swish of his cloak across his chest and a deep bow, "to welcome the daughter of my valued friend, The Cornplanter." Nathan saw Catherine bend in a boarding-school curtsey that seemed exaggerated into caricature.

"My father will be happy to hear of your kindness," she said, and in her eyes was a gleam which Nathan could interpret only as amusement, though he could not understand why she found the situation humorous. She stood erect beneath the gaze of Williamson, and her manner indicated such easy and impersonal detachment that the gleaming aura of the Captain's personality seemed suddenly to dim.

"We have already overtaken a dozen of the deserters," said Williamson, "but there are a few still ahead. Your scheme worked well and you and your companion shall receive a reward for bringing in one of the leaders. Will you join us now in continuing the chase?"

"I have promised to begin a portrait of The Friend," said Nathan.

"I congratulate you on so distinguished a commission," said the Captain, "and I hope you will forgive our failure to bring your mount with us. You will remember that we were in great haste. Perhaps we can find a horse for your return."

"You will need your horses," said Nathan, "and I can walk to Bath by sundown."

"We must be on our way, then," said the Captain briskly.

"Your pistol, Captain," Nathan said, presenting the weapon.

"Here's mine," said Whirl. "Sartain used it plenty without firin' it."

The Captain laughed.

"My man," he said heartily, "I'll be glad to lend both to you if you care to continue with the posse."

"My idee," said Whirl slowly, "was to settle in these parts, not go gallivantin' round after fellers that don't want to."

Williamson's laughter seemed forced and too loud, and his eyes blazed a contradiction to it.

"There's another barge on the way up the Susquehanna," he said. "It should arrive today. Perhaps you'd like to earn your way to Bath by joining the crew."

"That'd suit me down to the ground," said Whirl; "an' do Nate and I git our land when we git back?"

"As soon as I return," said the Captain smiling. "I haven't forgotten, Mr. Hart, that I promised you a cabin. Perhaps you and your friend here can share it until you desire to build handsomer quarters."

"I will not be able to pay for it, Captain," said Nathan.

"Be as long about it as you like," said Williamson impatiently. "In another few years, I warrant you, your acres will make you a rich man. I'll be glad to gamble your cabin on it. You will receive it in a few days." He turned on his heel and strode back to the store.

XVII

Nathan parted from Whirl and Catherine O'Bail at once. Whirl had waved a negligent hand:

"On my way to Nellie Fuller's," he said. "A woman an' liquor together don't come frequent in these parts. Bounden duty to take advantage of it."

"I am going to Squawkie Hill," Catherine said, "but I must stop here to see some friends for a few hours."

Nathan was embarrassed. He realized that her talk of a visit to friends was a device to give him a choice of making the journey to Bath with her or alone. Squawkie Hill, Elijah had told him, was an Indian village not far from Williamsburg. Stumbling over his words he explained that he wished to arrive in Bath as early as possible.

"I understand," said the girl quietly, and she turned away.

Nathan welcomed the long walk to Bath without a companion. It would give him time, he thought, to consider his new life and to establish recent events in a reasonable perspective. He was happier than he had been in many weeks. The humiliation of his arrest and its sequel had begun to seem a part of the far past, though less than a fortnight had elapsed since his escape. He was glad that so much had happened to make it seem distant. If he could satisfy his new acquaintances with his painting he might acquire more land and become, eventually, a teacher again, a respected member of a new and growing community. He realized that the Captain would know at once on looking at his work that he was no artist, but this did not disturb him. Charles Williamson thought only of the development of the lands in his care, and as long as men worked with him toward that end he would ask no more of them. Thomas Morris would know, too, that his paintings were worthless and there lay greater danger. Morris would suspect him, possibly accuse him.

Father Robert was a powerful man in Philadelphia and might cause a fleeing Whiskey Boy to be apprehended and returned to jail. I must be careful, Nathan thought, not to offend and I must establish myself as a dependable neighbor. Perhaps then I can settle down and be safe from the past.

It was a misfortune, he mused, that the only young women he had met in his new world could not logically be considered even as platonic companions in the program. He longed to look once more into the blue eyes of Rachel, to see the blue veins of her plump white hands, the curving rise of the deep breasts beneath the gray cloth of her dress. But he knew all too well the disfavor with which The Universal Friend looked upon his casual meetings with her chief handmaiden. As for the Indian girl—he had begun to call her that though she was partly white—any sort of relationship with her was out of the question. He had heard men of his father's generation speak contemptuously of such mixed breeds and of men who had married them. He must wait. There would be other opportunities if a young man could possess his soul in patience. But it was hard to wait—especially for a fellow whose body gave a patient soul short shrift when opportunity was at hand.

He did not remember later just when or where it was that his head began to hurt. He reckoned he had been walking for more than four hours when the change came. There was a moment when he was stepping briskly among the blackened stumps of the muddy road and thinking logically of his future— and there was the next moment when his brain was seared by a torturing heat and waves of blood were pounding at his temples. He stopped in the shade of an oak and rested. Though the noon was oppressive he knew that its heat could not have caused his condition. Suddenly the sunlight seemed to change its nature and he was colder than he had ever been in his life. His body was shaken by a storm of shivers, and his teeth beat against each other in an uncontrollable and incredibly rapid tattoo. Ahead of him lay a broad unshaded patch of road and he forced his body toward it. Before he reached it he was compelled to stop and allow his retching stomach to empty. Then when the sun was strong upon him he slumped to the ground in an agony of chill. He did not know how long he lay there shaking before the fever came. He only knew that there was an instant when his body lost its cold, and unbearable heat surged through his veins. The sunny spot in which he lay was a furnace consuming him as inevitably as licking flame.

Then he heard a smooth entreating voice that he hated and he rose and fled it through the trees. And though he ran as fast as he could, cursing the flitting shape behind him, always, when he halted, the voice was there, begging a boon he would not give. Sometimes the blaze within his brain was so great that he would fling himself once more to earth, trying to cool his burning forehead against the leaves beneath him. But the voice would grow more urgent and soon he would feel a hand upon his head and an upward pressure that would enrage him. Screaming wild oaths he would leap to his feet and be off, racing furiously ahead of his swift and inevitable pursuer.

Once, when the voice and hand had urged him gently to the right of the road and into a small path that ran beside it, he had had a cunning idea, and putting on a quick burst of speed he had dashed off to the left. This time he felt that he outdistanced the voice and he ran on, desperately trying to keep the advantage he had gained. Unexpectedly he was stumbling through high grass and knew he must be near a river. He shouted in the joy of his anticipation and drove forward, parting the tough stalks with his hands. In a moment he had reached the narrow stream and plunged his heat-crazed body into it.

At once the stream turned icy to his touch and the violent shivering returned. He made for the opposite bank, fearing with each stroke that his legs and arms would cease their thrashing from the congealing cold. He heard the hated voice calling, heard a splashing behind him, and flailed the water in an ecstasy of fright at being overtaken. He crawled out of the stream on the far bank, scrambling on all fours in his haste, and darted once more into the grass. He ran on, trembling lest he hear the voice, but he did not hear it.

Then, where the grass should have ended and the forest become visible, he stopped. There was a tall green wall on every side of him and he knew he could not go back over the way he had come. He felt his body once more begin to burn and he was filled with a great lassitude. He pulled up an armful of the grass and spread it out at his feet. In a few moments he had laid enough of the long green fibers on the earth to protect his body from the dampness below. He lay on them and lost consciousness.

The waning moon was drooping just above the high pinnacles of the grass when he came slowly awake. The fire was gone from his blood and he felt well save for a weakness in his legs when he moved them. The night air was strangely perfumed and there were flutterings among the near-by stalks. He thought at first that the low movement he heard beside him was that of a bird, but when it was repeated he turned and saw, lying on her red cloak beside him, Catherine O'Bail. Then he knew that the voice he had heard in his delirium had been hers and she had been the pursuer he had fled.

"Why are you here?" he said gruffly.

The black eyes, luminous in the dim moonlight, met his look squarely.

"You might hurt yourself."

"I was sick but I am well now. How did you find me?"

"I climbed a tree," she said. Nathan pictured her perched on a limb and watching without difficulty his frantic course through the grass. He was angry and abashed.

"It was not necessary. Naturally I'm grateful, but you need not have gone out of your way."

"You will be ill again tomorrow," she said. "You have the Genesee fever."

"What's that?"

"Almost every white man who comes to the Genesee Country has had it. Many die. Some people call this the valley of bones."

"But I have recovered. My fever has left me."

"It will come back tomorrow. You must have the Jesuit bark. It is the one cure."

"But where can I get it?"

"Only from Monsieur de Boui at Big Tree and he will not give it to all who ask. He brought it with him from the island of San Domingo."

"Where is Big Tree?"

"Across the valley from Squawkie Hill where I am to meet my father."

"I shall not need the bark," said Nathan. "I do not believe

the fever will come back. Bath is nearer and even if I am sick
again they can care for me there."

"You cannot find your way to Bath," said the girl suddenly; "you do not even know where you are now."

"Do you?" said Nathan.

She smiled. "Not exactly, but I know that if we walk west
we will come to the Little Canisteo River. We follow it up to
its source, then climb over the hill, and find the Canaseraga on
the other side. That will take us to Squawkie Hill."

"I prefer to go to Bath."

"Good-bye," said the girl, picking up her red cloak.

"Will you tell me how to reach it?"

"No," said Catherine, and she and Nathan stood looking
at each other.

"Why not?"

"Because you must have the bark. You may even die tomorrow before we get it."

Nathan was already weary when they reached the Canisteo.
His weakness made him sweat and pant as the girl moved
through the grass ahead of him and came out of it into the
forest. He dared not talk for loss of breath but trudged doggedly behind her as she stepped springily along. He resented
her sureness of direction, her positive diagnosis of his ailment;
yet he knew that she was right and that she sought to help
him.

When the sun was high above them she stopped and drew
from a pocket of her cloak a bag of white corn flour. While
he stretched himself on the ground in exhaustion she knelt beside the river and mixed the flour into little dabs of paste which
she fed to him one by one. The taste was cool and good and
after he had eaten Nathan felt stronger. He gazed at the girl
as she made little balls of the paste and popped them into her
own mouth. She went about it as gravely as a child and with as
much delight. He saw how easily her graceful, legginged legs
held her weight as she sat upon her haunches by the brown
water. A kingfisher dipped for a minnow a few yards downstream, and her eyes leaped and glowed as they watched the bird
struggle with his prize. She looks like a boy, he thought, a
little Chinese boy, except that her face is thin and pointed.
She is beautiful as a boy is beautiful.

"Why were you at Painted Post?" he asked.

"To get this shirt," she said, clasping a hand about her brick-red sleeve. "I like this shirt."

Nathan grinned. He was amused that despite her schooling she was so frank in her aboriginal tastes. She had set out to walk more than fifty miles and back to own a red shirt. Their eyes met and they both laughed.

The first hours of that afternoon were full of chatter. They walked beside the Canisteo, tumbling here and there over the rocky banks, and the girl told him many things about her life. She had first begun to learn of white ways when she was twelve. Then her father had let the missionary preacher Samuel Kirkland, who had been passing through the Genesee Country on his way to a meeting at Niagara Falls, tell her about the Bible. She had not understood what he told her but she liked the songs he sang. She had begged her father to let her go to Kirkland's Indian School, the Oneida Academy, on a high hill above the Mohawk River, and The Cornplanter had taken her with him to see the missionary and left her there for a few weeks. Then she had been so depressed by her teachers' frightening declarations that the world was full of sin for which all but a few would be punished that she had run away and walked home.

When she was fifteen she had talked with two Quaker men from Pennsylvania who had come to the Genesee to help the Seneca Tribe make treaties with the government in Washington. They had told her of Quaker schools in Philadelphia which received Indians as well as whites. Ebenezer Allen, old Indian Allen, who lived down by the great falls of the Genesee, had taken two of his daughters by an Indian wife to such a school. The Quakers had been interested in Catherine and had persuaded her father to let them take her back to Philadelphia.

She had liked the instruction at the school. There had been less of gloomy religion and there were tales like the Seneca religious stories which she had known since she could talk. She had stayed in Philadelphia two years. She had hoped to start a small school of her own in the Genesee Country after she came back, but both the Indians and the whites had felt mistrust of a school presided over by a teacher of mixed blood.

"Is your white blood only from your grandfather?" asked Nathan bluntly.

"Yes. My mother was a Seneca. She died in the year of the starvation after General Sullivan destroyed our crops. My father has been kind but my white grandfather does not know of me. The Cornplanter went to see him in Albany once. O'Bail admitted his son but he gave him nothing—not even food for the journey home."

Nathan found the girl's frankness engaging. For the first time since he had left the stone house in the valley he felt the urge to talk. He told her of his lonely life as a boy among the Pennsylvania hills. His parents had belonged to the Congregational Church before they came to the valley, and they were looked upon by their Calvinist neighbors as atheists. The other boys and girls at the log schoolhouse which he had attended had not been allowed to play with him. Of all the folk outside his family only the schoolmaster, a solemn scholar who loved Latin and whiskey, had been companionable. When, because of his drinking, the strict Presbyterian farmers had forced the teacher to resign he had taken his young protégé to his home over the mountains for a visit. There, in the town of Swarthmore, the teacher had got the boy a job grinding paints to color the big covered Conestoga wagons used to carry freight over the mountain roads. After a few weeks the apprentice had been promoted to doing the actual painting and soon he could decorate a wagon as well as anyone in the town. Advised by the schoolmaster he had saved his money until he had enough for a season of schooling at Philadelphia. Those had been glorious months. Student life had been carefree after the arduous studies of the day. There had been gay parties in the Refreshment Gardens of the town. There had been lovely girls and one in particular. And when his money was gone there had been an offer of a position as master of a small school in the western part of the state.

Suddenly Nathan was aware that he had talked enough. There could be no going on without revealing facts that must be hidden forever. He must never tell any one of his joining the Whiskey Boys and what it had brought about. He stopped, confused and uncertain.

"What happened to the girl?" said Catherine, and Nathan

realized happily that she had not been listening since she had heard him speak of the Philadelphia mother's-child. Hastily he improvised a story. Her parents had objected to his poverty, he said, and she had agreed not to marry him.

"Then she is waiting?"

Nathan laughed.

"Not she," he said.

"I hate her," said Catherine O'Bail.

XVIII

The Canisteo had become a brawling brook and now it was less than that—a quiet flow of waters from a wide marsh. Ahead of them they could see that the main stream would soon be unidentifiable among the many little rivulets that flowed out of the soft swampy soil. They made for high ground to their left and Nathan saw the side of a great hill rise before them. As they set out to mount it he despaired of reaching the crest. Before long he was climbing with dogged determination, putting one foot slowly, weakly ahead of the other and forcing his weight on upward.

The girl fluttered about him like an anxious partridge with a lone chick. He could see that she was being gay to keep up his spirit, that she would, if she dared, put both her hands at the small of his back and push him up the steepening slope. He could not talk, for his exertions left him breathless. His clothing was wet with sweat. At increasingly short intervals he stopped to rest, and as he looked up to the summit it seemed farther than it had been the last time he halted. The sun was far down the sky when, with a last straining effort, Nathan plunged to the little plateau of the summit and fell forward on his face. When, at last, he rolled over he saw in the black eyes of the girl above him the same look of compassion that had rested on the bound Frenchman the day before.

"We must go on," she said. "We must walk as far as you can before the fever comes again. Perhaps if we can reach the creek before it is dark we can follow it all night." Stumbling drunkenly in his exhaustion, Nathan followed her down the hill. A half hour later he heard her cry out in delight. She had found the bubbling current of the Canaseraga.

Dusk was a long ghostly hour after the sun had sunk below the westward hills. Night was a troubled dream that would not end. They groped in blackness until the tardy quarter moon was bright. Then they hurried along beside the creek or, barred from the bank by rocks and trees, they waded down its stony bed. But when big clouds obscured all light except the silver about their ragged edges they picked their way painfully from white boulder to white birch to white riffle in the water. Nathan was an automaton before morning, a sleeper who saw obstacles and avoided them and went on sleeping.

As the stars were turning into nothingness the girl led her companion out of the woods into wide grass flats once more. She was watching him constantly now, with a concentration that annoyed him. They were on a gently slanting hillside and the narrow Canaseraga flowed silently and swiftly.

"Hurry," said the girl. "Only a few hours more."

Down they went, bending aside the stalks that obstructed their path. At the foot of the slope a few acres of bare brown earth showed rows of short green sprouts. Off to the right Nathan thought he saw a gleam as from a cabin window and turned to look again.

"Come," said Catherine impatiently, and they hurried on.

Two hours later Nathan felt the first indications of the recurrence of his fever. Little shivers about his spine and a rush of heat within his brain filled him with dread. He pressed his jaws together with all his strength and held on. Catherine saw the muscles of his face tighten and dismay was in her eyes.

"It's only a few miles," she said. "Very soon we must cross the creek and keep to the east bank of the Genesee."

Where the Canaseraga bent to the east they waded it and made for the high ground on the horizon. A row of scattered pines upon a hilltop were a visible goal as they entered the waving sea of grass. The fever in Nathan was growing stronger with every step and he felt that he must collapse before they reached the river. His face was flushed and he sensed by the choked feeling in his throat that his pulse was racing. Tears of helplessness came to his eyes, and when the girl took him by the arm to steady him he did not draw away. He began to move forward in a series of short rushes, stopping to gather his remaining strength, then plunging ahead. In this manner they covered about a mile.

They were fighting now for every yard. The girl was constantly taking more of the burden. Time and again as Nathan was about to fall she held him upright and then pushed him gently forward a few more steps. Finally she put his right arm over her right shoulder and, clinging to his hand with both of hers, she dragged him onward.

When they reached the bank of the Genesee, Nathan was only partially conscious. On the next day he remembered wondering if what he saw there was a vision out of his delirium. For, stretched upon the muddy bank less than twenty paces from where they emerged from the grass, lay the almost nude body of an Indian. He was a tall, well-proportioned young man and his skin was a deep yellowish brown. His length was accentuated by his hair which, though cut to about six inches, was gathered into a braid at the top of his head and run through a short piece of silver pipe that stood away from his head. From his ears, bared by the upswept hair, hung little silver rings. His slender waist was circled by a wide beaded girdle from which hung a small, short-bladed knife. The girdle held in place a deer-skin breechclout. In his feverish state Nathan thought his bare feet, standing vertically from the heel and not spread fanwise like a white man's, were funny and he laughed. The girl frowned at him and, walking over to the prostrate one, grabbed him by the shoulders and shook him vigorously. He did not waken.

In disgust the girl grabbed the Indian firmly by the chin and wheeled his body about until his head was over the stream. Then she placed the palm of her hand flat on his face and forced it under water. The effect was obviously more than she had expected.

With a strangled yell and a convulsive leap the Indian was on his feet, and his scalping knife was out of his belt and glittering in the air.

The girl's reaction was equally swift. In the jumble of staccato syllables that rushed from her mouth it was evident to Nathan she was shouting invectives at her victim. Slowly the knife descended above her head but she ignored it, moving closer to the Indian and looking up at him with flashing, angry eyes. Nathan stepped forward, and at his sudden movement the man uttered an exclamation and turned the knife toward him. The girl laughed.

"*Seos cagena,*" she said. "He is a good man."

Sheepishly the Indian returned his knife to his waist. Nathan, watching the water drip from his wet hair down his long sensitive face, saw that his eyes were bloodshot and guessed the cause.

"This is Peter Otsiquette," said the girl. "He is an Oneida of the Turtle brotherhood."

"*Comment ça va?*" said Otsiquette, bowing from the waist. "*Parlez-vous francais, monsieur?*"

"Enough to know what you say but not enough to answer it," said Nathan.

Again Catherine O'Bail laughed.

"It isn't necessary to speak French to him," she said. "He always talks it when he's drunk. Peter was educated in France. The great General Lafayette took him to his home for seven years that he might become a teacher and leader of his people."

The tall man in savage costume drew himself up proudly.

"*Je suis l'ami de Lafayette,*" he said.

When he slowly came to consciousness later Nathan remembered that this was the point at which he had fainted, and he smiled to think that Peter must have believed his boast had caused a white man to drop to the ground. There was no more smiling for the day, however. Consciousness brought with it an attack of chills that racked his body again and again and he was too miserable to notice his surroundings. Fever followed the storm of shivering and it was so hot that it drove all sense from his mind.

A yellow flame in darkness was first evidence that he was once more aware of things about him. He tried to turn to face it and discovered that he was bound to the surface upon which he lay by deerhide thongs which would not loosen though his hands strained against them. The flame cast a flickering light, and Nathan could see that the fire was in the center of some sort of room. High above, through a hole in the roof, smoke hurried upward. He could see that along the wall on the other side of the chamber hung wide shelves covered with skins and he surmised that he lay on something similar. From a forked pole standing upright in a corner hung a haunch of venison. Dark figures moved between him and the firelight now and then. He felt a tugging at his bonds. Catherine O'Bail bent above him.

"You are well at last," she said, smiling. "We had to bind you to keep you here."

She loosed the thongs and he lay still, feeling again the weakness and the utter but peaceful exhaustion caused by the fever. In a moment Catherine placed her arm beneath his head and raised it. She held a wooden bowl of soup in which big exploded kernels of white corn drifted. He drank greedily.

"I do not wish to be cruel," she said after the bowl was empty, "but if you can go on to De Boui you should go at once. You must not have another fever like this one. I cannot get the Jesuit bark from him, for he hates all women. Peter could not get it because he would be suspected of wanting to sell it for whiskey. But Peter will go with you, and the cabin is only a few miles away on the flats by the river."

Nathan sat up and looked about him. On the dirt floor near his couch a dozen Indians crouched, gazing at him. One, a dignified old man with a kind weathered face, rose and addressed him.

"Me Blackchief," he said. "Me friend of Williamson."

Two other old men, four women, and a half-dozen small boys and girls looked at Blackchief respectfully.

"Give him a present," said Catherine softly. "He is the sachem of this village."

Nathan reached into his breeches pocket and brought out several coins. He fingered a half dollar.

"No, no," whispered the girl, "ninepence."

Nathan held the silver piece out to the old man and saw his face crack into an ecstatic smile.

"Thanks," said Blackchief, "you goddam strong man soon."

Peter Otsiquette rose from a seat beside the hearth and strode forward.

"I am ready," he said sulkily, looking at Catherine with dull eyes.

With Catherine and Peter helping him at each side Nathan came out into the open on Squawkie Hill. Close together on the summit stood about fifteen small log houses, each covered with bark. Smoke rose into the starlight from the central roof hole of each. The night was clear and the Milky Way was a pale drifting powder above them.

As Nathan began the steep descent he realized that Peter

and Catherine had not only ferried him across the river but borne him between them up to this height. He looked at the girl, not knowing how to express his gratitude.

"You can go on from here without me," she said sharply, and he saw that she had interpreted his glance and wished to avoid it.

"I would have died without your help," he said. "I want to repay you somehow. If you need money. . . ."

Catherine looked at him sullenly. Then her face was lit up with a fierce light.

"You fool!" she said, and her hand flashed through the air. Nathan was staggered by a stinging crack along the side of his head. His ear was deafened and his head rang. He stuck out an arm as if to protect himself from another blow, but the girl was gone and Peter was convulsed with laughter, bellowing to the stars.

When they had stumbled down the side of the hill the Indian set off through the grass at a swift pace. Though there was a well-trodden path Nathan had a hard time following and was sometimes obliged to rest. Whenever he stopped Peter went on without noticing, but he returned later, grunting contemptuously at his companion.

It seemed hardly more than an hour before they were at the bank of the Genesee and could see De Boui's tiny log house standing beside the lazy water. The cabin was about twelve feet square. It showed no windows on either side of its narrow door and a big stone chimney took up an entire wall. Around the outside, save for the entrance, earth was piled to a height of about two feet. The little clearing by the starry river looked lonely and deserted. Peter strode up to the door and knocked. There was silence for a moment and then a high voice said, "Who's there?"

"*C'est* Otsiquette," said Peter.

There was a colloquy inside. A deep voice grumbled and the high notes of the first speaker replied as if pleading to be allowed to admit the visitors. Then the door swung inward. As he and Peter entered, Nathan saw by the light of the fire and a candle on a table that the man who had admitted them was of a light-tan complexion and that he wore a faded green coat and short cream-colored breeches. He stood respectfully beside the door, saying nothing, and for a moment Nathan thought him an Indian. Then, observing his flat nose, rounded face, and short curly hair he realized that he was a mulatto.

"*Bon soir*, Joseph," said Peter condescendingly.

"What ees it? What ees it?" said the grumbling voice they had heard.

Beside the fire, on a wooden bench, sat a well-knit, bullet-headed man of about forty. His hair, cut very short, stood up on the top of his head like fur. His wide brow was etched by long, thin, parallel lines. His eyes were a pale blue. Lace dripped in tatters from the sleeves of a shirt that had once been elaborate and beautiful. His knee-length breeches were of homespun, but his sturdy legs shone in stockings of silk and there were silver buckles on his graceful shoes.

"My friend needs Jesuit bark," said Peter, "or he will die." He sat down, cross-legged by the fire.

"Must he live?" said the man coldly. "And why must I keep heem alive who do not care to live myself? Life! It ees not important."

Nathan was both embarrassed and angry.

"My name is Nathan Hart, De Boui," he said, "and I came here to buy medicine. If you don't want to sell I'll be leaving."

"Hart?" said De Boui. "Then you are the painter who helped *le capitaine* Veeliamson against Berezy. *Tiens, tiens.*"

"I was there," said Nathan shortly.

"You shall have the bark eef you weel be seated," said De Boui. "*Joseph, apportez-vous de quinine, s'l vous plait.* And you shall pay me by telling me why you weesh it."

"I have the Genesee fever," said Nathan, puzzled. "I may die of it."

"Why not?" said the Frenchman imperturbably. "I haf been in danger of dying many times and each time it would haf been better for me to haf met weeth death than to haf gone on."

Joseph, smiling, brought to the firelight a leather bag and a tall glass of water. From the bag he drew several pieces of shredded brown substance and offered one to Nathan.

"*Mangez, monsieur*," he said.

"*Mais non*," said De Boui. "Eat if you weel, but remember zat I tell you it ees a meestake. It would be bettair to die. Why do you not weesh it?"

In the uncertain light of the one candle and a two-log fire Nathan thought the scene unbelievably grotesque. The idea crossed his mind that the tall, nearly naked Indian, the green-coated mulatto, and the strange-talking Frenchman might all be products of his continued delirium. Part of a dream or not, De Boui, he decided, was mad and he had best humor him.

"I wish to live because I want to see what is in the future," he said. "Captain Williamson has promised me a cabin and land. He says the time will come when the land will produce so much and be so valuable that I will be rich and can have a fine home. I will have a wife and children and—"

"Bah!" The Frenchman had leaped to his feet and was striding nervously back and forth across the little room. "These are but eemages and dreams. The horror zat ees life—it ees not to be escape'. I keeled a man in Alsace for a dream called honor. I should haf die' then. A *lettre de cachet*—an' I am no more. But I flee to San Dominique, for I am young and weesh to live. I prosper *comme le capitaine* Veeliamson say you weel. I am reech an' respectable. One night black fiends keel *ma femme, mes enfants, mes amis,* and cut to piece. They keel almos' all *les blancs,* white people, in San Dominique. I am build a road through ze wood an' Joseph he come and guide me to ze ocean. I should haf die then weeth all my family and my friends. But where I go, death—she is not."

During all these words Joseph had been feeding Nathan the shredded bark. Whenever the latter faltered, choking over the bitter stuff, the mulatto lifted the water to his lips, and as soon as the glass had been set down the bark was once more in his mouth. Now, taking a moment's respite, Nathan said:

"But here you have land and a home and friends. Soon other people will come to this valley and you will be wealthy and successful. You are young."

De Boui laughed and there was nothing but bitterness in the sound.

"People?" he said. "It ees the people who keel *ma femme* in San Dominique. It ees the people who keel me now if I go home to *la France.* They are the wild beast of the worl'. They crouch now here in *Amérique.* But one day they weel spring."

"I do not believe you," said Nathan hotly, waving Joseph of the bitter bark aside. "The people will one day rule themselves for their own advantage, obtaining the greatest good for the greatest number."

"You are mad," said De Boui calmly. "Look around you. *Le Capitaine* Veeliamson would sell the beeg estate. He would make lan'lor' an' peasant. The Universal Frien'—she would make all obey ze Christ, an' she say she ees ze Christ. My own benefactor le Colonel Wadsworth weesh all the land for himsel' —all, all are mad, too. Each one would destroy ze other. The people de *l'Amérique*—zey are all ze same."

"I hate monarchists," said Nathan intensely and with the purpose of obvious insult. The Frenchman smiled and there was a cold glitter in his eye.

"*Moi aussi*," he said. "Kings are of all people ze worst; ze murderers, banditti, ze beeg outlaw of ze universe."

"But what do you believe in?" cried Nathan.

"Perhaps *l'anarchie*," said De Boui slowly, "but *assurément* death. *La mort*—it ees ze one content."

There was a sharp rap on the door. De Boui started from his seat and sank slowly back. His worship of death, thought Nathan, does not destroy fear. Joseph smiled and stepped over to lift the bar. The door swung in and for a startled second Nathan saw on the faces of both the Frenchman and the mulatto such stark and awful fright that he was himself panic-stricken. In the doorway stood a thickset woman in a dark dress and a white, close-fitted bonnet. Her face and her hands were blacker than the night behind her.

"Massa Bill an' I comin' back from Gershom Beach's house," she said. "Went to cook Missus Beach some herb tea. Massa Bill he say jest now step ovah to dat door dah an' axe de gemman kin I come in a whiles."

Massa Bill had not waited for an answer, for as the woman finished her message a tall, darkly frowning man walked past her into the cabin. He wore a tricorn hat, white stock, and a long blue military coat that hung below the tops of his shiny black boots.

"That'll do, Gin," he said curtly. "You can ride on home now."

"Not me," said the Negress emphatically. "I ain' ridin' nowhere with them hoot owls an' whippoorwills a-talkin'. I nebber liked this country nohow an' I ain' ridin' it without folks with me."

Nathan saw that his host and Joseph could not keep their eyes from the black woman, and he suddenly knew that their memories of escape from the Negro rebels of San Domingo had caused their fear. The tall newcomer paid the slave no attention.

"Good evening, Mr. De Boui," he said.

De Boui rose slowly.

"*Bon soir,* Monsieur Wadsworth," he said. "You know my guests, Monsieur Hart *et* Monsieur Otsiquette?"

William Wadsworth bowed. His face was thin and bold, and his beaklike nose was so prominent that it gave him resemblance to an enormous bird of prey.

"I will not interrupt you, gentlemen," he said. "I came in to ask Mr. De Boui if he would accompany me tomorrow to the mustering of the militia. His training in the regiment at Cape Haitienne has made him an admirable adviser."

"I weel go," said De Boui in a voice so melancholy that Nathan expected him to continue with an outburst of his pessimistic philosophy.

"I happen to have with me a small keg of West Indies refreshment," said Wadsworth. "I hope you will accept it. Ginny, bring in the rum."

"Gladly," said De Boui, bowing for the first time, "eef you weel join us in emptying it. Joseph, find us glasses. Perhaps we persuade my frien' Peter to recite for us a speech from the tragedies of the great Corneille or such verses of Racine as he remembair."

"I recite no more," said Peter sullenly.

"Surely you no refuse to drink weeth us," said De Boui pointedly, as Ginny and Joseph busied themselves with serving the rum. The Indian was silent, his eyes following Joseph about the room. As each man received a glass of the liquid except himself and he realized that he must recite or not be served his face set in angry lines.

"Mr. Morris has told me that you speak French verses beautifully," said William Wadsworth to him placatingly, "and though my French is inferior I would enjoy hearing them. Do you know the language, Mr. Hart?"

"Only a few words," said Nathan.

"You are the portrait painter of whom Captain Williamson has spoken, are you not?"

"I believe so. He thought you might be interested in sitting for me."

Wadsworth laughed.

"I am only a plain farmer," he said. "It is my brother who would be interested. He is a man of the world."

"A plain farmer," said De Boui mockingly, "who own most ze land to ze falls of ze Genesee."

Wadsworth grinned.

"Do you know more I can buy?"

"Only from Veeliamson."

Nathan saw the harsh features of the man darken in a frown.

"His price is high."

"To you, *mais oui*, for you tak' all his acres—two meelion eef you could be reed of him."

Angrily Wadsworth sprang to his feet. As he did so, Peter Otsiquette sitting stolidly by the fire gave up his struggle.

"I will recite," he said so hopelessly that first Nathan, then De Boui, then Wadsworth laughed aloud. Joseph at once handed Peter a glass of rum which he drained at a gulp and gave back for refilling. He drained the second glass before he spoke again.

"What do you wish?"

"Horatius to ze brothair of his wife," said De Boui promptly. "They haf been chosen each to fight against ze odder —Alban against Roman. You know ze part where he say to Curatius, 'Eef you are no Roman try to be jus' as good; eef you are equal to me prove it. Ze courage I make boast about haf no weakness. Ze honor mus' not look behind when she enter ze tourney. My misfortune ees beeg, beegest in worl', but I look him in face and I do not tremble. Let Horatius speak."

At once the Indian stood up. The little flames behind him played on his bare flanks and bronze shoulders as he lifted a long hand and began:

"*Si vous n'êtes Romain, soyez digne de l'être;*
Et si vous m'égalez, faites-le mieux paroître.

La solide vertu dont je fais vanité
N'admet point de foiblesse avec sa fermeté;
Et c'est mal de l'honneur entrer dans la carrière.
Que dès le premier pas regarder en arrière.
Notre malheur est grand; il est au plus haut point:
Je l'envisage entier, mais je n'en frémis point;
Contre qui que ce soit que mon pays m'emploie,
J'accepte aveuglément cette gloire avec joie;
Celle de recevoir de tels commandemens
Doit étouffer en nous tous autres sentimens.
Qui, près de le servir, considère autre chose,
À faire ce qu'il doit lâchement se dispose:
Ce droit saint et sacré rompt tout autre lien.
Rome a choisi mon bras, je n'examine rien.
Avec une allégresse aussi pleine et sincère
Que j'épousai la soeur, je combattrai le frère;
Et, pour trancher enfin ces discours superflus,
Albe vous a nommé, je ne vous connois plus!"

As he finished with a tragic renunciatory gesture, his companions burst into applause that continued for some time—the longest and loudest coming from admiring Ginny who obviously understood no word of the speech's content. Peter approached the little keg, glass in hand, and was rewarded by Joseph with two more full measures of rum.

"Zat was good," said De Boui. "I like ze ending. You onerstan' it, Monsieur Hart?"

Nathan shook his head.

"He say, 'I go where my contree send me weeth joy in ze gloire to be sent. I think of no else but duty. Rome chose me—it ees enough. I marry ze seester—I fight ze brother. Alba has chosen you—I do not know you again.' Now s'il vous plait—jus' one bit more."

Nathan thought he saw a purposeful gleam in the Frenchman's pale eyes as he went on. "Zee mourning of zee father for his dead sons and his shame for Horatius who flee away. I cannot say it good for you, but it mean, 'Do not weep them. Their father ees jealous. Throw fine flower on ze tomb. Ze gloire of their death pay me for everythin'. This happiness follow their beeg courage. Rome ees free an' they nevair see her made province or obey a master.' "

Softly the Indian began again, speaking each syllable perfectly and with feeling:

"*Tout beau, ne les pleurez pas tous;*
Deux jouissent d'un sort dont leur père est jaloux.
Que des plus nobles fleurs leur tombe soit couverte;
La gloire de leur mort m'a payé de leur perte:
Ce bonheur a suivi leur courage invaincu,
Qu'ils ont vu Rome libre autant qu'il ont vécu,
Et ne l'auront point vue obéir qu'à son prince. . . ."

Here in the midst of his recitation emotion began to overcome Peter. His voice turned husky and his lips trembled. Tears stood in his eyes, reflecting the candle's glow. Valiantly he struggled through the next line:

"*Ni d'un Etat voisin devenir la province—*"

but at the end of it he hurled himself against the door of the cabin, lifted the bar, and vanished into the night.

De Boui smiled, and in the certainty of his expression it was obvious that he had expected exactly this to happen.

"He should haf die *aussi*," he said. "Le Marquis sent him back to be Moses. He strike ze rock and ze rum—she pour out."

"But why did you ask for those passages?" said Nathan.

"So he be glad to die," said De Boui simply, "lak' all of us. He saw himsel' lak' Moses—an' his dream *est fini*. My benefactor Wadsworth see himsel' lan'lor' of all ze Genesee—ze eemage disappear. You see yoursel' how—it ees *la même chose*." He shrugged his shoulders.

"I have enjoyed this visit," said Wadsworth heavily. De Boui's philosophic remarks evidently bored him. "It is a pity that Peter should be overcome by drink, for his education should be an important asset to any community." Nathan was amused by the ponderous platitude, obviously spoken as an appropriate sentiment.

"Mr. Hart," Wadsworth continued, "will you ride on with me to my home? I have ample accommodation for you there and we might approach my brother about a commission for you."

"But Monsieur Hart stay weeth me," said De Boui quickly. "He eat more bark in ze morning."

Nathan felt that the Frenchman really wished him to stay, and the thought of returning fever frightened him.

"I am thankful to you, Mr. Wadsworth," he said, "and after my fever has left me I hope you will allow me to make the visit I am denied."

"My brother and I will look forward to it," said Wadsworth formally. The black woman was already in the saddle and calling to him excitedly as he strode out of the door.

XIX

The sun was high when Nathan awoke. There was no one in the cabin. A tension had broken within him and, except for a strange buzzing in his ears, he felt well. Strength was flowing back into his muscles and lazy warmth into his bones. Joseph bustled into the room smiling, and in another moment Nathan's mouth was filled again with the bitterness of Jesuit bark. But the aftertaste of clear fresh water was heartening relief and it was followed by such urgent smells from the fireplace that he rose and went outside lest he seem too eager for his breakfast. He splashed the river water on his face and let his hands and forearms soak for a while in the cooling current. Then Joseph called and he bounded into the cabin. One place was set on the crude wooden table before the fire.

"Where is Monsieur De Boui?" asked Nathan, and Joseph answered in a long speech of which his hearer understood nothing. Nathan laughed, and Joseph, seeing his puzzled look, laughed too, and began marching stiffly about the room, making sounds like a drum. Suddenly Nathan remembered that, on the night before, William Wadsworth had asked the Frenchman to attend the militia muster this day.

"*Oui, oui,*" he said to Joseph, and the mulatto rushed to the skillet on the fire and began serving up hot cakes of fried corn-meal mush. To his delight Nathan discovered maple syrup in a large decanter beside his plate and he made such a meal of the cakes and sweet sauce as he was proud of. And when he could eat no more a peaceful heaviness settled down upon his mind and he lay once more on the bed against the wall and dozed. After Joseph had made the room tidy he went out into the garden behind the cabin where, half-heard, his rhythmic hoeing went on and on. It is easier, thought Nathan, drowsily, to hold consistently to any philosophy if a slave provides you with the necessaries of living.

He was up and eager to be returning to Bath by midafternoon. Joseph tried to persuade him to stay, but Nathan was so elated over the return of good spirits and health that he ran happily down to the river. He meant to cross to the other shore and follow the short path to Williamsburg. Thence he could retrace his previous ride to Bath and reclaim his mare. Though his illness had prohibited his keeping his appointment with The Friend and with Elijah he hoped they would not cancel their orders for portraits. He must begin to earn his living.

But De Boui's canoe was safely tied on the eastern side and the river was too wide to cross without swimming. Nathan set out to follow the course upstream in the hope of finding a narrow channel filled with rocks on which he could cross without wetting his clothes. He had gone less than a quarter of a mile when he came to a sharp-jutting wooded point and there, calmly sitting with her back to a tall pine, was Catherine.

"I am tired of waiting," she said pleasantly and quite as if their last parting had been casual. "I came to paddle you up the river in my canoe for a few miles. It will make your return much easier."

"I don't need help," said Nathan stiffly, remembering the stinging slap and the fact that she had called him a fool. He suspected, too, that she was lying, for he was sure that the course of the Genesee was too far to the west to bring him closer to Bath.

For answer she slipped quickly down the bank to her landed canoe and set about pushing it into the stream. She made hard work of it, and Nathan, shamefaced at the memory of the miles the girl had helped him cover in his delirium, jumped down beside her. A few seconds later the long and ungainly dugout was in the water and Catherine was holding it steady for him to enter. Stooped above the water she looked up at him questioningly, and Nathan, wondering what he should do, finally climbed in and sat down.

"Did Peter recite his French poems?" she asked casually as she knelt and, skillfully swinging the prow into the channel, set the craft against the bubbling current.

He told her of Otsiquette's strange actions and she nodded understandingly.

"He is ashamed," she said. "The Messiah has become a drunk. I wish you could have seen him when he came back from France. I loved him then."

From the tone of her voice Nathan knew that she meant her last sentence to be taken literally, and he wondered what the love of these two could have been.

"He was a fool to lose you," he said sincerely.

In the black eyes shone a glint he did not understand.

"You think so?" she said.

Nathan watched the play of her yellow-brown rounded arms as she moved her paddle. The rhythmic swinging like her every other movement was effortless. On the red shirt, open at her sun-browned throat, shone the black braid of her hair. The full mouth was curved happily and her lips were slightly apart, as if she were vastly enjoying the moment and yet not quite aware of her own delight.

They had been hardly an hour on the river before Nathan could see that the shores were of a different character. The width of the grassy bottoms was growing less and the slopes beyond were steep and rugged. Nathan turned his face to look along the course ahead and saw a high and dark escarpment curving upward toward the sun. The canoe was entering a narrow canyon whose sides dwarfed the tall hemlocks at their feet. The east bank, still yellowed by sunlight, was a lofty mass of greening foliage; the west was a shadowy precipice. A perpendicular rocky barren, unmarked save where an occasional rooty shrub leaned out of the cracked and brownish rock, it towered to an eerie height. The canoe grated on the bottom. Catherine had sent it ashore and it lay in cool dark shadow at the foot of the high wall.

"I will not go farther," she said. "From the top of this bank I can show you the shortest way to Bath. There is a path a few feet from us."

She rose and stepped lightly ashore. Her short and garish skirt, lifted above her sturdy legging, bared the two straight tendons at the back of her right knee and the smooth widening curves of the tawny flesh above it. Nathan helped her pull the canoe on the stony shore and followed her as she eagerly set out to reach the far summit. The winding path was less steep than he had anticipated, and he was elated that climbing was not the agony of the past few days but a blood-stimulating joy. The lithe boyish figure ahead leaned forward and the moccasined feet were quick and dainty. Nathan's lank legs covered more distance with each step but he moved awkwardly, and the girl stopped to laugh at him when a shoe dislodged a rock and sent it hurtling downward.

Nathan was surprised when, after a half hour of steady progress, they came out on a broad plateau and there was no slope above them. Cautiously the two approached the sharp edge and looked down to the water. The girl shuddered and her firm hand reached for Nathan's and held it tightly. The Genesee had shrunk to a glimmering silver band laid haphazardly at the dark bottom of the ravine. The sun's rays had crept up the east wall and lighted now only the green treetops above its summit. Dusk lay in the canyon and its softness made the vast depth before them seem measureless.

A dark pine stood on the brink, its trunk curving over the abyss, its roots grappling for a hold in the rock-covered soil. No foliage grew on its landward side, but it held a misshapen green burden out into the air above the chasm. They stood beside it until the sun, a dull red ball behind them, had dropped into a nest of purple clouds at the edge of the world.

Nathan looked at Catherine. A star had struck through the darkening blue curtain above the eastern bank and he seemed to see its reflection in her eyes. Her hand tightened on his own and suddenly he tore it from her grasp and put his arms around her, holding her slim figure very close. He cupped the little childlike chin in his left hand and lifted it upward. He bent his head until his mouth was on her full lips, and they were moist and cool. Slowly they opened before his continuous searching pressure and his hand dropped from her chin to the resilient mound that lifted the left side of her brick-red shirt into little folds radiating from a single center. Her hands clenched into fists that rested on his chest as if to beat upon it, but they did not move.

He put both arms around her and lifted her for a moment, and, then, letting her toes touch the earth, he moved forward. She went down full length, slowly, flowingly. Tenderly he laid the shiny black head upon a patch of red clover that had struggled through the stones at the foot of the pine. His mouth once more on hers he stretched his long body on the ground. Her body was a seeking flame, licking against him, bidding the potential fire within him burst out and burn upwards in one blending, singing surge. The cracked and dirty leather leggings were gross cover for a stirring mystery, but above them lay such satin smoothness as no man could dream.

It seemed to Nathan that all the bitterness of his life since his arrest, all the outrage of his humiliation, all the nervous sense of continually being pursued might here and now be released from him forever. He had possessed a woman before and the experience had been hearty and wholly carnal and soon forgotten. But this girl had become by a process he could not explain a symbol of the imprisonment and torture of his spirit, and through her he might be free. He exulted in her suppressed exclamations, her knitted brows, her curled and bitten lower lip. She was a mated animal, no, an evil spirit in animal form whose spell would now, by God, be broken.

Fiercely he fought his battle, searching her brutally again and again, lest one vestige of his enemy be unconquered. But his was an enduring and elusive foe, a foe that must be overwhelmed time after time by a fierce and watchful adversary. Nathan was ruthless in his hate, returning with frantic violence every new effort to oppose him. Then suddenly he knew that he had won. Here was the last and bitterest moment of all, the crucial combat—but he felt victory rise within him on such a flood of elation as he had never known, and he welcomed the struggle with a cry. Somewhere below him the river canyon was a gash of darkness, soft darkness that must hide nothing from him if he would triumph. But light had come to aid him. Light was all about him, for his head was lifted into a tilted heaven and the stars were wheeling down its slanted planes.

They lay still for a long time, while their breathing slowed from quick desperate gasps to the long rhythm of the happily exhausted. And Nathan was suddenly ashamed of the bitterness of his thoughts of the girl. She was no evil spirit in animal form, no symbol of the forces that persecuted him. She was the dispeller of evil enchantment, the priestess who granted absolution. He had come to her sick of body and of heart, and she had cured first one and then the other. He put out a hand and rested it on the top of her head. She turned on her side and curled contentedly against him.

A few moments later Nathan was asleep. When he awoke the sky was streaked with dawn and his arms were empty. Catherine was gone. He stood up and looked about him. The scent of the wild grass far below was sweet on the morning breeze. The contentment which had lulled him to sleep was gone and in its place had come doubt and self-reproach. He had taken physical possession of the Philadelphia girl, but that had been when they had thought to be married and she had both expected and desired his advances. It was she, moreover, who had put an end to their wooing with her blind obedience to a silly, stupid mother.

This was different. He had heard older men joke about the days in western Pennsylvania when they said a squaw lay under every bush. Like them he had given way to the simple bodily reactions of lust. He was chagrined and full of self-distrust. He had taken this girl and had found in this action release from nervous torture. Now he was paying too high a price in humiliation and remorse.

What of Catherine O'Bail? She was no primitive savage but a beautiful, honest girl who had once saved him from a fevered death in the high grass beside the Genesee. He remembered the voice of his mother, "He got a lot of ideas I don't approve of—never strict about women." He had treated this friendly, loyal person like a squaw under a bush. He thought of the blue eyes of Rachel Malin and he was miserable and ashamed.

XX

"*Ye might think we'd lost old G. Washington himself,*" said Whirl Gragg, settling comfortably on the new cabin floor. "Cap'n Williamson was ridin' around in all directions like a phoebe bird when a young 'un flies off to the woods. 'We can't afford t'lose no artist,' he says. 'A painter,' he says, 'is proof to gentlemen of leisure of the polite civilization of the Genesee Country. A lot o' high-class macaroni'd buy estates here,' he says, 'if they knowed they c'd git their picter painted inside a day's ride. I don't see what could-a become o' the young man.'

" 'Perhaps he's caught the chills an' hots,' I says, 'what folks call the Genesee fever.' He puffs up like a black snake chokin' on a bullfrog. 'They ain't no sech thin' as Genesee fever,' he says. 'This here country's jest a-bustin' out with health an' strong constitution.'

" 'I won't say nothin' agin the Constitution myself,' I says, 'but I reckon a lot o' fellas that ketched the ague somers else has been givin' this valley a bad name.'

"So then I gits ready to come a-lookin' for ye when ye pile int' town with a story o' being saved by Injuns. Don't want t'hurt yer feelin's none, but it sounds all-fired tall t'me."

Nathan laughed joyously.

"It's as good as I could make up," he said. "When did you get the cabin?"

"Soon's we'd got back from lockin' up the Germans we caught. Had to build an addition on the Canandaigua jail to hold 'em all. Then I lit out fer Bath. 'There 'tis,' the Cap'n says, standin' out there in front o' the door. 'You an' Mr. Hart can occupy it till Hell freezes,' he says, 'an' longer if ye pay me the money.' So I moves in, an' the nex' day as sweet a drink o' white-collared gray ale as ye'd want to put yer mouth to comes a-knockin'. 'Is Mr. Hart t'hum?' she says, blushin' purty. 'No'm,'

I says, 'but there ain't much he kin do that I can't.' 'The Friend expected him,' she says—like you'd left the Holy Virgin standin' in the rain. 'I'll tell him t'come right over,' I says, 'soon's he gits back from where he's gone,' an' she went away."

Nathan looked about the cabin pridefully. A stone chimney and wide bake oven took up one whole wall. The two windows, one on each of the long sides, were already filtering the sunlight through greased-paper panes. Hewn rafters supported the floor of the little attic, and a square hole permitted entry to it from a ladder leaning against the center beam. The floor was of split and matched basswood, and the narrow door was one wide plank of pumpkin pine.

"Made by a genuwine Scotch carpenter," said Whirl, observing Nathan's interest, "name o' McKay. Most houses here look like the beavers built 'em."

"Did the Captain give us the land, too?" said Nathan.

"A hunderd acres fer you an' fifty fer me," said Whirl. "Most as fer as the eye can see, ain't it? I'm settin' out a couple acres o' the cleared land in wheat tomorrow."

"I'll help."

"No, ye don't. Ye can paint faster'n grain kin grow an' we'll be needin' real money afore harvest."

"Then I'll ride over to see The Friend this morning. On my way back I'll stop at Elijah's. If they keep their agreements I'll be paid twenty dollars for the two portraits."

Whirl whistled a long descending phrase of wonderment.

"Beats the Dutch what folks'll pay fer what they c'n see better in a mirror," he said. "I seen some picters to Philadelphy wunst. Wouldn't a give a pistarene fer the lot of 'em."

The white house above the blue lake had lost none of its luster when Nathan saw it for the second time. At the big mounting-block before the door he swung himself off the mare and tied her. He heard no voices as he went up the steps, bearing his canvases and brushes, and his knock seemed to resound through the whole building. There was no answer and after a long minute of waiting he knocked again. As the sound died out he heard quick footsteps coming down the narrow room that he had left wrathfully. He wished it were shorter, for both heart and breath seemed to cease until the door should open. Then mysteriously there was no door and blue eyes were leaping at the sight of him and his whole being was feasting on the picture of her standing there. They gazed at each other and neither knew how long. At last she spoke:

"We were afraid that you had come to harm."

"I was ill with the fever."

"If we had only known. The Friend has cared for many who have had it."

"Some Indians found me on the trail and cared for me. They cured me with the Jesuit bark." He was unhappy lying to her. Why had he not said "an Indian girl?"

"Oh, that was good," she said. "The Friend has found that Indians often bear less evil in their hearts than the white men who persecute her."

"Are you glad?" he asked bluntly, looking into her frightened eyes.

"We are always glad to find a lack of evil."

"You know what I mean. Are you glad that I am here?"

"The Friend is always—"

"No, not The Friend—you. Are you glad?"

The fright within her eyes had turned to panic. Seconds were too long to endure.

"Yes," she said very softly, and then in a clear sure voice, "I will tell The Friend that you have come. She will wish to see you."

Again Nathan entered the room with the chairs along the sides and at the end the carved wooden pulpit. He followed Rachel down its length, climbed the steps to the platform, and stood before a screen of gray homespun, edged with unpainted hickory.

"Wait," said Rachel, and she went behind the screen and through a doorway on the other side. Nathan could not hear what she said, but in a moment the clear cold voice of The Friend spoke decisively:

"Bring him to me!"

Rachel came out and beckoned, and Nathan went behind the screen and through the door. He found himself in a small, many-angled room of eight sides. Doors in four of them led to other chambers, and through one he could see a wide, sleigh-shaped, red and gold bed. Garish pictures of saints and apostles adorned the walls around him. A ponderous Quaker Bible lay on a slim-legged mahogany table in a corner. Beside it hung a long mirror in an elaborately carved oak frame and the carvings ended at the bottom in the swirling letters U.F.

In the exact center of the octagonal chamber stood a red-cherry dressing table, ornamented with exquisite inlays of white maple. Facing it in a pillowed armchair sat The Universal Friend. Nathan caught his breath at sight of her. A change had come to the regal face and the slim, strong body. The overlarge eyes were misted, and her cheeks hung loosely and were spotted with patches of red. Beneath her white morning gown her stomach swelled out, stretching her flowered waistcoat into wrinkles and giving her the ludicrous look of a man with too much paunch. But the jet-black hair had been carefully divided and curled into three ringlets, the white stock about her neck was trimmed at the throat with fine lace, and her white silk cravat was tied loosely about it with a negligence that might have been designed. In the ceiling above her an eight-sided skylight admitted the noon sun, and its rays, descending upon the upheld head, wreathed it in a gleaming halo. Nathan noted that with all the tragic difference in her appearance her assumption of sacred authority and her attempts to bolster it by artificial means continued.

"I am sorry you have been visited with the ague," she said, and Nathan knew she had spoken only words and allowed herself no concepts of them.

"I came as soon as I could," said Nathan. "If you would care to sit for an hour today. . . ."

A look of pain crossed her face.

"The Lord bespoke me in a dream, and said, 'Thy space in Time is brief.' "

"I wait your convenience," said Nathan.

"First you shall break bread with us," said The Friend. "Rachel, you may give the signal." The girl went quickly out the door and around the edge of the gray screen. Nathan heard the singing note of a small bell. At once there was a distant, broken, humming noise. The Friend rose and went out of the room, and Nathan followed, leaving his canvases behind. A moment later he stood with Rachel on the right of The Friend as she occupied her pulpit. In the short time since he had entered the octagonal chamber a table covered with a white cloth had been set in the long room. A swinging door at the far end opened, and with the clatter of many steps the six girls Nathan had seen on his former visit hurried into the room, each bearing a steaming platter piled with food. Behind them a black boy raced about bringing up chairs from the side walls. Their burdens placed on the table, the girls stood rigidly, each at her own plate. There was a silence—then the clangor of a great bell outside, so loud it seemed to shake the walls of the house. At once the outer door opened and a bearded short man in a tow shirt and homespun breeches slowly entered. Over his right shoulder hung a wide piece of stout webbing and at either end of it dangled an oblong tin trunk—bright proof of the quality of the shiny wares inside. Behind him walked two blanket-wrapped Indian men; then a shrinking, coughing, emaciated white man wearing a heavy greatcoat. All moved up to the table and the tin peddler would have seated himself had not one of the Indians restrained him. The All-Friend raised her hands and spread them in a gesture including all the people in the room.

"In the name of Jesus Christ," she said clearly, "I bless this food to the use of all who love and fear Him."

She let one hand drop and moved the other in a short gesture of benediction. "Come," she said sharply to Rachel, and Nathan found himself standing alone beside the pulpit. Embarrassed, he hurried down the steps and seated himself beside the peddler who was eating furiously. At once the Negro boy, whom the young women called Cuff, set each of the platters before him in turn. Nathan cut a large piece from a leg of mutton, sliced one side of the breast from a roast wild turkey, placed two baked potatoes on his plate, and covered the lot with gravy. When he had eaten these, glorying in the return of sharp appetite after his fever, he filled his plate with fresh greens, sprinkled them with vinegar, and devoured them. Again and again he emptied his glass, which Cuff generously kept filled with a refreshing drink that seemed to be made of milk and eggs and flavored with vanilla and nutmeg. When, finally, Cuff brought him a bowl of custard pudding he could hardly finish it. As the last spoonful reached his mouth he saw the peddler, who had also finished, draw a jackknife from his pocket and cut from the table a thin sliver with which he picked his teeth.

"Mutton sorta gits into the corners," he said genially. "Have t' spear it out. Wonder if you noticed a pecooliar flavor 'bout that there meat. I c'n tell it ever' time. Comes from usin' pewter dishes. Slow poison, that's what 'tis. More folks a-dyin' from cookin' their vittles in pewter today than o' Genesee fever. An' if they'd only knowed they'd a put in a complete stock o' health-givin' tinware—yes, siree!"

The tinkling bell had sounded from the pulpit again and there was a silence. Once more The Friend and Rachel stood upon the platform. The Friend had changed her costume. She wore the purple robe of her formal appearances.

"Those who follow The Friend," she said, "will come to her chamber as soon as the dishes have been removed from the table. Mr. Hart will come with them. God bless and keep you all."

At once all guests rose and left the room except Nathan. He sat and watched the girls at their work. They were not gay, as he remembered them. They looked at him out of the corners of their eyes and whispered seriously together. He could not tell whether or not they recognized him. In a few moments dishes and cloth were gone, and Cuff had placed a woolen blanket under the table legs and was sliding the whole thing to a far corner. Nathan saw that the girls expected him to go first, and so, feeling self-conscious, he rose and walked to the platform. Forming three pairs they marched behind him, and he felt very silly as he led the little company of gray doves up the steps.

The Universal Friend was again seated in the armchair in the center of the room. Rachel sat on a wooden stool beside her. The girls stood against the walls in a wide circle. Nathan faced the prophetess, but his eyes sought Rachel's.

The Universal Friend raised her eyes to a point above his head and spoke:

"I have told ye that the Lord is so displeased with the world that He would return The Friend to His heaven, there to await a time when the unregenerate are more receptive to His message. And I have told ye that I would leave behind a sign for your comfort that ye do not despair."

There was a distressed fluttering among the girls, a clasping and unclasping of hands, a few uttered syllables of distress.

"I have asked the Lord so to guide the hand of Mr. Hart that during the period I am absent from Time ye may have a likeness of The Friend and know that ye are in her thoughts as she is in yours. Do not misunderstand me. A graven image or a painted form conceived in vanity is an abomination before the Lord. But a likeness such as these—" she pointed to the colored pictures of the saints and apostles on the walls— "may be an inspiration and a solace. For thy sake, not my own, I leave a likeness behind me. I do so at the command of the Lord who appeared to me in a Vision and so directed me. I ask but one question of ye. Do ye wish it?"

For answer the girls burst into torrents of tearful protestations. One fell upon her face on the floor, sobbing convulsively. Two knelt before her seeking to touch her hands. Another lifted the hem of the purple robe and kissed it.

"Weep not for me like those who have no hope," said The Friend. Her eyes were set as if she were in a trance and the syllables fell from her lips in a rhythmic chant:

"Though I shall sleep I shall arise again
And when I part from Time I wish no hearse,
No pomp, and no parade, no rites save those
Sweet blessings you who followed me on earth
May bring, before you, too, leave Time and come
To join me in the New Jerusalem."

A stout, red-haired girl had become hysterical. Her voice rose in a high scream of anguish. The Friend spoke to her sharply.

"That will do!" The words cracked like a whip and the girl's screams diminished into a terrified whimpering.

"I will devote the next two hours to Mr. Hart's work," said The Friend practically. "I will sit for two hours each week at this time until the likeness is done. I will receive your reports on your work for the day as soon as Mr. Hart leaves."

All the girls except Rachel left the room. Nathan picked up a canvas and looked about for a convenient spot to place it.

"You may use the mahogany table to put your brushes

on" said The Friend, "and if you and Rachel can roll the pulpit inside it will hold your canvas while you paint."

Nathan allowed Rachel to grasp the top of the heavy lectern first. Then he placed a hand firmly on her own and swung the piece forward so that its base was on edge. An imploring look came into her eyes.

"You mustn't," she whispered softly, but as he released his hold he thought he felt the little hand press upward against his own. He waved her aside then, and unaided carried the thick column into the chamber.

As he entered, The Friend stood before her mirror peering earnestly into the glass. Her right hand lay on her right shoulder and its extended forefinger was within the curvings of one of her three ringlets. The big brown eyes that had been so bright when he first saw her bulged from their sockets in the intensity of her emotion. She once had great beauty, Nathan thought, and now she will not admit that it is gone, even to herself.

She dropped her hand quickly.

"You will stand there," she said, indicating a spot near the door. "Bring the table to him, Rachel. I will be here." She sat before the cherry dressing table. Again a shaft from the skylight descended upon her black hair.

"The light is difficult," said Nathan.

"The Lord has commanded me to sit here. If you would please Him you will paint me as I am now."

"But I cannot see your features distinctly."

"You may move about to obtain the likeness, but I wish the light to be as it is."

Nathan set up his canvas. He had scraped it and had prepared his paints. There was nothing to prevent his beginning to work at once and yet he dawdled. She could not accept a true likeness, he thought. An honest portrait would destroy her. Yet the tricks of flattery that a professional painter might know were beyond his skill. He would be lucky if he could make the portrait look even reasonably like its subject. He set out his lake, ultramarine, and umber on the white pine palette and began uncertainly to paint in the background.

Two hours later he slowly gathered his materials together.

"I prefer to take the canvas with me," he said. "There are touches I can make at home."

"Yes," said The Friend, and it was the first word uttered since he had begun to paint. Through the whole time Rachel had sat with downcast eyes, not looking up even to watch his brushes. The Friend had struck a rigid pose at first, but as the minutes passed she had relaxed and apparently gone into a not unpleasant revery.

As Nathan left the room Rachel followed. On the steps of the platform the six handmaidens waited demurely. They rose to allow their leader and the painter to pass. Then they moved on toward The Friend's chamber.

Rachel closed the outside door behind her. Like a voluptuous gray statue against a white background she stood motionless, her eyes looking straight forward and apparently fixed upon Nathan's throat.

"Good-bye," she said.

"I will come a week from today," said Nathan. "It will be a long time to wait to see you again."

"Seeing me need not interest you," she said coldly. "You are painting a portrait of The Friend. I am her companion while you do so."

"You said you were glad I had come," Nathan reminded her roughly.

"I was wrong," she said, and a set angry look came into her face. "Worldly and wicked feelings cannot find room in my heart."

"You have no heart," said Nathan savagely. "If you can't love a man, you can't love your saint-woman there or your God either."

"You need not be concerned," she said. "I am safe in the guidance of the Lord. In visions I have seen Him and He has counseled me."

"There'll be a day when you can't answer with fancy words learned by heart," said Nathan.

"You had better go," she said.

Nathan stamped down the steps and untied the mare. He was puzzled and angry. What did Rachel expect? Was she a woman or a nun? All he wanted was a one-word answer. If it were "no" he would recover. He stopped the mare at the edge of the woods and looked back. The haze that hung above the lake seemed to have drifted shoreward, and though the dwelling stood in sunlight its outlines were indistinct. The well house, too, was a blurred white spot in the yard. The whole clearing was a picture in a dream. Within those dim high walls were many women and something else not to be called by name—an influence not to be understood. Near at hand a thrush turned the notes of a squeaking pump handle into an exquisite harmony. He reined Lottie about and urged her into the forest. A few steps inside its shade Rachel barred his path, her eyes dancing, her breasts lifting and falling quickly. She must have run from the rear of the house into the woods and then on, unseen, until she intercepted him.

"I didn't mean it," she said, and her voice broke in a near sob. "Oh, I didn't mean it!"

Nathan swung off his saddle and took her in his arms.

XXI

Throughout the long days the yellow-throated warbler in the birches near Nathan's cabin cried "witchery, witchery, witchery." Throughout the short nights moons of enchantment waxed and waned. It was a summer happier than a young man's dream of summer. Every Monday Nathan's week began with two silent hours in the holy chamber of The Friend. And when they were over, and the pairs of demure doves had filed up the platform steps to the august presence, there was bliss among the hickories beyond the clearing.

There, with their arms about each other, Rachel and Nathan stood mouth to mouth until, breathless, they drew away in fear of the depths their kisses stirred. The passion of The Friend's high priestess was insatiable and undisciplined, yet it never compelled her to give herself over completely. There were moments when her body, overwhelmed by the storm of his desiring, writhed crazily and her eyes were fixed in a glassy stare. But if at such an instant Nathan dared so much as slip a hand between the buttons below her collar and try to touch a generous soft mound concealed there she would, with a convulsive effort, become coldly rigid and her voice would be hard and she would speak of wickedness and the laws of God. Then she would recall the teachings of The Friend, and at the name her eyes would fill with tears and sobs would rush into her throat. After that she would not let Nathan kiss her again but would walk away from him with bent head, leaving him miserable and desperate. But on the next Monday afternoon she would be frantically eager to renew their love-making, clasping him to her with all the strength of her arms, kissing him with a bruising pressure.

More than once as he held Rachel in his arms Nathan remembered Catherine O'Bail. The Indian girl had given him more of herself than had Rachel and she had done so in a conscious questing. She had frankly sought the maximum of delight for them both by making her slim body obey her will. The sheer madness of Rachel, the lack of awareness in her love-making, puzzled him. What she gave, she gave without design. She was not co-operative, she was simply automatic. She was incapable of self-control save for her inexorable enforcement of an incomplete and unsatisfactory ending.

After he had left Rachel, Nathan would ride down the trail to Elijah's. He had feared that upon discovery of the commission from The Friend the Prophet would cancel his own order and refuse to see him further. At the end of the afternoon on which Nathan had begun painting in the octagon room he had found Elijah at home and told him all that happened, laying especial stress on the twelve dollars The Friend was to pay for her portrait. At this disclosure Elijah's yells of rage nearly drove Nathan from the house.

"For thirty pieces of silver," he cried, "the true Prophet is betrayed."

"I must earn a living," said Nathan stoutly, "and take commissions where I can find them."

"It is a profanity," shouted Elijah, "for the same hand to portray that deceiving Jezebel and the sacred Elijah."

"You have been very kind to me," said Nathan slowly, "and if you wish it I will cancel my arrangements with The Friend."

Elijah was so taken aback at this suggestion that he could not summon enough breath for an outburst for some time. Then his voice shook the room again:

"She shall not have a twelve-dollar job and I an eight. I will pay fourteen dollars for my likeness and you must make the difference show clearly."

"I think I can guarantee that you will like it better," said Nathan smiling, and at that Elijah put an arm about his shoulders and guided him up the slope to the springhouse. There he loaded down his guest with a new cheese, a ham, a five-pound crock of butter—all for the larder of the new cabin in Bath.

"Did you say," said Elijah as they returned down the slope, "that the wicked female imposter says she wants her picture for those deluded fools to keep while she is absent from Time?"

"Yes," said Nathan.

"And then she'll rise up again and they won't need it any more?"

"That's about right."

"Would ye be willing to swear to that in a court of law?"

"It's the truth, but I don't know that I'd be willing to testify."

"I'll subpoena ye," said Elijah triumphantly. "If ye were forced to testify that's what ye'd say, isn't it?"

"I'd have to."

"I'm getting up a case against her," said Elijah. "I'm entering a charge of blasphemy and next time the state court meets in Canandaigua the wicked shall be confounded and the righteous Prophet shall receive his reward."

On his weekly visit to the Parker farm Nathan never failed to ask when he should begin to paint the portrait of the Prophet, but Elijah was always too excited over his current activities to listen. His black bees were swarming or his brindle cow was calving and he had no time for art. He talked as enthusiastically as ever about the picture but the day of its beginning did not come.

Of the hundred and fifty acres Williamson had given to Nathan and Whirl only twenty proved ready for planting. These, lying between the tall grass flats and the wooded slopes, had not been plowed, but before he had allotted them the Captain had ordered the surface broken with a heavy wooden harrow dragged by his own oxen. Seed was plentiful at the Captain's store and the two new settlers hurried to set out the whole tract in wheat, for the planting season was already at an end. Then they began to clear their bottom lands. Turning the sod under proved more of a task than they had imagined, for the roots of the giant wild grass were so entangled beneath the brown earth that they formed a stout fibrous net.

"Ye'll want a keen coulter," said a lanky, bearded neighbor in a buckskin shirt, as he watched Nathan drive a spade into his land, "and ye'll need about four yoke o' bullocks."

"I'm afraid we can't manage it," said Nathan despairingly.

"Course ye kin," said the bearded fellow contemptuously. "I'll lend ye the coulter if ye'll whittle it sharp, an' the Cap'n's got eighty yoke o' them cattle in the grass. All ye do is ketch 'em."

"I'll ask him if I can use them."

"Great Jehosophat," said the man. "I'm tellin' ye all ye hev to do is ketch 'em. I'm workin' for the Cap'n an' he lets me tell the new uns what to do. Name's Smith, Andrew Smith."

"I'm much obliged," said Nathan.

"Jest don't ketch no wild 'uns," said Smith. "Some o' them critters is so near human they jest won't work."

The next day Nathan and Whirl went down to the river at dawn. They found four oxen standing knee deep in the shallows. It took them the rest of the morning to round up four more. Once they had seen the grasses moving and had rushed to the spot, only to hear a startled snort and see a wild gray horse plunge frantically through the high stalks and disappear. And once Nathan, thinking Whirl far away, had mistaken him for an ox and had almost knocked him down as he dashed in upon him.

The wooden blade of Andrew Smith's plow was sharp with Nathan's carving when the four patient teams were finally in the spliced traces. Whirl goaded them forward and Nathan, pushing downward on the plow handles, felt a thrill of excitement as the coulter took hold. Suddenly there was a snapping, tearing sound, then a roar like that of continuous musketry. Nathan saw before his feet the parting of the braided roots of the grass as the coulter moved cleanly through them, and he knew that the noise came from their breaking. He grinned at Whirl and pointed to the steadily advancing wooden blade. Then, shouting at the straining oxen, the partners stepped happily forward, ripping the matted cover from their land in one long deafening racket.

After the first two days Nathan left Whirl to manage the plow alone and began setting out Indian corn, for the second week in May had begun and already neighboring plots were splattered with new green. Fifteen acres of the grasslands had been turned under when their plowing suddenly ended. The wooden coulter struck a heavy rock and split. Andrew Smith took the bad news philosophically. "Knew it'd happen when I loaned it to ye. Figgered 'twas a good way to git a new one cheap." It had taken Whirl four days to carve out a new one, four days that Nathan spent hoeing in the hot sun, and by that time both knew that further planting was useless.

There was less to do now, and Nathan and Whirl found that each could work three days of the week with the Captain's building crew. Some weeks their carpentry brought in twelve to fifteen extra dollars. Two sawmills on the Conhocton below the town were whining all day long, and the ox teams dragging the lumber sleds along the stumpy road to town were a long procession. Houses were going up in Bath as fast as thirty or forty hands could raise them. The big clearing about which the town was to center, Pultney Square, was lined with dwellings.

The members of the building crew were young men, mostly Scottish and Irish. Before the sun had climbed to noon raw whiskey gave their arms a stronger bent than they had had at dawn, and sunset found all rhythm running wild. At Metcalf's long, one-story tavern, when the light was failing, the builders gathered to devour great slabs of broiled and ruddy venison, and hominy cakes fried brown and drenched with maple syrup. Then in the moment before the stars broke out above the purple ridges the first reveler's horn would blare—its brash notes shivering against the wooden walls raised that day within the town. A musket shot would crack a fiercely gay reply and from a near-by cabin wild drums would sound. A flame would leap in the square, and in a moment the tavern and all dwellings would be emptied as dark groups of whooping, cursing men drifted about the yellow light. Then there would be more horns blowing, more drumming, drunken speechmaking, and sometimes swift, fierce fights that ended only when a man lay still and could not rise again.

Females stayed at home on roaring nights like these. There were not a half-dozen white women in the town, and kindly Mrs. Metcalf, elderly and English, watched over them like a mother. The very scarcity of them gave them safety, for if any man offered harm to one a dozen male protectors would spring to her defense. Indian women, too, learned to stay away from the square after dark—those at least who took no joy in a wild losing struggle underneath the pines when the fire had become red embers and the crowd had scattered. And even after there was stillness in the square there was no telling when a sudden blast might blow, a quick tattoo might sound from some awakened reveler who felt the lonely silence intolerable.

Nathan found Whirl gone one evening when he returned from working with the crew. The cabin was empty and there was no smell of cooking, no fire on the hearth. He walked down to the river and washed his face in the clear cold water. There would still be time to go to Metcalf's for supper. As he retraced his steps to the cabin he heard a great bumping and squeaking down the road and above it Whirl's high voice swearing prodigiously. Nathan stopped at the cabin door and waited. Floundering through the bushes, bouncing over logs, snubbing the stumps, Whirl rode behind a yoke of oxen in a chariot of his own devising. It was a box on wheels, a shallow bin that moved on solid wooden rounds cut from the big end of a curly maple log, and the screaming of its ungreased axles was more painful to Nathan's ears than he had believed a sound could be.

Whirl dismounted with a flourish.

"Built this down to White's sawmill today. Ef'n we had a boat now we could move our crops all the way from here to Baltimore, an' take a few extrys to market with us—fer a price."

"You couldn't float a heavy load from here to Painted Post," said Nathan. "River's dammed up with rocks and dead trees."

"Tain't nuther," said Whirl triumphantly. "The Cap'n's had some o' the boys workin' from t'other end to clear it. Come harvesttime we could make it—if we had a boat—an' I'm the feller to make it an' commodore it too. Wheat's a dollar in Baltimore an' it's only sixty-five cents in Albany. I'm goin' south with mine."

There was no more working with the building crew after that. Whirl spent every minute of daylight on the riverbank beside the sawmill, and Nathan, when he was not tending the crops or painting on the portrait, worked with him. A strange and awkward craft began to grow upon the slanting bank. Because the river was so narrow it could be only fifteen feet wide, but the builders could make up for lack of breadth by increasing the length. They felled their tallest pines on the slopes back of the cabin and dragged them to the bank. There they stripped them of their limbs and fashioned with them the flat bottom of a long box—a covered, river-going grain bin. A stout rudder-sweep at bow and stern and a crew shanty near the square prow which lay braced above the river on a pile of round logs were the only evidences of its watery purposes. "She'll take the whole shootin' match in her belly," said Whirl, inspecting the strange vessel in triumph. "Now the Cap'n's back home ye better go tell him what we got on our minds. Mebbe he'll help fill her up."

Nathan had not seen Charles Williamson since he and Whirl had begun work on their acres. One of the boys of the building crew had announced to them with a proud air of secrecy that their employer had gone north to the shores of the English Seas.

"Fixin' fer a settlement smack up under the Britisher's chin," he said. "An' jest let his Majesty open his mouth an' the Cap'n'll ram a dose o' gunpowder down his gullet."

"Ye ferget he was a cap'n o' the redcoats, himsel'," said a Scotch carpenter surlily. "Hoo do we ken he'll na sell us oot to the Canada governor?"

The next instant a doubled fist caught the doubting Scot fair on the chin, and he lay senseless on the pine needles for a long time while his companions went casually about their jobs.

Nathan and Whirl had been working on their boat when the horns and drums of the town had broken into hideous cacophony. They had guessed the cause but they had not quit work. As he walked across the big square toward the rambling one-story house, which looked like nothing so much as a child's building blocks lying in close disorder on the ground, Nathan wished he had been among the welcoming crowd. If he had been present to greet the Captain he would not feel so embarrassed at suggesting the idea of marketing the whole town's produce by means of the big boat.

The sound of his own knock, loud on the pine plank of the Captain's door, increased his self-consciousness. There seemed to be a hollow echo inside and it was followed by long silence. He rapped again. The short echo was like another rap in the stillness. He turned to go and then, out of impatience and with no plan in mind, he started to walk around the house.

As he reached the rear he beheld, standing in the shadowed corner made by the walls of two jutting rooms, a plump, blonde young woman and a little curlyheaded girl. They faced him and Nathan saw the woman straighten defiantly as she took the child by the hand. There could be no doubt that they had heard his knocking and had chosen to ignore it.

"I—I am sorry," Nathan stammered. "I had hoped to find Captain Williamson."

"He's not here," said the woman in a low, sullen tone. "He was not here all night."

"Forgive me," said Nathan. "I understood that he had returned from the north."

"He has returned," said the woman, and her voice was full of bitterness and fatigue, "but he went away again. He will come back today." Her short full lips curled in a pouting sneer. Nathan saw that her cheeks were round and pink, her nose prominent and straight, her forehead broad and white beneath her honey-colored hair. Her eyes, small and very light blue, held flecks of gold within their pupils. Her figure was full and stocky beneath a formal-looking dress of flowered muslin, the kind of long-sleeved, long-skirted gown Nathan had seen on Philadelphia ladies when they were making their calls in the early afternoon. He wondered who she was and why he had heard nothing of her. She was too beautiful, too obviously sensual, to have escaped the notice of the men of the town.

"I am Nathan Hart," he said. "My partner and I have built a boat to carry our grain to the southern market. I wanted to talk to the Captain about it."

"I am Mrs. Williamson," said the woman.

Nathan was suddenly amazed that he had never thought of the possibility of the Captain's being married. There was something in the graceful bearing of the tall cloaked figure, something in the genial courteous manner of the man's talk, that suggested gallant bachelorhood. His surprise at the woman's statement was badly concealed.

"You do not know of me," she said slowly, and after a pause she went on with ill-suppressed bitterness. "Nor does anyone else in this forsaken waste. I have lived here for months without speaking to a soul save the children and Indian servants. Why? Because the great man's wife must be above these wild and uncouth revelers. I am to be brought out, like a rare piece of china, when a traveling duke or an American gentleman of fortune condescends to visit our humble cot."

The little girl, terrified by the note of anger in her mother's voice, began to cry and the woman bent over her, wiping the tears away and speaking to her tenderly. Nathan realized that the long strange speech had been caused, not by his sudden appearance and evident embarrassment, but by some condition within the woman herself, occasioned by circumstances of which he knew nothing.

"There, run into the house, now," said the woman and, as the little girl obeyed, she turned her eyes on Nathan once more and he felt that he had never seen such misery and wrath compounded in a look.

"You are the painter, aren't you? But you're not good enough to paint the portrait of the agent's wife. Only the great may go beyond the office of this log hovel, only that dull Tom Morris and his doddering father and the rest. I must endure all this so that some day I may queen it over rolling acres and have a great house of my own. I'll be the Duchess of the Genesee and be received at Court."

She stopped for want of breath. Her voice had grown strident and her eyes flashed.

"I did not mean to intrude," said Nathan hesitantly. "I came on a matter of business."

The woman's laughter, high and uncontrolled, suddenly drowned his words.

"You didn't expect this, did you? Well, go out and tell those howling fiends that hammer all day long that their beloved Captain has shut up in his home a woman of flesh and blood. Abby Newell I used to be before they brought the prisoner Captain to my father's house in Boston—and I could dance and sing and carry on with the Yankee boys as well as any. But now I must be a lady and forget all that, while he rides up and down the valley being hearty with the men and gallant with the women. Yesterday afternoon he came home. Where is he now? I'll tell you where he is. Last night he rode on to that half-heathen yellow slut across the valley. Oh, he can wallow in the Indian's sty, he's done it often enough. But I—I. . . ."

Her voice faded into a whisper, for striding toward her

from around the corner of the house came her husband. Nathan knew that the Captain must have heard the last few words, yet he gave no sign of having done so.

"Madame Williamson," he cried, bowing low and sweeping the blue cloak about him. "I have returned early as I promised. Ah, Mr. Hart, are you and Mr. Gragg successful with your acres, and how goes the portrait of The Friend?"

The meaning of the woman's outburst had been slow to reach Nathan's brain because of the Captain's interruption. Now he was shocked at his reaction to what she had said. Catherine O'Bail is not the only part-Indian woman in the valley, he assured himself. And even if it were she whom the Captain had visited what did it matter? Nathan Hart had slaked his thirst at that spring and gone on never expecting to pass that way again. Did he begrudge another man like satisfaction? By his fast-beating heart and a sickening sensation within him he realized that he did—and he was ashamed. The Captain was looking at him impatiently. Nathan tried to concentrate on words to conceal the confusion in his mind.

"Whirl Gragg and I have built a floating bin to take our grain to Baltimore," he said, ignoring the Captain's questions. "I came to tell you of it and say that we've room to rent to others who have crops to send."

Williamson's eyes narrowed, and for a moment Nathan thought he saw in them a cold hard light. Then there seemed to be extra warmth in his voice as he spoke:

"Why, this is an admirable surprise! We seem to be continually in your debt! You build boats, you paint portraits, you catch malefactors. By the way, the fellow you caught and many of his companions are now working out their fines on the farms of Canandaigua."

"And what of Mr. Berezy?" said Mrs. Williamson slowly, and as if she were taunting her husband.

"He got through to Morris at Philadelphia and is trying to make trouble for me there and in New York," said Williamson shortly. He turned to Nathan.

"I fear Mrs. Williamson and I are remiss in our hospitality," he said. "Won't you come into my house and join us in a glass of Madeira?"

"I would be glad to," said Nathan, "but my partner and

I are working to finish our new barge and there is little time. I came to ask if you would aid us in completing the cargo."

"With the greatest pleasure," said the Captain emphatically, and then, as if an afterthought had occurred to him, "but I wonder if you would like to sell the boat. I take it that you would not plan to work it back upstream but would dispose of it in Baltimore for the lumber in it. If I were to give your crops free passage, pay you for the time and labor and materials that went into the building and add a pretty profit beside, would you let me have it?"

Nathan looked at the Captain in puzzlement. He could not understand the selfish motive behind this generosity, yet he was convinced that there was one.

"I will speak to my partner," he said.

"You'll sell," said Mrs. Williamson, again interrupting in her husky sullen voice. "They all do. The Baron of the Backwoods must keep his place."

The Captain laughed.

"My wife will have her little jokes at my expense," he said ruefully. "I hope you'll sell. I would find it easier than to make selection of the crops to be sent south. And if you and Gragg wish to pilot the boat south I'll be glad to pay you well to make the journey. Well, there's business to attend to now. Let me hear from you tomorrow." He bowed and turned on his heel. Once more the cape resumed its familiar slant as his long steps took him rapidly away.

The woman stood looking at Nathan, hot-eyed and contemptuous.

"You're a fool," she said and went into the house.

Nathan's mind was a turmoil as he walked back to the boat beside the river. Sternly he put down the torment that Mrs. Williamson's words had engendered. A jealous wife, he thought, might naturally attack a pretty girl of mixed ancestry without reason. The "yellow slut" was probably no one he had ever seen. And yet if it were the someone he suspected, he did not care. Still he somehow concluded that the Captain's wife had spoken of Catherine O'Bail, and he was heartsick at the thought. The starlit hour upon the Genesee's high banks kept returning to his memory as if it were a picture upon a revolving globe within his mind. He tried to convince himself that he had committed that night a sin which through the rest of his days he would repent bitterly—that his depression was due to this and to the fact that this wild girl had sinned again with another—but he knew that none of this was true. Through alchemy of her own devising the Seneca witch had converted the dross of cheap and degrading experience into an eerie gold. She had caught him, without his knowing it, in the thin, unbreakable webs of enchantment. There was but one way to meet such a situation. He thought of Rachel Malin and quickened his steps.

Whirl Gragg, Nathan was pleased to discover, also had doubts of the Captain's generous offer.

"There's somethin' about this I don't like, as the feller says when the Injun scalped him. We got to sell all right. We'd be damn fools not to."

"He could build a barge of his own and take all the cargo except ours away from us," said Nathan. "I can't see why he wants our boat. He'll lose money on it if he does all he says he'll do for us."

"He's keepin' us satisfied, ain't he?" said Whirl, "an' he's keepin' the right folks in the seats o' the mighty."

"This is a free country," said Nathan sternly. "Every man's got an equal chance here. The Captain would be the first to say so."

"Sure," said Whirl, "as long as he's out in front an' everybody's in step behind him. I was in a fight once back side o' Albany when a feller got out o' step—a fightin' son of a bitch, name o' Arnold. Old General Gates an' the rest made it so hot for him he damn near give the Britishers West Point."

"Well, anyway," said Nathan, "I guess we're agreed that we sell. I'm celebrating by not working this afternoon. You better do the same."

"It bein' a Saturday," said Whirl, "might as well git ready for not doin' nothin' tomorrow by gittin' drunk now."

XXII

The need to see Rachel at once had caused Nathan to forget that The Friend's teachings proclaimed Saturday as the Sabbath. When he came in sight of the white house he was suddenly aware of his oversight, for the yard in front of the door was black with people, and horses, oxen, wagons lined the edges of the clearing. He dismounted, hitched Lottie to a tree beside the trail, and advanced on foot. As he approached he saw that The Friend stood on the horse-block before her door. Two men in long black coats stood just behind her, holding with obvious effort a tremendous round white sunshade over her head. In the strong light of early afternoon it was a refulgent halo suspended above the shadowed features of the prophetess. Her black satin robe reached the floor of the platform, and the white stock about her neck echoing the whiteness of the shade seemed to separate her face from the rest of her body, leaving it suspended in a white mist.

At the right rear of the big block stood Rachel, her beauty stricken by the dark shadow from above. One of the dignified elderly men holding the wooden shaft of the sunshade wore a close-fitting black cap that covered his hair and most of his forehead. From the skirt of the other's coat dangled a little silver bell which tinkled gaily whenever a breeze from the lake set it in motion. Nathan noticed that when this happened irreverent listeners on the outskirts of the meeting were moved to almost uncontrollable mirth.

"Belled him like a goat, she did," giggled a young fellow, "'cause he peeked in her window late at night. The black cap come from being cheated in a hoss trade."

The voice of The Friend was distinct and clear above the crowd noises, though she did not seem to be trying to be heard.

"When I wrote to those who came to the New Jerusalem before me," she said with an air of quiet simplicity, "I said that I would come here to end my stay in Time, provided that I might be surrounded only by those who love me. Now the unregenerate and the profane, the blasphemous and the unholy increase about me. Strong drink, gambling, and the evils of the flesh have spread their nets and captured the ungodly. Yet the moment will soon come when the wrath of the Almighty Being will descend, and only those who have followed the teachings of Jesus Christ through me, his chosen vessel, shall survive. For behold! Last night I saw a vision—and in it I beheld countless millions of the ungodly standing on a dark and awful plain. And as I gazed, from rolling clouds above their heads, there came a rain of death. Yea—each and every one of the wicked was transfixed by the lightning lances of God and lay writhing in the throes of the damned who shall inherit eternal torment."

She paused, and her eyes, flashing the exaltation of the moment, lifted her spirit above the illness of her swollen body. There was a frightened murmur from the crowd. Even the curious who had come to jeer were caught up into the lowering fearsome mood.

"Listen to me," she said quietly, and utter silence answered her. "I am the messenger of the Christ and I say these things to you:

"Do not strive against one another for mastery, but all of you keep your ranks in righteousness as I shall allot them.

"Let not debate, evil surmisings, jealousies, evil speaking, or hard thinking be named among you, but be at peace among yourselves as I, the interpreter of God's will, shall direct.

"Do not inquire after news, or the public reports of anyone, and be careful not to spread any yourselves, that are not of the Lord. I will allow ye knowledge of those things which the godly should know.

"If ye will do these things the worldly and the wicked shall be driven from this land and the Genesee Country shall be a Canaan for the chosen—for those twelve thousand times twelve thousand who shall be called to stand with me upon the sea of glass—saved for all eternity."

She held up a hand and bowed her head. The crowd understood the signal. Many dropped upon their knees. Rachel Malin stepped forward out of the black shadow and knelt beside The Friend. As she did so Nathan saw her eyes look full upon him.

Her lips trembled and she looked frightened. There was a long, still wait. The sun was hot yet no one moved. Then The Friend lowered her hand and offered it to Rachel. The girl rose and clasped the hand in her own. The two stood for a moment, hand in hand, while the holders of the sunshade laid it aside and solemnly shook hands with each other. The handshaking became general throughout the crowd. The meeting was over.

Nathan walked into the woods. The air was hot and still and the minutes passed slowly. He heard the creak of wagons and the shouts of drivers to their horses and their oxen. Then silence came and it seemed to him that it had lasted a long time before he heard the little familiar noises that told him Rachel was coming. With arms outstretched she ran to him and held him close.

"Why are you here?" she said. "I did not expect you until Monday."

"Because I love you," said Nathan, "and I want to marry you."

She held him at arm's length, looking long into his eyes. Then she sighed.

"The Great Friend would welcome you into her family," she said wistfully, "if you would only become a follower. We could both live then as I do now—safe in her arms. We could be together every day, living in the peace that only The Friend can give. We need not marry then, for in The Friend's domain there can be no sin of heart or mind or flesh."

"Great God!" said Nathan explosively. "Don't you understand? I want a wife, a woman to love, a mother for children."

"The All-Friend says that children are evidences of sin."

"The All-Friend be damned," shouted Nathan and at once regretted it, for Rachel buried her head in her arms and, leaning against a tree trunk, sobbed bitterly.

"I'm sorry," he said, touching with his fingers the curving tendrils of brown hair at her temples. "I did not mean to hurt you. I have told you I want you to be my wife. I love you enough for that. Either you love me enough to give up your life here and be mine, or . . ." He paused not knowing how to go on. Suddenly she turned to him, throwing both arms about his neck and lifting her round, tear-stained face to his. The blue eyes sought his own eagerly.

"But I do," she said desperately. "Oh, I do. I cannot live without you."

In the dark shade of a purple beech then they sat for a hurried half hour, planning blissfully what they would do to bring their happiness to its fullest flower. The portrait would be finished by the end of Monday's sitting, said Nathan, and he could add the fee to money he had already saved to hire the building of a new and larger cabin on his land. Whirl could keep the old one. Perhaps, if Whirl agreed, she might go along on the big boat when it set out for Baltimore, and their honeymoon could be spent drifting down the Susquehanna and in the old city on the Chesapeake.

"When I come back on Monday," said Nathan, "I'll show The Friend her finished picture and you can tell her what we're going to do."

She looked so panic-stricken then that he laughed and kissed her.

"I'll help you," he said. "You needn't worry. After all she doesn't really own you."

Nathan sensed a curious tautness about The Friend when he came into the eight-sided room for the last sitting. While he busied himself arranging the pulpit easel and preparing his colors and brushes he tried to assure himself that he imagined the difference in her, but without success. She took up the pose naturally and held it, but her old serenity was gone and he felt nervous and baffled as he began his work. Rachel sat in her usual corner, her face as still as that of a doll, her eyes resolutely averted.

As he looked at the picture Nathan's heart sank. It was a likeness, but such a likeness as a mirror might give. It was the prophetess without her mystic quality. No one could imagine this obese woman, with the big nose and the dull, slightly protruding eyes, to be the lovely inspired creature who had galloped into the firelight on her shining black gelding the night she had saved Williamson's party from the Germans.

As he worked, retouching here and there, Nathan saw that he had painted the woman without compromise or pity. This was she as she sat there. Had he the tricks of a Court painter or the ability of the distinguished Philadelphia artist, Mr. Benjamin

West, he thought, he could have made her into the beautiful woman she had but recently been. And suddenly he knew that he was offering himself specious excuses. Had he the flattering tricks he would not have used them. This was the picture as he wanted it. It was something he had to say to her. He would not change a single phrase of it.

"I have finished," he said.

Without surprise The All-Friend lifted a hand as if to delay his approach.

"Before you show it to me," she said, "I wish to say something to you." She paused and fixed her eyes steadily upon Nathan's. "Why did you come to the Sabbath meeting? Was it because you felt the need of spiritual guidance?"

Nathan was silent. Her attack had been so sudden he could think of no defense. He had not believed that she could see him at the meeting.

"I will tell you why," she said heavily, rising from her chair and taking a step toward him. "It is because you have cast the lustful eye of sin upon the chosen servant of The Friend." Rachel moaned and, putting both hands to her face, began to weep. Inexorably the prophetess went on:

"You have dared to covet the holy vessel into whose keeping I will soon commit my mission. And I say to you this is the New Jerusalem, this is the Vale of Kedron, dedicated to peace under the laws of Christ as administered by His representative. Let you and all the others like you who have invaded my land heed my warning. Lechery and licentiousness, strong drink and evil passions, rebellious utterances against God and His chosen will of a single moment be cast from us forever." Her voice which had grown strident suddenly softened. Her body stiffened and the words came from her mouth in a measured cadence:

> "For The Friend has had a dream!
> And in it she beheld
> Swift horses racing on a grassy plain,
> Vain actors mouthing oaths within a theater,
> Proud men and women dancing to the devil's music,
> And on an instant
> The earth yawned and swallowed up
> All sinning souls."

Out of the silence that followed then came the dry, heavy sobs of Rachel. Nathan's mind was in a tumult. He felt that if he were not so much in love with the girl, and if the manner of The Friend were not so impressive as to send shudders down his back, he might want to laugh. And on the heels of this strange impulse came a cold and bitter anger. He whirled about and grabbed the heavy pulpit behind him. With the strength of overwhelming wrath he lifted it and moved forward three tottering steps. Then, twisting it about so that the painting faced its subject, he let it drop to an upright position at her feet.

With the thunder of the pulpit's fall ringing in her ears The Universal Friend looked upon her likeness. For a long moment her eyes beheld the portrait, and it seemed to Nathan that they would bulge from their sockets as she became aware of what she saw. When she turned to him again he was startled by the utter fury of her look. In her face was such a mixture of malevolence and agony as he had not dreamed that human features could express. But her glance rested on him for only a moment. It moved to her mirror, and he saw her look into it and turn again to the picture as if hoping that one or the other would give back the image she desired. At last she spoke, slowly and hesitantly, as though the shock of seeing the painting had destroyed her power of concentration.

"The Friend is grieved that depravity and wickedness have possessed so young a man. While yet she dwells in Time she prays for her enemies and all who spitefully use her."

She took a few slow steps toward the door of her bedchamber, then turned suddenly and walked swiftly back to the portrait. Picking it up in both hands she made off with it as though she feared that Nathan might follow her. The door of her bedchamber slammed behind her. Nathan turned to find Rachel standing before him, her face contorted with grief.

"You have hurt the dearest of all souls," she said hysterically. "You have profaned the holiest of God's beings. Pray that you may be forgiven as I do now and shall until I am called from Time. Pray as I do now that we may not see each other again." She rushed to the door of the Friend's chamber and tried to open it. It was immovable. She sank to her knees before it.

XXIII

Whirl Gragg sat on the cabin doorstep reading aloud slowly and painfully. A long narrow broadside splotched with black printer's ink rippled from his hands to the ground.

" 'There will be held at Williamsburg at the Great Forks of the Genesee River, an annual fair, for the sale and purchase of cattle, horses, and sheep, to commence on Monday, the 23d of September and continue on Tuesday.' *And* so on, *and* so on. Nate—are you a-payin' me any mind? Nate, you long-legged, thatch-topped ole—"

"Go on, go on, I hear you."

"Ef'n ye do it's the first time in a week. Might's well have the swamp shakes as the mullygrubs. Git more action out'n 'em."

"I'm listening, I tell you."

"Fer what?"

"Shut up, damn you, and go on!"

"Well, it says somethin' about fat bullocks an' workin' oxen bein' showed. An' then it says, 'On Wednesday tresol will be run for over the race ground a purse of fifty pounds, and also a subscription purse. On Thursday there will be run for the sweepstakes, and races for small prizes. On Friday there will be shootin' matches and foot races.' And so on, and so on. Air ye listenin'?"

"Yes, I'm listening."

"Well, day before yistiddy the Cap'n says to me, 'Mr. Gragg,' he says, 'Mister Gragg, whaddyesay we launch that goddamned ol' ark o' yourn on the day after the last hoss racin'— that's Saturday—an' we'll ketch some o' the crowd at Bath on their way home.' An' I says right back to 'un, 'Cap'n,' I says, 'while the inelegance o' your language annoys me considerable, ef'n you say start commodorin' of a Saturday why that's when I start commodorin'.' "

"Whirl," said Nathan. "I don't want you to think I'm not thankful to you for trying to cheer me up. Any other time I'd think you were funny. You probably were just then, but right now—"

"Nate," said Whirl, "'member the time you an' me was bein' firmly escorted down the streets o' Philadelphy, an' I says to ye, 'Bet ye're mixed up with a woman'? Well, all I'm sayin' now is 'ditto.'"

"It's not the same," said Nathan. "I didn't give a damn about that girl or her fool mother. I love Rachel Malin—and something keeps us apart. I don't know what it is. Maybe it's religion."

"Now there's the macaroni of 'em all," said Whirl. "Religion c'n take a gal from ye quicker 'n more unexpected than a dead possum c'n bite. Whoever ye been wooin' I know ye ain't been outa sight o' this cabin fer ten days. Never seen nobody put in so many solid licks with a hoe. All that time ye been lettin' religion sew her into her winter drawers. Likely won't be out agin 'fore spring."

From the woods below their clearing came a snatch of song. A rich male baritone gaily let it go into the morning air though the beat of his horse's cantering hoofs punctuated it at inappropriate intervals:

"Through the woods I'll go,
Through the boggy mire,
Straightway on the road
Till I come to my heart's desire!
Eyes as bright as coal,
Lips as red as a cherry,
And 'tis her delight—
To make the young folks merry."

A few moments later the tall, white-wigged Captain on his rangy mount, riding with his hat in his hand, wheeled before them. His long right leg swung in a gracefully draped arc under the blue cape and he stood on the ground.

"Good morning, gentlemen," he said. "I am here to complete my bargain for your boat and to congratulate you on having outdistanced my most sanguine dreams for water transport. All the Genesee Country is in your debt." He drew a long purse from under his cape. "I hope you will be satisfied with a hundred dollars apiece for the craft and your labor."

Whirling Gragg gave out a long whistle of surprise. There was a note of disparagement in his voice as he spoke.

"Ye can't make money that way, Cap'n."

Williamson laughed.

"I'm glad you think me generous. You are right in saying I shall profit little. But your boat is only the forerunner of a fleet of hundreds that shall bear the wealth of the west to the market of the south. The Genesee Country is closer to its rich destiny than the nation dreams. Our religious friends on Crooked Lake will soon be outnumbered now. I have had great news this morning, great news."

"Kin we hear it?"

"Indeed you may. Letters by the Pennsylvania Post inform me that two cavalcades from the southern states will ride to Williamsburg Fair. Major FitzHugh of Maryland and Colonel Thornton of Virginia, with their families and retainers, have signified their intention of being present. I could not ask for a happier omen. Should these gentlemen purchase estates of me it will be the beginning of even greater prospects. Gentlemen of leisure from all the eastern coast will find here fertile lands and build fine homes upon them. The Genesee Country will be as rich and powerful as any state in the nation. Need you wonder at my satisfaction?"

"Captain," said Nathan, "you said the Genesee Country will be powerful. Are you aiming to keep it separate from the rest of the state it belongs to?"

"Why not?" said Williamson promptly. "All boundaries in the nation are not yet permanent. This country is by nature unsuited to belong to the region of the Hudson. Let the Dutchmen trade the Jews out of their money at Albany. Let Kingston and Poughkeepsie ship their inferior crops to New York. These wide fields and rich harvests shall provide abundance for master and servant. Stately houses such as may be found now only in England will shelter the gentry of America. Bath will be the capital, a city of spacious streets and gracious living, the center of the nation's genteel living."

"It sounds like British monarchy," said Nathan obstinately.

"Not monarchy," said Williamson smiling, "but a free aristocracy such as already exists in some parts of Virginia, the kind of society Mr. Adams and my friend Mr. Hamilton now advocate."

"This is a republic," said Nathan bluntly. "There's no place in it for aristocrats."

"I am sorry to hear you say so," said Williamson, and there was an edge to his voice though he still smiled. "I'm afraid you will find few of your philosophy about you. We are all Federalists here."

"There is time to remedy that."

"Mr. Hart," said Williamson, and he had stopped smiling, "we need intelligent men like you in this new country. You will not deny, I believe, that I have been generous to you. But some intelligent men, like fine horses that have been mishandled as colts, have had unhappy experiences in their youth that embittered them, making them ever dissatisfied and rebellious. I would hate to feel that you are one of these. But if I were to be convinced of it I should not hesitate to suggest that you finish your conflict with authority where it began —in the affected counties of western Pennsylvania."

Nathan saw the figure of Whirling Gragg sag helplessly over the printed broadside, and suddenly he was aware that his mounting anger was caused more by the danger to his friend than by the realization that at last his own situation stood revealed. The sick hunted feeling that had tortured him through the weeks following his escape was gone. Almost exultantly he faced the Captain.

"Your threat does not frighten me," he said. "And if your aristocratic friend Hamilton wants to send the army after me as he did before, I'll go back to Pennsylvania. You must have known of my escape before now. Why did you welcome me here?"

"I knew of it before your arrival," said Williamson, "through a letter that came by direct post from Mr. Robert Morris. He described it to me as one of the more exciting incidents of a dull day in Philadelphia. As for your welcome I saw no reason to let your views on liquor taxation interfere with that. But I have my work to do here and it must not be hampered by malcontents." He struck his clenched right fist into the open palm of his left hand. Then he went on in a rational, almost a pleading tone. "All that I ask is that those who work with me have faith in me or, better yet, that they see the future of this country as I see it. I am not the only one who would have my prophecies come true. My employer, Sir William, Mr. Morris, Mr. Hamilton who provided me with introductions upon my arrival in this country, and, since the conception of the Genesee Country as a separate state, the distinguished Mr. Aaron Burr—"

"Great God," said Whirl Gragg, still sitting dejectedly on the steps. "Better send yer gal on a three-year whalin' v'yage with a young crew than let *him* into the country."

The Captain threw back his head and laughed unrestrainedly.

"Up Maine way few years back," said Whirl reflectively and obviously pleased with this appreciation, "they was talk about Aaron enj'yin' a little red meat in his diet—daughter o' one o' them Kennebec Injun chiefs. I been thinkin'—"

Quickly the Captain interrupted. For once his ever-ready aplomb had deserted him. His voice was formal and his eyes stared straight ahead of him. Nathan watched him maliciously, wondering what strange facts lay behind his embarrassment. At least I am not concerned, he assured himself. Catherine O'Bail may be his private torment but she is no longer mine.

"Fortunately Mr. Burr has other abilities to be respected quite as much as those you mention."

"If he is for a separate state I do not respect him," said Nathan, "though he claims to belong to the right party. I hate Hamilton. If they agree on your plan I am against it."

"You misunderstand the Federalists," said the Captain, "and my own ambitions for this country."

"I understand this," said Nathan emphatically, "that I never asked you for the generosity you are so satisfied with. I fought your Germans for you and you paid me out—but I'd rather live under the tyranny of a man like Berezy than be beholden to a rich neighbor. You've bought the good wishes of everyone about you with your British money and your friendly ways—for what? To make another England of a free valley in the American Republic. Well, you can take back the acres you gave me and report me an escaped Whiskey Boy. I'd rather rot in a Philadelphia jail—"

"Wait, wait," said Williamson placatingly, hands upraised. "You are too rash. I have no intention of doing either. You may hold what opinions you please in this country. All that I ask is that you do not interfere with my administration of the lands entrusted to my care. Stay on here and we shall see that you prosper. Young and radical ideas change with the coming of new responsibilities. I am glad we have had this talk. Now we understand each other." He swung to his saddle and slapped spurs to his mount. The horse reared and bounded forward, then wheeled and trotted back stiffly under pressure of rein and knee.

"I almost forgot," said the Captain gaily as though nothing of importance had been spoken. "The black boy Cuff brought to my office yesterday messages to you from The Friend's Settlement. I had difficulty in persuading him that I would deliver them. He had been directed to give them to no one but you." From a saddlebag he drew a small cloth bag, and then, tossing it to Nathan, gave rein to his impatient steed. Before he had reached the edge of the forest Nathan's trembling fingers had loosed the strings of the bag. He heard the chink of money and saw twelve metal dollars lying below two folded oblongs of paper. He unfolded the upper one and read:

"These twelve coins are in full payment for value received from Nathan Hart. Signed, Rachel Malin for The Universal Friend."

Nathan felt that he dared not look at the other sheet. The slim, perfectly formed characters were a blur of ink on the white surface. Slowly he forced himself to focus his eyes and his mind on the writing:

My dear, dear Friend:
    Though even this communication be wicked I write to say I cannot endure my sojurn in Time without you. If you still wish it I am ready to fulfill the promises I gave. May God forgive me if this be a sin against Him and His servant.
                        Your unhappy Rachel.

At the bottom of the sheet he read, in tiny script, "Monday at the accustomed spot."

"What in tarnation ails ye?" said Whirling Gragg.

XXIV

Now Nathan lived in bliss, wrapped in the sweet haze of sum-
mer's end. Each day he was long in the yellow field, cutting
and binding the bearded wheat, breaking green ears from the
tall whispering maize. At sundown he would not know how
much his aching body had done, though Whirl marveled and
made remarks about a man's endurance increasing once he was
in love. Yet, for the lover, time did not seem to pass. All life
seemed to have been slowed almost to stopping, seemed to be
caught in autumn sunlight as if in slowly hardening amber.

The meeting with Rachel at their rendezvous among the
hickories had been almost hysterical with relief for both. After
their first desperate, breathless kisses Rachel had wept and
begged Nathan to forgive her for the cruel things she had said.
She had felt sorry for The Friend, she told him, and her pity
had moved her to anger against him. When The Friend had
finally come out from her chamber, hours after Nathan had
left, she had been cold and distant and had spoken of punish-
ing Rachel—though for years they two had been as one being
in God's sight. Only after a week had passed had the old relationship been renewed, and by that time Rachel was suffering
so from the realization that she might never see Nathan again
that she could hardly attend to her usual duties. It was The
Friend, she said, who had insisted on sending Cuff with the
money—though the picture itself was never mentioned. And
after Rachel had sent the black boy off with the coins and the
explanatory note she had called him back, written what was in
her heart, and sent that, too.

Then Nathan, exulting in this proof of the girl's love, told
her of the sale of the boat, of the harvest, of the fair the Captain
had planned for Williamsburg, and of the launching that would
take place at Bath on the Saturday after the fair was over. He

would speak to Whirl immediately and plan with him for all three to float to Baltimore on the vessel's first voyage. At first Rachel demurred. Baltimore, she had heard, was a sinful and licentious city, and The Friend had said that such worldly places were to be avoided. But at mention of The Friend, Nathan had suddenly become silent and morose, and Rachel, noticing this, had put her arms around his neck and said she would go anywhere if it were only with him.

At that their happiness was completely restored, and Rachel, counting on her plump white fingers, said there were but three Mondays before the Saturday of the launching and on each of them she would meet him at this time and place. On the day of their departure she would plead to be excused from the platform during the meeting and seat herself in the audience. If the preaching were to be outdoors she could lose herself among the crowd after it was over and find an opportunity to run to him. But if the weather made an indoor gathering necessary she would rise as if to go to the kitchen to attend to something forgotten and, while The Friend was engrossed in her own words, she would climb out of the window behind the stove and join him.

"But why is it necessary?" said Nathan. "Why not pack your clothes in a bundle and walk out and tell them all what you are doing. There's nothing they can do."

At this tears came into Rachel's eyes and she said that he must allow her to act as she thought best—at least until she reached his side. Nathan finally agreed, and he rode back along the trail to Bath in a cloud of happiness so thick that he even forgot to stop off to see Elijah and plague him about his oft-deferred portrait.

Whirl had not seemed at all surprised when told of the prospective marriage.

"Heerd tell pious women are wildcats," he said approvingly. But when Nathan broached the subject of taking Rachel on the voyage he proved difficult.

"A female on a boat is tarnal bad luck," he said. "I know it's a hell of a boat but the principle is jest the same."

Nathan had to use all the arguments he could muster to get Whirl to agree.

"Ye won't be no good on the sweeps," he said. "Run us

aground as sure as shootin'. An' when I'm on a boat my cussin' is enough to make a young bride blush herself to death even if she's been practicin'. Ain't goin' to change it nuther."

At last, however, the whole thing was arranged. Nathan would ride his mare and lead a horse borrowed from a farmer whose wheat was to go on the boat. He and Rachel would ride straight from The Friend's Settlement to the river. They would arrive by three o'clock in the afternoon. The launching would be set for the same time. The farmer would take care of his horse and Nathan's, and before sundown they'd be well on their way downstream.

The long craft was ready two weeks before the beginning of the fair. The Captain had had the idea of launching it early in the morning and filling it with its cargo on the same day, but Whirl objected.

"Take more'n one day to fill her up," he said. "I'll git me some oxen to pull that pile o' logs out from under her an' inch her down into the water. Then we can build a sorta fence around her and fill her up and have 'er ready to start when we want to. When we're all set we can knock down the fence, blow some horns an' beat some drums, an' she'll be launched jest as good as if she'd slid down off the mountains."

The partners were glad they had decided on this course of action, for the long bin had no sooner slipped into the river than it developed leaks in unaccountable places which only a week of carpentering and of steady soaking could stop. Nathan worked on, day by day, from morning light to darkness, thankful when physical exhaustion shortened the nights by giving him sleep. When at last the wheat and corn had been stored and each farmer's bushels carefully measured, when the furs of wolves and foxes, coons and wildcats had been tagged and instructions noted for their disposal, the fair was still ten days away. Now Nathan lived in a quiet and almost deserted town. The building crew was in Williamsburg repairing the cabins of Berezy's Germans, erecting long shelters, and clearing the fair grounds themselves so that foresighted arrivals who brought tents might pitch them there. Already a cavalcade of shouting, horn-blowing Pennsylvanians in three shining Conestoga wagons had jingled through Bath on its way to the great event. Whirl Gragg was in a fever of excitement.

"Ought to be there now," he grumbled. "Need t'git my ear to the ground a good week afore a hoss race."

But Nathan, impatient with any interruption of his dream, found trifling things for both to do in preparation for the long journey. The days went by in dull procession, each a monotonous round, like the slow circles of a high-sailing hawk. A week passed. Now the road from Painted Post poured a steady stream of gay fairgoers through the town. Each night found Metcalf's little inn crowded with eager, excited travelers. They were sleeping fifteen to a room, both men and women, and poor old Mrs. Metcalf was getting blear-eyed from watching her patrons all night long lest her house lose its respectability.

On the day of the fair's beginning Nathan found Rachel thoughtful but determined. She said The Friend had been greatly troubled by the coming of new, worldly people to the region. Until now she had not felt the whole danger of Captain Williamson's campaign to her purposes. She had planned, as new recruits gathered about her, to buy more and more of the Captain's land, until the whole Genesee Country should be one godly, peaceful company of friends. With nearly three hundred followers already established in their cabins and more coming from the New England states, from Pennsylvania and Rhode Island each month, she had felt safe from the difficulties Williamson and his little handful might create. But the gathering of the sinful at Williamsburg had caused her great sorrow. The time when her prophetic vision of a great catastrophe would be fulfilled must now be very near. She was aghast and filled with pity that so many souls should perish in torment— but their sins allowed no other course. She begged of her followers to keep themselves uncontaminated by communication with those who lived outside the settlement and to follow rigidly the teachings of Christ through The All-Friend.

"I was moved to confess all to her," said Rachel, "and tell her of our plans, but I could not. After we have returned from our journey I feel sure that she will forgive us as she has others who have offended her."

"I'm not asking her forgiveness," said Nathan.

"But she is kind and good," said Rachel pleadingly. "She is the spirit of the Christ in the human form. I will always love her—even though my love for you burns all thought of other feelings from my brain."

Then Nathan took her in his arms and kissed her and made her promise for the last time that on Saturday she would come to him from the meeting at the earliest possible moment. He would arrive among the hickories after the services had begun, lest anyone should think it strange to see a young man riding to meeting and leading a saddled horse. She must try to join him by noon, for they would have to ride swiftly to Bath to be on the boat before the launching. They looked long into each other's eyes as they parted. And when Nathan had ridden a little way into the woods he turned and looked back. She was standing among the hickories, as straight and still as they, watching him out of sight. He waved and she made a queer, taut little gesture of farewell with her right hand.

He did not forget Elijah on his way home, but when he rode into the Prophet's clearing it was empty. The cattle had disappeared and Nathan feared they had been stolen, until he remembered that there were to be exhibitions of livestock at Williamsburg. Then he deduced that Elijah, with his usual roaring optimism, must have set out for the fair with wife, children, and all other living things belonging to him.

When Nathan came to his own cabin he found Whirl hard at work fitting new wheels to his wagon. A yoke of oxen stood patiently beside him.

"Found these wild beasts in the grass," he said. "Depend on 'em t'git me to the fair. Figger ef'n I start tomorrow ought to be there by Thursday night fer the big doin's."

"You'll get there before then," said Nathan. "They're Williamson's oxen."

"How'd I know that?" said the little bald man, wide-eyed. "I trapped 'em in wild country. They look mighty ornery t'me." He paused for a moment's reflection.

"Nate," he said, "they ain't a human bein' twixt here an' Harris's Ferry 'ceptin' a few hundred crazy pious fools that ain't agoin' t'that fair. Why, it's a man's bounden duty t'go. Ef'n it's goin' t'up the price of land—our land goes with it, b'God. What's more, they tell me they's goin' to be folks there all the way from Virginny an' I figger it's up to us to make 'em feel at home just like they'd do the same if we was down there."

"You won't need me for that," said Nathan grimly. "You and the Captain between you ought to be able to handle it."

"Ye mean y'ain't countin' on goin'?" said Whirl.

"You know I'm not. You've known it for weeks."

There was a silence.

"Nate," said Whirl plaintively. "You know jest as well as me I'm agoin' to git drunk. I ain't even pertendin' I ain't. An' ef'n I git drunk I might stay drunk a long time—long enough to miss my commodorin'. Now you an' me can't afford that, kin we?"

"So I have to ride fifty miles and back to get you to the boat?"

"I knew ye'd do it," said Whirl triumphantly. "Allays said ye had somep'n to ye."

XXV

Nathan welcomed the next days of loneliness and silence. The stream of travelers on the road had become a punctuated trickle, then stopped altogether. The nights had suddenly turned cold, and he wakened Tuesday morning to stillness and low-lying mist struck through by spears of sunlight. Outside the cabin window the maples and oaks were windless torches of red and gold. Now and then a Baltimore oriole, full-throated and sure, whistled a syncopated snatch of song. Nathan cooked a breakfast of cornmeal cakes, bacon, and coffee, and ate it listlessly. Then he wandered down to the river. The long boat rode easily behind the board screen that Whirl had erected. The water was clear and brown. Already yellow leaves were tumbling from the willows to ride the ripples in winking brilliance. He was happy that he was taking Rachel south to more summer days. He turned upstream and walked the bank toward town.

Pultney Square was deserted. Nathan looked about it, remembering the day he and Elijah had heard the beat of a lone hammer rising from this spot to the wooded hills where they stood. Now there were nearly twenty cabins in the settlement. He noted one large empty lot in the very heart of the town—at the corner of Steuben Street and Morris Street—and he smiled. The Captain's theater was to be there. He wondered if it would be built and how the Captain would get players to come to this western wilderness.

From the south road came the sound of a horn—no such horn as his ears had become accustomed to in the past months. The notes were clear and high, surely played on a brass instrument of full tone. A thin voice shouted something—a man's voice—and then Nathan could hear the sound of wheels and the jingle of harness. Into the square two horsemen trotted, each resting a yellow trumpet on his right knee and holding his reins in his left hand. The men wore long blue coats, high-fitting, yellow waistcoats, tight white breeches that ended below shin-length, shiny-black riding boots. Wide, three-cornered black hats shaded their faces. A shaft of sunlight, reflected from the brass horns to their cheeks, showed their skins to be black as ink. About thirty yards behind them, drawn by four beautiful chestnut horses, one team ahead of the other, swayed a shining, silver-trimmed chaise. A black boy in livery like that of the outriders held reins and whip above them.

Heavy wooden rods had been tied lengthwise on each side of the carriage, and four other Negroes ran alongside holding to the rods and trying to soften the jolts for the sole occupant of the back seat. This was a gentleman of ample proportions and handsome costume. His face, large and moonlike, seemed hinged upon his torso without the formality of a neck. From his chin downward spread a vast ocean of white ruffles, each whiter than snow and stiffer than birch bark. His fat legs, tightly limited by fawn-colored short breeches and silk hose of the same color, stretched out to the seat facing him where they ended in small slender feet cased in slippers such as a dancing teacher might wear. An enormous white wig sat askew on his spherical, almost bald head. At first glance he seemed to have no eyes, for his brows and lashes were of a pale shade and the lids seemed to cover at least half of the space allotted to his little green pupils. As his conveyance rolled on over the uneven road he grunted and swore petulantly. Behind the chaise a young man and a young woman rode tall, exquisitely proportioned mounts, a bay and a roan, dancing skittishly. And thundering into the square now came two tremendous Conestogas, their boxes as blue as the sky, their covers as white as the fleecy clouds.

At sight of Nathan standing amazed at the foot of the square the fat man cried out in his thin voice and waved a hand. One of the Negroes raised a trumpet and blew five notes. At once with a great deal of shouting and pulling of reins the whole cavalcade came to a halt. The fat man said something to his driver who urged his horses slowly forward until the chaise was beside Nathan.

"My man," said the thin voice, "what in the name of

Jehovah and the Continental Congress is this forsaken hell-hole?"

"This town is Bath," said Nathan shortly.

"Bath," said the fat man. "Bath," and the white sea of his shirt ruffles was shaken by a series of falsetto giggles. "Gad, sir, you may lead me to the pumproom! And is the Duchess of York perchance in attendance? My sweet niece," he called to the girl riding behind him, "this is Bath. Shall we stop here and partake of the waters?" His giggles choked off further utterance.

Nathan turned his back and set off across the square.

"Wait, wait," called the fat man. "I want further information."

Nathan kept on. There was a sound of hoofbeats behind him. Then the girl whirled the roan about to face him.

"Can't you hear my uncle speaking to you?"

"Perfectly," said Nathan.

The girl's brown eyes flashed.

"You are insolent," she said furiously. "It is what we have learned to expect in these Yankee woods."

Looking up at her Nathan thought she is all one color, a golden brown, except for her white teeth and the clear whites of her eyes. Her face was long and narrow, a tawny oval in which her long prominent nose shadowed a short upper lip. Her forehead was shortened in its center by a strongly outlined peak of brown hair. Her cheeks were lean and her chin was firm and slightly protuberant. She was not beautiful, nor even pretty, but the strength and regularity of her features gave her distinction. In her gracefully draped riding habit, the color of a late autumn leaf, she sat the restless roan easily. The tan plume in her brown velvet hat nodded as the horse moved impatiently about.

"I regret," said Nathan ironically, "that in these Yankee woods we have not kept up the genteel practice of fawning servility in the presence of superior beings."

He saw her long tan fingers clutch her rein. He thought she was about to attempt to ride over him. At the instant a lazy, rich voice sounded:

"What's the matter, Nell?"

The young man who had been riding with her had slowly trotted to the girl's side.

"This—this—yokel has insulted me."

The young man laughed, and Nathan saw that he looked like his sister, save that her features seemed caricatured in him. His face was thin and lantern-jawed, his body long and his legs too long to be gracefully stirruped even on his tall mount.

"This yokel, as you call him, uses a scholar's vocabulary," he said. " 'Genteel practice of fawning servility' indeed! I'll wager our uncle couldn't understand him."

"Are you going to punish his impertinence?" said the girl.

"Sir," said her brother, addressing Nathan, "both my uncle and my sister have been rude to you. For this I apologize. As for me, if you will allow me to present myself, I am Major Peregrine Fitzhugh of Arundel County, Maryland. I am traveling with my sister, Eleanor, and both of us are a part of the cortege of our distinguished uncle, Colonel Jonas Hogmire, also of Maryland. We have come all the way from the banks of the Patuxent with a few fast horses to try their speed against the Yankee nags at Captain Williamson's great Genesee Fair. We have been on the road much longer than we anticipated, and naturally we wish to know how much farther we must go before we reach our destination."

"Fifty miles," said Nathan.

Major Fitzhugh looked expectant, obviously waiting further words. None came. Once more he threw back his head and laughed. The sound was so completely infectious that Nathan grinned in spite of himself.

"I don't know who you are, tall fellow," said the major, "but I have an idea that if we are ever thrown together again we shall get on very well." He clapped his loose, widespread knees to the bay and moved briskly off. The girl's eyes were sharp, her mouth hard, as she looked down at Nathan.

"If I ever see you again," she said quickly, "I trust I can command the protection of a gentleman instead of my brother." Stung by her sharp boot in his ribs the roan leaped forward. Already the horns of the cavalcade were sounding, the chaise was swaying, Jonas Hogmire was cursing, the Conestogas were rumbling.

XXVI

*Williamsburg was asleep when Nathan finished his long
journey.* It was after midnight when Lottie bore him into the
little town. In the clear starlight he could see many tents pitched
on the flats by the river and the high white curves of the covered Conestogas standing beside them. From the woods behind
the town came a wild whoop, suddenly stilled, and Nathan
guessed that a drunken Indian had been hushed by sleepy companions. He rode directly to Starr's tavern but, on dismounting
and opening the door, he found there was no hope of staying
the night there. The floor was covered with sleeping forms, so
close to each other that it seemed impossible for one to turn
on his other side without compelling all the others to do like-
wise. Nathan led his mare up the slope into a clump of pines,
hitched her, and lay down among the pungent needles. He was
soon asleep.

A long blast from a wooden raft-horn wakened him. As if
it had been an awaited signal, hubbub began. Bugle calls sang
across the valley. Drums pounded. A long falsetto whoop from a
cabin was interrupted by a gust of staccato yells from the woods
near Nathan where evidently Indians were encamped. On the
flats the Conestogas and the tents poured out men, many of
them Negroes. Yellow fires began to glow against the background of the tall grass. High above the little flames at their
base the green tips waved in slanting amber sunlight.

Nathan rose and began to look for Whirl. He was not long
finding him. Where the highest blaze licked upward, where the
shouting was loudest, the laughter most raucous, the little man
squatted drinking his coffee unconcernedly from a wooden mug.
At sight of Nathan he sprang to his feet:

"Listen, you Susquehanna hyenas," he shouted, "you black-
hearted Canisteo cannibals, this long-legged string o' wildcat

gristle is the fellow I been tellin' ya about—the greatest picter painter west of Philadelphy. He kin paint a jug o' rum so good that lookin' at it'll give ye a thirst an' tiltin' it'll make ye drunk. He kin—"

"He kin sit an' eat hearty," said a heavy voice, "an' praise the Lord fer the chance."

A giant of a man in tow smock and homespun breeches reached out a long arm and presented Nathan with a steaming mug.

"God bless the food an' you, stranger," he said. "I'm Andrew Grey, preacher to the most sinful crew of rapscallions ever met in one place."

As he sipped the hot coffee Nathan looked about him. In the circle around the fire squatted a group of sun-browned, roughly dressed men—obviously farmers and rafters. Many of them were already drunk and noisy.

"Here's your hominy, mister," said the preacher, handing out a generously filled wooden bowl. "Ye better down it 'fore things begin to happen."

The bowl was but half-empty when the movement to the flats began. The entire clearing was suddenly alive with men drifting down toward a level area on which the grass had been cut. Already the preacher and his flock had vanished. Whirl looked at Nathan appealingly.

"I've enough," said the latter, and the two hurried after their breakfast companions.

A wide path led them to a narrow bridge across the little river. It was jammed with eager men, shouting and singing. Nathan could see that on the far side an elliptical course about twenty feet wide and apparently a mile in circumference had been mowed through the grass and leveled off. The grass inside the course had not been cut save for about one acre just in front of the bridge. In this two small concentric circles had been fenced off and about the larger of these hundreds of men were already gathered.

As they came off the bridge Nathan and Whirl heard a shout of disappointment. On coming near they saw a horse dragging a cart on which lay the inert body of a small black bear. Apparently it had not proved ferocious enough to kill a sturdy red bull which now stood inside the ring, horns lowered, awaiting an

antagonist. There was a quick rush away from the barrier as he
charged against it, but the move gave his owner a chance to
throw a cloak over his head and tie him while he was blinded.

As the bull was led reluctantly away a long weird cry
sounded from the slopes behind and across the bridge raced a
crowd of Indians, perhaps fifty in all. Most of them were naked
save for breechclouts and moccasins, and their hair, cut short and
wound into a tuft that stood upright above the crown of the
head, made them seem tall and menacing. One of them, powerful and thickset, had painted his body in grotesque red and
blue patterns and then greased it until it shone in the sunlight
as if he had been varnished. He leaped into the ring and began
strutting about it, shouting in his own language.

"That's their wrastler from Squawkie Hill," said Whirl.
"They think he could throw Sampson, but I've heerd tell he's
got a surprise comin'."

At Whirl's mention of Squawkie Hill Nathan's mind went
back to his visit there, the tribe's kindness to him when he was
ill, to Otsiquette, and inevitably to Catherine O'Bail who had
left him one night long ago on the high banks of the Genesee.
The feeling of miserable shame that had come to him at the
end of that night enveloped him. He wondered if Catherine
were somewhere in the crowd. He hoped he would not see her.

As the Indian stalked about, uttering sharp yells and making horrible grimaces, an angular, shambling young man, naked
to the waist, strolled into the circle. At sight of him a shout
went up from the white spectators.

"It's Eli Stephens," shouted the tall preacher. "Lay the
heathen low, Eli."

"Smartest man with his hands in the country," said Whirl.
"Lives with his paw an' three brothers back up the Canisteo."

The Indian and the white man approached each other
awkwardly. When they were within six feet of each other they
began circling slowly. Suddenly the Indian leaped forward. He
was too quick for his opponent who toppled like a falling tree
and just managed to twist to the side as he fell. But as he twisted
his long arms went out around the Indian and held him
close. Then, as they lay face to face, Stephens, with feet straining against the earth, tried to roll over on the Indian. He was
moving slowly and surely. With a sudden flickering movement

the Indian was out of his grasp and away, rolling swiftly to his feet. His greased body had slipped out of Stephens' grip.

The white man was quickly on his feet but he did not rise to his full height. On his haunches, leaning forward slightly, he awaited the next attack. Nathan saw his hands working in the dirt before him, searching for grit that would keep his hold from slipping. The Indian saw them, too, and at once launched himself again. He threw his body low and hard, endeavoring to push Stephens over backward. For a moment it seemed that he would succeed. But the lank legs of the white man straightened like hawsers snapping taut and the Indian suddenly found himself hoisted into the air. A long right arm went between his legs, catching him firmly in the crotch, and a viselike left hand caught the erect tuft of hair on his head. With burden held chest-high, Stephens took one mighty step to give impetus to the throw, and with a quick effort dumped it to the ground. There was a sharp cracking sound and then a groan. To his complete astonishment, Nathan saw that the fall had fractured the Indian's hip. A jagged edge of the bone was breaking through the flesh.

There was a cry of triumph from the white men. Nathan, shouting with the rest and looking at the helpless Indian, was suddenly reminded of another such prone figure, of Otsiquette coming up dripping out of a stream with a knife in his hand. Afterward he decided that it was this memory that made him step into the circle and toward Stephens. It seemed that his mind had hardly had time to signal a premonition of danger when he moved, yet some quick logic drove him forward, made him look upward. There, above Stephens' head, hung the expected instrument, a short, hatchetlike weapon—its blade already descending. Hands upraised, Nathan dove for it, clutched it, hung on. Suddenly it was left in his grasp, and the young Indian who had raised it had leaped into the midst of his own people.

At once all the Indians moved away from the circle in a body. Some looked bewildered and frightened, others angry. Many of the white men had drawn knives and pistols. Several were racing across the bridge and up the hill for their rifles. Stephens stood looking stupidly at Nathan.

"Much obliged," he said in a wooden tone. "Ef ye'll stick by me fer a few minutes now mebbe I can return the favor."

But a tall man had moved into the open between the two groups. Nathan saw that he was an Indian clad in leggings and ornamented breechclout, and that over his thin muscular chest hung a short crimson coat of the sort worn by officers of the British grenadiers. It was stained and the frogs across its front were greasy, but he wore it with dignity.

"By the great hornspoon, it's Red Jacket," said Whirl.

The tall man lifted a hand. The gesture was at the same time commanding and filled with indefinable grace.

"It is not the Indian's fault that he cracks like a dry stick," he said. "If the white man would have good wrestling let him fill the Indian's bones with sap." He pointed to the bridge over which at that moment two white men were carrying a gleaming brass kettle. A bellow broke from the two groups at the same moment. Whites and Indians, roaring as they ran, scrambled for mugs, descended on the rum kettle in a thirsty horde. Behind them four Indians bore their unlucky champion away on a deerskin stretched between two poles. A white man, evidently a doctor, walked beside him.

"Saved a massacree," said Whirl softly, "you an' Red Jacket. Smartest Injun they got—'ceptin' mebbe Cornplanter."

Again, at the mention of the name of Catherine O'Bail's father, Nathan felt an uneasy premonition. With resolution he put it aside. He would not be troubled by this girl. If he were to see her he would be unmoved. She was a character in an incident he would soon forget in the joy of his new life with Rachel.

Now a group were gathered at the near end of the bridge, shouting to the rest to join them and clear the field. Even as they moved toward the spot a heavy-headed wooden maul sailed through the air and, barely missing the head of a drunken Indian, plunked to the soft earth a dozen yards from the tall grass. As Whirl and Nathan approached, a heavily built fellow whom they recognized as one of Williamson's blacksmiths at Bath grasped the handle of the retrieved maul and, swinging it in two vertical arcs, let it go. It dropped less than ten feet from the line of the grass. There was a gasp of amazement and a cheer from the Captain's building crew, who began collecting wagers they had won.

One of the men with whom Nathan and Whirl had break-fasted sauntered aimlessly from the crowd at this moment. Timing his remark to the exact moment when it would be heard by the greatest number he said carelessly:

"Us Canisteers got a preacher kin beat that all hollow."

There was a roar of laughter.

"Bring on his reverence."

"Miracles barred."

The Canisteer seemed unperturbed.

"Over the mountain where we come from," he said seri-ously, "that heave's a boy's work. Even a preacher kin beat it."

"I've got three dollars that says no."

"Done," said the Canisteer.

With a whoop the crowd closed in—money in hand. The hardy group from the Canisteo were ready for them. Nathan was suddenly horrified to see that Whirl Gragg had joined them and was matching his money against that of his former comrades on the building crew. He fought his way over to the little man.

"You'll have no money left for Baltimore," Nathan said.

"Wait and see," said Whirl. "I got my ear on the groun' sooner'n I expected."

In a few minutes the money of the Canisteers had been covered. The betting was over.

"Where's the man o' God?" jeered the blacksmith. "Bring on your sermonizin' hammer slinger."

Andrew Grey stood out from the crowd, maul in hand. At sight of his great frame there was a cry of rage.

"He ain't no preacher."

Grey dropped the maul and lifted his hands above the crowd.

"Oh Lord," he said, "give me strength to conquer the wicked as easy as I'm goin' t'beat that last throw. Amen."

There was silence. Everyone seemed convinced by this evi-dence of the man's religious vocation. He wasted no time. Seizing the maul he swung it twice to get the feel and balance. Then with a lightning-quick motion he let it go. Its flight seemed gradual. The big hammer appeared to hang motionless for a moment high against the blue of the sky. Then it began its descent. No one saw it strike the earth, for the tall grass re-ceived it. The shouting of the Canisteers was deafening.

XXVII

As he turned away from the scene of the Canisteer's triumph
Nathan wondered why he had caught no sight of Williamson
nor of the strange trio of the Virginia cavalcade. He strolled
about among the crowd but found only the bully boys of the
river valleys. He went back across the bridge and saw, beside
the Conestogas and the tents, a crowd of black servants polish-
ing harness, washing clothes, and currying horses. Crossing the
Genesee proved a lucky move, for he was among the first at the
Starr's tavern table when the dinner bell brought a rush of
hungry revelers to attack big sides of venison, roast quail, and
steaming hominy in wooden trenchers.

It was a full two hours before the feasting and drinking
began to decline and the drift down the slope to set in again.
Then Nathan understood why he had not observed the Captain
and the Virginians for, while he was noting with amusement the
new door of Miller's cabin as he passed, it swung open and
out of it paraded Eleanor and Peregrine Fitzhugh, Jonas Hogmire, and Charles Williamson.

"Damned excellent Madeira, Captain," the beruffled fat
man was saying. "Indeed the quality of your life here astounds
me. By gad, with faster horses this country might be another
Virginia."

"If the filly I bought from you this morning does not belie
her Virginia breeding," said the Captain, smiling, "the time is
near. And, by the way, may I respectfully request permission
to change her name?"

"To that of a Yankee beauty, I'll wager," said Hogmire,
giggling and poking a fat elbow at Williamson's ribs. "Come,
Captain, reveal the current of your affections."

"If I may be so bold," said the Captain, looking at Miss
Fitzhugh, "I should like to call her Virginia Nell."

Nathan saw the girl's eyes drop a moment, then rise to meet the Captain's. She was smiling happily.

"As pretty a compliment as ever was turned, by Gad," said Hogmire. "You'll find no objection to that from her former owners, I'll be bound."

The girl curtseyed, the golden-brown plumes on her high riding hat nodding gracefully.

"Thank you, Captain," she said in her sure low voice. "I hope she will bring honor to her new master and her name."

They had come to the end of the slope, now covered with a scattered, hurrying crowd.

"I took the liberty of ordering your mounts led across the bridge," said Williamson. "You will find that Colonel Wadsworth has them in charge."

In the pushing jovial crowd on the narrow span Nathan lost the little group and overheard no more. When he arrived at the racecourse it was already lined on both sides of the long straightaway and even partially around the first bend with eager spectators. Near the middle of the straightaway he could see the towering figure of dour, unsmiling Colonel Wadsworth on a magnificent black horse. Beside him Hogmire tilted his round head quizzically upward on its insufficient neck. The fat man was riding a long-limbed chestnut mare with a white star on her forehead. As Nathan caught sight of them Williamson rode up to join them. He seemed moved out of his usual smiling calm. The near-by crowd, scenting a controversy, closed around the three. Others ran up to listen.

As Nathan came nearer he deduced the reason for the dispute. In front of Hogmire and Wadsworth stood Red Jacket and another Indian as tall as he, though stockier. Between the two stood a rat-tailed, rough-coated gray gelding. His head was down; his mane full of burs; his fetlocks were uncurried; there was an air of complete dejection about him. Nathan heard Williamson's voice. It held a note of annoyance which its owner was too obviously trying to check.

"But the main race is for the horses of pedigree and owned by gentlemen."

Red Jacket's companion spoke.

"I am a chief of the Seneca Nation," he said. "I am The Cornplanter and I own the horse. The Indians here ask to have a horse in the big race." As he said "the Indians here" he turned his face toward the crowd and Nathan saw the face of the father of Catherine O'Bail. It was round and full, in strong contrast to Red Jacket's sharp, lean features, and it was light in color, paler than the complexion of his daughter.

"Let him be entered in any of the other races," said the Captain placatingly. "Surely you do not think he can compete with Virginia and Maryland stock."

Colonel Wadsworth's sallow, hawklike features set a trifle more grimly. If the Captain wishes anything, Nathan thought, Wadsworth is against it.

"I see no objection," said Hogmire genially. "It will serve as an excellent lesson in the benefits of scientific animal breeding to the people of your country, and the race will be the better for not being confined to Southern horses."

"I agree," said Wadsworth saturninely.

"The judges make the decisions," said Williamson smiling wryly, "and I obey them. Let us get on with the race."

At a signal from Hogmire his two black buglers blew a long call. Cornplanter and Red Jacket led their horse into the mowed land where the morning contests had taken place. They were immediately surrounded by Indians. Nathan saw that a few yards away from them, during the dinner hour, a high tent had been erected, and he guessed that it held the Southern horses. The bugles sounded again, and from the tent loped the two horses that the Fitzhughs had been riding on the day they had passed through Bath. Now two black boys, so alike in wiry figure and size as to be twins, sat them surely as they nervously danced about.

Williamson, cantering down the middle of the straight-away, his long cloak fluttering behind, suddenly reined in and held up a hand.

"The great race of the day," he shouted, "will be run for a purse of four hundred dollars by Colonel Jonas Hogmire's bay mare Maryland Girl, bred in Washington County, Maryland, Major Peregrine Fitzhugh's roan gelding Light Horse Harry, bred by Colonel Presley Thornton of Virginia, and—" he stopped, realizing that he had forgotten to find out the name of the Indian's horse. The crowd parted and Red Jacket stepped out lithely into the course. The Captain leaned down to hear him and then, raising his hand again, went on, "—and Chief Cornplanter's gray gelding, Tom the Tinker, bred around and about."

There was a roar of laughing approval from the Susquehanna raftsmen and the Canisteers. Some of the more intoxicated began waving money about and shouting "Tom the Tinker." There was a rush toward them. Suddenly Nathan wondered if Catherine O'Bail had named the horse. Though he had never told her of his connection with the whiskey riots she might know of it and be trying to annoy him. Williamson might have told her, he thought, and he was filled with rage.

"Nate," said the voice of Whirling Gragg, and Nathan looking down on the bright bald poll of the little man saw it nodding back and forth uncertainly. "Nate, I may be awash but I want to say something."

"Go ahead," said Nathan.

"Never trust an Injun when he lets ye see jest how it is. I thought that up in time to bet all I got on the gray."

"Don't be a fool," said Nathan.

"I reckon it ain't occurred to you," said Whirl, "that if an Injun wants to he can slick a horse up so's he shines as bright as a white man's. What I want to know is why he ain't got ribbons on his mane an' tail instead o' cockleburs. An' I know the answer already. Jes' have a look at Cornplanter an' Red Jacket."

Nathan saw the two tall Senecas standing side by side and shaking their heads negatively as they were pressed for bets. One shake, two shakes—and then, with great reluctance and a deprecatory smile, each surrendered to pressure and gave up more money. Again and again they were persuaded, obviously, almost too obviously, against their better judgment.

The bugles sounded once more and the black boys bounced out into the course. The rider of the roan wore a shirt of yellow silk, white breeches, black boots, and black cap. The boy on the bay was similarly dressed except for a shirt of bright blue. Both carried riding crops and wore heavy spurs. Out of the milling crowd of Indians trotted the gray. He was saddleless and the Indian boy on his back bobbed about like a leaf on a rippling stream—an autumn leaf, for his shirt was a startling red. He held a leafy twig indolently in his hand. About his head was wound a wide red cotton ribbon from which a single hawk feather protruded toward the back.

At the starter's post Williamson was once more holding up his hand.

"The race will start with the single tap of the drum," he said. "The horses are now ready, the judges in their places. Colonel Hogmire will give the signal to the drummer."

There was a moment of silence. Both black boys were having difficulty in holding their dancing mounts behind the starting line. The gray stood quietly but he had pricked up his ears and was looking down the stretch. The boy in the red shirt leaned forward. There was a sharp thud on the drum head.

Maryland Girl took the lead at once. Her bay flanks flashed into a long stride as the boy held her to the inside and made for the first curve. The roan was close at her heels, his rider content to wait. Down the middle of the course bounded the gray, neither horse nor rider appearing to take the contest seriously. As they rounded the curve Maryland Girl first became aware of the tall grass lining her path and, startled, moved away from it. The boy on Light Horse Harry saw the opening and drove for it. The Southern horses were neck and neck as they went out of sight behind the grass. Tom the Tinker was a good length behind.

At once the few trees near the straightaway blossomed with eager humans. Men took turns holding each other on their shoulders to catch a glimpse of the progress of the race.

"Nate," called Whirling Gragg, "this away!" Nathan raced across the course and, grasping Whirl's hand, leaped to the seat of his cart. Oxen and cart were covered with men.

"Figgered we'd be needin' this," said Whirl. "Had a boy geein' an' hawin' 'em into this spot ever since dinner."

Standing on the seat Nathan looked across the grass. He could see only the colored shirts of the riders above the blowing tips. They had reached the middle of the backstretch but had changed position only slightly. Now he could see more clearly. The black boys were tautly stretched along the necks of the Southern horses, but the gray head of Tom the Tinker was still high, and the boy in the red shirt still rode carelessly, bobbing up and down. He was a length and a half behind now and losing ground.

"There goes your money, Whirl," said Nathan. "You'll have to come right back from Baltimore."

"Ef'n ye knew a hoss from a rattlesnake," said Whirl, "ye c'd see that Injun ain't tryin' yit."

The horses were crowding the third curve now and Light Horse Harry once more put on a burst of speed. Nathan could see the roan head and blue shirt move out in front and a yellow-clad arm raised as the rider of Maryland Girl brought his whip down on the mare's flanks. He looked for the Indian and was surprised to see that the gray had made up a half length and was running easily at the mare's tail. The boy had given up his easy bouncing seat and was leaning farther forward. Slowly the red shirt crept up the outside of the blue. Now one, now the other color showed ahead as the horses plunged on. They were coming to the turn that led into the straightaway.

Suddenly Nathan saw the Indian's head go down to the gray's ear and saw the red shirt shoot forward leaving the blue behind. And at the same instant came the knowledge that somewhere and sometime a shirt of that very brick color had meant something to him—something pleasant and exciting. As the horses turned into the stretch his mind was racing through his memory like an eager bird dog working a field. At that instant the color flashed into his brain: a brown girl sat on her haunches beside the brown water of a river, her right hand curved about her left sleeve, saying "I like this shirt."

The horses were pounding down the stretch now and his eyes sought them out, straining to see if by some miracle the owner of that shirt and the Indian rider could be the same person. She looked like a boy, he said to himself. I remember thinking she looked like a boy. The yells of the crowd at the upper end of the stretch united into a roar. The boy on Light Horse Harry, knowing himself a length ahead of Maryland Girl, was confused. His quick black head snapped to the side to look behind. As it did so, above the wild shouting of the watchers sounded the high yodeling falsetto of the Seneca rider's war cry. The gray responded. With his rider crouched close along his neck he rocketed down the course. In a dozen strides he had caught Light Horse Harry, and for a few moments the two geldings seemed to be moving in the same rhythm as one animal. Then it seemed as if the Virginia horse were galloping helplessly on a treadmill as Tom the Tinker surged forward across the line.

When Nathan came out of his own coma of excitement over the miracle of the race he discovered that Whirl was hanging from his neck and kicking out like a frog, shouting unintelligible syllables. Roughly removing him Nathan set out for the finish line where he could see Williamson and the judges in earnest discussion. The crowd about them was thick, but he pushed his way through, determined to see the face of the Indian rider. As he came within hearing distance Peregrine Fitzhugh was drawling a remark to his uncle, a wry smile on his long face:

"Well, uncle, shall we now deliver our lecture on the breeding of fast horses in the Southern states?"

Jonas Hogmire giggled nervously.

"I will not believe, sir, that the gray was not bred for speed."

"But, uncle," said the contralto voice of Eleanor Fitzhugh, "he has not the build of our fast horses. Moreover I do not believe he is as fast as the horses he defeated. He was simply ridden better."

Loud jeers came from the crowd, and she drew herself up in her saddle and looked steadily down at her annoyers.

"We ought to be able to settle the argument easily," said Williamson. "Ask The Cornplanter to come here."

There were shouts of "Cornplanter." Almost immediately the chief appeared, stalking through the lane made by the spectators, his right hand on the shoulder of the rider of Tom the Tinker. From beneath his brilliant blanket came a chinking sound, and his wide Oriental face was firmly set as though he were trying to repress a smile. Nathan gasped as he saw the little rider. The wide red band about the black head obviously concealed the long braids of Catherine O'Bail. She was clothed in the red shirt, a girdle, and a breechclout, and her legs and feet were bare. She looked very tiny standing beside her father and smiling like a delighted child.

"May we offer the congratulations of the judges, Chief Cornplanter," said Major Fitzhugh, and his uncle, suddenly rousing himself from revery, murmured, "Quite, quite." The Cornplanter inclined his head with dignity.

"We are all curious about the breeding of your horse," said Williamson pleasantly. "How did you happen to own him?"

"I got him honest," said The Cornplanter belligerently.

"Of course, of course," said the Captain in haste, "but where?"

The Cornplanter waved a hand dramatically toward the tall green jungle. "He was wild in high grass," he said. "I ran far to catch him and I brought him to my daughter."

"My father," said the rider beside him, "since it is as you say that you got him honest we could tell another and truer story."

The Cornplanter considered the suggestion solemnly. Then he smiled.

"New Jersey," he said.

"What?" said Williamson, Fitzhugh, and Hogmire all at once.

"When I brought my daughter home from the school in Philadelphia we came to New York, to Albany, to the Genesee. At Weehawken beside the great river we saw the horses run and I bought the gray for my daughter."

"What was his name then?" said Fitzhugh eagerly.

"Blowing Cloud," said the Cornplanter.

Colonel Hogmire cleared his throat. His little eyes danced like stars in the big round of his face.

"I have heard of the horse," he said triumphantly. "He was bred for speed, but why did you change his name?"

"A friend of my daughter," said The Cornplanter impassively, and the crowd bellowed mirthfully. Nathan felt his face grow hot with rushing blood. He looked at Williamson and saw the blue eyes blazing down at the little rider. Even in his own embarrassment he felt satisfaction that the girl had been able by reference to himself to arouse the Captain's jealousy so successfully.

"I still say," said Eleanor Fitzhugh impatiently, "that he could not have won if it had not been for the riding of your boy."

"My girl," said The Cornplanter, and as he spoke his unsmiling reserve broke down and he chuckled. As if the first sound of his delight were a signal the whole troop of Senecas, standing apart from the group about the judges, began to laugh.

To the Indians it seemed an incredibly funny joke that an Indian girl should have bested the skilful Negroes. They guffawed and jumped about, striking at each other. Some of them rolled on the ground in their ecstasy. They seemed to be trying to point out by their contemptuous mirth that the best riders the whites could furnish were black boys who were no match for a red girl. Their antics were so infectious that the entire throng were smiling, though many ruefully.

The eyes of the judges and all the group about them were on Catherine O'Bail.

"Good God!" said Hogmire.

"My congratulations," said Eleanor Fitzhugh as calmly as though she were not surprised. "You ride exceedingly well." She said that, thought Nathan, as if she were speaking to one of her Negro servants.

"Thank you," said the girl and smiled composedly.

Nathan, still watching the burning gaze that Williamson directed upon her, saw her raise her black eyes to meet it fairly.

"Perhaps," said the Captain, "we are missing the opportunity to honor the fortunate fellow for whom you named your animal. Is he among us?" As his keen blue eyes looked about over the crowd Nathan thought, His voice shows he's suffering and it's not merely from jealousy. Beneath that jocose manner his pride tortures him. He's ashamed of his wife if she's to be believed, but he's more ashamed of whatever it is that has happened between him and Catherine O'Bail—just as I am ashamed. Moreover he wants to punish me because of some feeling of guilt within himself. The blue eyes were on him now—and so were the black. He had not prepared himself for this. Catherine had known where he stood and had turned directly toward him. Stonily he glared into the ebony depths where once his self-pity had found solace. In desperate concentration he willed her not to speak. Finally words came from her mouth in a tone that was dull and listless.

"My father joked. There is no one."

Nathan turned and strode off, stumbling in unseeing haste through the crowd. She had saved him, yet he hated her. When he reached the oxcart Whirl was invisible, but from the bottom of its deep box he heard deep rumbling snores. He went up the slope to the grove, untied Lottie, and rode her back down to the cart. Turning the oxen about and using Whirl's goad as a kind of lance he started them out on the Bath road. It lay along the sloping edge of the wide shallow valley. Though September was at an end the air was soft and warm. The sun was sliding down the west toward a nest of billowing white thunderheads that lifted only partially above the blue hills at the horizon. Out in the plain of waving green, scattered elms raised yellowing arms into a light that turned their topmost reaches to a gleaming bronze.

By the time the shouts of the fair had dimmed to indistinct echoes the thunderheads were lined with changing light. A high fleck of white-gold, the first star, struck into sudden contrast with the yellow glow flooding the sky. Impatiently the mare kept trying to move out ahead of the slow-swinging oxen. Whirl snored on contentedly.

Over the stilling grass darkness was a soft blanket quilted with stars. Nathan's spirit was comforted. After all, the accident which had brought about his brief association with Catherine O'Bail was not to be blamed on him. He had, it was true, lost control of himself at one unfortunate moment. Perhaps Williamson kept much the same secret. Perhaps other men. Somehow he knew this last thought could not be justified. Catherine had told him that she had once loved Otsiquette. That she had been something more to Williamson than he wished to admit seemed certain. But even to give himself peace of mind Nathan could not think of her as dishonest or indiscriminate.

Why, then, had he resented the very thought of her possible relationship with the gallant Captain? Why had he been angry that she had named her horse for him and had apparently considered saying that she had done so publicly? Because, he decided, he belonged so completely to Rachel that the thought of a moral lapse, whether by himself or another, was repugnant to him. And why had he left the fair almost a full day earlier than necessary? Because he found its boisterous, raucous gaieties distasteful. Because Whirl was already unconscious and could no longer enjoy it. Because he must not run the risk of being late on Saturday. Not because he did not wish to meet Catherine O'Bail alone and face to face.

All night he urged the oxen on toward Bath. A late moon turned the stumps along the roadway into crouching grotesques, misshapen animals, silvery grief-torn ghosts. It went down, and an hour later on the black gurgling water of the Conhocton he saw the first uncertain reflection of the light of dawn. Still there would be four or five hours of steady going before they were at home. When the sun's rays finally hit the bottom of the cart they roused the sleeper who looked about him and burst into a long, heart-rending wail.

"Why, ye lovesick cub, ye half-witted barn spoiler, ye've lost me a fortune. I'd jest got my ear to the ground."

"Look in your pockets," said Nathan, "and then tell me if you ever came away with more."

For a few moments then Whirl rode in silence, interrupted only by the chink of metal on the floor of the wagon box. Then the shiny bald head appeared above the side.

"It's sixty-two dollars an' ninepence," yelled Whirl. "I'll buy Baltimore an' make 'em throw in Pittsburgh." Hastily he climbed from the cart and ran ahead of it and down to the river. He lay at its brink for a full minute, drinking steadily. Then he rushed back to the cart and resumed his recumbent posture.

"I fergive ye," he said benignly, and went back to sleep.

XXVIII

Whenever he waked during the day's long slumber Nathan thought of Rachel. He wondered what she was doing on this, her last day in the big white house by the lake. He was thankful that exhaustion from the long night trip had brought him deep sleep, for he knew that if he was sufficiently rested he would be nervously wandering about, incapable of calm. Whirl, too, slept the day through in the cabin and neither of the two men rose from their beds until sundown. Then, while they were cooking their supper, an evening wind began to blow from the north. By nightfall it was a steady roar through the woods. They went down to the river and looked at the long ark. Its timbers creaked and groaned against the wooden barriers, but it rode easy despite the rushing air. They made their way back to the cabin through total darkness, for clouds had obscured the stars. Each new blast from the north seemed colder and more ominous.

"Nate," said Whirl later, as the two sat by the fire. "Are ye sure ye want this pious gal?"

"I am."

"Ye answer too quick," said Whirl. "A question like that needs thinkin' over." He was silent a while.

"Did I ever tell ye how I come by my unfittin' first name?"

"No," said Nathan, "and you know it."

"My mother come here from England 'round '60," said Whirl, "when I was five. Don't know who my pappy was. Guess she did, but she never said. After I was borned she jined up a crew over there called the Shakin' Quakers. Had a woman to the head of 'em jest like this bunch over at Crooked Lake. My maw was havin' a hard time, bein' single with a little bastard to feed, and this bunch took up a collection an' sent her over here where she could be a widow lady. So to please 'em she changed my name from what it was—I can't even remember—to Whirling, 'cause that was the way they worshiped—dancin' and whirlin' round."

"Sounds like some folks we had down in Pennsylvania," said Nathan.

"Ain't the same," said Whirl. "All them folks that helped my mother is over here now—near Albany. They call 'em Shakers and they're still whirlin'."

"And why aren't you one of them?"

"My mother died afore they come over. She tried to send me back to the woman that runs it when she knew she was dyin'—but I was fifteen then an' I wouldn't go. And when that woman come to this country she tried to git a holt on me. Sent folks atter me an' said I belonged to 'em an' I was to come an' live with 'em. 'How many young women ye got there?' I says, fer I was twenty then. 'Well,' they says, 'we got young women, but they live separate from the men an' nobody gits married or fools around none 'cause Mother Ann—that was the head woman—she don't hold with that sorta business.' 'Well, I do,' I says, an' that ended it."

"Whirl," said Nathan, "what's all this about? Why are you telling it to me?"

"My maw thought the world an' all o' Mother Ann," said Whirl. "Guess she had good reason to. But she had a chance to wed up agin when I was 'bout seven an' she wouldn't do it 'cause he was a man that knew what he wanted."

"And you're warning me to look out for the same kind of trouble?"

"Yep."

Nathan laughed.

"You needn't worry," he said. "You just keep to your end of the boat tomorrow night."

In the morning the wind still blew. Twisting red and yellow leaves rode the fitful cold waves of air. Above the treetops gray clouds hung low, striated by fierce currents. Nathan and Whirl were silent while they prepared their breakfast. Finally, over a steaming mug of coffee, Whirl spoke:

"Never thought the time'd come, did ye?"

"No," said Nathan. "I felt just this way that day in Philadelphia, as if I were making a lot of unreal motions in a dream."

"Mebbe y'are," said Whirl darkly. "Mebbe y'are."

"I'll be starting," said Nathan, rising. "By the time I get the other horse I should be on my way to The Friend's. I'll meet you at the river a half hour before you cut loose."

"Be sure," said Whirl. "Captain's bringin' a lot o' folks from Williamsburg to see us start. He won't stand fer no waitin' round. Come four o'clock we better let go or he'll be wantin' to know why."

"I'll be here," said Nathan, walking to the door.

"Nate," said Whirl, and stopped.

"What?"

"Nothin' much. Sorta hate to see ye go."

"I want to give you my half of this cabin," said Nathan slowly, "just as soon as Rachel and I get settled in the big new one I'm going to build."

"I'm mighty obliged to ye. I like this place real well, now we got it t'lookin' decent."

"Maybe you'll be finding a woman to live in it with you."

"Never seem to get close enough to a woman like that— one worth livin' with."

"I'm going to get one like that now."

"That's fine," said Whirl. "Hope everythin' goes as slick as a soaped eel."

XXIX

Nathan went about his preparations with forced deliberation.
Patiently he explained to his neighbor why he wished to use
an extra horse. Whirl wanted to ride with him up the Conhocton a few miles, he said a little self-consciously, to see a
farmer about shipment of a last few bushels of grain. Again and
again he inspected the saddle and harness of the borrowed animal. Then he rode slowly toward the junction of the main north
road and that leading off to The Friend's Settlement. When he
was near it he turned into the woods and halted his mare. In
the leafy silence he could hear the creak of wheels and shouts
of a lategoer hurrying his oxen. They must have passed only
a few minutes before and he waited until he could no longer
hear the sounds. The Friend's service would begin in less than
three hours. No one would be likely to set out for it now. He
spoke to his mare and tugged at the lead rein of the other
horse. At last he had taken the road that would lead him to
Rachel.

The sky was a solid, dark cloud cover. Scarves of lighter
mist rode the wind below it. The colors of the leaves about
him, garish yesterday in the brilliance of the sun, were softened
by the grayness through which they tumbled. With each moment the air blew colder. Nathan was shivering, but in his
throat he could feel the quick surging of his blood. Beneath
his ribs he felt a vast emptiness. Time passed and he did not
know it. When finally he saw what was about him he was
among the tall hickories and The Friend's house was white
beyond the clean silvery trunks. He dismounted and tied the
horses. He seemed to be moving so slowly that action was
hardly perceptible. He walked to the border of the forest.

The windows of the house were rows of sullen gray eyes.
Beyond and below them the somber lake stretched into a light-

less infinity. The animals that had brought men and women
to the meeting were tied to trees at the edge of the clearing.
Oxen and horses stood as motionless as the high-wheeled carts
and long box wagons in an air of chill enchantment. He tried
to picture the scene inside the long room. The chairs along
the walls now stood in solid phalanx before the rostrum, each
bearing a listener. Behind the pulpit that had served as his
easel The Friend in her purple gown and white neckcloth was
speaking. The three curls trembled about her face and the
brown eyes were full of glancing lights. Behind her, at her
right, stood the gray-clad spirit of the Prophet Daniel operating
in the female line—the loving, full-bodied, eager girl who would
that night be possessed by her lover. In a few minutes now
she would be coming to him, hurrying along the way she knew
so well.

Nathan turned and walked back to the horses. He inspected the knots he had tied carefully a few moments before.
Then he walked aimlessly about among the trees. Pulling a
knife from its deerskin scabbard at his belt he cut a small
branch and whittled at it desperately.

He marveled that his mind could race so swiftly over
many courses during the little measure of time that was passing.
In a few hours, he assured himself, she and I will be floating
south in sunshine. In Baltimore the autumn days will still be
warm, and there will be soft nights under the stars. The hard
hickory twisted beneath the wounding pressure of his blade
and he threw it from him.

Perhaps, he thought, on the way back we can stop for a
day's visit with the old people, show them the stuff of which
their grandchildren will be made. His mother would welcome
Rachel, he knew. The two women would find warming comfort
in their common piety. His father would look at Rachel more
realistically. He might not approve a girl who had been so
strenuous a disciple of a woman prophet.

The sound of many voices came from the direction of the
house and Nathan wheeled about and ran back to the wood's
edge. The congregation was singing. From behind the dull
windows came the words of the hymn—sometimes almost indistinct as the majority of the singers uncertainly followed the
sure rhythms of a few:

The spirit breathes upon the Word
And brings the truth to sight;
Precept and promise still afford
A sanctifying light.

A glory gilds the sacred page,
Majestic like the sun;
It gives a light to every age,
It gives but borrows none.

Let everlasting thanks be Thine
For such a bright display
As makes a world of darkness shine
With beams of heavenly day.

A sudden gust poured through the clearing as if to carry the last note into oblivion. Again Nathan began his nervous pacing. With each step I take, he thought, a portion of time is gone. Actually minutes are passing, completing the slow hours.

He had so resigned himself to interminable waiting that sudden chatter startled him. Once more he hurried to his post. The meeting was over. Men and women were crowding out of the big door and down the steps. A horseman was already on his way home, urging his mount carefully through the crowd. As Nathan watched, families piled into the long wagons. The drivers shouted at their oxen. The road to Bath filled with slow-moving teams. There was a shrill squealing of axles. Now she will come, he thought. It is hard to believe, but in a moment I shall see her. I wonder if her face will be strange to me, for I feel as if she were someone whom I do not know.

The last stragglers gossiped leisurely beside their wagons. Then they moved out and were lost in the woods. Another gust arrived bearing a spatter of rain. Then a watery veil slanted downward. The lake disappeared. The trees at the forest's far edge were dimmed to shadowy masses. Only the white house kept its strong clean lines against the blowing mist. Except for the limitless whisperings of drops on the leaves there was no sound.

Nathan stood at the clearing's edge until he felt the cold

trickling of the rain upon his shivering body. His eyes burned against the water that dripped into them. Unbelievingly he stared at the house, standing stolidly, holding its secret. No door opened. No window moved. There was less light now. The afternoon was waning. He thought of Whirl Gragg waiting anxiously beside the boat. If she were to come now they could not ride to Bath in time to go aboard before the launching. There would be no floating south in sunlight, no wandering the streets of Baltimore. If she were to come now—

And suddenly he knew she was not coming.

He strode across the clearing and clumped up the wet steps. The streaming boards of the door sounded to his knock. There was no reply. Again and again the blows of his clenched hands struck hollow thunders through the house. There was no sound of steps inside the great room. Desperately he threw himself against the solid barrier before him. It was as firm as stone.

He ran a few steps back and turned to charge. He would make a battering ram of his body. Either he or the wooden panel must break.

But the door was moving. It was swinging slowly inward and for a moment it seemed to be opening on utter darkness. Then, as the gray light of the clearing struck inward, Nathan saw The Universal Friend. She still wore the purple of her public preaching and she stood rigid, strong hands clenched at her sides, her eyes blazing.

"Nathan Hart," she said, and her voice trembled out between lips that she seemed unable to open widely enough to allow the passage of her words. "You have desecrated the Lord's annointed. Judgment shall be the Lord's."

"I've come to get Rachel," said Nathan thickly.

"The spirit that ministers unto The Friend has been beset by the forces of evil," said the prophetess evenly, "but she has won the victory and come into the light of eternal day."

"You're lying," said Nathan. "You're holding her against her will."

The woman smiled, the upper lip of her broad mouth curving in contempt.

"The followers of The Friend are guided only by love," she said. "There is but one way of salvation. Renounce the way of the flesh, accept the way of God as His messenger showeth it." Her eyes sought Nathan's and suddenly became intent.

"Ye may yet find the peace that passeth understanding," she said persuasively. "It lieth here in the Vale of Kedron under the will of Christ as He revealeth it to me, His servant. If ye will accept of His bounty through me ye may be one of us. Ye shall dwell beside the sacred brook and become a worker in the Master's vineyard. Heavenly love shall replace the carnal in thy heart and ye will thank God." Her voice had become soft and pleading and her look tender. Her arms were stretched out before her.

"I thank God that I am a man and I will live like one," said Nathan roughly. "And if you don't let that girl out of there I'm coming in after her."

Convulsively the hands of The Friend clenched and returned to her sides. Without turning her head she spoke sharply.

"Rachel Malin."

At once Rachel, who had been standing in the big room just out of Nathan's sight, stepped forward to stand beside The Friend. The white collar above her gray dress was rumpled and soiled. The blue eyes stared coldly from tear-reddened rims.

"Speak," said the prophetess.

"The Friend's morning word burned away the sin in my heart," said Rachel, as if she were reciting a sentence she had not well learned. "Even as she spoke I had a vision—I saw an evil, horned monster about to devour a white-robed child. Before it was too late I confessed my sin to The Friend and she has assigned me penance. Now my soul is at peace. I will not see you again. Expiate if you can the evil you have done." Her eyes filled with tears and a sob came into her throat.

The Friend smiled tenderly.

"Do not refuse the offer of God's grace," she said. "Live here with us in the happiness that comes only to those who put aside the world. Ye may love Rachel Malin here even as ye love all other of God's children. The Friend will guide you to eternal peace."

"No!" shouted Nathan. "You can have your girl and to hell with her and you. You've won a fight but, by God, you'll take no prisoner!"

He turned away and walked slowly to the horses. He was a long time untying the careful knots.

He did not remember later his ride down the darkening road. He did not feel the sting of blowing rain upon his face, the tug on his arm of the weary horse behind him, or the swing of his mount beneath him. Nor did he know whether he or Lottie made the decision to turn aside into Elijah's clearing. A fire was growing in his veins, a merciful burning that bit by bit destroyed unbearable consciousness. Before the fever had completely won, however, he saw certain things clearly—the white robe of Elijah with firelight flickering upon it, the wide eyes of frightened children, and the hands of Mrs. Parker holding a bowl from which steam was rising. He heard a few things, too—his own voice rising and falling in monotonous repetitions of some statement he felt was very important, and the voice of thundering Elijah replying each time, "I know. I know. But the wicked shall yet be confounded!"

1794

Farewell to Whiskey!
(Song of the 1790's)

I

Elijah stood on a wooden platform in front of Williamson's
low, widespread house. Above him at the top of the swaying
Liberty Pole, a banner, bearing thirteen long stripes and fifteen
stars that were herded into a blue field at its upper left corner,
flirted in the warm wind. From the folds of the Prophet's new-
laundered robe a big hand suddenly emerged and moved to a
point behind his right ear.

"Hark! what sounds are those which arise from the lowering north?"

The little crowd of men and women before him listened
for a menacing roar from the sunny woods beyond them. They
heard only the wind among the August leaves.

"While we were celebrating a month ago the anniversary
of our hard-won independence the prize was already threatened.
Lo! the great unicorn of Albion moans in Canada's forest shade
and that other red quadruped which rides rampant on the
British shield growls from the bristling ramparts of Toronto.
Black war elephants raise their dusky backs from the blue
waters of Lake Ontario and shake their death-white tusks. A
Canadian Hannibal threatens to march across our mountains,
lay waste our lands, capture our leader, and, emerging from our
forests with drums, clarinets, and feathers, parade him in chains
through British streets. Once more we stand and hurl defiance
into the teeth of the British lion. Let him come ravening down
—we await him undismayed!"

Nathan, standing on the ground before the platform, led
the yelling that greeted this announcement. As the noise continued he began to fear that the crowd would get out of hand
and, accepting Elijah's last words as a conclusion, drift back
into the two taverns to resume their drinking. Soon, however,
he knew that he need not have worried. For while the right

hand of the Prophet had sought his ear the left hand had been beneath his robe tugging at his girdle. Before the long shout had died out Elijah's belly had begun its customary miraculous distention. The nerves of the beholders grew taut as the Prophet's skin while they stood awaiting the explosion that seemed inevitable. Still the balloonlike swelling increased beneath the white robe.

"I am filled with the wind of prophecy," said Elijah solemnly, and many sighed with relief as his slow deflation began. "I see a mighty champion, sword in hand, face threatening Simcoe and drive him cringing to his northern lair. I see the waves of blue Ontario's waters lie down beside the smiling land because that champion brings us peace and plenty. He is the David of the Genesee, the Moses of our western Canaan, Charles Williamson."

As the roar of the crowd began Nathan saw the lithe figure of the Captain push its way to the edge of the platform and leap lightly upon it. Tricorn in hand, cape falling carelessly from his shoulder, Williamson waited for the noise to subside. It grew louder, and he waved the hat toward the audience in a deprecating gesture. There was thunderous response. He bowed his head in a gesture of humility and gradually the shouting died. He stepped forward and there was silence.

"My hearty thanks to the distinguished speaker. You and I extend to him, I am sure, sincere congratulations on his decision soon to exchange the white robe for the black, and we now happily greet him as Judge Parker." Renewed yelling brought a self-conscious bow from Elijah, who then seated himself firmly in a big, ladder-back rocking chair at the rear of the platform and swayed back and forth, fanning himself with an end of his robe.

"I called this meeting for a special purpose, my friends," said Charles Williamson confidentially.

"Because I have tried to find land for all who wish it, and because I have tried to increase the value of your acres here by opening the rich tract on the shores of Ontario, the Governor of Canada boasted last month that he would send me to England in chains. A few days later he seized by force of arms a few wagonloads of flour I bought north of the border for your sustenance. You have seen how our Seneca friends are decked

out in new blankets and jewels. You have seen their new guns
and you know that they come from the British fort at Niagara.
Governor Simcoe is buying Iroquois support for the Indians
of the Ohio country against the gallant force of General
Wayne."

"Hooray for mad Tony!" came a voice, and the crowd
cheered.

"If Wayne is defeated," said Williamson seriously, "we
can expect the governor to try to pay us a visit and bring his
friends with him."

"Let 'em come," shouted Whirling Gragg, his bald head
glistening in the sun, as he leaped into the air so that his
audience could see him. "We'll give every one of the bastards a
six-foot lot."

Williamson held up his hand for silence.

"I have been greatly hampered in my efforts for your defense," he said. "Because I was once a British soldier some
of our neighbors, even some of you, suspect me of treason."

There were cries of "No, no," followed by embarrassed
silence. The men in the crowd cast furtive, suspicious looks at
each other.

"Every road I talk of building is said to be for the purpose
of admitting the invader. My enemies say that every musket
I get for you is to be handed over to the enemy. I bought a
few bags of grass seed to sow upon our square here, and they
were seized at Albany lest they be gunpowder for the British."

The hulking form of the wrestling champion, Eli Stephens,
climbed slowly to the platform, and the Captain, seemingly
confused, hesitated to continue.

"Guess I c'n take keer o' anybody says you ain't a patriot,
Cap'n," said Eli slowly.

Nathan saw Williamson's head go back as his hearty laughter rang out over the crowd. He wondered why he could not
put his full faith in the Captain. Was it because here was a
grace such as no other man he knew possessed? Was it envy
of his perfection? There could be no question, Nathan thought,
of Williamson's honest desire to develop his employer's lands
without interference. Why did this tall, dark, smiling fellow,
so unassuming, so full of good will toward his companions,
create in him only a vague distrust?

"Eli," said the Captain, "after what you did to that greased Seneca last fall I don't believe anybody is going to challenge you." He smiled and Nathan saw on the faces around the platform responsive smiles of confidence and affection. The Captain took a step forward and his face was solemn, his manner earnest. There's something noble about him, thought Nathan, or is it just a look of nobility?

"I have news for you," said Williamson. "Tom Moffat has ridden here from the shore of the lake to tell us that Governor Simcoe has done me the honor to send his representative to call on me. Unhappily I was not present at Sodus when he arrived. Tom says he left instructions for me to meet him next week at the same place."

"It's a bear trap, Cap'n," called Whirling Gragg. "They'll surround ye an' take ye back with 'em."

"Tom says they had a dozen grenadiers with them," said the Captain, "and he thinks they thought to find me without guards."

"Don't go, Cap'n," said Whirl.

"I'm going," said the Captain, looking far out over the treetops at the edge of the clearing.

"Don't go," shouted the crowd.

"I must," said Williamson. "I wouldn't let them think I was afraid to come."

"Hooray for the Cap'n."

"Give 'em hot shot, Cap'n."

"And I want some of you to go with me."

"Hell, we'll all go."

"That will not be necessary. I want ten good men—and, for fear my enemies will accuse me of plotting with the governor to surrender this country to him, I want men who served against His Majesty."

"I was a captain of militia," shouted Elijah, jumping from his rocking chair and saluting, though not so smartly as he had intended because his hand caught in the folds of his robe.

"I fit 'em," shouted Whirl, leaping into the air again. A few hands went up from the crowd.

"Though most of us have come to this country since the peace treaty," said Williamson, "we love it as well as if we had been born here. Nevertheless my guard must be soldiers of the Revolution. How many volunteers have we?"

"Eight," said Elijah, counting the raised hands.

"Mr. Thomas Morris, now a guest at my house, will be of the party," said the Captain. "He did not serve, but in view of his father's record we need not doubt his patriotism." The crowd laughed.

"One more," said Elijah looking about. "Nathan Hart, did you not serve in Pennsylvania?"

"No," said Nathan. "When I was fourteen I marched out to protect our valley from the Tories and Indians, but I wasn't a soldier."

"I'm sure we all agree that Mr. Hart's experience is sufficient," said Williamson, smiling.

"Never thought I'd git a sight o' the English seas," said Whirl complacently. He sat the broad back of his horse as if it were a raft drifting crookedly.

"Don't call 'em that," said Nathan. "Our side belongs to us."

"Workin' fer the Cap'n suits me," said Whirl, disregarding the interruption. "Never stayed so long in one place before, an' it's because he keeps sendin' me away from it. Last year to Baltimore,"—he looked apologetically at Nathan—"and this year to the English seas."

Williamson and Thomas Morris lolled in their saddles. Nathan could hear behind him the steady beat of hoofs and the heavy voice of Elijah addressing all who would listen. The little party had left Canandaigua Lake behind early in the morning to amble along the narrow east road through the woods. Sunlight sifted through the August foliage, but the air was still cool and permeated by the smells of the dark hours. In Canandaigua, Morris had entertained the Captain at his tall, white frame house during the night, but the rest of the group had slept, five in a bed, at Mrs. Sanford's log tavern. Refreshed by their rest after the weary day of riding up and down long steep hills they rode lazily over gentle slopes.

"Look a-there," said Whirl abruptly, with a wave of his arm. They had trotted through a dark hollow, walked up its far side, and now reached the far-stretching summit of a long ridge. Below them lay a narrow lake, and their road bore to the left, running parallel to the shore.

An irregular row of unkempt cabins squatted close to the water line just where the curving of the bank indicated the lake's end.

"Mr. Hart," called the Captain, and Nathan spurred his mare forward.

"Mr. Morris and I wished you to join us that we might be the first to show an artist one of the most beautiful sights of this new country. Indeed this long body of water surrounded by hills reminded me so much of the beauties of Lake Leman that I named the little town we are about to enter 'Geneva.' We hope that one day you will paint us the scene that lies before us, Mr. Hart."

"It is very beautiful, Captain," said Nathan. "I wish I were capable of painting it well."

"We have faith in your future, Mr. Hart," said the Captain lightly, "and we have faith in the future of Geneva. I have already begun to build a great tavern here. It shall stand at the entrance of the Genesee Country to welcome the weary traveler to the comfort, the wealth, and the luxury that lie within it."

"Captain Williamson has just been telling me," said Morris easily, "of his plan to combine here the civilized ways of Europe with the native materials of the Genesee. He is building an English tavern out of our native trees. He is importing an English chef to prepare our American roasts."

"The best venison I ever ate," said Nathan, "was roasted by my mother. An Indian taught her."

Williamson laughed and Nathan grinned at him. His reaction to the Captain's mirth surprised him. A year ago, he thought, I would have been angry when I said that, and I would have been sullen after I said it. I am changing. It is not that I distrust the Captain less. Perhaps it is because Whirl went back to the valley on his way home from Baltimore and saw my father and found out that I need no longer fear pursuit. Perhaps it is because I am no longer tortured by thoughts of Rachel. Perhaps it is because Whirl and I are thriving and our crops are large. At any rate I wouldn't have grinned at the Captain a year ago.

Before the party reached the curving of the lake Williamson called a halt. Before them on a wide knoll a hundred sturdy
timber uprights stood like a naked but well-drilled army. From
the far side of this nude forest came the clangor of hammers
and the singing of saws. Here and there among the posts Nathan
could see men going about their work, disregarding the little
band of mounted spectators.

"Before the year's end," said Williamson in a voice for
all to hear, "this skeleton shall be clothed, and we shall open
the great hostelry of the Genesee with a ball that shall befit so
great an event. Gentlemen, you are all invited."

"Whoopee," yelled Whirl, bouncing on his saddle. "Cap'n,
could ye import about a yard an' a half o' tender female fer
me to favor on that evenin'?"

"There will be ladies, I trust, for the pleasure of us all,"
said Williamson a little stiffly. "Let us ride on."

When the rippling waves lapped the white curve of shore
at the north boundary of blue water the party turned north.
They rode silently now over undulating woodland. All seemed
to realize that their adventure had begun. The scents of the
night had disappeared and the air was hot and motionless.
Through the narrow open space above the road the riders could
see white billowing clouds drifting in the sky to the north,
thunderheads above great Ontario. Nathan had dropped back
to ride once more with Whirl and the six pairs of horsemen
kept up a steady fast walk. At their left a brown stream splashed
and gurgled pleasantly, or disappeared and became silent as its
frequent meanders took it away from their path.

It was about noon when they heard the distant whine of
a sawmill. It grew louder and was punctuated by the beat of
hammers. Soon they rode into the open. The low, weather-
beaten mill stood beside the stream at the near edge of the
clearing. The water rushed fast here, plunging through the
millrace and down to join with another larger stream that met
it in a sharp-angled fork. Near the mill a big flat-bottomed
boat lay upside down on log braces. Three men were working
energetically to patch the craft's broad bottom. Captain Williamson and Thomas Morris rode swiftly toward them and their
companions followed.

"Good day to you, gentlemen," said the Captain. "It's

good to see the Stancells and Jack Featherly so industrious. But why do you mend the old bateau? Are you planning to drag her to Ontario for the fishing?"

"Beggin' your pardon, Captain," said the eldest of the three, a stocky gray-bearded man in deerskin coat and home-spun short breeches, "but I think you know why we mend her. We had enough of Injuns on the Mohawk to know when to git out."

"What's that?" said Williamson sharply. "What do you mean?"

The older man looked at him boldly and, Nathan thought, with an air of condescension.

"We know the signs, Captain. We went through it all back there in the Fort Stanwix country. Brother Bill here served with Sullivan when we paid 'em back fer Cherry Valley an' the rest o' their murderin' tricks. After that we thought it would be safe to come on here."

"Of course it's safe," said Williamson impatiently.

"Ye listen to me," said the man. "There ain't a man-Seneca in this whole country at this minute. They's plenty o' their womenfolks around—with their pretty new red blankets an' shiny beads an' some on 'em even a-wearin' Christian clothes. We don't need nobody t'tell us what that means. We been through it before. The bloody Britishers 've bought 'em agin. We've seen war parties a-sneakin' west through here. The Six Nations are jinin' up with the Ohio Injuns t' massacre Wayne. They've probably done it already."

"Nonsense," said Williamson, so sternly that the talker was silent.

"It ain't nonsense," said the youngest of the three hotly. "Me an' the Stancells ain't waitin' fer 'em t'come back with scalps t'their belts an' a-lookin' fer more. We're takin' our wives an' startin' east soon's this bateau'll float us."

Thomas Morris laughed.

"It's the same way with some of our outlying farmers near Canandaigua," he said. "They rushed into town the other day, packed and ready to flee for their lives. They changed their minds when they saw I was having my house painted. They tried to frighten us all, but the painters just went on painting so placidly that finally the scare subsided and the farmers went home and unpacked again."

"The more fools they," said Jack Featherly. "When ye can't find no Injuns around but squaws—look fer trouble. Larned that at m'mother's knee."

"You're wrong," said Morris. "It's probably true that the Indians are gathering, but it is to talk over the treaty meeting at Canandaigua next month. President Washington has ordered Colonel Pickering to summon them for a last peacemaking, in order that all their grievances may be heard and friendship permanently established."

"Mr. Morris is right," said Williamson quickly. "We know the chiefs of the Seneca Nation to be favorable to us."

"Seen 'em lift the hair o' their best friends," said Featherly sullenly.

Williamson laughed.

"Not Red Jacket," he said, "nor Farmer's Brother nor The Cornplanter. I wish you would take my word for it that Indian troubles are over in the Genesee Country. But just to make you doubly sure I'll have this rumor looked into. We'll be coming back through here from Great Sodus in a few days and I'll be able to tell you then what the situation is. Meanwhile don't worry."

"We may not worry, but we'll keep hammerin' on this ol' boat," said Featherly.

Williamson cantered down the slope and the cavalcade jounced along behind him. A narrow ford, marked by big rocks painted white, crossed the little stream just above its junction with the other. On the bank he waited for his companions. As they joined him he waved a hand toward the meeting of the two currents.

"It is a miniature likeness of the meeting of the Rhone and the Saône," he said excitedly, "and so I call the town I have planned here Lyons."

He has already forgotten what the men said about the Indians, Nathan thought, as his mare's hoofs splashed into the stream. His dreams of this land crowd all other thoughts from his head.

But Nathan was not quite correct in his conclusion. The

Captain had suddenly wheeled his horse about and ridden back to join him.

"Mr. Hart," he said. "Have you any particular knowledge of Indian discontent at this time?"

"Just such as we all know," said Nathan.

"I have a vague memory of your being considered a friend of The Cornplanter and his family."

Nathan flushed.

"His daughter once saved my life when I was out of my head with fever and lost in the grass."

"Ah, yes. I am beginning to remember. And she named that streak of lightning she calls a horse after you, didn't she?"

"She called him Tom the Tinker."

"I beg your pardon. I did not mean—"

"I don't mind, Captain. Whirl tells me the Federalists already regret their persecution of honest farmers."

Williamson smiled.

"You are too quick for me, sir. I do not wish to seem over-curious nor to offend you, but I had thought that perhaps through your friendship with The Cornplanter's family you might have valuable information about the Indians." His blue eyes sought Nathan's in a look that seemed at the same time penetrating and appealing. Nathan felt a sense of triumph rising within him. The Captain has not seen Catherine O'Bail in many months, he thought, and he is miserable for fear that I am her lover.

He returned Williamson's look directly.

"I have not seen The Cornplanter's daughter for more than a year," he said.

The gaze of the Captain wavered. He seemed about to speak again and then to stop himself from speaking. At length he began with what seemed to Nathan a forced joviality.

"Indeed if you have not deceived me you have not associated with any young woman since religion lost its hold upon you on the shores of Crooked Lake."

Once more Nathan grinned. I'd have killed him for that a year ago, he thought.

"I'm a backsliding sinner, Captain. I live in hope of new conversions."

Williamson's laughter rang through the woods. He's happy

now, thought Nathan. He's been really worrying about me and Catherine.

"Mr. Hart," his companion was saying, "I like you and I do not understand why we have not been better friends. I am grateful to you for many services. I regret more than I can say my having been obliged to send Gragg off to Baltimore without you a year ago. We waited as long as we dared, but eventually our distinguished guests at the landing became restless and demanded action. Now that you have no further fear of unpleasant consequences as a result of your taking refuge in this country can we not associate more pleasantly?"

"My only objection, Captain Williamson," said Nathan, "is that I hold a bad opinion, not only of your political faith, but of your plans for the future of this country."

"Surely you do not suspect me of treason," said Williamson incredulously. "I had given you credit for more common sense. I am as loyal a citizen of my adopted country as you or any other."

"There's a higher treason than betrayal to the British," said Nathan hotly. "No, I do not suspect you of dealing with Simcoe. The British hate each other when they thwart each other as you and Simcoe are doing. But you will not deny that you are trying to make another Europe of your land. The very names you give your towns—Bath, Geneva, Lyons—are proofs of it. But it isn't the names that trouble me. It's the fact that you would make a state of English shires out of the Genesee Country. You would have big estates, with lords to own them and peasants to till them."

"And you would have every man a king," said Williamson contemptuously. "We have too much of that spirit in this country now for our own good. We have too many kings."

"I would have every man own his own land and work it," said Nathan in a fury, "and no man touch his forelock to a master."

"It is impossible," exclaimed Williamson. "You would destroy gentility and build a nation of barbarians. Since we have few aristocrats we must build an aristocracy in order that the arts of living may be preserved. These are dangerous doctrines you recite so glibly, Mr. Hart."

"You will find them the doctrines of the majority of the citizens of this country, Captain."

Williamson sat straight in his saddle. His eyes were set and anger burned in them.

"I will not argue with a madman," he said. Clapping spurs to his mount's flank he was away to rejoin lone Thomas Morris.

Nathan rode on for a few minutes in a white rage. Then he was suddenly amused. This was the fellow who could no longer anger him, the man at whom, after the calming passage of an uneventful year, he could grin. He heard a grunt beside him and turned to look at Whirl. The little man was bobbing peacefully up and down on his fat nag. His cherubic face bore a look of mingled satisfaction and admiration.

"Ye'd tell the Lord how t' run the Kingdom," he said.

The sun was setting and the woods were cooling when Nathan saw to his left the glint of a rapid stream.

"Salmon Crick, if they tell me true," said Whirl. "Look to yer right an' y' might see Great Sodus."

Nathan's eyes caught the shine of sunny water to the east. Evidently the party was riding along a wooded promontory. The horses, sensing the journey's end, broke into an eager trot, veering away from the creek toward the fitful gleam beyond the dark trees. The eastern light began to widen and grow brighter. It spread to the north and on into the west. The woods were thinner now. Suddenly the riders came out on open high land. A calm blue sea stretched out before them. Far to their left, just above the sure line of the horizon, hung the red sun. Even while they looked its lower edge seemed to touch water and a flamelike ray shot over the placid surface. The horsemen reined in on a tall bluff. Its lakeward bank shelved steeply down to white sand, edging the water. On its other side gentle terraces slanted to Great Sodus Bay. Narrowing the harbor's mouth, tongues of land stretched toward each other from the mainland. Behind them, in the wide, still reaches, lay pine-covered islands, black in the sunset light.

"I call your attention to the fact," Nathan heard the Captain saying, "that the first view of this place strikes the eye of the beholder as one of the most magnificent landscapes the human eye can picture. If only Mr. Hart could catch and hold on canvas for us this very moment, we should be forever his debtors."

Nathan looked at the smiling Williamson in amazement. No trace of the man's recent anger showed in his frank, interested face. He seemed completely to have forgotten that he had just been so enraged as to call one of his companions a madman. Nathan wondered if the Captain believed himself so superior to his associates that he might play with them as a cat plays with a mouse.

"What do you say, Mr. Hart?"

"Nature has painted a scene too beautiful for my skill."

"Your tongue is as facile as your brush, Mr. Hart, when you choose to use it. I hope that may be oftener in—"

A yodel from the bay side of the bluff interrupted him. A tall man stood beside a widespread low cabin on the shore and waved excitedly.

"That will be Joseph Colt," said the Captain. "He is surveying the town I plan here. Let us ride down to meet him."

II

The air was still that night. After their dinner of roast venison and boiled maize the men had stumbled about for a time on the little round stones of the beach, their eyes straining into the darkness to catch by starlight some further knowledge of the new region about them. Then, tired by the long ride, they undressed, stretched themselves beside their muskets on Joseph Colt's floor, and slept. In the loft above, Colt and Williamson rested on the cabin's one bed.

Nathan, lying naked beside the barred door, heard the ceaseless lap of water on the sand outside and did not sleep. Again and again he went over in his memory his quarrel with the Captain. Each time he recalled it the name of Catherine O'Bail sent his mind back to moments he had spent with her. The room was hot and two of the men were snoring. Restlessly he turned from one side to the other. The floor was hard and the blanket on which he lay made him warmer without adding to his comfort. Silently he rose, lifted the door bar from its sockets, and leaned it against the wall. He picked up his musket and swung the door open. It creaked loudly and one of the men stopped snoring. With an inexplicable sense of panic Nathan stepped outside and shut the door behind him.

At once he felt the blessing of coolness on his skin. His bare feet sank into soft sand. He walked to the water and stood where the ripples of the bay just touched his toes. Across the silent surface came an intermittent dull rumble, the breaking of waves on the shore of the great lake. He began to walk on the firm smoothness of wet sand toward the mouth of the bay. Stars lay in the water and just above the headland before him swung a powderhorn moon. Time seemed not to exist and he did not know how long he had been moving when his course curved below the bluff and he stood beside Ontario. The moon had laid across the slow-moving water a rolling silver path that ended at methodical intervals in eruptions of white froth as a wave went home. A sudden high meteor streaked downward and died before it reached the dark horizon.

Nathan lay on the sand. It had not lost all the heat of the day, and the air, blowing gently, was full of warmth and wet softness and the smell of the lake. The Milky Way was a vague white above him. He felt happily weary and the exhilaration of extreme well-being took hold of him. He nursed the stock of the gun lying beside him, running his hand over the smooth, oiled wooden surfaces. He had not known such peace as this since the long days of boyhood, nor such exultant joy since the moment the Pennsylvania wagonmaker had set him to painting pictures on the sides of the Conestogas. The nervous fear of pursuit and the sense of disgrace, which had made him taciturn and irascible when he came to the Genesee Country, had faded out as the succeeding days brought only security and the friendship of neighbors. The enchantment by which Rachel Malin had enslaved his body and tormented his mind had been destroyed. Living lonely in his cabin during the long months of Whirl Gragg's absence he had at last suspected the struggle that had gone on within Rachel, and one day he had realized that he pitied her. After that her spell was broken. Whirl had returned with profane outcries against Nathan for having missed the launching of the ark and with gay, incredible stories of the loose ways of Baltimore girls. On his way back to Bath the little man had gone many miles out of his way to see Nathan's father and mother and to find out from them whether or not their son was still considered a fugitive. Then he had hurried home with the reassuring news. Nathan smiled into the star-whitened sky as he thought of Whirl and his friendship.

Something had broken the rhythms of the night. The melody of the slow waves had been decorated by grace notes. Nathan rolled over on his belly and grasped his musket. Out beyond the gentle surf there was movement. He listened intently. As regular as the wave beats but in quicker time came the soft plashing. A man or an animal was swimming toward the mouth of the bay. Already the sound was growing fainter as the swimmer moved on to round the headland. Nathan rose and picked up his gun. If he waited for about a minute, now, he would catch the invader close to land as he slipped into the calm water of the bay. Painfully he tried to count the seconds; then he leaped to his feet and dashed for the inlet. His momentum as he reached his goal took him into the water up to his knees. Within a few feet of him a hand rose from the water.

"Come out of there," said Nathan harshly, lifting his gun, "or I'll kill you."

There was a moment of silence and Nathan stepped forward. Then a body rose beside him and stood waist-deep.

"Nathan Hart," said a voice that Nathan remembered. There in the dim light of the stars and the quarter moon stood Catherine O'Bail. Her long straight hair fell about her face and partially covered the strong young swellings of her breasts. Her tawny skin gleamed wet and smooth.

"I came to find you," she said softly and waded swiftly to the white sand. As she approached him Nathan saw that she was breathing rapidly and her deepset eyes showed wide white areas about the shining black centers.

"They plan to take him," she said in a low, tense tone, "and the war parties will come back from the Ohio and kill all of you."

"Take whom?"

"The Captain," she said impatiently. "The British will capture him and it will be the beginning of Indian war. They say that tomorrow General Wayne's army will be massacred. Then the Seneca warriors will return, killing the whites as they come. Governor Simcoe says he will bring an army to help."

"Who told you this?" said Nathan fiercely, moving close to her.

"I heard my father talking to the old chiefs left behind."

"And how are they going to take Williamson?"

"The British officer is bringing a boatload of soldiers."

"How many?"

"About twelve—not many more men than you have."

"How do you know?"

"My father has known everything from the day it was decided."

"And why are you here? What were you doing out there in the inlet?"

"I was coming to tell you. I was afraid to come by land. They are watching."

For the first time Nathan realized both were naked. The shock of the girl's news had occupied his mind. Fear and excitement had overwhelmed his sense. Now he looked on Catherine and remembered her, remembered the tousled black hair, the straight, sturdy young body which he had possessed, and a sudden feeling of gratitude for her continued loyalty took hold of him. But another memory was singing into his mind. He was standing behind the Captain's log house and a plump girl with a discontented face was saying petulantly: "I'll tell you where he is. Last night he rode on to that half-heathen yellow slut across the valley."

"You risked your life to save the Captain," he said harshly.

All light seemed to go from the girl's face. Her eyes were dull, like burned-out coals.

"To prevent a war," she said stonily.

Nathan grasped the slim rounds of her shoulders.

"To save your lover."

"It is not true."

He shook her and her head dropped back until her eyes looked into the stars, reflecting them, and her hair hung straight, not touching her back. She was smiling.

"I don't believe you," he said.

"Does it matter? Do you object that I am loved?"

Once more she was in his arms and his lips sought the yielding mouth they remembered. It was cold and immobile.

"Catherine," he said, and the yearning of a year's loneliness was in his voice. She stepped back and looked at him compassionately.

"Did the prophet girl hurt you so much?" she said. "You are a fool."

"How did you know?"

"Because I am a fool too."

They looked at each other, trying to span the gulf of time and life between them, trying to call an old mood into re-existence. Then, clasped in each other's arms, they were sinking to the sand. It received them tenderly. And Nathan knew that this was no reconstruction of a past moment. He lay with no enemy to be destroyed, as once he had lain above the dizzy, dark gorge of the Genesee. He lay with a spirit as generous as this open arch of sky, this star-reflecting watery plain. It seemed to him that they had somehow become part of all that white-stained immensity. The night held the rhythm of the waves on the soft flanks of the beach, the rhythm of the heavens syncopated by the beat of a shooting star, the rhythm of two bodies joined, infinitesimal and yet a part of the world's endless movement. All marched toward a moment of unbearable beauty, a chord of such harmony as had never been. Suddenly it was upon them. . . .

They lay long in the warm sand, their faces lifted to the sky, their bodies blown upon by gentle changing winds. Light was spreading above the eastern rim of the lake when Catherine rose and walked to the water's edge. She stood ankle-deep for a moment, shivered, and ran back to Nathan.

"Promise me that you will be careful," she said. "Do not let your plans fail."

He held her close for a moment, and then she was slipping away from him, slowly, bit by bit. She was a bobbing black head among the little waves—and she was gone.

III

"*This is a strange story, Mr. Hart,*" *said the* Captain, *stretching* his unbooted legs toward the hearth fire. "It grows more and more incredible."

Nathan looked at him.

"It is true," he said shortly.

"I am not questioning your report," the Captain said quickly and with a chuckle in his voice, "but the Indian's. You haven't left anything out, have you?"

"You have all the information given me."

Williamson stared at his stockinged foot.

"He must have been lying," he said meditatively. "The days of Indian trouble here are over. He must have been trying to frighten you."

"Why?" said Nathan.

"The Indian sense of humor is, to say the least, peculiar. Because it would amuse him to make us prepare for a crisis that will never come."

"In this case," said Nathan slowly, "that could not be."

"I have the feeling," said Williamson still looking down, "that you have not given me all the facts on which you base your judgment. 'An Indian' you say, but what Indian? There must be some reason which you have not given me for your trusting his tale."

There was a long silence. The Captain's high boots, standing beside the flaring fire, made an odd dark pattern on the cabin walls.

"You're right," said Nathan at length and very quietly. "I know I heard the truth. I don't want to tell you how I happen to know. But for our safety and your own we must believe this."

"It is all very puzzling," said the Captain dully, and Nathan suspected that his quick mind had guessed the explanation of the warning and shut it from his consciousness, "but after all, it will do us no harm to act cautiously." He rose and walked to the door and opened it.

"Tom," he called, and Morris, who had been awaiting the end of the interview, came in.

"Mr. Hart informs me there may be an effort to seize me today," said the Captain, "and if it is successful there may be some Indian disturbances. While I doubt that the Senecas would be so foolish we had better see to it that Governor Simcoe's envoy and his men do not make off with me. I would suggest that you march the guard down to the shore when his boat appears. Then, attended by Mr. Hart, you will bring the governor's messenger to me here. I will await him in the corner behind this table on which I will have laid cocked pistols. The guard will stay on the shore and see to it that none of his men approach us."

Thomas Morris's eyes grew large with excitement. "What if they rush us?" he said. "Suppose they take me prisoner?"

"The guard will come to your rescue," said Williamson a little impatiently. "In a difficulty of that sort, of course, I will join you and we'll fight it out. If there is to be an effort to take me I believe it depends upon surprise. Once we show we are ready for it there will be no trouble."

"But suppose they outnumber us—" Morris began, when a long halloo from the shore interrupted him. He turned and plunged out the door.

Williamson turned to Nathan.

"I think we might put the experienced Judge Parker in command of the guard," he said. "Perhaps you will be good enough to arrange the details with him and report to me. Will you help me move the table into position? Thank you. And now while you are arranging matters outside I will pull on my boots and examine my pistols."

As Nathan's long legs took him down the sand he saw a white boat round the west headland and enter the mouth of the bay. Eight oars flashed in unison and the uniforms of the rowers made an irregular splotch of crimson against the blue of the lake. At the water's edge the Americans waited, a voluble knot of excited watchers.

"Elijah," said Nathan. "The Captain appoints you to command the guard. Form them and march them to Mr. Morris. He and I will go with the British officer to the cabin as soon as he lands. See to it that none of the redcoats go near it."

"Nate," said Whirl, stepping forward, "we ain't goin' t'let them bastards land, be we?"

"We have to let the governor's man deliver his message."

"Takes only one on 'em to do that. Me an' Cap'n Elijah an' the boys here don't want no Britishers marchin' on American soil, an' we ain't goin' t' have 'em."

Growling, the men of the guard surrounded Nathan and Whirl.

"My scheme," said Whirl, "is to sneak up into them trees jes' behind the beach. Our guns 'll be in a few feet of 'em when they land—an' they'll be pinted right into their noses."

"The Captain wants a guard to march behind me and Mr. Morris down to the boat," said Nathan.

"That's a plumb British idee," said Whirl in exasperation. "Ef'n we do what I been tellin' ye they won't know they's only a few of us, an' them gun barrels stickin' out from the trees'll be a mighty convincin' argument agin' landin'."

"If I command the guard," said Elijah sonorously, holding up a monitory hand, "we'll do as Mr. Gragg suggests. Like Moses, Simcoe's man will find truth waiting for him in the burning bush. Forward men, double time."

Guns at trail, the guard loped off to the thin line of trees and undergrowth behind the narrow beach. Morris nervously striding up and down a few yards away called to Nathan distractedly.

"What are they doing? Why don't they form a guard?"

"They're bound to do it their way," said Nathan. "They're getting ready to ambush them if they come ashore."

"It's preposterous," fumed Morris. "We'll be laughed at. We should present a dignified appearance, not act like a lot of savages. It's humiliating."

"You may be glad it's to be as it is," said Nathan drily. "Their boat will be grounding in a moment. We'd better go."

As the two young men walked briskly down to the water the bobbing boat moved steadily nearer. About twenty yards from shore the two oarsmen nearest land shipped their oars and rose to their feet. At a sharp command a moment later both leaped into the water, landing waist-deep. Holding the prow they steadied the craft and dragged it slowly landward. As it grounded about nine feet out, four other redcoats shipped oars and jumped overboard, lightening the bow so that it once more swung free. Foot by foot the six dragged the heavy wide craft to dry sand. Then one by one the rest of the crew disembarked, disclosing at last, seated in the stern, an elegant, bewigged gentleman in the uniform of a British lieutenant. Slowly he rose to his feet, taking the hand of a soldier on either side of the boat. Then he allowed himself to be led daintily from one rower's bench to another until at last, with a little jump, he landed on the shore."

"Beach the boat," he said in a high precise voice, "and form at once."

Seeing Thomas Morris watching him with interest the officer advanced a few paces in his direction and bowed.

"Lieutenant Roger Sheaffe, at your service, sir," he said. "I bear a message from His Excellency the Governor of Canada to one Captain Charles Williamson whom I expected to see here at this time."

"I shall be honored to escort you to Captain Williamson, sir," said Morris in a thin voice. "He asked me to receive you and conduct you to him."

The lieutenant drew back, obviously surprised and displeased.

"I do not understand such procedure, sir, but I assume that it is based on honorable intention." He turned to the detail of soldiers drawn up behind him. "Follow on," he said. There was an ominous rattling of guns in the bushes. At the sound Morris turned white and was obviously incapable of speech. Nathan stepped forward.

"If you will excuse me, sir," he said, "Captain Williamson expressly requested he be allowed to meet you alone. No guard will be necessary."

"Nonsense," said the lieutenant, waving his right hand in a limp gesture. "I do not move an inch without my guard."

"We can guarantee your safety, sir, only if your guard awaits you on the water," said Nathan.

"What sort of barbarous American conduct is this? I come

as a peaceful envoy on a matter of business and I am treated as a hostile invader."

"I hope you will forgive us," said Nathan ironically, "but the guard of barbarous Americans whose guns you see protruding from the underbrush insist upon looking on you in just that light. If you wish to avoid bloodshed, you'd better order your men back into the boat."

For a moment the lieutenant looked coolly ahead into the steady barrels of eight muskets. Then he turned to the British guard.

"This is ridiculous," he said, "but we will oblige. Wait for me fifty yards offshore. I will return within an hour. If I have not done so I shall expect you to come after me."

The sergeant in command of the detail saluted smartly and gave a sharp order. In a minute's time the eight oars were lifting again as the boat moved out against the waves. A single catcall sounded from the bushes.

"Now," said Lieutenant Sheaffe.

As Nathan walked up the sand toward the cabin he looked curiously at the British officer. Under the frogs of his crimson jacket his torso was obviously slim and boyish. His face, pink and blank, bore out the impression that he looked much younger than his probable age. Beneath the gold braid of his smart hat brown curls, carefully arranged, surged about his brow. His blue eyes were placid as he slouched along in an affected military swagger.

Morris knocked at the door of the cabin and at once Williamson answered "Come." Morris swung the door wide and Sheaffe stepped up to the threshold, teetering back and forth.

"Charles!" he exclaimed.

There was a moment's silence—then Williamson's hearty voice:

"Well, Roger—this is a strange reunion for a pair of His Majesty's late subalterns!"

Sheaffe walked in and Morris and Nathan followed. Williamson held out his hand cordially, but Nathan noticed that he did not come forward to greet the visitor. As the men met, their hands clasped above the cocked pistols lying on the table.

"And a strange business I find you in," said Sheaffe jocosely.

"I represent a most respectable English realty firm," said Williamson a little stiffly.

"I know, I know, but there's more to it than that, as you are well aware."

"May I ask, what more?"

"You know Governor Simcoe's position—that so long as the peace treaty remains unexecuted, so long as British subjects are still prevented by law from collecting debts owed them before the American rebellion—"

"I prefer the word Revolution," said Williamson.

"You did not prefer it in 1775."

"I did my duty faithfully while in the service of the Crown. Now I am a loyal citizen of the United States."

"As I was saying," said Sheaffe, "so long as the treaty is not complete, the governor claims proprietary rights in these border lands. Papers protesting your settlements here have been prepared, and I am commissioned by Governor Simcoe to deliver the papers and require an answer."

"I repeat," said Williamson, "I am a citizen of the United States, and under their authority and protection I possess these lands. I know no right that His Britannic Majesty or Governor Simcoe has to interfere with me or molest me." His voice rose and Nathan guessed that the words he spoke had been carefully considered and as carefully learned in the last few days. They poured from Williamson's mouth in loud continuous flow. "The only allegiance I owe to any power on earth is to the United States; and so far from being intimidated by threats from people I have no connection with, I shall proceed with my improvements; and nothing but superior force shall make me abandon the place." He paused, then said in a conversational tone. "Is the protest of Governor Simcoe intended to apply to Sodus exclusively?"

"By no means!" said Sheaffe. "It is intended to embrace all the Indian lands purchased since the peace of 1783."

"And what are Governor Simcoe's intentions, supposing the protest is disregarded?"

"I am merely the official bearer of the papers. No explanation of them was given me and I am not authorized to give one."

"You may tell Governor Simcoe for me," said Williamson

slowly, "that I will pay no attention to these papers but will continue to settle these lands as if no message of protest had been received."

The entire conversation had taken place with all four men standing. The finality of Williamson's last statement occasioned a silent pause. Finally Sheaffe spoke, laughing softly.

"You haven't changed much, Charles. You're as obstinate about surrendering this land as you were about sharing the general's mistress when we marched through Devon."

Williamson smiled.

"The cases are not very different. Your governor would seize the lands I administer, but he may find that its English owners will have his knuckles rapped for him."

Sheaffe looked at Williamson quizzically. "You'd like to see that, wouldn't you?"

"Yes, Roger, and so would you."

Sheaffe laughed.

"I'd advise you and the rest of your fellow citizens not to try it yourselves. If the Crown wants to call him off the scent he'll obey. But you know how he's felt about Washington and his satellites ever since they killed John André."

"I know he's a tin soldier," said Williamson shortly.

"The very butcher of a button," said Sheaffe.

The two men looked at each other smiling.

"I regret that I must return with so unsatisfactory an answer," Sheaffe continued. "I'd prefer your giving it in person."

"No doubt," said Williamson, "but I hope you will forgive me if I do not accompany you."

The British officer's gaze dropped to the pistols on the table.

"This isn't a very friendly reception, Charles," he said reprovingly.

"Come again, Roger," said Williamson, "when we can entertain you more fittingly. You must be my guest at the December opening of my hostelry at Geneva. The Genesee ladies will atone then for our present lack of warmth."

Sheaffe looked at him intently. "I hope I shall be able to accept," he said significantly. "And now shall we go down to my boat—I must be returning."

"Not we, unfortunately," said Williamson. "Mr. Morris

and I beg you to pardon our not saying *bon voyage* on the shore. My second Genesee Country Fair begins almost immediately and we must be returning to Williamsburg at once. Mr. Hart here will be our representative and pay our respects when you embark."

For a long moment Lieutenant Sheaffe stood silent. It was obvious to the Americans that he was considering his next action. He seemed to realize this but appeared not in the least embarrassed. Then he held out his hand.

"Good-bye, Charles," he said.

"Good-bye, Roger, and better luck."

The Briton's face was impassive for a moment. Then he smiled. His hand snapped upward in a stiff salute. Smartly he faced about and marched from the cabin. Nathan fell in behind.

Sheaffe had stepped only a dozen paces before he resumed his customary slouching walk, slowing his pace that Nathan might catch up with him.

"Hart," he said, "is a good English name. Have you lived long in America?"

"All my life," said Nathan, "and I am of the third generation of our family to do so."

"Once an Englishman, always an Englishman," said Sheaffe.

"My father's mother was Swedish," said Nathan, "and my mother's mother was from Holland."

"A villainous mixture," said the Englishman, grinning in comradely fashion. "And may I ask how you maintain yourself in this new world?"

"I am a portrait painter and a farmer."

Sheaffe threw back his head and laughed. "You Yankees will destroy me yet," he said. "A portrait painter and a farmer! It is too much. Does the plow or the brush provide you more handsomely?"

"The plow in summer, the brush in winter," said Nathan, and Sheaffe laughed again.

"And how does a court painter progress when governed by a thousand kings instead of one?"

"Well enough," said Nathan, remembering that Williamson had said to him almost these identical words, "except for a lot of Federalists who talk as you do."

"A majority may be as tyrannical as a single king," said Sheaffe significantly. "I hear there are oppressed souls even in your free country of the Genesee."

"I don't know what you mean."

"I think you do, but in case you've forgotten there is a band of worthy German colonists who were lured by false promises, then attacked and beaten, given a prejudiced trial on trumped-up charges, and finally bound out as servants—slaves, rather—for periods too long for a free man to contemplate."

Nathan was amazed. At first he could hardly believe that the English officer was speaking of Berezy and his followers. It had been months since he had thought of them. Now he realized that this account, which Sheaffe obviously believed, was someone's version of the previous autumn's events. He laughed and the lieutenant smiled at him questioningly.

"I'm afraid this story comes from a prejudiced source."

"Prejudiced as are all Englishmen against the enslavement of honest men," said Sheaffe seriously. "And I may say, I believe, without violating a confidence, that His Excellency is aware of the pitiful state of these persecuted people, these white slaves of Canandaigua."

"We shall look forward to receiving his advice on governing them," said Nathan ironically. "He and his kind set us fine precedent on governing colonists a score of years ago."

"*Touché,*" said Sheaffe smiling. "You have a mordant wit. If you run out of patrons in this western wilderness come across the lake. There are more of the sort of people who appreciate a quip or a portrait in Canada than here. We need a portrait painter."

"Not so much," said Nathan, "as you need the promoter of the Genesee lands."

Sheaffe looked into Nathan's eyes blankly. "You are playing a game of riddles, Mr. Hart," he said. "I am not in the mood for playing."

They approached the spot where Sheaffe had disembarked. There was a sudden metallic rattle in the bushes behind them. Sheaffe simulated a shudder.

"Your invisible army gives me the creeps, Mr. Hart," he said. "Do you mind walking between me and those ghostly muskets?"

The white boat was returning now, the oars lifting and falling precisely. Once more the landing process was repeated, save that the men overboard did not pull the boat up to the sand. They waited while their sergeant and two of their comrades splashed ashore. The sergeant saluted.

"You may take me aboard," said Sheaffe.

"No further orders, sir?" said the sergeant in evident disappointment.

Roger Sheaffe looked about him. Far up on the bank the cabin looked shut and deserted save for a thin trickle of smoke from the chimney. From the line of trees and underbrush a few yards away the long guns of Elijah's little command were stiff parallel lines of black within the green foliage.

"No," said Lieutenant Sheaffe with a dry little laugh. "No further orders."

The two British privates clasped their hands about each others wrists to form a seat for him and the lieutenant sank gracefully into it. Sturdily they bore their burden over the water, the sergeant following behind and turning fearfully now and then as if he feared treachery.

"Good-bye, Mr. Hart," called Sheaffe, limply waving a lace-fringed hand. "I hope you won't remember this scene well enough to paint it."

Tenderly his men placed him aboard the craft and then climbed in after him. The sergeant lifted himself in. The oars resumed their clocklike motion. From behind Nathan came a shrill hoot—then the crash of a volley of muskets. The tempo of the rowers out on the water took a swifter beat. Nathan turned indignantly as Elijah leaped toward him.

"Just a salute to the envoy of a foreign power," he said solemnly. Whoops of laughter came from the bushes. The men danced about hugging each other, firing their guns in the air as fast as they could load them.

IV

Two days after Roger Sheaffe had made his strategic retreat into the waters of Lake Ontario, Nathan stood in the big front room of Thomas Morris's house in Canandaigua.

"I hope, Mr. Hart," said Morris, crossing his legs but otherwise rigidly holding his pose, "that my summoning you to paint my portrait at this time has not inconvenienced you greatly. You are missing Captain Williamson's public games, it is true, but now that Colonel Pickering and his aides have arrived we can expect to be regaled with Indian spectacles of interest."

Nathan, lifting his brush from the canvas, turned to look out of the big square-paned window behind him into the waning light of the afternoon. At the end of the long slope down to blue water the lake slept in a soft dull haze.

"I have attended one of the Captain's fairs," he said dully, remembering his ride from Williamsburg to Bath the year before. "How many Indians have come to Canandaigua?"

"Sixteen hundred," said Morris, "and you'll think there are many more tonight. They'll not let a man sleep with their yelling and dancing and racing their horses beside the lake. While you were on your way to Bath to get your paints five hundred of them raced into town behind Farmer's Brother. The Oneidas, Cayugas, and Onondagas drew up on one side of General Chapin's door and the Senecas on the other. Chapin was so weak from jaundice that he could hardly move, but he stood in the entrance and gave the signal for the whites on the steps to fire three volleys. The Indians answered with three rounds and wheeled into a big circle. Then Farmer's Brother made a speech and handed strings of wampum to the general. Pickering answered for Chapin and ordered out the kettles of rum. There hasn't been a quiet moment in the town since."

As if to cap his last sentence a long whoop followed by many short, staccato howls sounded near the house.

Nathan turned from the window to look again at his work. His brush moved to the mixtures on the pine palette and hung above the canvas.

"Are their women with them?" he asked. Morris laughed.

"I've never seen such colors and fantastic dress. You must come with me to the council fire tonight."

"Look," said Nathan.

A procession was passing the window led by a stocky Indian in buckskin, one feather drooping above the matted hair that hung down back of his large head. His short arms held close to his body two brass kettles which he tried to keep level lest he spill their contents. From each of his hands dangled a bottle. Behind him six companions bore a long pine box, obviously a coffin. A dozen or more whooping, dancing Indians followed.

Morris laughed again.

"It's Old Beech Tree's funeral," he said. "His friends use his burial as an excuse to get drunk. You'll hear three volleys soon. Then there'll be a rush for the rum kettles and bottles. Old Beech Tree won't be the only one of them lying stiff and unconscious before the evening's over. Well, the council fire will be burning soon. Let's rest, eat, and dress."

He pulled a cord that hung beside the door and a bell tinkled in a distant part of the house. Nathan heard doors opening and heavy footsteps. A big man who wore a long apron above a white shirt and homespun breeches entered the room. Out of a gross fat face little eyes glanced about discontentedly. As they rested on Nathan a look of amazement and fear jumped into them. The slow footsteps stopped abruptly, a grunt escaped trembling thick lips. Nathan stared, fascinated. This was the man whom he and Whirl had surrendered, bound, to Williamson's posse over a year ago.

Morris was speaking.

"You will serve dinner early and—" he broke off suddenly as he saw the expression of his servant's face.

"You have seen this man of mine before?" he said to Nathan anxiously.

"He was one of Berezy's Germans."

"Oh, that!" said Morris with a relieved little laugh. "Yes,

he's working out his fine here. He's not a bad cook—I hope you'll agree—and now that the misunderstanding is over he's perfectly harmless, aren't you, Bucky?"

"*Jawohl*," said Buckendahl, trying to force a smile, his gaze avoiding Nathan's. "*Ich bin* honest man."

"You'd better be unless you wish to be a bond servant all your life," said Morris lightly. "And you'd better have our dinner ready in an hour. Come, Mr. Hart, let's go up."

As he walked slowly up the stairs Nathan wondered if he should report to Morris and perhaps to Williamson the facts Sheaffe had told him. He wondered why the Governor of Canada had so interested himself in Berezy's Germans and how he had obtained the distorted account of their fate. He dismissed the matter from his mind later at dinner as he watched Buckendahl awkwardly moving about the table serving the meal.

When Nathan arrived with Morris at the place of meeting the fire was already flickering on hundreds of solemn, painted faces. The two men found a large stump at the outskirts of the clearing and climbed upon it. From its height they could see the old councilors and chieftains standing near the fire and behind them the elaborately painted warriors. The women and children stood in an irregular circle surrounding all.

"Pickering is making his first speech," said Morris excitedly. "He's got to make amends for the murder of a young Seneca last summer by a white man. The chiefs are using it to put us in the wrong before the treaty bargaining begins."

Nathan could see Timothy Pickering in full uniform striding about the fire. He was a giant of a man, and he was moving deliberately. The flames of the council fire glinted on the gold braid of his buff and blue uniform. Near him stood a short Indian who held a yellow blanket wrapped about him. As the tall colonel gestured the Indian interpreted his actions loudly in Seneca.

Bending over, the colonel fixed his eyes sorrowfully upon the ground. Then gently he grasped with his right hand an invisible something and drew it slowly upward.

"He's taking the hatchet out of the murdered young man's head," said Morris.

Slowly the big man knelt and put his arms beneath the imagined form of the crime's victim. With straining muscles and with his long face set in lugubrious lines he rose to his feet and walked a few heavy steps. Once more he sank to his knees, bending far over to show that he was laying his burden tenderly beneath the ground. He pushed at unseen piles of earth, watching as they tumbled down into the unseen grave. Then his big hands smoothed the surface above it. He rose and walked about, stopping here and there to pick up real leaves from the ground. These he brought to the grave, spreading them over it carefully.

A wave of low sound spread among the crowd.

"*Entaw,*" said an old man sharply, as if he were suppressing strong emotion. The other Indians took it up. "*Entaw,*" they said, and repeated it again and again, "*Entaw.*"

Pickering walked up to a small pine tree standing in the clearing and with one wrench of his powerful arms tore it from the earth. In the gaping hole left by its roots he hurled an invisible something.

"The hatchet," said Morris.

Back into the hole went the tree and the colonel knelt to fill in the earth around it.

"*Entaw,*" said the crowd in low tones.

Leaving the tree once more upright the colonel pulled from beneath the jacket of his uniform a square of white cloth. He approached the interpreter and bent over, moving the cloth about as if he were wiping a surface only a few feet from the earth.

"He wipes the blood from their beds," said Morris.

Now the cloth was at the cheeks of the interpreter.

"And the tears from their eyes."

Pickering pointed to himself and to the interpreter and then to the east. The interpreter nodded his head and the two men walked into the crowd together.

There was a chorus of "*Entaw,*" as the Indians opened ranks to receive them.

An elderly Indian of powerful frame stepped into the circle and said a long sentence. His words came very slowly and he ended abruptly. The interpreter, returning to his post, hurriedly spoke in English.

"Farmer's Brother say his white friend and his Seneca

brother take the path of peace together. They keep both ends of it open as long as the sun shall shine."

"*Entaw*," said the Indians at once. At the same instant two pairs of white men appeared in the circle bearing gleaming brass kettles. There was a shout and the whites were nearly knocked down by the rush of Indians. Farmer's Brother looked at them contemptuously. From his right arm he took a folded blanket, slowly opened it, and spread it beside the leaping blaze of the central fire.

"He is covering the council fire," said Morris. "The meeting is over and the rest of the night will be all rum and caterwauling. I hope the chiefs recover in time for my dinner tomorrow night. I'm expecting you, of course. A portrait painter ought to enjoy seeing white soldiers, red sachems, women prophets, and pious Quakers seated at the same board."

"Women prophets?" said Nathan, trying to sound casual.

"Colonel Pickering is determined to meet The Friend—out of curiosity, I think. She accepted my invitation by stating that she and three of her followers would come. It will be a long table. Some Philadelphia Quakers who have come here to see that we don't cheat the Indians will be there. So will the Indians—Red Jacket, Cornplanter, Farmer's Brother, and more. You might get a commission from one of them if the treaty results in a land purchase. You'll have to work fast to get their money ahead of the rum merchant."

"I'd like to paint a chief," said Nathan, wondering the while if he could bear to look upon Rachel again.

"Perhaps The Friend will recommend you," said Morris. "Didn't you paint her some time ago?"

"Yes," said Nathan, surprised to find himself grinning, "but she didn't like it much."

In his bedroom in the big white house Nathan lay awake a long time. The darkness outside was alive with sound. From down by the lake came the shouts of racing riders and the excited barking of dogs. Brass kettles were banging and horns were blowing in Canandaigua's central square. Scattered shots sounded in an almost continuous fusillade.

Nathan had felt that seeing Rachel again was inevitable, but each time the idea had come into his mind he had fearfully put it aside. Though a year had passed, the memory of the

anguish she had caused him made him wince. The thought of
refusing Morris's invitation he impatiently put aside as cowardly.
And once he had decided he would attend the dinner he specu-
lated eagerly on what attitude Rachel and The Friend would
assume toward him.

He waked in the morning to a sudden change in the
weather. The night before had been clear and mild and the air
had seemed soft like that of a warm evening of mid-September.
Now low clouds scudded over the lake and a fitful wind blew
through the little town. Morris had ordered fires built on the
hearths, but these and the thick, brick-filled walls of the house
could not banish the cold. Nathan worked alone at the background of his painting in the morning while his host fussed
about, anxiously directing preparations for the big dinner.
Shortly after noon Morris came into the front room and posed
for a time, but both men proved too distrait for progress on
the portrait. Nathan could not divert his thoughts from Rachel,
and Morris, crossing and recrossing his legs, turning his head
again and again to look out of the window, was a difficult subject. Before the light began to wane he impatiently rose and left
the room. Nathan put down his brush. On a table beside him
lay a volume and he picked it up and glanced at its title: *A De-
fence of the Constitution of Government of the United States
of America.* Idly he thumbed its pages:

". . . it must be remembered that the rich are *people* as
well as the poor; that they have rights as well as others; that
they have as clear and as sacred a right to their large property as
others have to theirs which is smaller; that oppression to them
is as possible and as wicked as to others." He turned to the title
page. I should have known, he thought, that John Adams wrote
that. He picked up a pamphlet that lay beside the book—*Gazette
of the United States*—and found himself in the midst of an
article entitled "Discourses on Davila":

"Take away thrones and crowns from among men and
there will soon be an end of all dominion and justice. There
must be some adventitious properties infused into the government to give it energy and spirit, or the selfish turbulent passions of men can never be controlled."

He flung the journal across the room, just missing the fireplace. It lay crumpled and disorderly against the wall. A move-

ment outside the window caught his eye. Three Quakers, holding
their big black hats and leaning against the wind, were slowly
walking up the path to the house. Behind them the coat of Red
Jacket was a spot of brilliant color. The tall Indian walked
gracefully and with no effort, his bearing making the labors of
his somber-clad companions seem almost ridiculous. Hastily
Nathan strode from the room and up the stair.

He did not come down again until he had heard the door
open and close many times and a sound of numerous voices
welled up the stairway. Morris, standing in the hall, saw him
diffidently descending and came to the foot of the steps to take
his arm. He was somewhat surprised to find that Morris evidently looked upon him as a social asset and in making introductions spoke of him as "the well-known painter who is my guest
while at work on my portrait." The three Quakers seemed to
try to make it obvious that they were not impressed by this
evidence of vanity. Some of the Indian chiefs appeared not to
understand the designation but made polite sounds. The Cornplanter and Red Jacket stood together near the door of the
dining room, and when Morris presented Hart to them with
the by now well-worn clause of explanation they looked into
each other's eyes a moment as if in furtive amusement. Colonel
Pickering, towering above all present and very handsome in full
regimentals, vouchsafed a deep bass. "Very interesting," as if
he thought the idea of Morris's portrait a significant historic
event.

"And now," said Morris, "the most charming of our guests
are having tea in the pantry with Farmer's Brother." He opened
a door and pushed Nathan forward.

On the straight ladder-back chairs of the dark room sat
three people cosily sipping tea. As his eyes accustomed themselves to the changed light Nathan saw that the largest of the
three was the big chief, Farmer's Brother. At his left sat The
Universal Friend and at his right Rachel Malin. As he stared at
Rachel, Nathan was hardly aware that Morris was speaking. He
saw the Indian rise and incline his head and mechanically he
answered the salutation. In the dim light the whites of Rachel's
eyes seemed luminous and the blue eyeballs darker than he had
remembered them.

". . . a long cold ride, and so I insisted that they have a

hot drink at once," prattled Morris, "and Farmer's Brother joined them because he likes tea." The Indian nodded his head solemnly.

Rachel's cheeks were fuller than they had been a year ago. There was a tautness about her mouth and one corner of it seemed now to be drawn down slightly, giving its lovely fullness a petulant expression. As she recognized Nathan a look of fright and sudden hatred flashed over her face. He turned to look at The Friend. In the half-light she was beautiful. The long curls had been carefully tended and they fell about her high cheekbones to make a curving plastic frame for the great dark eyes. There was a serenity about her and at the same time an eager look, as of a child pleased by being at a party. Nathan guessed that she considered him no longer likely to thwart her, and that she had decided not to let his presence be disturbing.

"As soon as you have finished your tea," said Morris hesitantly, unaware of the reasons for the silence but feeling that it was awkward, "we will go in to dinner."

At once The Friend rose and Rachel walked to her side as if seeking her protection. Morris and Nathan bowed them out of the room. Farmer's Brother looked into his cup, swung it in a circle a moment to cool its contents and drained it at a gulp. He stood and looked about him with a twinkle in his eye. Then with stately tread he followed the two women.

Seated near the end of the long, candlelit table Nathan felt excitement rise within him. Servants, laden with steaming dishes, were hurrying about behind the diners. Buckendahl stood near the door to the kitchen, arms folded, directing them importantly in German. Obviously they were fellow members of the Berezy expedition. Nathan looked at Morris sitting stiffly at the head of the board, at Colonel Pickering's noble head inclined above the curls of The Universal Friend, at Rachel rigidly erect between two gray-coated, black-hatted Quakers, and at Red Jacket, watching The Friend's voluble mouth with amusement.

Cornplanter, directly across from Red Jacket, was just above Nathan. Below him sat other chiefs, Fish Carrier, Little Beard, and Clear Sky, facing two male followers of The Friend, Daniel Waggoner and Enoch Malin. The huge bulk of Farmer's Brother occupied the whole narrow end of the table. Suddenly at a remark in Seneca by The Cornplanter it began to shake. At the same instant Little Beard guffawed and the chiefs on either side of him began to giggle. Morris leaned forward.

"May those of us who do not understand the native language of The Cornplanter be allowed to appreciate his humor?"

The Cornplanter spoke up at once—as if he had even hoped for the question.

"I tell chiefs of warrior no friend to the Fifteen Fires. On battle day he speaks good speech—makes chiefs mad and they run out to kill white man and take scalps. While they fight runner comes into empty Seneca town—sees brave speechmaker kill neighbor's cow and cut up for meat."

Again Farmer's Brother was convulsed with mirth. The giggles of Clear Sky and Fish Carrier turned to raucous bellows. Little Beard laughed until tears stood on his bronze cheeks. Only Red Jacket was silent. Nathan suddenly realized the reason for his lack of mirth. The chief sat looking straight ahead, an embarrassed grim smile on his handsome face. The other Indians, save for the teller of the tale, cast covert glances at him, looking swiftly away again. The Cornplanter was looking directly at him and smiling significantly.

Morris, not finding the story amusing, was smiling politely and looking confused. Nathan saw Timothy Pickering's face grow serious. It was evidence that he understood the situation and realized that something must be done to save the alleged cow killer further embarrassment. He leaned forward and spoke:

"The Friend has been telling me that she highly approves the Seneca custom of determining lineage through the female line. She is herself an example of such female intelligence and ability as to justify such action among us all."

The eyes of The Universal Friend widened with pleasure, and spots of rose color appeared over each high cheekbone.

"Perhaps The Cornplanter will tell us," continued Pickering, "how the practice came about."

The Cornplanter looked up the table toward The Friend.

"Indians watch seed spring from earth," he said. "Not know sower."

There was a silence. Nathan, grinning inwardly, saw Rachel's mouth set in a hard line that he had never seen. Across from her The Friend's eyes were blazing.

"You speak as a child of abomination," she said sharply to The Cornplanter. "Such thoughts betoken unrepentant wickedness."

Composedly The Cornplanter answered her, but the faces of his hearers grew blank. He spoke at length and in Seneca. On and on went the long-voweled syllables. Obviously he was talking rationally and without emotion. Suddenly, as if in the middle of a word, he stopped. The Friend's mouth twisted in anger and contempt, and her voice was cold with malice as she fixed her snapping black eyes on Red Jacket and demanded:

"What does he say?"

Red Jacket leaned across the table toward The Cornplanter and said a few words in Seneca. Another long flow of calm argument answered him.

"The Cornplanter say he has often heard the white woman is the Spirit of Jesus Christ and speaks for Him."

"It is true," said The Friend, impatiently. "I am the Spirit of the Christ and I speak with His knowledge and authority."

"Then he say," said Red Jacket placidly, "you mus' know what he has spoke because Jesus Christ knows all languages."

This time Morris caught The Cornplanter's meaning at once. A look of helplessness spread over his thin face. He seemed desperately searching for something to say. Nathan admired Pickering as he came smoothly to the rescue. The big soldier launched himself into a recountal of funny misunderstandings between French and American officers during the latter days of the Revolution. Then he told how Baron von Steuben had boasted to General Washington that he had caught a whale in the Hudson, but doubting companions had discovered that he meant an eel. The Friend was gradually recovering her composure as he talked. There was a fixed look about her eyes but she smiled when the soldier expected her to. Rachel was not eating. She sat motionless, a look of sudden shock upon her face. The Quakers spoke casually among themselves, their "thees" and "thous" sounding strangely loud and out of place. In Morris's silver candelabra each slim wax pillar bore its separate flame, and the long mirror behind his chair reflected them all, making the table seem endless. In their flickering light the chiefs ate heartily, their jaws moving in slow rhythms, a look of polite amusement on each leathery face.

V

The wind was whistling about the house when the diners rose.
With its sudden gusts came a thin rattle upon the window-
panes. The first snow of autumn was blowing down upon the
little town. Morris bade all hurry into their coats, for the council
already awaited Pickering and the chiefs. As the party poured
out of the house Nathan tried to join the Quaker Savery whom
he hoped to question about Philadelphia and his home country.

A hand on his arm detained him. He looked down at the
plump white fingers and knew that he had kissed them often.

"Friend Nathan," said Rachel, "will you walk with me, for
I wish to speak with you."

He stalked by her side in silence, waiting long moments
for her to begin.

"I wanted to ask you to forgive me."

"It is not necessary. A year has passed since you broke
your promise."

"But I am not asking you to pardon that," she said sweetly
and patiently, as if she were explaining to a child. "That was
a good action. It is the promises themselves I hope you will
forgive—the promises and the fact that my wish to serve you as
I would serve all good souls could not overcome your worldly
desires. I know now that I should not have allowed you to be
near me, for you could not check your carnal nature and at
times your sinful wishes even confused me. It led to suffering—" her wide blue eyes searched his face as if for evidences
of his misery—"and for all the unhappiness I have caused you,
my dear friend, I ask forgiveness in the name of her who has
ever been my refuge and my strength."

Nathan stopped abruptly. He looked at the round face
of the girl he had loved and he wondered why he had ever loved
her. She had once plunged him into a fevered agony of self-pity,

and now she excused herself on the grounds that she was irresistibly desirable and asked for pardon in the name of the woman on whom she centered her whole existence.

"In the name of your refuge and your strength," he said ironically, "I forgive you."

The new hard line at the corner of her wide mouth deepened.

"Through repentance I have expiated my sin and found peace," she said. "You will never be happy until you repent."

"I have repented," said Nathan.

She looked eagerly into his eyes.

"If this is true I am very happy. I feared that without wishing to I had brought bitter and wicked thoughts into your mind."

Nathan felt pity defeating all other emotions within him.

"I am sorry that I ever loved you," he said gently.

"Ah, but you still love me," she said with the pathos of a child, "as all of God's creatures should love each other."

Nathan was saved the embarrassment of a reply by their arrival at the council fire. In the center of the great circle the wind tortured the dry logs into fitful sheets of red light that leaped far sideways before they rose toward the barren limbs of tall trees. Already Timothy Pickering stood before it, lifting his big hands high above his head in salutation to the crowd. All about him the rich colors of the Indian robes alternately flashed and dulled as the snowy gusts blew up the blaze or left it smoldering. Behind them stood a scattering of Quakers in gray garb, farmers in butternut and gray homespun, and, here and there, knots of Berezy's Germans in their gaily variegated though threadbare clothes.

"The Fifteen Fires keep their end of the silver chain of friendship very bright," said the Colonel loudly. "One who gives it great brightness dwells near you and is your friend. You have given her the name of Shinnewanagis-taw-ge because you know she speaks truths that are good for all men to hear. Shinnewanagis-taw-ge speaks now."

The Universal Friend stepped to the center of the circle. A leaping flame revealed the strong white face, the long, snow-spattered curls swinging about it, the purple robe billowing like a sunset cloud below it.

"The Lord hath sent me among ye to bid ye beware His wrath, repent, and be saved," she said, and her voice was strong and harsh. "Before The Universal Friend came among ye ye lived as heathen, bowing down to false gods and graven images. Ye lived in wickedness and ye died condemned to eternal despair. Since The Friend has dwelt within the Vale of Kedron she has offered thee salvation but ye have heeded her not. Thy wickedness ceaseth not. Thy ways are an abomination in the sight of God. In His name I call upon ye to repent."

Nathan heard a sudden grunt beside him and, turning his face toward it, saw Red Jacket striding through the crowd, fiercely pushing aside those in his path.

"Repent!" shouted The Friend, raising a white-cuffed hand above her head in a threatening gesture. "Repent or feel the wrath of a jealous God!" She turned and walked back to the side of Colonel Pickering, who stood looking at her as if he could not believe that he had heard her words.

"She needs me," said Rachel. "I must go to her." She ran toward The Friend, losing herself in the crowd. As she did so Red Jacket shot out from the crowd into the open space where The Friend had been standing. His braided coat glowed in the firelight. Near it a deeper red, rich as blood, fluted in the wind. Nathan's heart leaped. The chief was dragging a slim cloaked figure behind him. His long right hand was clasped about the wrist of a black-haired girl who struggled desperately to free herself. It was Catherine O'Bail.

Through the fierce blowing air the voice of the chief was clear and hard with rage.

"Is it so ye brighten friendship's silver chain?" he said, and there was a stillness all about him. "Ye have heard the white woman call on my people to repent. Has the white woman done nothing to forgive? The captain who comes from the Great White Father has said that she speaks true. I ask him now to hear another truth. I ask him to let a Seneca woman bid the white man repent. The Genesee grew corn for the Iroquois. Beside it the Senecas lived happily and their mouths were filled. Each year now the Fifteen Fires push us westward. The pleasant valley of the river is ours no more. Soon, though we look to the east, we cannot see the flowing waters. Let the daughter of the great sachem, The Cornplanter, speak. She will say in the white man's words the sins of the white man. Let her tell him to repent."

The girl had ceased to struggle as the meaning of the chief's words became clear. He did not relinquish his hold on her, but now she stood quietly beside him. To Nathan she looked very small beside Red Jacket. He saw a frightened, appealing look come into her eyes, saw her fighting for control of her emotions. A sweet and dignified seriousness triumphed at last on her face.

Colonel Pickering stepped forward. His face was set firmly and it was obvious that he realized that the treaty he had been instructed to bring about was in danger. He spoke surely and decisively.

"The Great White Father's messenger did not know what Shinnewanagis-taw-ge was to say. He removes it from the council fire. Let it be gone with the smoke. It has not been said."

There was a chorus of approving exclamations from the Indians.

"It is cold and stormy," said Pickering. "Let us leave important matters until tomorrow. Let us cover the council flame and warm our stomachs."

From the rear of the crowd came the familiar shout of the kettle bearers. Eagerly the Indians made way for the rum. In an instant the open space beside the fire was filled with Indians. Red Jacket and Catherine O'Bail were swallowed up in the crowd. Pickering had averted a crisis. Nathan heard a voice beside him and looked into the round, stolid face of The Cornplanter.

"Council fire shoots sparks," he said. As he spoke The Universal Friend brushed by him. Her robe, floating behind her, brushed his arm and he put it roughly aside with a gesture of distaste. The Friend was walking swiftly and her eyes were bright with feverish rage. Behind her hurried Rachel, her face drawn in distress. Two of the men of The Friend's Settlement followed.

"They burn bright," said The Cornplanter. He turned and looked full at Nathan.

"Remember horse race?" he said.

Nathan laughed.

"My girl named horse for you—good horse."

"I know," said Nathan. "Where is the horse?"

"Sold to Sheriff Dunn. Different name now—Silk Stocking. Beat all other horses yesterday at Williamsburg. Captain Williamson was mad."

Nathan laughed again.

"Can your daughter speak truths as well as she rides races?"

The Cornplanter grinned. He looked about at his yelling countrymen.

"She can speak," he said. Nathan saw his face change suddenly and a look of shock froze his expression. A white man in buckskins was coming toward him through the crowd. The man looked sick and tired. His face was very pale and the look in his eyes was dull and hopeless. The Indian went quickly toward the man. They met and shook hands, and the white man spoke to The Cornplanter in a low tone, his mouth close to the chief's ear. The Indian's shoulders slumped suddenly, and his hands lifted a bit and then fell limply at his sides in a despairing gesture.

The voice of Colonel Pickering was thundering out over the crowd. Even the eager knots of men about the rum kettles were mute at the sound. Though the council fire was covered the white man would be heard. He strode toward the new arrival and, stopping suddenly, pointed a finger at him in a wrathful gesture.

"How dare this British spy come here? The Fifteen Fires blaze in anger. The Six Nations, their Quaker friends, and I are deeply offended. This agent of our secret enemies shall leave this place or the council fire shall not again be uncovered."

The soldier was in deadly earnest. His eyes were fires of contempt and his voice cut sharply through the silence. The Indians who had gathered about the white visitor seemed gently to disappear. Only The Cornplanter still stood beside him. The man turned on Pickering a look of utter fatigue and despair.

"I am only an interpreter," he said slowly, in a voice hardly audible. "My name is Johnson."

"I know who you are," said Pickering grimly.

"I will do whatever you say," said the man, and Nathan could see in his face the look of a man who believed he was surrendering his life.

"Do not let me see you again," said Pickering shortly.

The man looked at him incredulously. He turned and walked a few yards, then wheeled as if he expected to be shot in the back if he took another step. Then doggedly he walked on. The Cornplanter, wrapping his blanket more snugly about him, followed. Nathan saw a figure detach itself from the rear of the crowd and drift towards Johnson. It reached his side and fell into step with him. In the light that lessened as they marched farther away Nathan saw a sturdy, erect back, clad in a dark military jacket, a square-looking head topped by swirling hair. He had seen that man before—at Williamsburg, the day of the fight in the cabin. Suddenly he realized that the figure was that of Berezy. Then a voice that Nathan knew well spoke in his ear.

"The Colonel need not be frightened. He does not know that the end of Indian dreams and British hopes has come."

Nathan looked down into the clear eyes of Catherine O'Bail.

"He's from the west," he said triumphantly. "Wayne has beat them."

"I have not said so."

She looked steadfastly into his face. A warm feeling of affection for the sturdy, sure girl at his side surged through him. Ever since he had first seen her bravely confronting the thieving Buckendahl he had felt the firm consistency of her character. Whenever since then his life had run tangent to hers he had been benefited. She had rescued him from death in delirium beside the river. She had found him remedy for the fever and nursed him to health. At Sodus Bay she had warned him of the danger of British attack. But more important to him than these examples of her loyalty had been her surrenderings of herself to him and the solace they had given his spirit.

"I want to see you again," he said.

She smiled and there was a look of deep happiness in her face.

"I will walk where the brook comes into the lake tomorrow afternoon," she said, and she slipped away through the crowd.

Nathan was amused when he arrived at Morris's house to find that all doors and windows had been barred. A little light streamed from the cracks in the blinds of the owner's bedroom and Nathan beat upon the front door until he heard his voice calling "Who's there?" While Buckendahl, aroused at last, made slow progress to open the door, Morris explained from the open window. Pickering had warned him that the arrival of the British spy, Johnson, might be the signal for an Indian attack —particularly if he brought news of Wayne's defeat in the west. One could not be too careful.

Nathan assured his host that he had obtained evidence of Wayne's victory, and Morris was so delighted that he sent Buckendahl stumbling through the snowy wind to tell Pickering of the rumor. A few minutes later the Colonel was himself outside the door, and after Morris and Nathan had welcomed him the three men sat beside the fire until after midnight. Nathan did not tell who had intimated to him the content of Johnson's message but he said he had faith in his informant. Pickering was jubilant. The treaty would go well now, he said. The Iroquois would be less arrogant. He would complete satisfactorily the mission on which President Washington had sent him. At this Morris happily ordered out a keg of his best Madeira and the evening grew the mellower for the whistling of the cold wind outside.

By noon the next day the air had stilled and the sun had warmed it to gentleness. Nathan worked on the portrait until the sitter begged off in midafternoon. Morris hurried off then to find Pickering and discover if he had had word that their surmises of the previous night had been correct, and Nathan strolled down to the banks of the brook. Catherine was waiting where the brown water tumbled into the blueness of Lake Canandaigua.

The days raced with each other after that. Hardly had they dawned in yellow light above the frosted carpet of fallen leaves than they seemed to be sliding down a flaming sky, and starpinned darkness was settling uncertainly as a veil drops through the air. No moment together held enough of time for these two, trying to know each other. Only the morning hours, while Tom Morris posed restlessly in his big chair and Nathan gazed bleakly at the canvas before him, went slowly.

Catherine had read many books while she had been in the Friends' school at Philadelphia, she said, and Nathan discovered that, without knowledge of their historic settings, she had formulated strange though sometimes very wise ideas on their purposes and meanings. He was amazed that she had read Tom Paine's *Common Sense*. She said that it had been so strenuously denounced by the faculty of the school as atheistic that she and some of her companions had smuggled a copy of it within the walls and had perused it secretly with delicious shudders at their own wickedness. Nathan fetched his own worn copy from his saddlebags the next day and they read portions of it together —stopping now and then to watch the kingfishers, like blowing bits of blue sky, swoop down upon the lake.

Each day as the light died out above them and a cold breath came from the water they walked hand in hand along the path beside the brook and came to the hemlock grove where Farmer's Brother and his people had built a temporary village. As they walked the new-lighted fires were amber gleams behind the dark wall of the forest, and the sound of the water drums was spreading like the tattoo of raindrops at the breaking of a heavy shower. The long, leaf-covered houses were small round-topped volcanoes erupting the blue smoke of burning hickory. From poles as high as the rooftops hung tawny haunches of venison. Above the chuckling of the drums rode the high voices of playing children and the clear ringing of bells; there were hundreds of bells on every baby's cradle, Catherine said.

As twilight came Nathan and Catherine had to leave the well-trodden path beside the brook, for ballplayers from the lakeside fields were racing homeward over it and groups of shouting horsemen, having left their sandy coursing, now and again almost rode them down. When at last Catherine stood near the house in which she lived she stopped and put up eager lips for a parting kiss. Nathan treasured their shadowy farewells in the fire-dotted dusk. She would not see him at night. Whenever the treaty council fire was uncovered she stood thoughtfully in her place with the women of her tribe.

Once at the end of a sun-drenched afternoon, just as sullen grayness tinged a shadowed strip of beach, Nathan dared to speak, as casually as he could, of Charles Williamson. It seemed strange to him that he should care so much to know what her relationship had been to the Captain, when he had accepted without emotion her revelation that once she had loved the drunken Otsiquette. But as soon as he had asked his question he understood his feeling. When she told him of Otsiquette it had been obvious that whatever had been between them no longer troubled her. She spoke of her love for the educated Seneca as objectively as if it had been the affection of a stranger. But when Nathan spoke of Williamson she rose suddenly and waited for him to stand, and then took his hand and looked at him with troubled eyes.

"When he first came to the Genesee Country," she said, "he was even more beautiful than he is now. When he leaped upon his horse without touching his stirrups and dashed off through the forest with his blue cloak flying behind him I felt that my heart was being ground into dust by a giant pestle. He came often to my father's house the summer after I returned from school. One day my father had gone to Niagara and I was alone. The Captain said many things to me then. I do not remember them all—but he said that only the chiefs and the women of the chiefs of all nations should mingle. He was sad because while he was a captive he had allowed himself to be joined to a woman whose father was only his guard. Now he knew how greatly he had been mistaken. Though he was chief of all the Genesee lands the woman who lived in his house could not help him to govern them.

"I knew how he felt. Otsiquette had planned to teach the Iroquois wiser ways and I had believed I could help him. When he stayed drunk a week I knew I had been a fool. Out of my sorrow over that and out of my worship for the beautiful white Captain I gave him what he wished.

"And a strange thing happened. I saw him beautiful no more. I knew he had spoken untruths to earn a reward he thought of little importance, though he had let me think it great. Now that he had got it I knew that what I had given was worthless to me because I found him weak and pitiful. But he had found a value I do not understand. Ever since that day he has been unhappy because an Indian girl comes into his mind when he does not want her there."

Silently Nathan and Catherine trudged down to the brook. Dusk lay about the birches beside the brown water.

"I must go," said Nathan, surprised that his voice was loud and hard upon the quiet air. She took his right hand in her lean brown fingers and lifted it to her lips.

"I do not ask you to stay," she said. "I will be here tomorrow if you come."

He turned and walked to the shore of the lake. He stood staring at the headlands on the far side until he could see them no longer.

The next day he waited long at their meeting place before she joined him. Her mouth was serious and her eyes were sad.

"I am going away," she said.

"Where?"

"I will be a teacher for the missionary Kirkland on the high hill where he has made a school for the Oneidas. He has been with the Quakers at the council fire for many nights. Now his work is done. Tomorrow he goes back along the Mohawk and I will go with him."

He looked down on the straight line that parted her thick black hair. She did not look up and he put his hand beneath her chin and lifted it.

"Don't go," he said.

As if she feared what he would say next she spoke.

"When I was a little girl my mother told me a story of a young man who thought that none of the girls about him were beautiful. One day he saw a strange girl at a dance in the village and after that he was often with her. Moons passed and she said she must go to her own people. He went with her into a land of flowering fields and blossoming forests. And toward sunset of the last day of their travel they came to a wide-spreading low house. In the dusk they could see many people entering the house and already the sound of feasting had begun. The girl said 'This is my home,' and they went in and joined in the feasting and were happy all night long. The next day was like today. The hunters of the sky had wounded the heavenly bear and his blood had stained the falling leaves. Then the girl said 'I must go away. Do not be sorry. I will see you again in the spring.'

" 'You promise?' he said. 'You will not forget?'

" 'I promise,' she said and suddenly she had vanished, and the house and all of her people had gone, too, and he was alone in the midst of a marsh and all about him many frogs were crying. It was not until then that he realized that his companion was a frog-woman. He felt very badly after that for many days, but when the spring came he had forgotten her and he never went back to the spot where he had lost her to see if the frog-woman had come as she promised."

There were tears in her eyes when she finished. Nathan was silent, turning his head away in a sudden desire to hide from her the working of his face. He did not know how to answer. There could never be peace for either of them, he thought, if they were to continue their relationship. Too many factors were at work to keep them apart. In a frontier settlement in the west country, perhaps, a man might still have an Indian wife and fear no difficulties with his white neighbors, but not in a world of Charles Williamson's building. Indian girls had been good wives to hundreds of settlers in the old days, yes, even a generation ago. Others were even now marrying their white lovers on the banks of the Ohio, the Kentucky, the Mississippi —but not the Genesee. If he chose to stay in this land of his choice he must find a wife of his own race. Catherine must find an Indian husband. They must not see each other again. He knew that through the happy days he and Catherine had been together this moment had been casting its shadow on his mind and hers. He knew that she was meeting it more bravely, more realistically than he, and as he turned his head back, prepared to tell her so, he saw that she was running up the homeward path beside the brook.

VI

Nathan was pleased with his portrait of Thomas Morris. The face had more fullness than he had intended but the effect was flattering. He had caught some of the delicacy of the young man's hands, the swagger of his uplifted chin and the gleaming eyes, the elegance of his coat, the grace of his arms and curving wrists. He had dared to use brighter colors than those he had employed on his portrait of The Friend, and the whole effect of the painting seemed to him brilliant and rather charming. For a wagon painter, he thought, it's not a bad job even though there are some portions that would seem more fitting on a Conestoga board than on an artist's canvas.

Morris hovered about the painting as if he were a hen that had produced her first egg. His head cocked first on one side and then on the other, he made eager but vague gestures with his hands—suggesting a stronger line, a deeper shadow, a paler hue. Nathan saw underneath all this concern that he was pleased and that he regarded the thirty dollars he had promised for it as well spent.

The treaty meeting was dragging to a close now. A post rider from the west had finally arrived with confirmation of Wayne's victory, and the certainty of the news had made the chiefs at last eager to sign lest the victorious whites should ask for further concessions. The boundaries of the Seneca Nation had been set, perpetual peace and friendship firmly established, and the right of way of the white man over Seneca property secured forever. The last details of the document were being drawn up. More than two months had elapsed since the September day which had been designated for lighting the council fire. Only a few of the chiefs were left in Canandaigua now. The Philadelphia Quakers stayed on, knowing how often a white man's trickery had outwitted a red man's scheming. The sharp clear days of late October when Nathan had been happy with Catherine had gone now. Sky and lake seemed one color as the first days of November brought penetrating cold. Fringes of clear ice formed among the pebbles that lined the brook. All the larger birds of the Genesee woods seemed to have left them— the flickers and robins and orioles, the ducks and red-winged blackbirds. The nuthatches and chickadees, the little and less colorful birds, were near though, moving restlessly up and down the trunks of leafless trees.

Nathan was glad when Morris finally announced that he considered the portrait complete. Canandaigua had seemed a prison since Catherine had left. Only once had he walked down by the brook. The town of Farmer's Brother was deserted, the leafy huts turned brown and blown open here and there by the winds. There was no sound of drums or children's voices or tiny bells.

His paints and palette once more in his saddlebags, he turned Lottie north along the road to Bath. It seemed that he had been gone from his own cabin a long time though it had been but a few weeks. His thoughts were confused as he rode along the high shore toward the head of the lake. The mare took her own pace and it was midafternoon before he rode down into Watkinstown—a small group of scattered cabins at the bottom of a bowl of hills. Darkness had come before his halloo brought answer from the lighted doorways of the stately house of William Potter. The owner of the farm, a dignified quiet man, came out with three of his sons beside him and made the lonely rider welcome. Exclaiming over Lottie's extraordinary length the boys led her into the massive barn that loomed high against the heavens, and their father took Nathan at once into the big kitchen where a quarter of venison, still hot from its roasting, made smelling almost as happy as tasting.

After Nathan had eaten a hearty meal he and his host sat near the great brick oven and talked. Nathan was surprised to discover that this refined and highly educated gentleman had come to the Genesee Country as a follower of The Friend. He had known Rachel Malin in Rhode Island before she had followed the prophetess to the Genesee, "a chancy girl who could never use her mind because her feelings got in the way." Elijah,

Judge Parker now, was an old friend. "Never thought he'd give up making his belly swell even for a seat on a judge's bench."

At first Will Potter would not speak of The Friend. Whenever the talk approached her he grew silent. But when he saw that Nathan was antagonistic to her the dam he had put upon his speech overflowed. More and more bitterly he recited his charges, and with each one he gave corroborating details. The oven was no longer hot when he finished. Cold air seemed to be coming through the floor in a continuous wave. Nathan shivered. "I'm sorry," said Will Potter. "I get to talking about her and I can't stop. She is the only truly wicked person I have ever known."

Nathan slept between feather beds that night. In the morning the Potter boys had to melt the ice from the pump with kettles of boiling water. The great oven was hot again and the fire on the hearth roared up the chimney. For breakfast there were buckwheat cakes as big and round as the plates they were served on. Maple syrup dripped from two tall pitchers.

Lottie whinnied and set out at a brisk trot as Nathan began his ride. The air was sharp and clear and each breath was a delight that set his blood to racing.

He had not realized, as he rode into Bath a few hours after noon, that he would be the first courier from Canandaigua since the town had certain knowledge of Wayne's victory. He could hear hammers and axes while he was still far down the trail, and when he came in sight of the outskirts of the town he saw a log blockhouse already risen to its wide, overhanging, second story. About twenty-five men were at work on it and while he watched them he saw his own oxen, goaded by Whirl, patiently dragging new logs to the site. On seeing his partner the little man crowed like a mighty rooster and beat his arms against his sides as if they were a cock's wings. Nathan trotted the mare over to him and saw that he was pointing to the right sleeve of his shirt which bore awkwardly sewed chevrons.

"I'm a sergeant in the army of the Genesee," he announced proudly, "an' I'm so rough an' ready they won't let me give no orders 'ceptin' to wild beasts like this here yoke o' bulls."

"And where do you expect to find a battle?" said Nathan. "Who's going to try to storm the new blockhouse?"

"The Britishers an' the Injuns, jest as soon's they've scalped Anthony Wayne."

Nathan laughed.

"Wayne's beat 'em," he said. "The British won't dare come down on us now. There won't be any fighting around here for a long time."

"Shet up!" said Whirl. "I've been sellin' 'em our hillside stand o' pine for this here blockhouse an' fer the stockade around Pultney Square. Ye better not tell the Cap'n 'bout Wayne till we get a few things built around here. Tain't good business." He whooped loudly. "Wayne's chawed 'em to soup," he shouted to the men at work on the blockhouse. Wild shouting answered him.

A few moments later Nathan stood at the door of the Captain's house, looking into the sullen, lovely face of the girl from Boston.

"He's not here," she said in her husky dull voice. "He's never here since the fancy Virginia lords and ladies came to his races. The town might be burned and all of us scalped and murdered an' he'd never know it. He lives with the gentry on the hill below and can't be annoyed by unpleasant things like the scalps of his wife and child."

"You mean he's on the south road?" said Nathan.

"In more than one way," said the blonde woman bitterly. "It's a far jump from Indian hussies to Virginia hussies but he made it—easy. You'll find him being tended by a dozen black slaves. Now that you've painted his lordship Tom Morris perhaps you've had enough practice to aspire to a Virginian." Abruptly she retreated into the house and shut the door. Nathan urged the mare on out of the square and headed south.

He could see the skeleton of the house on the hill before he had ridden a mile. He had been accustomed to the sight of roomy structures in Pennsylvania. The stone farmhouses of his father and his neighbors were not small. Some of the residences of rich Philadelphia filled large lots. But this was a house to cover a wide hilltop—bigger even than the tavern the Captain was building at Geneva—and it already had an air about it. The plan had a grace and spaciousness, a distinctive quality which Nathan did not recognize. As he turned off the road to climb upward to the site of the house he was surprised to see that all of the builders—and there were, he guessed, about fifty of them—were black men. There was a song on the air, a strangely cadenced, high-voiced wail that met now and then a short, deep answer from many throats.

"It's the schoolteacher," said a hearty amused voice above him, and Nathan looked up into the smiling eyes of Peregrine Fitzhugh. The Virginian edged his horse up to Nathan's and held out a huge bony hand at the end of an incredibly long arm.

"Welcome to Springfield House," he said. "I've been hopin' to see you again ever since you gave my uncle and my sister a dose of Yankee bitters."

Nathan grinned.

"I was ruder than I should have been."

"Not much ruder—perhaps an iota. At any rate, you didn't drive us off. We're back and two uncles this time—Uncle Jonas, whom you know, and Major Presley Thornton, whom you don't. Uncle Presley is building a Virginia house, Springfield House, in Yankeeland. So is Uncle Jonas when he can get around to it."

"I bid you welcome," said Nathan.

"You've turned courtier," said Peregrine Fitzhugh, his mouth stretched wide in an ironic grin.

Nathan laughed.

"I don't seem to be able to keep my words going for long. As soon as my idea is in the open my mouth shuts up."

"It's lucky you're a Yankee," said Fitzhugh. "You wouldn't be very successful in Virginia, not with that sort of talk and with a horse longer than a Federalist political speech. I suppose you're here to see Colonel Williamson, aren't you?"

"Colonel?" said Nathan in surprise.

"Of the militia of the sovereign State of New York. Governor Clinton has defeated the British invasion by that one appointment."

"They're beaten anyway," said Nathan, "and that's what I came to tell him. Wayne settled the argument out in Ohio."

"I'm delighted," said Fitzhugh. "Let's go find the unnecessary Colonel."

They found him standing beside the tall, brown-eyed girl

whose imperious manner Nathan remembered as vividly as he did her big nose and her strong, firm-jawed chin.

"A replica," Williamson was saying, "of the planting at Blenheim would suit the flat terrain of your east garden. It will—"

"Here's news," said Peregrine Fitzhugh, interrupting, "that's better even than that which gave Marlborough the chance to plant Blenheim. Wayne has routed the Indians. There'll be no invasion."

Williamson's face grew ecstatic. Nathan thought he had never seen him so moved. He grasped Nathan's right hand in both of his own.

"Is it true, Mr. Hart? Then my happiest dreams will soon be realized."

Nathan nodded solemnly—with a glance at the serious face of Eleanor Fitzhugh.

Williamson laughed joyously.

"All goes as I hoped," he said. "The arrival of the Virginia and Maryland families for the races, the sale of large estates to them, the thwarting of England's last threat, the transportation of our grains to Baltimore by Mr. Kryder's arks—at last my works bear fruit."

"The world dances as you pull the strings," said Fitzhugh; "even my headstrong sister."

"We shall all dance with her," said the Colonel jubilantly, "at the Christmas Eve ball in Geneva. It shall usher in a new era in the Genesee Country. With it shall begin the age of prosperity and fine living I have planned." He stopped talking suddenly and looked at Nathan, as if he realized that he might now have caused an outburst of Republican sentiments. Then he went on quickly and blandly.

"Miss Fitzhugh, forgive my clumsy delay and allow me to present my friend, the Genesee Country's distinguished portrait painter, Mr. Nathan Hart."

The girl looked startled. Nathan bowed.

"A painter?" she said.

Her brother laughed.

"Yokel," he said, "is the word by which you presented him to me."

"I don't understand," said Williamson. "Have you known Mr. Hart before now?"

"No," said Eleanor Fitzhugh coolly, and Nathan saw that her brother seemed to find it wise not to carry his joking further. "I am glad to see Mr. Hart and I am not surprised to find that Colonel Williamson has provided his precious new country with even so exceptionally civilized an attribute as a portrait painter."

"I am not a very good one," said Nathan, remembering the Conestogas.

"He is modest," said Williamson. "Our most respected citizens require his services. I hope that you and he will give me the benefit of your artistic advice on decorating the Geneva ballroom in December."

"It will be a pleasure," said the girl, "if Mr. Hart can abide the undependable taste of an amateur." She smiled at Nathan. Her even teeth were a white gleam in the gold-brown of her long face.

"I shall be honored," said Nathan.

"Well I'm damned," muttered Peregrine Fitzhugh.

VII

Snow covered the Genesee Country early that year. The hame
bells were jingling ahead of the sleighs by the tenth of December. Sledding weather seemed to bring a happy release to all
the settlers. Now the long, slow drag on the rutted, mud-trapped
roads had ceased as if by sudden magic, and the settlers slid
swiftly and easily along behind their trotting horses. The barns
covered what harvest there had been. There was little work to
do except make dwellings more secure and mend harness. It was
easy to track deer through the snow. Venison and pigeon, maize
and potatoes, crowded the dinner tables.

Whirl and Nathan, with time on their hands, rode down
the road to the big house and asked for work as carpenters.
Jonas Hogmire came out to greet them, giggling nervously.

"Many of our slaves are skilled artisans," he said. "They
are better acquainted with the artistic turning of wood, the nice
fitting of joints than any of your Yankees. I might employ Gragg
here as foreman of hauling operations, but as for Mr. Hart . . ."
he shrugged his shoulders and waved a languid fat hand.

"Surely there is some work I could do," said Nathan.

"Not until the master of the house or one of its occupants
may wish a portrait in his new surroundings," said Hogmire.

"But—" said Nathan.

"Menial work here is done by our slaves," said the fat man.
"You aren't suggesting that you join them, I'm sure."

"I'm suggesting that," said Nathan.

Hogmire laughed uproariously.

"Mr. Hart," he said, "it is fortunate that I am a man of
the world who understands an artist's flights of perverse fancy."

He turned and walked back toward the house.

Whirl looked after the waddling squat figure in dismay.

"Run along," said Nathan. "Maybe I'll get a job on the inside while you're adorning the out."

"It goes agin the grain," said Whirl doubtfully.

"Go ahead."

Whirl set off at a slow pace. After he had gone a few steps he whooped loudly and Hogmire stumbled, frightened by the sudden noise behind him.

"I'll build yer shanty fer ye," shouted Whirl.

The Williamson Tavern was a sparkling jewel between black velvet covers of sky and lake. Below it the night was a vast jangle of hame bells. Sleighs had been arriving all day long and now that darkness had come long lines of them jammed the narrow roads. From as far east as the Cross Widow's and as far west as Ganson's the musical tinkling had rung the horses over the snow into the huddled town.

There was a whisper that some rich folks from Utica had warmed themselves with so much rum on the way that they had whipped up their horses and treated fellow travelers to the sight of a first-class runaway. The sleigh had upset on a turn, spilling them all into the snow, and had smashed into splinters against a tree. Undaunted the merrymakers had set out afoot after their horses and found them stopped by obliging friends a mile or so along the road. Then the gay Uticans had mounted and ridden the rest of the way without saddles, to find upon arrival their appetite for dancing considerably diminished though greater than their desire to sit and watch.

A big fire blazed in the center of the stableyard and the hubbub of the hostlers seemed to rise toward the stars on its leaping flames. Blanketed horses, breathing streams of white mist, stood patiently along the hitching rails. A yoke of oxen, drawing a long wagon box fitted to wooden runners, slowly ambled to a stop in the rosy light. A dozen bundled figures climbed out to the accompaniment of catcalls and whooping from following sleighs, delayed by their slow progress.

Nathan stood at the foot of the steps of the huge white tavern, and looked down the slanting road to town. As far as the moon's light would let him see it was black with teams and sleighs. He had ridden his mare to Sanborn's in Canandaigua the previous day. He had called on Morris in the evening and had had the satisfaction of seeing the portrait he had painted, now handsomely framed in gilt and hanging above the mantel in the big room in which it had been completed. In the flicker of many candles the picture had looked rich in color, and he congratulated himself that he had made a reasonably good likeness. Morris had seemed pleased, indeed rather vain about it, and had asked him to spend the night in the room he had previously occupied, but Nathan had refused. He could see that Morris now looked upon himself as the patron of an artist, and he felt his usual and characteristic resentment. He walked back along the snowy road to Sanborn's, well pleased with himself. He had painted a satisfactory portrait and he had let its proud owner know that he was an independent workman not dependent on beneficence. This was a finer result than he had achieved at the end of his painting the likeness of The Friend. He still remembered the stricken look with which the prophetess had greeted her first sight of her portrait.

The ride from Canandaigua had been a pleasant one. He had been hailed by many parties, singing along in the sunlight behind their jogging teams. His heart warmed to these people. They did not consider him one of them—he had an education and a talent for painting while they had neither. But they respected him and seemed proud of him and friendlily disposed. With a smile he remembered his loneliness and his bitter sense of being a fugitive when first he had come among them.

The door at the top of the steps opened and the chatter of the crowd within shot out above his head as though it had suddenly been released from encompassing pressure. He turned and walked slowly up the steps toward the great flaring of light above him. He wondered when he would see Eleanor Fitzhugh. Whirl had told him that the cavalcade from Springfield House had left Bath amid a shrill blowing of horns and barking of dogs three full days ago. Hardly had it thundered out of sight up the road than·Whirl had sneaked off to his horse, ridden home for such adornments as he had been saving for the occasion— blacked and well-greased boots, a white broadcloth shirt which he insisted on wearing, smocklike, outside his breeches, a pair of beaded doeskin leggings he had obtained in trade for sharpening a neighbor's plow—and galloped off in the wake of his employers. Nathan had not seen him since.

The great room of the tavern was filled with people. Waves of heat billowed from two wide fireplaces at either end. A queue of men stood beside the one in the east wall, regardless of the heat, awaiting entrance to the taproom, long since crowded to overflowing. Deep male laughter sounded from its doors and the men in the waiting line looked wistfully ahead.

A Negro boy in fantastic green livery figured with gold was diving here and there through the crowd calling in a high voice, "Mr. Nathan Hart! Mr. Nathan Hart!"

Nathan touched the boy on the shoulder.

"I'm Nathan Hart," he said.

"My master, Mr. Jonas Hogmire, presents his compliments, sir, and begs you to join him and his companions in their chamber."

Nathan followed the boy up the wide staircase that led to a windowed landing over the west fireplace and vanished in an upward slant toward the second floor. At the door opposite the end of the stair the boy, with a flourish of a black fist, knocked twice. The petulant voice of Hogmire bade him enter and the boy threw open the door, bowed, and with a wide sweep of his right arm announced:

"Mr. Nathan Hart."

Nathan stood, blinking a bit, in the doorway. Two heavy silver candelabra brightened the wide, white surface of the table with many little upward-bound arrows of fire. Beyond the second of the candelabra he saw Eleanor seated at the end of a long table. Her dress was a redder flame than that of the candles. Its sleeves, very full at the top, flared balloonlike above her shoulders and tapered downward to be tightly bound on the firm rounds of her arms just above her elbows. It had been cut away from her slim neck in a deep oblong that ended just below the little hollow that showed the division between her breasts. The oblong was edged with ivory lace that gently protected his eyes from the strong contrast between the fire of the dress and the whiteness of her skin. As Nathan entered the room she rose and moved around the end of the table to face him as he approached. Her skirt was a billowing sea of gleaming taffeta that rustled as she walked.

"Gad, Mr. Hart, you're late," said the voice of Hogmire, and the fat man suddenly lurched into Nathan's view—his

breeches and coat vast expanses of mulberry, his shirt front as
ever a frothing sea of white ruffles. His wig of powdered snowy
curls was a trifle small for his enormous head and was tilted
saucily over his right eye.

"We had been hoping you would accompany us from
Bath," said Eleanor, "but your man told us you could not leave
till yesterday."

"My man?" said Nathan, startled.

"It was good of you to lend him to us," said Eleanor.
"I'm sure he's doing very well."

"Peculiar fellow," said Jonas Hogmire reflectively.

"Whirl Gragg is my partner," said Nathan bluntly.

"No offense meant," said Hogmire genially. "Very worthy,
I'm sure."

"May I offer my congratulations, Mr. Hart!" said Charles
Williamson, stepping forward quickly. "The portrait of Morris
is exceptional—the face—the hands—the grace of your true aristocrat. He is greatly pleased."

Nathan was dazzled by the splendor of Williamson's appearance. He had never before seen him out of the role of an
active man of affairs. He knew him as always immaculate—
even at the end of a long ride he possessed the faculty of appearing freshly clad. The long blue cloak, the long clean boots,
the white stock about his neck, and the tricorn hat were familiar
to everyone in the Genesee Country. But Nathan was not prepared for the newly made Colonel in ballroom dress. His long
throat was a gleaming, white satin pillar rising from a foam of
starched ruffles. A yellow waistcoat, crossed by faint red lines in
a diamond pattern, was a gay answer to the dignity of his long,
darkly amber coat. Lace, translucent and intricate, fell from his
sleeve ends almost to the tips of his long fingers. The candlelight caught on the folds of his silken breeches, so tightly con-
trived as to suggest the strong line of his thighs, and above the
silver blaze of his shoe buckles his slim ankles swelled into
strong, well-muscled calves, intimately revealed beneath the
sheen of his stocking. A wig of dazzling whiteness fitted so perfectly upon his head that the piled-up coiffure seemed actually
to have grown there. Nathan suddenly realized that in his more
than two years of association with him this was the first time he
had seen Williamson at leisure.

He is too perfect, thought Nathan as he made a long-limbed, awkward imitation of the Colonel's graceful bow. Looking up then he saw with embarrassment that Peregrine Fitzhugh, standing in a shadowy corner, glass in hand, was grinning at him. Peregrine's wig was a trifle big, his coat a little short, his stock slightly awry.

"Glad to see you, Mr. Hart," he said, and Nathan felt that these were the first unstudied words he had heard in the room. "My uncle, Colonel Presley Thornton," said Fitzhugh, and Nathan turned to bow to a tall man in a black coat. His hair was gray and his serious regular features were somewhat like those of President Washington. Colonel Thornton nodded his head and made a slight inclination that would pass for a bow. These Virginians are negligent, thought Nathan, and Williamson is meticulous. They care little for forms they are accustomed to. The Colonel cares too much.

"We regret that you have not been with us for dinner," said Hogmire pompously. "Colonel Williamson has suggested that the other guests await our arrival to start the dancing and wishes to propose a last toast before we join them. Bring Mr. Hart a glass."

The black boy in the green livery hastily filled a glass from a decanter on the table and presented it to Nathan. Williamson lifted his glass.

"To the Genesee Country," he said. "May its beauties lure so many gentlemen of leisure like yourselves to seek homes within its borders that it shall become the very seat of American aristocracy."

The glass was already on its way to Nathan's lips when the meaning of Williamson's words reached his brain. His first impulse was to dash the glass upon the floor. His hand trembled as it slowed to a stop below his lips. Already the others were drinking. As he hesitated Hogmire set his glass upon the table.

"Now let us partake of the more widely enjoyed festivities," he said.

His hand still shaking from the violence of his feeling Nathan returned his full glass to the table. He looked at Williamson as he did so and saw that gentleman smiling whimsically directly at him. He steeled himself for reply if attention were called to his refusal to drink. At first he thought that only

Williamson had noticed his defection and had decided to ignore it. The rest of the party had gathered about Eleanor as she prepared to leave the room and seemed completely unaware of his action. But in the shadowy corner where Peregrine Fitzhugh stood Nathan saw a quick movement. The long-legged Marylander had taken one step to the side of the table. His glass was slowly descending upon the white cloth. It was full to the brim with yellow wine.

VIII

The ballroom filled the entire right wing of the second floor.
On a small platform at the far end sat a half dozen black
musicians tuning their banjos and fiddles in the light created
by three enormous chandeliers, which hung at regularly spaced
intervals from the ceiling. Twelve tall windows, six to each of
the long sides, provided shallow recesses in which little groups
of guests had formed. In one, surrounded by a number of the
young Scots whom Williamson had brought with him to Bath,
Nathan saw with amazement the beautiful, moody face of Mrs.
Williamson. Her eyes, catching the entry of the Maryland party,
glanced from her companions to the door and back many times.
She forced a heavy-lipped smile at the remark of one of the
young Scots and shook a finger at him. Nathan was glad that
Eleanor had chosen to enter on the arms of her two uncles.
Behind the three Colonel Williamson stalked alone. Then came
Nathan and Peregrine, the latter sauntering slowly a little to the
rear of his companion.

As soon as the party had entered Williamson moved ahead
and led it to a corner beside the music platform. Having seen
that Eleanor Fitzhugh was seated he moved to the center of the
room. As he did so the crowd that had been on the floor below
began to race into the room. While he stood smiling, turning
about to greet the loud cheers of each new group, the walls were
quickly lined four deep with eager onlookers. Finally Williamson held up an admonitory hand for silence and at once the
merrymakers were under his spell.

"I am happy that you are all here tonight," he said gaily,
"to celebrate with my companions and me the opening of this
great new hostelry at the gateway of our land of crystal lakes,
our garden home, the Genesee Country."

The crowd cheered lustily.

"Couldn't say it better meself, Cap'n," shouted a drunken male voice, and Williamson laughed. The crowd roared again.

"We have made every effort to give this tavern all the comfort and luxury that the best of foreign inns possess," he said, "and we have been most fortunate in obtaining from London the services of mine host of the famous Thatched Cottage, Thomas Powell. Mr. Powell and his good wife have served many of the great literary and political figures of England, yet I dare say never a more distinguished group than here gathered. I want you to see Powell and his spouse who have provided so generously for us tonight. Let them come forward."

Haltingly a huge man advanced into the room from the door through which Williamson and his party had entered. His face, ruddy from thousands of kitchen fires, was thick-jowled, fat-cheeked. His head was shining bald but beneath a small, budlike mouth sprouted a beard of disciplined and curled luxuriance. His eyes seemed small behind the rolls of fat that threatened to engulf them. His pudgy right hand clasped the wrist of a shrinking, worn little woman who held her apron to her face with her free hand in an agony of modesty. The pair advanced into the room a few steps and stopped, abashed by the shouted applause. When it had subsided a bit the big man spoke. His voice was high and thin.

"H'm h'overcome, Hi am. Completely h'overcome. Hi eyen't received no such honor since Hi entertined Sir 'Orace Walpole, not since Sir 'Orace." He subsided into a head-shaking revery for a moment and then dragged his wife, still masked by her apron, into the grateful oblivion outside the door.

"We are to begin our delights of the evening," said Charles Williamson, once more lifting a lacy wrist above his head, "with a minuet to be danced by the gentlemen and ladies of my party. The music is most thoughtfully provided for us by Colonel Presley Thornton who has lent his servants for the occasion."

Nathan saw Thomas Morris move out on the floor with Mrs. Williamson. At the same moment Colonel Hogmire led from the crowd along the wall a simpering, ample woman, stricken speechless by this sudden honor. Peregrine Fitzhugh reached out an arm and dragged to his side a red-faced, brown-eyed girl who had been flirting with him industriously in order to effect just such an outcome. Williamson turned to offer his arm to Eleanor.

"May I have the honor?" he said.

"Unless Mr. Hart has forgotten," said the girl calmly, "I am promised to him for this beginning."

Williamson flushed and Nathan saw in his eyes the fierce look that he had come to associate with the man's moments of disappointment and frustration.

"I—I have not forgotten," said Nathan, "but I am not familiar with dances of the gentry. I once saw a minuet danced in Philadelphia, but—"

"And that is quite enough," said Eleanor firmly, "for anyone who has ever seen the silly thing can step it. Come—I will help you through."

The black musicians had already struck up the slow, sweet introduction to the dance as they walked to the center of the floor. I wonder, thought Nathan, why I do what she wishes. Rachel could never make me do what she wished. Yet this girl assumes I will obey her and willy-nilly I do it. Somehow, then, with the aid of the girl on his arm and the smiling whispered advice of Peregrine and his ruddy partner who danced near him, Nathan plodded through smooth steps, turns, and curtsies. As the music ended on a long chord, he bowed low, greatly relieved that he had come through without loss of dignity. He stood erect again and saw Williamson once more advance to the center of the room.

"Your patience now wins reward," he said. "All of you are invited to join in the dancing and I expect no refusals. Let the music begin."

White fiddlers leaped to the platform as he spoke, hurrying the leisurely Negroes who were preparing to leave it. Magically a weird figure appeared before Nathan. It was Whirl, his white shirt concealing most of his breeches, his legginged legs performing strange quick gestures beneath him.

"All chaw hay," he shouted, grabbing Colonel Hogmire's buxom companion from him and swinging her about him in a circling arc.

"Anchor your sweeties, let your wife drift downstream," he shouted and leaped high into the air, beating his heels together.

His bald head shone brightly beneath the forest of candles and his blue eyes brimmed with delight.

Nathan heard a quick exclamation beside him. Eleanor's mouth was closed in a thin firm line. Contempt blazed from her. Then the music started a bouncing, vulgar, quick-beat tune, and Whirl, recognizing it, began to prance to it, singing drunkenly in a raucous voice:

> "Farewell to whiskey
> And everything frisky!
> Farewell to whiskey, farewell."

"This is my kind of dancing," said Nathan. "Will you honor me?"

Eleanor's voice was strong and sharp.

"You may take me to my brother."

"I danced your dance with you. You should oblige me."

"Mr. Hart, you may not use the word 'should' when you speak to me."

Furiously Nathan turned from her and stalked half the length of the room and out of the door, down the stair, and into the dark night. He heard a clatter on the steps and the slam of the door behind him.

"Cooked your goose, didn't I?" said Whirl. "I'm drunk as a hoot owl an' I'm goin' home."

"You're not going home," said Nathan. "I'm done with her and the rest of 'em. I'm done with myself. The Whiskey Rebel dances about with the Monarchists while the low-born rabble waits."

"Let 'em have their fun," said Whirl. "We have ours an' there's more chaw to it." He began to sing:

> "Hi, Betty Martin, tip toe, tip toe!
> Hi, Betty Martin, tip toe fine!
> Never found a man to suit her fancy—
> Never found a man to suit her mind."

A high uneven note was breaking in on this husky bellowing. Nathan did not know when he began to hear it. Suddenly, it was there—a wild, appealing, soprano chant wavering across the night.

"Tip toe, tip toe," Whirl sang and stopped to listen. A woman's voice, fast and desperate, somewhere below there by the stables—a voice that caught at his memory, though he had never heard any woman speak in a tone so strained, so close to hysterical outcry.

Whirl had already staggered down the steps from the entrance and was making remarkable speed in a zigzag course toward the strange sound. Nathan followed. Sleighs were still moving in long procession up the hill. On one of the five-foot stone columns that formed the gateway to the stableyard stood a woman in a long gray cloak. Her hands were stretched out before her and she was pleading frantically. Nathan ran forward. Around the column pressed a crowd of men—the hostlers, curious latecomers, and drunken early arrivals. As he reached them Nathan knew for certain what he had somehow been feeling since the sound had reached his ears. It was the voice of Rachel.

"Ye tempt God in his heaven," she screamed, her face a white, grotesquely moving mask in the light of the stable lanterns and torches. "Beware eternal wrath. The Friend has dreamed of doom—doom upon ye all because ye sin in carnal dancing and forget the Lord. Now retribution waits—even now it is at hand. Ye have built a shrine to Baal and it shall fall about ye and all shall be destroyed."

"Don't be afraid, lady," called a voice from the crowd. "We'll pertect ye."

"*Ja und* I vill hiding blace find—*für* you *und* me." The sentence ended in a burst of guttural laughter.

"The Friend will rule this land as God will have it ruled," screamed Rachel. "Speak against her and ye blaspheme God Himself."

"To hell with her, it's you I want."

"Come *hinunter* down, mine *Vögel*, or I vill after *kommen*."

Nathan saw the man with the German accent embrace the gate pillar and begin laboriously to climb it. His body was so big that it completely hid the base of the column. He reached up and grabbed Rachel's skirt.

"Buckendahl," said Whirl, and suddenly he was gone from Nathan's side. His short, round body doubled forward as he ran, and his bald head was a white cannonball in the light of the stableyard torches. From his mouth came a threatening roar. At the sound behind them the crowd turned, saw the speeding round projectile, and gave way. Whirl flashed through. His head caught the big German full in the small of the back, crushing him against the column. Buckendahl's grasp loosened. He fell backward, screaming. As he hit the ground a man stepped in close to Whirl and sent him spinning with a blow to his jaw. The little man stumbled over Buckendahl's prostrate body, fell, and lay still. Nathan, discovering that he had followed in the wake of the charge, leaped forward and struck. The man who had hit Whirl went down. Fiercely the crowd leaped on Nathan. He went down.

It seemed that he had been in darkness a long time when the press of bodies lifted from above him, and the rain of blows on his back and head mercifully ceased. He climbed to his feet and found himself in the middle of a circle of threatening faces. He looked above them to the gate column. Rachel was gone. Apparently she had chosen the moment when all attention was diverted to him for her escape. Beside him stood a slender straight figure in a familiar green coat of military cut. Once more he beheld the way of Berezy with a mob. It was different this time—the technique had improved. The man was surer and there was a sort of humorous finality about him as if he realized that he held an excess of power. He was smiling gently.

"Not so fast, my children," he said. "These men are not important—a rumpot and a painter of women and sickly aristocrats."

Buckendahl groaned and rose to his knees.

"Take that blundering fool away," said Berezy sharply. Three men pounced on the big man and dragged him out of the crowd.

"Mr. Hart," said Berezy calmly, "I save your life again. I grow used to your ingratitude. Go back to the patrons from whom you beg a living—the crazy prophetess, the tyrant Williamson, the rich Mr. Morris—and give them a message from me and my comrades."

Most of these stableboys and hostlers around him now, Nathan thought, must be the same men he and the rest of

Williamson's companions had fought off in the cabin at Williamsburg.

"Tell them," said Berezy, "that their rule is short. They have persecuted and enslaved my people, but soon our places will be reversed and they will serve us more diligently than we now serve them. We are not afraid of The Friend. She is a mad woman who relies on her God." Berezy laughed mirthlessly and then his face grew stern. "Her God can give her no power. And Williamson and those strutting Southern fools will have no more than she when I have done with them. The rights of those who follow me have been taken from them. I shall restore them. The promises made to me when I came to the Genesee Country shall be fulfilled."

An angry muttering grew in the crowd. One of the men stepped toward Nathan and Berezy held up a restraining hand.

"Mr. Hart," he said mockingly," is less than any of these. He is a Democrat-Republican, an anarchist believer in rabbles without leaders; he would give this land over to the beggars. Let him hold his miserable acres until we take them from him."

Nathan knew as he struck he would never forget the savage joy of the blow, the deep satisfaction of feeling, the soft crumple of Berezy's face as the strong fist smacked into it. The man went down with the swiftness of a dropping stone and Nathan felt only content as the crowd closed in once more. He knew that he faced death, but the triumph of the moment obliterated all other sensations. Instinctively he parried the first blows struck at him. Suddenly there were no more. A voice beside him, a woman's, low and contemptuous, had begun to speak.

"Stop! I'll have the lash on the bare back of any one of you that touches him. Stand back, you filthy beasts, or you'll be skinned alive!"

The presence of the woman and the sharp impact of her words brought sudden silence. The men nearest Nathan looked curiously, fearfully about for the source of the stinging sentence. There in the light of the torches stood a girl—her cheeks as brilliant as her flame-colored gown, her eyes loosing arrows of hatred and scorn. For a moment only the men stood motion-

less; then one laughed, threw his arms about her shoulders, and
dragged her into a bear-hug embrace.

Abruptly, close by, came the short, swift crack of a pistol
shot. Panic seized the crowd. Eleanor's assailant dropped her
and ran. The rest, stumbling over one another, followed. Then
the yard was empty save for two figures lying in the snow
and a huddled three standing near them—Eleanor and Nathan
and Peregrine. In the moment of recognition—as Nathan and
the girl saw the smoking pistol in Peregrine's left hand and the
unfired pistol in his right—the green-coated figure rose from
the hard-trodden white ground and slunk off into the darkness.
The sound of sobbing, terrible dry sobbing was with him as
he went. He has every courage except that of bearing physical
pain, thought Nathan, and there was a trace of pity in his
mind. Eleanor stood rigid with rage and disgust, still feeling
the repugnant arms about her.

"Seems to me," said Peregrine Fitzhugh to Nathan, "you
and I are about the only sort of folks that haven't been heard
from tonight. Hope there's a lot more of us in this country
somewhere."

"Here's one," said a voice from the ground as Whirl opened
a cautious eye.

1795

Liberty, Equality, and no King!
(Rallying cry of the Democrat-Republicans)

I

Spring came early to the Genesee Country that new year of
1795. Hardly had Nathan and Whirl realized that they needed
a new almanac when the first bluebird was a promise of spring
sky above the frozen savannahs of withered grass. There was
the late February day when the trees on the mountains across
the river stood blackly silhouetted in warm sunlight above the
snow. On the next morning bits of bare ground spotted the
far-spread whiteness and little streams were foaming down the
steep slopes into the swelling river. At once Whirl gave up
his job at Springfield House and joined Nathan in the task of
tapping the hard maples in their upland acres.

One afternoon Nathan found Whirl busily arranging a
series of wooden troughs of his own manufacture in such a
way that the syrup, dripping into them, flowed in converging
streams into one big pipe that led to a vat at the foot of the
slope. For the three following days the scheme worked beautifully. By midafternoon of the fourth day, however, the warm
sunlight had warped the boards in the troughs, and they had
spilled several quarts of the precious sweet liquid on the ground
before Whirl had discovered their defection. Disgustedly then
the partners went back to the old-fashioned way of collecting
their syrup in buckets hung under each tap.

By mid-March floods were spreading through all the valleys, rising inch by inch on the high yellow stalks, roiling over
the cleared fields on the flats. The Genesee at Williamsburg
was reported to be a mile wide. Du Boui, the melancholy
Frenchman who had cured Nathan's attack of Genesee Fever
with Jesuit bark, had been driven out of his cabin by the rising
waters. He had proposed to stay and drown, but the good
mulatto, Joseph, had finally persuaded him to move into a

cabin deserted by one of Berezy's Germans who was now working out a fine in Canandaigua.

A month later an inky glue had stuck to everything that showed above the receding liquid surface. Streams ran once more in their channels, but their banks were two inches higher, two inches of black silt, rich enough to grow bumper crops of anything. The killdeer, building their nests in the open fields, called to each other all day long. The wide acres of tall grass were alive with quick sound and quicker movement. The black and white reed birds—Whirl called them skunk-birds, fluttered swiftly from stalk to stalk, singing the while the song that gave them still another name "bobolink, bobolink." Robins, fat and weary from a day of pulling long worms from the damp, dark soil, perched high in the lonely spreading elms at sundown and yodeled for rain.

Whirl borrowed a yoke of oxen from Colonel Williamson and drove them over to Williamsburg. There he convinced William Wadsworth that he was an authority on the growing of hemp, flax, and tobacco and traded his knowledge for a load of seed. By the time their maple sap had been boiled down and cooled to hard sugar the partners were readying their acres on the flats for the sowing. They worked incessantly from sunrise until dark, and Nathan found himself no match for the short fat man, who chattered amiably while his hoe lifted and fell, lifted and fell. Many times they planned that on the first moony night they would ride down to Springfield House to see what progress had been made. Clear weather was precious, though, and at the end of each fair day they found themselves too weary to move. By moonrise both would be sound asleep.

Eventually they got reports from the big house on the south road. On a day of alternate drizzle and soaking rain a horseman rode up to their cabin, dismounted, and tied his steed in the new shed where Nathan's mare was quartered.

"It's Peregrine Fitzhugh," he called as he rapped smartly on the door, and Nathan bounded up from his reading beside the fire to let him in. Peregrine seemed to take in all the interior of the cabin at a glance and he nodded as he saw Nathan's dog-eared *Rights of Man* on the table. Then he sighed, took his pipe from a damp pocket, and lit it with a strip of fat-pine kindling which he ignited over the fire.

"It's hell living with a Federalist family," he volunteered. "They think I'm crazy, call me traitor, beggar, Leveler." His long frame slithered to the floor and he propped his head on his elbows and stared into the flames on the hearth. Nathan found it easy to fall into his mood. This was a man to whom he could talk. He had a simple, honest way of speaking.

"It isn't the political opinions of people like your family I resent," said Nathan, "it's the acceptance of inferior station by people like me and Whirl here."

"Who, me?" said Whirl rising from the bench on which he had been napping, and clenching his fists.

"Not you," said Nathan hastily, "but people like you and like me. Why do they accept such contradictions as the use of the word aristocracy in a democratic Republic? Why did we let them establish the Society of the Cincinnati? Why do we—"

"I'll tell you why," said Whirl, lying down once more on the bench. "It's because they ain't worth botherin' with. Do they enj'y 'emselves up to the nub or do we? C'n they git drunk with impunity—er lift a skirt without a'bowin' and a-askin' by your leave madam? Let 'em have their fancy ways an' their wigs an' satin pants. Ain't no blood under 'em."

Peregrine Fitzhugh laughed. "If that were all," he said, "I'd be of your mind. Unhappily there is a nasty quality of acquisitiveness that goes with the aristocratic turn of mind— rather it's the other way round. First acquisition—then the sense of superiority."

"I don't like it," said Nathan positively.

"Sir," said Peregrine Fitzhugh, "you sound like a *sans culotte*, an atheist, and a traitor. In fact I like you and feel that you would be a good influence on my family, particularly my headstrong sister. Therefore I am here to ask if you will come— if both of you will come—to Springfield House as my guests whenever you feel so disposed. I hope it will be often."

"I've been there often already," said Whirl, "know every damn' puddle in the road an' every damn' board in the walls personal. Besides, Nate's got ahead o' me down thataway, with his fancy dancin' an' his slick tricks."

Peregrine laughed, and both he and Nathan looked at

Whirl with amused respect. He has the sensitivity of a courtier, thought Nathan, and the integrity of an honest man.

"I'm afraid your sister finds me too rough and untutored a companion," he said, "for a Virginia lady."

"Whatever companionship you offer," said Peregrine, "she values it, or she wouldn't have walked into that little hurly-burly in the stableyard the other night—and she in her second-best gown."

"I was coming anyway," said Nathan hastily. Peregrine looked at him quizzically. The two men grinned at each other.

Three days later, when the sun was still above the far rim of the valley, Whirl leaned a moment on the handle of his hoe.

"Figgered on ketchin' a fish or two 'fore it's too dark," he said, "but I'd feel like I was shirkin' if I left ye here a-pluggin'."

"We could finish up easy tomorrow," said Nathan casually. "I might trot over to see Fitzhugh while you're fishing."

There was a silence. Then Whirl said:

"I'll save ye some speckled trout fer tomorrow's breakfast. Won't be expectin' ye t'eat home 'fore then." He shouldered his hoe and started for the cabin.

"Yes," said Nathan absently.

After that the spring went rapidly. Nathan made the short ride to Springfield House more and more often. Wild cherries bloomed along his way, fragrant in the soft dusk. Routes of yellow butterflies, like animated blossoms, danced along the evening breezes, causing Lottie to prick up her ears and take a dance step or two. The horse chestnuts were towering white candelabra in the moonlight when he rode home.

He liked the approach to the big house. First he would catch a glimpse of its tapering white pillars, lovely white-robed sisterhood standing on the rounded summit of a hill which sloped gently upward from the valley. By the time he could see it again from the road yellow light would be streaming into the dusk from the tall windows. From the moment he turned off the main road and took the upwinding trail to the entrance he was accompanied by a retinue of high-voiced Negro children, begging for the privilege of leading his mare to the stable when he dismounted. A gray-haired black man would open the big door with a smile. And Peregrine Fitzhugh, grinning comfortably, was always nearby to offer a welcome to what he called "the newest caucus of the Republican-Democrats of the Genesee Country" and to suggest rum or whiskey "after so arduous a ride through the Federalist wilderness."

The high-ceilinged reception room of Springfield House held only six chairs, all brought in the big wagons from Maryland. Nathan and Peregrine would sit beside the high mantel of the fireplace for a half hour or so before Jonas Hogmire, fuming and giggling and smoothing his white ruffles, bumbled down to join them. Colonel Thornton, severe and conservative, would arrive a few moments later. Dinner would have been announced by the gray-headed old Negro before there would be the sound of a door opening above and a firm step on the stair. Then Eleanor Fitzhugh would arrive, cool and gracious and somehow giving the impression of youth and vitality held in control by a firm mind. Swiftly the black servants would whisk the chairs into the dining room. Then Nathan would offer Eleanor his arm and lead the procession to the table. There, while silver platters filled with steaming foods were borne to their plates, the company would talk of progress in building the rest of the house, of planting new crops, and of news that had come up the Susquehanna road through the medium of the Philadelphia *Inquirer.* Inevitably there would be talk of swift horses and good-natured teasing of Nathan over his ownership of long-bodied, awkward Lottie.

Only one evening had been devoted to discussion of politics. Nathan and Peregrine had found themselves sore beset by all their companions on that occasion and had been unable to keep the argument impersonal. Colonel Thornton had quietly retired to his room, Major Hogmire had sputtered pompously about the dangers incurred by the whole country when gentlemen sided with rabble, and Eleanor Fitzhugh had demanded of her brother where he got the dangerous radical ideas of a demagogue. Nathan knew then that she would have said as much to him if he were not a guest, and rose to go. At this Colonel Hogmire had said "Enough of this nonsense, egad!" and asked Nathan to go out to the stables with him to look over a new gelding which one of his Negroes had ridden up from Maryland. Nathan had accepted the invitation and Peregrine had come along. The three men had been surprised a few moments later when Eleanor had appeared in the circle of lanterns held by the slaves and had acted as though she were not aware that her remark had caused a difficult moment for them all.

After that there was no more talk of politics at Springfield House, at least while Nathan was there.

II

The hemp and the flax were green shoots above the brown
earth and the tobacco leaves had begun their ungainly sprawling
when Nathan saw the little man riding by. There was grace
in the way he sat his fine bay mount—a subtler, quieter grace
than that of the dashing Colonel Williamson. His dark-blue
trousers, tapering from the knee and binding his calves tightly,
made smooth entrance beneath his riding boots. His short
cloak was the color of a bluebird's wing and it was crossed in
front by braided frogs of a light and misty green. Above his
smiling mouth, his handsome regular nose, his gleaming black
eyes, and his smooth wide forehead, sat a hat, a jaunty, gleaming tricorn topped by a cockade like a bursting bur, spilling red,
white, and blue on the spring air. Behind him rode a man in
somber black, obviously his servant. The sun poured a shower
of yellow light upon the tall elms through which he came, and
as his horse ambled toward the tobacco patch where Nathan
was hoeing the little man whistled a snatch of song. Nathan
leaned on his hoe and watched the two men approach.

"Good morning, my friend," said the little man in a warm,
friendly voice. "I hope that you can give me guidance to the
home of the distinguished Colonel Charles Williamson."

"I can tell you where it is," said Nathan smiling. "This
road leads to the village square and Mr. Williamson's house
is the one with the Liberty Pole in front."

"I am surprised that it still stands in a country of Federalist
complexion," said the little man, smiling the while as if he
would readily withdraw the words if they should be resented.

"If your sentiments lie that way," said Nathan, "you have
joined the most exclusive society in the Genesee Country. On
its behalf I welcome you."

"A Republican," said the little man, triumphantly, and he

slid from his horse and held out his right hand eagerly. "A Republican-Democrat as you call it in these northwestern lands. I am delighted, sir, to meet a man whose brain works so truly. Indeed I owe much to men like you who have honored me with their trust. I am Senator Aaron Burr."

"I have heard of you," said Nathan after a moment of surprise.

"And nothing good I'll warrant." The shiny black eyes twinkled and the strong mouth twisted into a whimsical half smile.

"You have said that you know this country to be Federalist," said Nathan.

Burr laughed and Nathan saw that he really seemed to enjoy the intimation of his unpopularity.

"Our friends must learn to know us better," he said, clapping Nathan on the shoulder, "before they pass judgment. Unhappily a Federalist feels so high and mighty these days he doesn't even try to reason—just depends on his kingly intuition."

Nathan grinned, and the Senator happily plucked a long green shoot from the side of the road and slapped at his shiny boots with it.

"We must have a rallying of the people of right thought while I am here," he said, "if Colonel Williamson and his friends would not consider it treasonable for men of democratic principles to associate with one another."

"He won't," said Nathan. "There are hardly a dozen of us in the region."

The black eyes snapped.

"A dozen good men can accomplish miracles, sir, when called upon to perform them. I must be on my way now. Will you be good enough to tell me your name that I may inquire for you later? I shall spend a few days in Bath."

"I am Nathan Hart."

"I shall look forward to seeing you again soon, Mr. Hart. Meanwhile, a modern Daniel, I go to beard the lions. Good day, Mr. Hart."

As he spoke the little man rose effortlessly into his saddle, slapped his horse affectionately on the flank, and continued his ride. Nathan looked after him for a moment, but Aaron Burr was completely hidden by the wide black back of his servant.

"The Colonel better keep an eye peeled," said Whirl at supper two nights later, "er he'll be a-nursin' a little Democrat bastard at his wife's bosom. I've he'erd tell Aaron Burr has a quicker trigger in his pants than you'll find on a pistol. He's laid more eggs in somebody else's nest than any cowbird in the Genesee Country."

"It isn't any of our business if he has," said Nathan sharply. "I respect him because he's stood up to Hamilton and Adams and he's defeated the fancy Federalist patroon Schuyler over in Albany. For that I'll forget any skirt lifting he's been up to."

"Seems like you two are a couple o' peas in a pod," said Whirl innocently, "though you'd make three o' him in size. 'Member I told ye he'd manufactured an extry half-breed or so up in the Kennebec Valley? An' they tell me he tried to git revenge on Benedict Arnold by growin' horns on 'em while takin' his pretty Tory wife to Philadelphy in a stagecoach."

"But why are we peas in a pod?" said Nathan impatiently.

"An Injun's an Injun," said Whirl, "a Tory's a Tory, whether he's fer the British er hell, married er single."

"I don't know what you're driving at."

"Guess I got mixed up then. Jest thought I seen some sort o' faint likeness," said Whirl rising from the table. "Must be goin' blind."

The next morning a boy brought Nathan an invitation from Colonel Williamson. Would Mr. Hart dine with him on the evening of the following day at five-thirty? Nathan accepted. He planned to go to Springfield House to find out if Peregrine and the others of his family were also invited, but a thunderstorm broke the warmth of the afternoon and ushered in an evening of such wind and rain that he did not leave his fireside.

When he tied Lottie outside the sprawling group of connected cabins that was Williamson's home yellow lamps were shining through the cool clear dusk from each house on the square. The heavy door swung open at his knock and a bowing servant took his hat. Colonel Williamson strode down the room to greet him.

"Welcome, Mr. Hart," he said jovially. "I am glad to be able to furnish you with such congenial company. Indeed, I'm hoping Senator Burr may help to modify the rigidity of your

political attitude. I find him more inclined to reason than most
Democrats."

"And I find our host singularly democratic for a Federalist,"
said Aaron Burr laughing lightly. "So far he has not said he
wished to rule his Genesee Country from a throne."

He shook Nathan's hand, and the warmth and charm of
his greeting seemed to permeate the room.

"We are awaiting the arrival of Major Fitzhugh and his
sister," said Williamson. "I shall have beauty on my side then,
though we shall still be outnumbered."

As he spoke there was the sound of voices outside and a
moment later the door opened again. Eleanor Fitzhugh swept
into the room, her eyes sparkling, her cheeks showing deep rose
beneath the clear brown of her skin. Nathan had never seen
her so radiant and alert. She bowed briskly with smiling lips
as Williamson presented Aaron Burr, and she stepped forward
and greeted Nathan eagerly and with friendly intimacy. Peregrine followed her lazily, in his usual slow good humor.

A servant said dinner was ready and the host, flushing a
little, said, "Madame Williamson has asked me to give you her
cordial greetings. Unhappily she is not well enough to join us."

It seemed to Nathan whose glance rested that moment on
Burr that he saw on the handsome face the faintest sign of
surprise and displeasure. Even as it appeared it was gone and,
with ineffable grace, the bland guest of honor was offering his
arm to Eleanor. As Peregrine and Nathan closed in behind
them in the march to the dining room the latter was glad to
notice that the girl was almost three inches taller than her
partner. Peregrine looked at them, then at Nathan's lank height,
and winked. Behind them Colonel Williamson moved in stately
grace, conversing with facile tongue:

"You may be pleased to know that our dinner this evening,
save for the wine, was grown entirely from the soil of the
Genesee Country—the ham, the beef, the turkey, the beets, the
salad, and the pudding."

At dinner the talk was gay. Williamson with mock solem-
nity declared that he had news of serious and ominous import
to Mr. Hart—another painter had bought lands beside the
Genesee and expected to occupy them soon. He was none other
than the famous Colonel John Trumbull.

"I trust," said Nathan, "that I can outdo him at farming by as much as he excels me at the easel."

"Nonsense," said Burr delightedly. "Trumbull is no artist. He has not one-tenth the talent of John Vanderlyn, to whom I have had the honor of being patron. Trumbull was a good soldier, though two strict a disciplinarian. Now he is a crochety, self-centered old pretender. I'll guarantee his portraits are worse than Mr. Hart's no matter how bad they be." He smiled at Nathan mischievously.

"He will be a welcome addition to our population," Williamson said happily, "and his coming encourages the plans we have already discussed. No state will have within its borders so select a company as we shall draw to the valley of the Genesee."

"We are all good friends here," said Burr, "and all hope for the prosperous future of the land. I am sure you could tell us more of these plans since we have already discussed them together."

Williamson looked startled and uncertain for a moment. His glance wandered about the table and he did not speak.

"Come," said Burr pleasantly, "surely there is no harm in telling your adherents and fellow countrymen here your ambitions for the improvement of their community."

"You will be surprised," said Williamson, leaning forward then and addressing himself to Peregrine and Eleanor, "to discover that I am already deep in my arrangements for an enterprise which will take place a little more than a year from now. I am planning for September of 1796 a great Genesee Country Fair."

"But why not have it this year?" said Eleanor.

"It is already too late for the kind of undertaking on which I am planning to engage—a fair of such proportions that it will lure patrons from all the fifteen states and from Canada as well. I shall announce in all the newspapers of our large cities that gentlemen are invited to bring their fastest horses to compete on the new racecourse at Bath. I have planned a large theater and expect to employ a fine company of players to perform in it. Our best farm animals will be shown, there will be games to be enjoyed, and there will be everywhere evidence of the abundance of riches and beauty and opportunity in the Genesee Country. Every detail will be calculated to have its influence on the gentleman of means and his family. I shall send courteous guides in each direction to the cities nearest us, to bring in companies of gentlemen and their families who will attend. And once these good people have seen how perfectly this land is suited to division into large country seats I shall have no difficulty in completing my labors as the administrator of the Pultney lands."

"It's a glorious idea," said Eleanor, enthusiastically.

The eyes of Colonel Williamson seemed to catch fire from her words and to glow with a blue flame. Aaron Burr leaned forward. There was a tenseness about him and his words were clipped and eager.

"And then?"

Again Colonel Williamson hesitated. He glanced down at his plate, his eyelids quivering slightly.

"I will tell you myself what then," said Burr triumphantly. "Once we have filled this region with citizens of the best type this nation boasts, the Genesee Country shall apply for independent statehood. This country has no common interest with the shopkeepers of New York or the penny-pinching Dutch bargainers of Albany. It shall be a greater Virginia, a finer Massachusetts."

"But Mr. Burr," said the slow, easygoing voice of Peregrine Fitzhugh, "how would you reconcile this idea with your political beliefs? You would be establishing an aristocratic state?"

"You misunderstand me," said Burr eagerly. "Every state desires to have as its citizens people of education and of virtue. Such a state as we contemplate—" his smile included Williamson as his partner in this idea—"would function more easily than any other on the principles of a democratic Republic. The fate of Democracy rests upon the intelligence of the masses and their ability to use their intelligence to govern themselves."

"The people whom I would lure to this land of lakes and fertile river bottoms," said Williamson, quickly availing himself of Burr's pause at the end of a sentence, "are members of families already well established in this country, men of property, gentlemen of leisure, ladies who are accustomed to polite usages."

"And these paragons," interrupted Peregrine Fitzhugh, drawling again, "are capable of keener political thought than,

let us say, the poor apprentices, the shopkeepers, the dirty
Dutchmen of Albany and New York?"

"Naturally," said Williamson.

Aaron Burr laughed—a little artificially it seemed to Nathan
—and plunged on.

"I'm afraid I would not entirely agree with Colonel Williamson," he said, "but I'll leave it to my friend and fellow Republican here, Mr. Hart, to answer whether or not a community
may rightfully try to improve itself by attracting families of
learning and refinement."

"Of course it may," said Eleanor Fitzhugh excitedly, her
head nodding, her eyes aglow. "Oh, Nathan, say it may."

All the men laughed. Nathan was pleased almost to an
ecstasy by the proud girl's sudden deference. This was the first
time she had called him "Nathan," and the fact that she had
done so in a moment of enthusiasm gave him reason to think
that she thought of him by the intimacy of his first name. He
was still smiling as he spoke.

"I can see no objection to it," he said, "providing each
citizen may have his voice in the government."

Eleanor clapped her hands while Peregrine groaned in mock
anguish. "The spider has caught the fly," he said, half in earnest.
"The web is so delicate it is hardly visible, but it holds with
the strength of iron chains."

"Are you still perverse?" said Burr smiling, "when even a
Republican-Democrat senator assures you that his party principles are not violated by the scheme?"

"This land shall be an Arcadia," said Eleanor dreamily,
"and we shall live happy in it beside our lakes and rivers."

"I had scarcely dared suggest the plan," said Williamson.
"Mr. Burr and I have talked of nothing else for two whole
days. Now that you all approve, with the exception of Major
Fitzhugh" (he bowed to Peregrine), "I am inspired to re-
doubled efforts toward the success of my great fair. I shall see
to it that no gentleman of fashion in all the countryside shall
dare absent himself. The flower of Philadelphia, the cream of
New York, the—"

There was a slow knocking at the great door of the house.
The sound broke ominously upon their mood, echoing hollowly
through the big room they had left and reaching the dining

room with an overtone of dread. The diners were silent listening to the hasty tread of a servant, the groan and bump of the door swinging back on its hinges. They heard the low expostulations of the servant rising in pitch and volume as the unseen visitor evidently became more insistent; then followed a sharp exclamation and a quick padding sound growing louder in the big room. Suddenly the door of the dining room was flung open and a white woman in the buckskin skirt and shirt of an Indian came in. She walked swiftly to the head of the table and stood looking down at Williamson who was slowly preparing to rise. Her head and shoulders seemed set slightly forward at the top of her short, slim figure—as if for years they had been straining against weights greater than her own. Her face was sharp-featured and deep-lined. Her hair, dark brown and streaked with gray, hung in two short braids in front of her ears.

"The White Woman," said Williamson in amazement as he rose to his feet.

"Aye," said the woman, "if you like. I am Deh-he-wa-mis, wife of Hiokatoo of the Senecas. You know me. I am Mary Jemison. I live on the flats of the Genesee."

"We are honored by the visit of Mary Jemison," said Williamson calmly and pleasantly, "and we shall be happy if she will sit and eat with us."

The woman looked at him intently.

"Your people are dying at Ganundasage," she said. "Ebenezer Allen—Indian Allen—told me but he would do nothing. They need doctors. Dr. Adams is sick. Dr. Coventry came from across the lake and now he is sick. They say Polydore Wisner, Deodat Allen, Peter Bortle, and Gamaliel Wilder will not live."

"Surely you are mistaken," said Williamson smoothly. "I returned from Geneva—Ganundasage—only a few days ago and all were well; a few cases of the fever perhaps, but—"

"This is no Genesee fever," said the woman, "it is a plague. My husband calls it Onoityiyende and says it comes from witches. Three women and a man are dead in the houses at the bottom beside the lake."

"Have they no help at all?" said Aaron Burr anxiously.

"Kirkland, the missionary to the Oneidas, was there when it began. Some of his Indians have joined him. They help."

"Indians from his school?" said Nathan.

The woman looked at him.

"I have seen you," she said. "You did not know it. You had the Genesee fever. It was at Squawkie Hill."

"Who is with him?" said Nathan excitedly.

"She is there."

"Who?" said Eleanor Fitzhugh.

"He knows," said the woman darkly.

"I must get doctors at once," said Williamson. "I hope, Miss Fitzhugh, that you and our other honored guest, Mr. Burr, will forgive my leaving the table. I must call Dr. Stockton."

"I will ride to Faulkner's after Dr. Schulz." Peregrine Fitzhugh quietly rose and walked from the room.

"They will need help," said Mary Jemison. "I am riding to Ganundasage."

"I regret that it is impossible for me to go," said Aaron Burr, "but, as Colonel Williamson knows, I must join my daughter and the rest of my party at the falls of the Genesee tomorrow. I have already kept them waiting for a day."

"You are most generous," said Williamson, "but I think it unnecessary for any of us to go, once the doctors have been despatched. There are many good, kind people near Geneva who will assist. Now if you will excuse me . . ." He followed Peregrine Fitzhugh.

"I am going," said Nathan.

"You mustn't," Eleanor's voice was sharp and determined. "It isn't necessary. The doctors will do all that is needed."

Once more Nathan was elated by the girl's forgetfulness of her usual cool decorum and her evident regard for him. For a moment he contemplated the delight he would experience in riding home with her beside the little moonlit river. Then he looked into the eyes of Mary Jemison.

"I'm going," he said shortly, as if the white woman had questioned him.

"But why?" said Eleanor. "Only the doctors will go from here. You have just heard Colonel Williamson say you need not."

Nathan smiled at her.

"I'm afraid I have to make my own decision," he said, "and I've made it."

Eleanor's eyes flashed angrily.

"You are rude," she said. "You enjoy contradicting men who are your superiors."

"You don't understand," said Nathan confusedly.

"I understand too well. I can't understand how my brother endures your dangerous theories and your worse manners. You have poisoned his mind against his elders and given him the ideas of a Leveler."

She walked to the door and turned to look back.

"I am returning to Springfield House alone," she said. "I shall find it a pleasanter residence during the next few days at least." She was gone.

Aaron Burr looked at Nathan quizzically.

"I don't know that you are interested, my young friend, but you may take the word of an old campaigner that a besieged force talks most belligerently when about to surrender."

While he was speaking a woman had entered the room. Nathan saw with surprise that she was Mrs. Williamson. With flushed face and downcast eyes she walked slowly to the table. Ignoring Nathan and Mary Jemison she stood before Aaron Burr and spoke in her low-pitched sullen voice.

"My husband tells me you have been left alone. He asks me to express his regrets and to beg you to continue your interrupted dinner in my company if you wish it."

The little man's eyes flashed. With the manner of seating a princess he conducted her to a chair beside his own and bowed as she sat on it.

Mary Jemison turned. Her moccasined feet took her from the room so swiftly that she seemed suddenly to have vanished. Nathan followed and, turning at the door to say a farewell if it were expected of him, saw Aaron Burr seated beside Mrs. Williamson, gazing fixedly at her. As if compelled by a psychic force the bowed blonde head was slowly lifting. The two looked into each other's eyes. Nathan went on without speaking.

III

Nathan heard only the hooting of owls and the occasional howl
of a wolf on the long ride through the night. Mary Jemison
rode steadily, silently, and he followed at a regular pace, keeping her always in sight. Reflections of the stars lay in the inky
depths of Canandaigua Lake when they reached its shores.
Dawn began somewhere ahead of them as they neared the town.
By the time they had reached it the water was gray, and a pile
of light-bordered clouds hanging above the eastern hills seemed
about to burst into flame. As they passed Thomas Morris's tall
house Nathan grinned, remembering the fantastic dinner party
during the treaty negotiations. He wondered if Morris had heard
of the plague at Geneva.

It was almost noon when they saw the huge white mass
of Williamson's Tavern rising against the soft blue of the spring
sky. Mary Jemison turned in her saddle and looked at Nathan.

"I thought you'd come," she said with a trace of a smile
on her sharp, grim face. "The Cornplanter told me you could
be depended on."

Nathan felt a warm glow of pleasure that the Seneca chief
had spoken well of him.

"His daughter once saved my life."

"She is a good girl," said the white woman. "I know white
folks and I know Indian folks. She is better than most."

"You like Indians better than whites, don't you?" said
Nathan, urging his mare forward that he might ride beside her.

"I made my choice," said Mary Jemison, "and I never
regretted it. I always liked the Indians—that is after the first
year or so when I was a prisoner. I was only sixteen then."

"Why did you choose to stay with them?"

"A man."

"Are you still his wife?" She looked at her questioner sharply. Her mouth tightened.

"No," she said. "He died."

"I'm sorry."

"Now I have Hiokatoo . . . He is good and kind and a fine man."

They were riding on the high ridge along the lake. The big hotel loomed above them. Below on the flat bottom land beside the water huddled the cabins of the earliest settlers. The cracks between the logs of the walls had been filled in with whitish clay. They looked, thought Nathan, like a picture he had seen once in a geography—a herd of zebras resting beside a water-hole.

"That's where the trouble is," said Mary Jemison. "They need us down there."

"You've had a long ride," said Nathan. "You'd better get some rest."

The woman snorted with contempt.

"I walked from the Ohio to the Genesee with my new child in my arms after my first husband died. Do you think this is harder?"

She swung her horse to the right and urged it down the shelving slope. Below them a dozen little fires were burning in the spaces between the cabins. Smoke was pouring from each chimney. A bundled figure hastened from one door to another. A few minutes later the riders were on the narrow street between the cabins and the shore of the lake. They halted and tied their horses.

A door opened and Catherine O'Bail came out to them. Nathan was surprised that she gave him no greeting. He had expected the same look of warm affection in her eyes that had marked their last meetings. Now she was grave and direct, wasting no time.

"We need vinegar to wet the blankets," she said. "Mr. Kirkland said it would prevent the spread of the disease if it proves contagious."

"I'll get some at the hotel," said Nathan.

"They won't let you," said Catherine. "They're afraid to let anybody from down here come up there."

"I'll get it," said Nathan and strode away.

Fat Thomas Powell came out on the porch and waved him back.

"You can't come 'ere," he shouted.

"Roll me a keg of vinegar down those steps or I'll come up there and roll you all the way to the bottom."

"There ain't enough for my guests as it is."

"I'm coming."

"No, no, I'll roll it. Stay right where you are."

In a minute the keg was tumbling down the steps. Nathan picked it up and started off down the hill at a slow trot.

Catherine looked surprised and smiled when she opened the door and saw him standing there.

"I'll get a tub," she said. "De-heh-wa-mis has gone to get all the blankets."

She rolled a wooden tub out of the door, went back into the house, and returned with an ax. Nathan set the keg in the middle of the tub and split it. The vinegar gurgled out. The White Woman was staggering toward them loaded down with blankets. Nathan took them from her and laid them in the tub.

As he did so the White Woman turned to Catherine.

"I can cure this," she said. "I think I can."

"How?"

"The medicine man's spell against Onoityiyende."

Catherine stamped her foot in impatience.

"A superstition," she said, "while people are dying."

"It cured me once. I have seen it cure others."

"What is it?" said Nathan.

"A brew. I took it for nine days and I was well."

"They wouldn't take it," said Catherine.

"I'll find it first," said the White Woman. "After that somebody may take it." She walked off toward a grove of trees that grew down to the lake's edge.

While the blankets soaked in the vinegar Catherine led Nathan into the cabin. As he entered the smell within stifled him. He coughed, strangling on the odor. On a husk bed in the corner lay a bearded man. His eyes were open and glittering with fever.

"Do you feel better, Peter Bortle?" said Catherine.

"Of course he doesn't," said a querulous, high-pitched voice from another corner. Peering through the half-light of the cabin Nathan saw a hatchet-faced white woman regarding him intently. "The doctor's too busy to see him and he don't know nothin' anyway. It's a fine how-de-do when the only person with human kindness in 'em turns out to be a heathen savage. Everybody's locked himself up in his house and won't come out. I declare I don't know what to do."

"Help is coming," said Nathan shortly, angered at her reference to Catherine.

The Indian girl walked up to the woman and put her hands on her shoulders. Gently she forced her to sit on a wooden settle by the fire. The woman burst into tears.

The man on the bed began to thrash about, his arms and legs moving in swift, uncontrollable jerks. His lips stretched taut showing his teeth in an animal-like snarl. His tongue protruded from his mouth and a hoarse rattling sound came from his throat. With swift, silent strides Catherine went to him, lifted his head, and spoke soothing words. Suddenly his emaciated frame grew rigid. His eyes protruded from their sockets. There was a moment of utter agony and then a snapping noise as if some sinew had been stretched beyond the breaking point. As the limp body dropped, seeming to flow into the irregular hollows of the bed beneath it, Nathan knew that the man was dead. The wife stopped her weeping and looked dully at her husband. There was a long moment of silence. Catherine looked down on the inert figure in dismay and horror. Then the woman spoke in her dry, harsh voice.

"I'm goin' with him," she said. "I've had it fer a day already but I'd not be worritin' him with it. Nobody'll have to take up no collection fer me now."

She rose to her feet slowly and Nathan could see that her physical endurance was at an end. The whites of her eyes were yellowish and bloodshot and the pupils held a beady glitter. She took four steps forward and fell across the body of her man.

Mary Jemison entered the cabin. In her two hands she carried a dozen brown and white sheets of wrinkled bark. She broke them and stuffed the pieces into the kettle of hot water that hung simmering above the embers in the fireplace. From beneath her shirt she drew a doeskin bag and untied the leather thongs about its neck.

"You are too late for the man," said Catherine O'Bail, "but his wife is sick now."

The older woman nodded without speaking. Her fingers went into the bag and came out crooked about a brown, thickly granulated substance. She dropped to her knees before the fire and cast the stuff on the flames. At once the room filled with the odor of burning tobacco.

"*Esnwaiyigwa shownie odeha*," chanted Mary Jemison. Then the clear voice of the Indian girl joined in:

> "*Dyasawa goduk Hawenio*
> *Cici dade gaoya geteiojo.*"

To Nathan standing between the singing women at the fireplace and the sick wife lying quiet above the corpse, the scene was like a nightmare. He stood motionless for a long time, not knowing what to do, feeling that he might offend by moving. At last he heard a swelling of volume in the song and then the final word "*Daneho!*" At once Mary Jemison took the kettle from the fire and poured some of its contents into a tin cup on the table. She saw a bucket by the door and motioned to Catherine to get it and follow her. Then, cup in hand, she approached the woman on the bed.

"Here," she said, suddenly grabbing the woman by the shoulder and rolling her over, "drink this."

The widow sat up blinking dazedly. Obediently she put the cup to her lips and drank. Mary Jemison tilted the cup.

"Drink it all," she said sharply.

The liquid choked the woman and for the first time the taste of it reached her senses. She gagged and strangled but Mary Jemison was inexorable. Both her hands forced the lower edge of the cup strongly downward, though the woman clutched at it and tried to divert the stream pouring into her throat. With a great cough and a convulsive sidewise leap she finally got away.

"You've poisoned me," she cried.

"Maybe," said Mary Jemison. "Heard ye hollerin' you was goin' to die anyways. Probably this won't make no difference nohow."

The woman sat looking at her strangely. Suddenly her shoulders moved convulsively upward and a look of surprise and fear shot into her face. Swiftly Catherine presented the pail. In a minute it was nearly half full. Again and again the woman retched—struggling pitifully against the inevitable recurrent heavings. It was at least fifteen minutes before she lay still, white, and inert.

"Carry her to the other bed," said Mary Jemison sharply. Nathan, moving as if in a dream, did as he was told.

"Take his spade and bury that in the ground at least two feet deep," said Mary Jemison, and Catherine, holding the pail at arm's length, went out the door.

"Now go up to the hotel," said Mary Jemison to Nathan, "and tell 'em they've got a funeral to tend to. I'm goin' next door with some more o' this Injun liquor."

When Nathan came back down the hill the White Woman and Catherine were seated on the doorstep of the cabin next door.

"Won't let us in," said Mary Jemison.

A broad-shouldered man strode along the bottom land toward them. He was so tall that the cabins looked like toy houses as he came among them. He looked down at the lined face of the White Woman.

"What ye givin' 'em, Mary?" he said.

"Witch hopple," she said shortly. "I peeled the bark upwards an' I burned tobacco to make it work."

"Great God!" he said. "I druther die an' they probably will. Let's see 'em."

"Only one, so far, Tim," said the woman. "Get the young man to take ye in to see her. I'm stayin' here. Don't mind the man—he's dead."

"I'm Dr. Timothy Hosmer," said the tall man to Nathan. "Come along."

Inside the cabin the doctor put a hand over the dead man's heart and then closed his eyes. He walked over to the bed where the woman lay. She was sleeping peacefully and her cheeks had lost their sallow, sick look. He lifted her eyelids. The yellow had gone from around the pupils. The feverish glitter had disappeared. The woman waked.

"Let me be," she said fretfully.

"Jest a minute," said the doctor, poking at her to keep her awake. "Answer me a question. Has there been any time lately when most of the folks have had the same meal. A big shindig for the whole town or something like that?"

"No," said the woman. "Why should there be?"

The doctor was silent for a time.

"Is there any place 'round here where everybody gets his milk or his butter or his meat—one store where everybody trades?"

"There's three stores," said the woman. "But nobody keeps no meat. Everybody shoots his own. It's all hung together in the shed down by the water."

"Eureka!" shouted the doctor. "It's spiled meat, that's what it is. It ain't no cholera nor plague. It's pizened meat. No wonder that fool woman's tricks are workin'." He turned to Nathan. "Don't ever misbelieve an Injun trick," he said. "Most o' their tomfoolery turns out based on plain ordinary sense. Now let's get out o' here an' pour that damn witch-hopple beer down the throats o' Geneva. I'll make 'em cough up everything they got 'ceptin' my pay."

For the next three days the two men and two women worked almost without ceasing. Dr. Hosmer and Nathan appropriated the lakeside cabin of a lone settler who had died before they arrived. To be safe, at the doctor's suggestion, they had emptied their bed of its ill-smelling husks and burned them. They had cut balsam boughs for new bedding and they had white-washed the inside walls—all this late at night when their patients were likely to be sleeping and when they themselves were so tired that they dropped off into unconsciousness while at work. Mary Jemison had found a Seneca family living in a ramshackle cabin at the head of the lake, and its many occupants had somehow made room for her and Catherine O'Bail.

Every morning at sunrise the four had met at a cabin where there was work to do. Hosmer had succeeded after long argument in getting Mary Jemison to brew her emetic potion in the Indian cabin before daybreak and bring it to him in pails which he warmed at the firesides of the stricken. Mary had said it would not work unless brewed in the patient's home, but the strenuous, sometimes violent objections of the sick to swallowing "Injun magic" finally convinced her. She never failed to burn tobacco as he boiled the bark, however, nor to repeat her Seneca invocation, and she always insisted that Catherine chant

it with her. As soon as he began administering the medicine
from the pails the doctor began calling it "tartar emetic" and
his patients were better satisfied. "It don't sound so heathenish,"
said one and the rest agreed.

A man and a girl of sixteen died one day after they had
drunk of the healing draught. Apparently the poisons had so
weakened them that the exertion caused by the emetic resulted
in a complete and fatal collapse. At once gossip raced about
the town that Hosmer had poisoned them with Indian witch
potions. Dr. Schultz who arrived on that day from Williamsburg helped the rumor along by agreeing that the witch-hopple
bark was poisonous and more likely to kill than to cure. He
added that it was his belief that the disease, whatever it was,
was "catching" and that the settlers gave it to each other.

Emboldened by this a settler went down to the meatshed,
seized his quarter of beef which hung there, and started for
his cabin with it. Dr. Hosmer met him on the way, knocked him
down, and threw the meat in the lake. That night the doctor
and Nathan surreptitiously bore armloads of fat pine into the
meatshed and waited in its shadow until moondown. Then
Nathan ran to their cabin and brought back a few live coals
in the fire shovel. He and the doctor were in their beds before
the crackling of the blazing shed roof awakened their neighbors. Hearing shouts the conspirators rose and went out to see
the results of their plot. The shed burned to the ground and
cooked all the meat within it to a crisp. The next day two of
Dr. Schulz's patients died and the tide of public favor flooded
toward Hosmer again. The burning of the shed against which
many had muttered profanely in the morning had become a
heroic deed by nightfall and, though those who had done it did
not confess, most of the townspeople suspected them.

Catherine sat with Nathan on the bluff south of the big
hotel. The end of the third day had come and the sun was dropping swiftly toward the bank of clouds that seemed to rest on
the blue hills across the lake. Nathan was abruptly aware that
this was the first time he had been alone with the girl since his
arrival. He looked at her and was amazed at the sweet calm of
her face, the clear white and shiny black of her eyes, the firm
line of her mouth. She had worked untiringly and with only
a few hours sleep for three days, yet she seemed fresh and un-

wearied. The colors of her blanket skirt had faded and blended into each other, but it was clean. Her hair was neatly braided. He looked down at his stained shirt, his ash-covered breeches, his dirtied stockings.

"I don't understand it," he said. "I feel as tired and as filthy as I look. You've worked as hard but you're as easy as a new daisy."

She laughed delightedly.

"I am learning to be a good nurse at the school. Mr. Kirkland tells me what to do."

"I thought he was here," said Nathan. "They need him for all the burying."

Catherine's face grew solemn. "He did what he could. Then he was sick. He said he would not stay to make more trouble—he would go back to his home and let his Indian students take care of him. I hope he is well now."

A horseman was loping along the road to the hotel. There was no mistaking his identity. The blue cloak fluttered out behind and as always the tall figure sat straight as if on parade. Suddenly the rider saw the two sitting on the bluff and turned his horse toward them. In a moment he had reined up and was dismounting.

"I am more happy than I can say to see you both well," said Charles Williamson. "I came as soon as it was possible. Tom Morris delayed me for some hours in Canandaigua."

There was an awkward pause. Neither Nathan nor Catherine was able to think of a suitable reply. The man's words seemed completely out of keeping with all that they had just experienced. As if sensing their uncertainty Williamson went on quickly:

"I have heard already of Dr. Hosmer's miracles, in which I am sure you both bore part. I knew, of course, that these poor people suffered from no contagious disease. The Genesee Country is far too salubrious for that. Indeed, there is no part of the states where the health of citizens is at a higher level."

To Nathan, looking up, the tall man seemed to be speaking almost automatically. His eyes were fixed on Catherine and there was a look of suffering in them. In his face were taut lines that Nathan had never seen there before. Memory of what Catherine had told him of her former relationship with this man flooded into Nathan's brain. He is still in love with her, he thought. It is against his reason and his will—yet he cannot help loving her. Then his deductions were interrupted by further words, amazing words:

"I bear you a message, Mr. Hart. The lovely Miss Fitz-hugh, from whom you parted somewhat unceremoniously, bids me tell you have a care for yourself among the dangers that surround you. She bids me say she has repented the sharp words she spoke and that you will be a most welcome visitor at Springfield House next time you ride that way."

Catherine had risen to her feet when Williamson mentioned Eleanor and had stood facing him while he continued. Now she turned her eyes on Nathan and he was startled by their blazing intensity.

"That Maryland girl," she said slowly, and as if she were repeating a shocking epithet.

"Yes," said Williamson simply and looking at her directly and significantly.

Suddenly she was gone, racing down the slope in a shower of small stones dislodged by her swift feet.

"Catherine," Nathan called after her. She did not reply. While the two men stood stupidly looking after her she reached the flats by the water. In another instant she had dashed into the shed in which she had that morning tied her horse. Nathan turned his back on Williamson and began to walk down toward her. As he did so the horse bounded out of the shed. The girl bent low above him, her mouth close to his right ear. At once he settled into a long gallop along the hard gravelly surface beside the water. As they reached the curve at the head of the lake Catherine swung the racing animal into the west road. Green willows received them, hid them from sight.

Nathan turned. Williamson's face was impassive. The cold blue eyes were fixed on the point where the brown road entered the willows, but there seemed to be no expression within them.

"As I was saying," Williamson said dully, "you are eagerly awaited at Springfield House."

He swung onto his horse and rode a few yards toward the hotel. Then he wheeled about and trotted slowly back to Nathan.

"I had a talk with Mr. Gragg," he said, "before I left Bath.

I have been planning to build a sloop here this summer—a vessel large enough to carry heavy loads of supplies and many travelers who may prefer to come to Geneva by sail from the southern end of the lake. If you are willing to agree, Mr. Gragg will superintend the building of the craft and will captain her at her launching. I am planning to make that event a celebration for the entire Genesee Country." He was silent for a moment. Nathan stared at him.

"Well, Mr. Hart, do you agree?"

"Yes," said Nathan absently. The man uses his passion for this country as a refuge, he thought. No matter how deeply he may be troubled he can always turn to launchings and fairs and races, and forget.

"When the great crowds come for next year's biggest fair of all many of our prospective residents will sail into the port city of Geneva."

"Yes," said Nathan.

"It will be a beautiful sight," said Williamson happily. He reined his horse about and gently urged him forward. He had ridden slowly almost to the hotel before Nathan began his lonely walk back to the cabins by the lake.

IV

A kingbird had routed a robber crow from the limbs of a plane tree and now darted angrily above his clumsily flopping victim. Nathan, riding beside the drowsy Conhocton in the heat of mid-afternoon, watched the two of them out of sight. A little breeze set up against the current and the surface of the stream broke into ripples. There was a smell of tansy; then the air was still again and the river flowed smoothly. Lottie, plodding patiently in the deep dust of the road, lifted her head and whinnied. Down the straight road, perhaps a half mile, Nathan could see the familiar rise of land on which lay the path to Springfield House. He lolled in the saddle, letting his long legs drop from the stirrups and giving himself up to the lazy untroubled mood of the summer day. He tried to imagine the scene that was soon to take place.

Eleanor would come down the stair, looking like a tall young boy at a masquerade. She would look at him with the straight, slightly scornful glance that he had come to expect from her. Since she had sent him an apology she would probably shake his hand brusquely to confirm it. It is hard, Nathan thought, not to accept her at the valuation she puts upon herself, for she is honest and intelligent and she deserves respect. If it were not for Peregrine's easy way with her and his quizzical smile when he looks at her it would be impossible for me to see her in any other light than she sees herself. She is a Diana, a goddess bred from two generations of the easy life of the Maryland families and perhaps, back of those, more ancestors among the squires of English country life.

As he turned into the path toward the house a group of five little Negroes raced toward him with whoops of joy—then solemnly led Lottie to the mounting block before the big door. The old butler came out without awaiting his knock and ushered him into the hall. Then, white teeth shining from his black face, he disappeared into the depths of the house without announcing the new arrival. Nathan, standing hat in hand in the hall, realized that his coming had been anticipated. Minutes passed, however, and there was no sound within the house.

At length he heard the click of a latch from somewhere on the second floor, quick footsteps, and Eleanor Fitzhugh stood at the top of the stair. As Nathan gazed at her he was amused by his previous picturing of this moment. Here was no masquerading boy. The slimness of her body was hid in the full flow of a flowered tabinet gown. A smile trembled on her lips, spreading happy curves about her eyes and mouth. Slowly she came down the stair and her gaze was full on Nathan as she came. Not until she stood upon the floor below did he step forward. As he did she raised her hand and held it toward him as if she expected him to take it and bow over it. Embarrassed he attempted as best he could this manner of greeting. Her smile grew broader then and she spoke:

"I was hateful at that stupid dinner. I hope you have forgiven me."

Nathan looked long into the brown eyes, seeing a light there that pleased him. He wondered if he were beginning to understand this girl. The look of scorn was gone. Perhaps this was because he had disregarded her imperious assumption of power over him. The thought that his defiance might have struck fire within her filled him with surprising exultation.

"Shall we walk a while?" she said, and without waiting for an answer she went to the big door and opened it on a patch of starry sky. The last gray light of dusk hovered like smoke about the tall white pillars, but darkness had fallen on the slopes below.

They strolled across the clearing and entered the wood's shadow where a winding footpath slanted toward the river. They found the sky again beneath the ripple of water whence stars looked up out of a depth as vast as that above them. Nathan looked at the girl beside him and smiled. She was so straight and independent, both in her carriage and in her ways, that she gave the impression of continuous sturdy aggressiveness. Yet he knew now that under her imperious manner at times lay an arch and pliant femininity which she strove eagerly to hide.

"Peregrine and Colonel Thornton go back to Maryland tomorrow," she said. "Father is so pleased with their reports of this country that he plans to come here as soon as travel is easy in the spring. Colonel Williamson has commissioned my brother to sell lands to our friends in the South. He hopes many of them will come to the Genesee Country with him."

Nathan walked on a while without speaking. The prospect of losing the company of Peregrine through the autumn and winter was disheartening. Except for Whirl Gragg he had come to care more for this wry-mouthed, loosehinged Southerner than for any other man in all Williamson's Woods. Loneliness struck at his heart as he realized that the long evenings of good wine and thoughtful talk at Springfield House had come to an end. As if she were reading his thoughts the girl at his side spoke again:

"My uncle and I would be honored if you would consider us as much your friends as Peregrine," she said, and there was a dogged note in her voice—as if she were trying to get something said for results that would bring pleasanter moments than this. "We want you to come to see us as often as ever."

Nathan smiled again as he thought of fat Jonas Hogmire giggling to himself in his chair beside the fireplace. Give him a listener, any listener, and a pitcher of liquor, and he would be happy.

"Why are you amused?" said Eleanor Fitzhugh. Her voice was low and her eyes sought Nathan's in a sidelong look.

"Would you be willing to take your brother's place?" he said. "Your uncle is not inclined to associate with a man of my political temper."

"You would not ask me to sacrifice my own convictions," said the girl, looking down at the water streaked by the image of the Milky Way, "but I would take my brother's place."

At this he stopped and, turning to her, put both hands upon her shoulders. She stood straightly, almost against him, and the long oval of her face was upturned and her eyes were bright.

"I love your brother," he said.

She was silent and she did not move. It was as if she knew that, having set a course, the consequences were inevitable and she need only wait.

Nathan put his mouth against hers. Her lips were cool and sweet.

"Eleanor," he said, and he put both arms about her and kissed her again. A little shudder shook the slim form in the heavy gown. Then she drew away from him and looked directly into his eyes.

"Perhaps we had better return to the house now," she said. She turned from him and hastened up the path. She said nothing to Nathan's puzzled protests, but when she arrived at the foot of the steps she stopped and waited for him, holding her left hand out behind her. Hands locked together they walked up the steps and through the big door. Only when they entered the drawing room and saw Peregrine standing there grinning in knowing fashion did Eleanor loose her clasp.

V

That was the summer Squire Fred Bartles built the two arks
on Mud Creek. Whirl went over from Bath and offered expert
advice if he and Nathan might ship their crops free. The squire
agreed and so Nathan was left alone to harvest the hemp and
tobacco down by the river. He made a hard work of it. The
hemp rake became incredibly heavy before night and the hot
sun of late summer made him dizzy by noontime, but he stayed
at work doggedly.

Then one evening Eleanor came down the stair and found
him asleep in a chair by the fire. Laughingly she waked him and
accused him of a lack of ardor. But the next day when he went
down to the fields, dreading the pain of more long hours, he
found there five black slaves skillfully completing the work he
had expected to be doing throughout the next week. He protested to Jonas Hogmire and his niece, but the fat man pooh-
poohed him, obviously willing to take the credit of a kind deed
though not quite sure what it was, and Eleanor put her long
smooth fingers against his lips silencing his feeble remonstrance.

When Whirl returned he was full of praise for the look
of the harvest and Nathan said nothing about how it had been
accomplished. Squire Bartles's arks were ready, Whirl said, and
he had been made captain of the fleet. Perhaps, he said wistfully, they could hire somebody to look after things and Nathan
could at last make the trip to Baltimore. But Nathan shook his
head, remembering with a shudder the agony of a year ago when
it had seemed to him that Rachel's weakness had destroyed all
hope of happiness for him until death.

Now he realized that the prospect of the autumn and winter
in Bath was pleasing. There would be work to do—and after
it the ride to Springfield House, and Eleanor waiting. Suddenly
he realized that he had come to love the little, twenty-cabin

town that lay in the shadow of the great bluff across he river. The strange antagonisms and uncertain fears which his arrest and escape had caused were almost as if they had never been, or as if they had been the emotions of a character of whom he had read. And his later differences with Charles Williamson and Thomas Morris and Eleanor Fitzhugh—these had lost importance. He belonged in this gay river town. The wild horns blowing, the crazy beat of drums, and the shouts of young men about the flaring fires in the square made a happy background through which he rode nightly to seek beyond them all the smile of a woman.

The men of Bath, the carpenters and farmers and tavernkeepers, had come to accept him now almost as one of them. From his first appearance with Charles Williamson and from the fact that Williamson and Morris treated him with obvious respect, they had been uncertain about him. When they had found out that he was a school teacher turned portrait painter they had been reserved and shy. But his friendship with Peregrine Fitzhugh and the residents of Springfield House had placed him in their minds as a young fellow who by artistic achievement had won a place above the station to which he had been born, and they were happy over it. They had all heard that he stuck up for his Democrat-Republican principles even in the midst of his aristocratic Federalist companions, and this had delighted them. As more and more of the Susquehanna raftsmen and farmers had settled in and near Bath the anti-Federalist sentiment grew stronger and stronger. Charles Williamson was no longer the unquestionable God of the Genesee Country and many of his devotees had fallen away. Both Whirl and Elijah (now Judge Parker) had encouraged the popular conception of Nathan.

"Mebbe he's a leetle long for sociability," said Whirl, "but when he lets out a word up thar, it's a good 'un."

"A Gideon without a trumpet," said Elijah cryptically, but everybody who heard him decided that he meant to be complimentary.

When Nathan rode through the dusk on the way to Springfield House that autumn the early roisterers in the square would greet him shyly.

"Hello, Nate," they would say, grinning up at him. "How much ye expect Whirl'll git fer our wheat to Baltimore?"

"More'n the measly six shillings you can get around here," Nathan would say, and the men would laugh and shake their heads sociably.

Peregrine's departure did not cause as much of a sense of loss as Nathan had anticipated. He was surprised at how easily and quickly the pattern of life at Springfield House was adjusted to the absence of two of its usual occupants. Jonas Hogmire was always giggling over his brandy in the drawing room when Nathan arrived. There had been awkward moments in his conversations with the fat man, for the colonel was intolerant of democratic ideas and felt that the country was honeycombed with mad French terrorists. Gradually the two learned to avoid talk of politics. Hogmire's other favorite subject was the breeding of horses and he never failed to remark upon "that incredible phenomenon," his guest's long-backed mare. Nathan was sometimes uneasy when his frank dissertations on Lottie's strange antecedents continued long after Eleanor entered the room. The girl seemed not at all annoyed, however, waiting patiently until her uncle finished his embarrassing anatomical remarks before she welcomed Nathan and offered him refreshment.

Always, if the night were clear, Eleanor and Nathan walked beside the river before he left. They saw the beginning of the fall of leaves, the last yellow gleam of them on the black water, and the lace of bare limbs reflected in the light of December's new moon. They heard the choked gurgling that followed the autumn rains, the hiss of heavy snow upon the surface, and the sharp cracking of thick ice on evenings when a south wind brought abatement of January's bitter cold.

And always, when they returned to the house and warmed themselves beside the fire and drank some hot and heady mixture prepared by the grinning black butler, Eleanor would stand close to Nathan as he said goodnight in the hall, and he would put his arms around her and feel the shiver of her as his lips rested on hers. That shiver he thought was a promise of something more, perhaps—on a moment when she should decide to let it be. And he was willing to wait for that time to come, for he was troubled in his mind and heart about this girl. Sometimes he thought he loved her, and then he would dream of long, happy, sunny days with Eleanor, straight and eager, sometimes rebellious, by his side. But he always woke from this vision with the unhappy, uncertain feeling that she would never feel as he felt about life and its purposes. And so, perhaps because of his doubting, the moment of further surrender did not come, though the river broke its ice bonds on a warm noon in February, though there were hours in March that went masked as golden days of mid-April.

Whirl came back late in December faithfully bearing Nathan's share of the profits from their harvest though he had spent all of his own. His return with Squire Bartles had been the occasion of great rejoicing and drunkenness at Bath, for the cargo of the arks had been sold for good prices at the end of Susquehanna water. A thousand pounds of cheese had brought a shilling and sixpence a pound, wool had brought five shillings a pound, hemp tuppence a pound, rye five shillings and sixpence a bushel. It was a good three days before the horn blowing and drum beating abated to its usual irregularity, and by that time many a farmer had drunk up most of the returns of his reaping.

Colonel Williamson rode over from Geneva as soon as he heard of Bartles's arrival and collected such payments on the farms as he could. Many of the settlers paid then and there for half of their lands, though their contracts did not call for that much until three years had passed. The Colonel was triumphant. Bath, he said, would soon be the great city of the Western Lands. All the vast harvests from the Genesee to the Ohio would be brought here to be shipped down to Chesapeake Bay. He urged the settlers who had just received money for their crops to invest in more land. They could have six years' credit if they made small down payments. They need not begin to pay interest on their mortgages for eighteen months. In just a few years every man who bought land now would be master of hundreds of acres—lord of an estate. The men cheered and trooped to the Captain's office to sign for more property—but they saved out enough money to celebrate the purchases with a night's wild carouse.

VI

Whirl had been back some weeks before he spoke to Nathan of his father and mother.

"I went up to the farm on the hill while Bartles was in Philadelphy," he said one bitterly cold morning after he and Nathan had eaten their breakfast.

"Why didn't you tell me?" said Nathan in surprise.

"Been tryin' t'git up gumption. Dunno how t'say it 'ceptin' straight out. Yer maw's dead."

There was a long silence in the cabin. Whirl went about the few chores of the morning and left Nathan sitting by the fire. Nearly an hour went by before Whirl spoke again.

"The old man won't live nowhere else. Tried to git him to come along o' me but he said no. Said to tell ye he was doin' all right and not to worry none. Can't work the place no more, an' he said if you wasn't gittin' along too good t'come on back an' he'd deed the whole farm over to ye. Said he ain't goin' t'live more'n a year or so an' ye wouldn't begrudge him his vittles."

Tears came to Nathan's eyes. He hurried from the cabin and walked swiftly down to the shore of the little river. It was so firmly locked in deep ice he could hear no sound of moving water. The loneliness of his father in the stone farmhouse moved him as deeply as the loss of his mother. He had known that such a message must come eventually, yet that fact proved weak armor now. His mind pictured scenes of his boyhood— his mother standing in the sun-dappled doorway calling him to come from plowing the field below—his mother turning away from him suddenly after she had told him to be a good boy and do what the wagonmaker man in Pittsburgh said—his mother holding a gleaming white cake aloft and smiling. He was surprised to find himself weeping. Tears were cold upon his cheeks and his chest heaved again and again in quick and uncontrollable sobs.

Now she was gone and the old man was alone, unable to plow or reap, living a dreary round of days. Nathan yearned to see him. Perhaps it would be better to give up this new life and go back. The hill farm would just about make a living. He shivered, aware that he had come out into the cold without his greatcoat. Then Whirl stood beside him.

"One thing the old feller said I forgot about. After he told me ye could have the place he said 'He'll never take it though. That boy ain't never backtracked yit an' he won't be startin' now.' "

Whirl waited a moment, then put a hand on Nathan's sleeve. "Colder'n Jehosophat," he said. "We better be gittin' back."

That night Nathan told Eleanor the news Whirl had brought. When he came to the old man's offer of the farm she looked at him quickly and with an expression he could not understand.

"You aren't going," she said.

"I thought of it."

"You own land here. You will own more. You will have high place here both as a planter and as an artist."

"The Pennsylvania farm would bring me a living," he said defensively.

Her eyes flashed and the old look of scorn returned.

"You and your farms," she exclaimed derisively. "Can't you get your mind above dirt and animals and what you call a living? This country gives you an opportunity to own thousands of acres. In twenty years the Genesee Country will equal the finest plantation lands of the South. Colonel Williamson is no dunce. Give us time here and we will build houses finer than this, finer than General Washington's Mount Vernon. Each one will stand in the midst of an estate. You have your choice now between being a white overseer and a gentleman."

"I'll be an overseer," Nathan said coldly.

"I believe it," she said fiercely. "You haven't the quality of a gentleman. You'd rather spend your days with that silly little bald clown of yours than associate with the men of this house or with Mr. Morris or Colonel Williamson. Oh, I don't understand you! These gentlemen respect you. They are willing to take you in as one of them. And you rebuff them—you who could own lands and a fine house and slaves and—"

Nathan rose from his chair beside the fire. He could feel the blood leaving his face, the sick helplessness of being fiercely angry with a woman.

"I'll keep my station in the future," he said. "I prefer it—as you say. You needn't trouble yourself about my association with gentlemen, for I shall not continue it. The bald little clown is worth the lot of them."

Suddenly Eleanor burst into tears. Nathan was startled and alarmed. He had not believed it possible for her to show such emotion. Involuntarily he stepped toward her, and as he did so she rose and threw her arms about him, clutching him convulsively and sobbing on his breast.

"You fool! You fool!" she said. "You just won't understand."

1796

"This Sylvan Home"
(Charles Williamson)

I

It was a different Nathan who rode beside Conhocton water in that spring of 1796. He had taken his savings and nearly all the money Whirl had brought him from Baltimore over to Williamson's office one day in February. There he had had a long talk with the Colonel about buying more land. It had not been entirely satisfactory, for the Land Agent had done his best to sell him lots in the unbuilt city of Bath. Eagerly he had brought out plans showing the wide streets, the river docks, and—at the corner of Morris and Steuben Streets, the big log theater which was to be built that very summer. The city lots would more than double in price, he said, during the Genesee Fair in September. Thousands of visitors would be clamoring for them, then, and there was no knowing how high prices would go.

When Nathan suggested that he preferred tillable soil the Colonel became even more charming and cordial and, with the air of an old personal friend doing a very special favor, he suggested that he confer the title of five thousand acres of his own best bottom land on Nathan. The money at hand would serve to secure him the use of these for a six-year period, and by that time they would have paid for themselves and brought him a handsome profit as well.

Nathan insisted that he wished to buy his land outright and Williamson at once became less intimate in manner and not so inclined to part with his more fertile acres. He was surprised and pleased, however, when Nathan insisted on including in his purchase twenty acres of wooded upland. It had not occurred to him that a prospective buyer would be interested in timbered slopes and he was willing to sell them at a shilling an acre.

Nathan rode away proudly, the possessor of the slope be-bind his home and two hundred acres of bottom adjoining the land which he owned in partnership. He found Whirl in the fields and told him what he had done. The little man was delighted.

"Corn'll grow so fast in that muck it'll be ticklin' yer feet while ye sow," he said. "An' I know a hired hand that'll do the sowin' for ye ef'n ye want to take him on."

Nathan told Eleanor about his action and she had at first been pleased. But when he told her of Williamson's other offers she had been stirred to anger.

"Why must you always plod like a peasant?" she said, her eyes flashing. "You could have owned five thousand acres as easily and as surely as two hundred," and the evening had ended as many did that spring in a coolness between them and no kisses at the doorway when Nathan said good night.

II

"Gentlemen," said Charles Williamson, rising from his seat at the head of his long table and looking about him, "I have invited you here to consider affairs important to us all. September is nearer than we think and our plans for the Great Fair of the Genesee Country will brook no further delay."

"Hear, hear," said Thomas Morris from his seat at the Colonel's left, looking about him brightly at Jonas Hogmire, Nathan Hart, John Johnson, Thomas Powell, Sheriff Dunn, and the enormous bulk of the guest of honor, Colonel Jonathan Trumbull.

"Within the next few weeks," said the Colonel, consulting the manuscript held in his right hand, "I will have stationed at Utica, Albany, and New York City on the east; at Northumberland, Easton, Harris's Ferry, Carlisle, Lancaster, Philadelphia, Baltimore, Alexandria, and Richmond on the south; and at Montreal, Quebec, Niagara, and Presque Isle on the north—trusty and civil guides who will meet and conduct gentlemen and their suites to this far-famed city upon the upper waters of the Susquehanna, in the lands of crystal lakes and memorial parks, located at the garden home of the lately vanquished Six Nations, whose dominions formerly extended from Canada to the Potomac and beyond."

"Gad," said Jonas Hogmire, "the man should write romances."

"Gentlemen owning fleet horses, wherever they may be," Williamson continued, waving his left hand for silence, "are cordially invited to come with their families and friends, their wives and daughters, and enjoy the hospitalities of this sylvan home."

"And lose their fortunes," said big-faced, gray-headed John Trumbull somberly.

Williamson laughed. "We are honored, Colonel Trumbull," he said, "in your company, and there is not one of us who does not know that your purchase of land on Allen's Hill will do as much as all our plans to make new converts to the Genesee Country."

"I hope not," said Trumbull dryly. "A painter needs solitude and cares little for people who go mad over land schemes."

The aplomb of the tall smiling Land Agent did not desert him. Lightly he turned toward Nathan.

"Surely not all painters agree. Our own Mr. Hart has but recently purchased more acres on the river bottoms. The Genesee Country provides landscape for all tastes. Colonel Trumbull may find solitude on the heights of Allen's Hill while—"

"Richmond Hill," grunted Trumbull, "I've changed it to Richmond Hill."

"Richmond Hill," said Williamson pleasantly, "and perhaps Mr. Hart will tell us what joys a painter finds on the low flats."

"I have earned a few shillings with my paints," said Nathan, "but I'm no painter."

"If I am to judge by that portrait of Morris I saw in his house in Canandaigua," said Trumbull sourly, "I agree with you."

There was a silence. Nathan smiled—then leaned forward.

"I am a farmer, Mr. Trumbull," he said, "and it will interest me to see if the crops of the painter on Richmond Hill do as well as the paintings of the farmer of the Bath bottoms."

Trumbull cleared his throat aggressively.

"I am no farmer," he said. "I had hoped to retire to a home so remote as to be untroubled by the Frenchified ideas of American Levelers. I see that is impossible. Colonel Williamson assured me when I bought my land that the poison of the French philosophers had not seeped into the Genesee."

"You should have bought nearer to Geneva," smiled the fat chef, Thomas Powell. "I assure that my tavern is patronized by a more 'igher class of men than you find in this town. Never in my entire career 'ave I been 'ost to a more distinguished gathering than at the opening ball, not even when I myself served Sir 'Orace at the Thatched Cottage. Never in my—"

"In this country," said Williamson good-naturedly but

with an anxious glance at Nathan, "a man may hold such political opinions as he pleases. It may please you, Colonel Trumbull, to know that Mr. Hart is in the minority here."

"At this table—yes," said Nathan hotly, "but your votes count no more than those of the farmers and carpenters and blacksmiths who were not invited here tonight."

"They should," said Trumbull shortly. "I doubt that you gentlemen know the woods to the south of us are white with placards attacking Mr. Washington and Mr. Adams. We all know who put them up—Mr. Hart's farmers and blacksmiths and carpenters. It's the result of wild French notions and of that treasonous Western Liquor Insurrection. That damned Frenchman Adet with his infernal tricolor cockades and crazy Gallatin with his damned Whiskey Boys would turn this country into a blood-thirsty madhouse."

A gasp went round the table and many eyes flashed on Nathan. He knew that all the men at the table except Trumbull had come to know by now the events that had brought him to the Genesee Country. Slowly he rose from his seat, his gaze fixed steadily on the little piercing eyes of Trumbull.

"As Colonel Williamson remarked," he said, and he was surprised to find that his voice was even and clear, "I am in the minority here—so much so that I hope you'll not think me cowardly if I retire. Before I leave, however, I want to express a sentiment in which none of you will join me. I am told that it's very popular among farmers and blacksmiths and carpenters. I join them in shouting 'Liberty, Equality, and no King!'—and I go now to sew the tricolor on my hat."

He strode from the room, took his greatcoat from the table in the hall, and walked to the door. The tall figure of Williamson overtook and passed him, then turned about.

"Mr. Hart," said the Colonel. "You and I have had honest disagreements before and remained friends. I hope it may continue to be so. I hope, too, that you are not greatly offended by Colonel Trumbull's frankness. I give you my word he knew nothing of your adventures in Pennsylvania."

"I know that," said Nathan, "and you know that I have a temper I do not easily control. I'm leaving before I lose it."

Williamson laughed lightly.

"I understand," he said. Then he put a hand on Nathan's

shoulder. "I hope when next you see her you will present my respects to Miss Fitzhugh," he said earnestly, "and tell her the mare I named Virginia Nell shall defend the honor of the Genesee Country against all challengers at the great September Fair. I have entered her in a few races in the vicinity. She has won them all without effort and in amazing time. She has become, I honestly believe, the fastest horse in America."

Nathan stared at him. Then he grinned.

"I don't believe you ever really think of anything except selling land," he said.

Williamson smiled.

"Perhaps not."

"Is Virginia Nell faster than Sheriff Dunn's Silk Stocking?" said Nathan.

"Silk Stocking is three years older than was Tom the Tinker."

The two men looked at each other solemnly but lights danced in their eyes.

"Good night," they said in unison, and then the younger walked out to the hitching post where, stamping her hoofs in the soft spring earth, Lottie waited patiently.

III

Nathan had ridden less than a quarter mile in the moonlight
when a sound on the damp April air broke in on his angry
reflections over the conversation he had just terminated. It
grew louder and his ears made out the rhythmic plunging of
hoofs on the soft river road behind him. He urged his mare
to the little rise at the side of the wagon ruts and waited. In
a moment he could see the horse rocking along. An open space
let in a quick flash of moonlight and Nathan drew in his breath
sharply as he saw the rider was a woman in a gray cloak. Her
horse was streaked with white lather and breathing loudly in
distress. Nathan clapped heels to his mare and she started forward directly in the path of the rider. The woman tried to make
her mount swerve to the side, but the laboring animal refused
and came to an abrupt halt.

"Rachel!" said Nathan.

"Let me go! Let me go! I must save her," cried the woman
hysterically. "I must tell them in Jerusalem of her danger."

"Rachel," said Nathan sternly, and he leaned forward to
grasp her plump forearm, "what has happened? Say it."

An attack of shuddering seized her for a moment. Then she
was still.

"They were found in sin," she said at last in a thin doleful
voice.

"Who?"

"Benedict and Susannah."

"And you want to save Susannah?"

"No, no. It was Thomas Hathaway who found them. And
he denounced them then and there above their sinful bed. Then
he ran to tell The Friend."

"And why does that bring you galloping to Jerusalem at
this hour of the night?"

"You don't understand. Benedict Robinson lives outside Jerusalem on a big farm. The Friend had been warned not to leave the settlement for fear wicked James Parker would have her arrested for blasphemy. He has tried it many times but we have always protected her. Now it is too late. I must go on— we must save her." She burst into tears.

"What happened?" said Nathan impatiently. "No one can help you if you can't tell what's wrong." He wondered how he could ever have been so desperately in love with this silly-minded girl.

"I begged her not to go, but God had told her she must rebuke Benedict and Susannah for their great sin. So I rode with her. James Parker heard about it and guessed she would be coming. He met her with deputies and I could not fight them off. I tried to all the way into Bath, but they have lodged her in the jail and James Parker stands guard himself."

"He has the law on his side if he issued a warrant," said Nathan.

"Not God's law."

"Perhaps not, but you won't help her by getting your friends to storm the jail."

"What can I do? What can I do?" wept Rachel, wringing her dimpled hands.

"Go home to bed. Come back with your friends in the morning if you like, but come peaceably. I'll go back and talk to Elijah."

"He is no longer Elijah," said Rachel sternly.

"I call him Elijah. Now run along. I'll see what I can do."

Nathan wheeled Lottie and spurred her into a brisk trot along the way he had just come. He did not look back. And as he rode back over the short distance into town his irritation with himself for having allowed Rachel so completely to dominate his life changed gradually into amusement that he could now dismiss her so brusquely. As he entered the square he heard the voice of Elijah. Diagonally across the wide clearing he could see the lights of Williamson's house still burning brightly and he grinned. There was more excitement out in the open this night than those plotters of the September doings suspected.

As he drew near the square log jail he saw two horses tied

to the hitching post before it. One was obviously The Friend's famous black gelding. Then Elijah's voice came clear and resonant and he stopped to listen.

" 'How beautiful are thy feet with shoes, O prince's daughter! the joints of thy thighs are like jewels, the work of the hands of a cunning workman. Thy navel is like a round goblet, which wanteth not liquor: thy belly is like an heap of wheat set about with lilies.' Now that's in the Bible and it's not wicked and all Benedict was doing was singing the same song."

As he spoke the rhythmic words of the old Hebrew lyric Elijah walked a measured beat before the door of the tiny shadowed prison. He set his feet down sharply to emphasize important words and, musket over shoulder, he did a precise about-face at the ends of clauses. And when Nathan rode up he brought the gun smartly off his shoulder and thundered menacingly, "Who goes there?"

"You know very well," said Nathan. "And I'll bet you know I've come to ask you if you make war on women."

"No trumpets now," said Elijah, "these walls shall not fall no matter how many times a Gideon walks 'round them. They hold no woman but a profane monster who condemns the highest purpose of man—the art of begetting. And I can prove her wrong by book and verse—as wrong as the priests of Baal." He paused for a moment. "Listen to this one, you in there," he shouted, and began his quoting and his marching at the same time:

" 'Thy two breasts are like two young roes that—' "

But the strong, deep voice of The Universal Friend came out of the little barred window and it seemed to fill all the square, silencing her tormentor:

" 'The wise men are ashamed, they are dismayed and taken: lo, they have rejected the word of the Lord; and what wisdom is in them?' "

Louder then, as if to drown her out, spoke the marching Elijah:

" 'How fair and how pleasant art thou, O love, for delights! This thy stature is like to a palm tree, and thy breasts to clusters of grapes.' Ye know I'm quotin' true, so how can ye persecute Benedict and Susannah? It's plain blasphemy to go agin the Bible, ain't it, Nathan?"

"Leave me out of this," said Nathan, entranced.

Stronger came the voice of The Publick Universal Friend.

"'Therefore will I give their wives unto others and their fields to them that shall inherit them; for every one from the least unto the greatest is given to covetousness, from the prophet even unto the priest every one dealeth falsely.'"

"'Many waters cannot quench love,'" shouted Elijah, fairly dancing up and down in wrath, "'neither can the floods drown it.'"

"'Were they ashamed when they had committed abomination?'" said The Friend petulantly, "'nay, they were not at all ashamed, neither could they blush.'"

"'Make haste, my beloved,'" screamed Elijah. The strange argument had begun to waken people in houses nearby. There was a sound of banging doors, of people talking. Above it rang the woman's voice, filled with the sheer joy of vengeance:

"'For behold I will send serpents, cockatrices among you which will not be charmed, and they shall bite you, saith the Lord.'"

Then Nathan saw Charles Williamson striding across the square in long, soundless steps. He did not run, but his pace seemed swifter than the running of most men. In a moment he had stopped before Elijah.

"Judge Parker, what does this mean?"

"A blasphemer brought to justice," said Elijah promptly; "the downfall of a taker of the name of the Lord in vain."

"You mean The Friend is in there?" said Williamson incredulously.

"I pray for those who despitefully use me," said the voice of The Friend.

"She's in there legal," said Elijah triumphantly, "on a warrant issued by Judge James Parker or, in other words, me."

"I care not for the persecutions that have fallen upon me," said The Friend, "but I am moved to wrath that I was not allowed to rebuke those children of abomination who have defied the Lord's command as given through me, His faithful servant."

"What's she talking about?" said Williamson to Elijah.

"Tom Hathaway found Benedict Robinson enjoying the natural way of living with his housekeeper," said Elijah, shifting his musket to his left shoulder. "I knew she'd be after 'em so I laid in wait with a posse."

"Is this true?" said Williamson in a low voice to Nathan. "I have been told so."

" 'They shall rue this day,' " announced The Friend. " 'There shall be wailing and gnashing of teeth!' "

"But Benedict is a good and honest man," said Williamson.

"He is a defiler of God's laws, as interpreted by me, His prophet."

"Blasphemer!" shouted Elijah.

"Surely it is not a sin against God for a man to sleep beside his wife," said Williamson easily.

"The way of the flesh is the way of the Devil," said The Friend, "and these unregenerate children indulged their hellish carnal natures without divine or secular consent."

"Forgive me," said Williamson sweetly, "for making a correction you will be happy to hear. As you may have heard, only three days ago I became a justice in this district—and my first act in my new office was to wed Benedict and Susannah. Tom Hathaway should be ashamed of himself for slandering two upright and honest people."

"Well, I'll be confounded," said Elijah.

In the barred cell there was only stricken silence.

"And now," said Williamson cheerfully. "We must do something about getting The Friend out of jail."

Nathan rode forward until he was close to the sentry.

"Elijah," he said confidentially, "what you want is that The Friend appear at court to answer a charge of blasphemy, isn't it?"

"It is."

"Will you take her word that she will appear on the date set for the trial?"

"W-e-e-ll—yes. She don't lie about things like that."

"And will The Friend give it?" said Nathan anxiously.

"I shall stand before Pilate," said the voice behind the bars, "and shame him and the multitude."

"Will that do?" asked Nathan.

"It'll do," said Elijah.

"Get her out of there," said Williamson, "before my guests and the rest of the town decide to investigate this business."

As The Publick Universal Friend rode silently out of the square Nathan turned about, ready to start once more for home.

"Mr. Hart," said Williamson, looking up at him. "Though a man with a temper you have twice performed miracles of tact this evening. I thank you and I wish you a better night's rest than I shall have, for I have a long ride yet before me—"

"A ride tonight?" said Nathan, puzzled.

"To marry Benedict and Susannah," said Williamson wearily, and he strode away as swiftly as he had come.

IV

As the summer drew on, a calm settled on the Genesee Country,
a calm that all knew was indicative of great events. Throughout
May, Nathan and Whirl worked frantically to get their seed
into the ground. On the first of June, Colonel Williamson rode
by to tell Whirl he was needed in Geneva where the lake's
first big schooner was taking shape on the stocks. She was to
be of forty tons' burden and she would carry passengers and
freight from Geneva to Catherine's Town and back. If all went
well she would be launched in August in time to carry many
of the gay parties coming to the Fair. With a gay light in his eye
Whirl set out, leaving Nathan to await the July harvest.

News of the success of Williamson's posters began drifting
into Bath. People were coming, hundreds of them, from every
direction. Already two great caravans had been announced as
ready to start from Virginia. Almost the whole state of New
Jersey would soon be on its way and all set to wage its bottom
shilling on Silk Stocking. New Englanders were waiting until
the last minute to set out—no foolish waste of money on the
road for them, but they would be there! Every raftsman in Pennsylvania and every man of sporting instinct would be on hand
and looking toward paying for the trip with money won from
the rich Southerners. A rumor flew about that a big party would
arrive from Canada, so big indeed that it might be dangerous—
perhaps sent by Simcoe in a new secret effort at invasion. Fears
were laughed away, however, when it became known they were
bringing a horse. No one, said the merrymakers, could be
bothered with international treachery when he had a nag to
race.

The price of land went up at the very thought of the
oncoming multitude. Settlers who had given Williamson bonds
that they would pay in full at the end of six years tried to buy

the bonds of their neighbors. Farms bought at six shillings an acre two years before were selling at four and five dollars an acre.

Elijah rode to Bath to see Williamson. He must know when the schooner was to be launched at Geneva, he said. He wanted to get the date of The Friend's trial set two days before so that it could be attended by folks on their way to the launching. Williamson laughed and said he would set the date of the launching two days after the trial if it were possible, but all depended on the arrival of the judge from Albany.

The Genesee Country began to seethe with excitement. The trial and the launching and then the Fair. No part of the United States could boast more doing in two months.

Nathan had found it impossible to keep his acres and Whirl's productive while Whirl worked on the Geneva sloop. Though he rose early and worked late his increased property defied the efforts of one man. He tried to hire help on a share basis, but all his neighbors were too eagerly at work on their own land or too busy trading lots and bonds to consider such arrangements. Finally in despair he had approached Jonas Hogmire with the idea of renting from him the services of some of his slaves.

"Nonsense," said Hogmire in his high, thin voice. "Take 'em, my boy. We have more than we need and the lazy rascals aren't earning what they eat. Feed 'em and they're yours for as long as you like."

At first Nathan refused, but as time went on and he saw his crops weed-infested, untended, he felt himself forced to reconsider.

"They're as happy working for you as for us," said Eleanor impatiently. "What difference does it make?"

He tried to explain to her how he felt about the relationships between men. When he quoted "All men are created equal" to her she laughed. "If you knew more about that ridiculous Mr. Jefferson you'd understand," she said. "He owns slaves himself. He just likes to play with ideas." That angered Nathan and they had another of their frequent quarrels. It ended as all ended now, in reconciliation, and after that two black men worked every day in Nathan's fields—hearty, singing field hands who grinned whenever he spoke to them and seemed to think the world a fine joke and did not seem to mind being slaves.

Eleanor and Nathan rode longer than usual one late June night. There was a new moon to watch above the cliffs and it made a shivering gold sickle in the river water. The air was soft and warm. Thunder muttered in the distance. Perhaps it drowned other noises, for the couple heard no strange sounds until on an instant there was a hullabaloo to the south of them —a rumbling of wheels, the barking of dogs, the notes of a song lifted by many men's deep voices, and the high ta-ran-ta-ra of a brass horn.

"It's Peregrine and Father," said Eleanor, and she sent her horse galloping toward the sound.

When Nathan caught up with her she was leaning from her horse to embrace her grinning brother.

"Where's Father?" she cried.

"Still selling off the old place," said Peregrine. "He'll be on in a few months, but he wasn't quite ready to leave. Uncle Presley stayed on and will come back with him."

The girl was silent in disappointment. Nathan held out a hand and the long arm of the Marylander reached toward him.

"I've missed you," said Nathan.

"The Federalists haven't got you?" drawled Peregrine.

"Not a whit."

"He doesn't know it yet," said Eleanor, bravely smiling, "but's he's in the trap. We haven't sprung it."

"I'm counting on you," said Peregrine, and Nathan was surprised that he spoke solemnly, ignoring his sister's joking. "Do you see those men behind me?"

As far as Nathan could see down the road the white balloons of Conestoga tops gleamed in the night. Beside each team stood a black man in white shirt and dark, short breeches, and each held a light-pine flare. They had stopped their singing and stood motionless, the whites of their eyes looking big in the torchlight.

"Yes, I see them."

"Forty freemen—candidates for an African colony along the Genesee. They were my slaves but I gave them liberty if they would come with me to enlist in my great sociological experiment."

"You're mad," said Eleanor slowly.

"That's what Father says," Peregrine chuckled, "but to-morrow I'm buying them enough land to get started on—not the best land of course, for I can't afford it." His eyes gleamed with excitement. "I shall prove that any man in this country— no matter what his station—may become a free, independent, self-supporting citizen."

Nathan thought of the black men who had worked in his fields all that day without hire and he felt uncertain and self-conscious.

"Let's go on," said Peregrine happily. "I'll never get the whole lot bedded before midnight. And how have you and my royal sister here been progressing against the tide of your mutual disagreement on all important subjects? It's only incidentally a Federalist trap she's laid for you, Nathan. She's a woman trap."

V

The courtroom in Canandaigua was hot and sultry, but every seat was occupied and about a score of men and women stood outside the entrance. Nathan, sitting between Eleanor and Peregrine, looked through a window at the misty blue streak of the lake. Peregrine saw the direction of his gaze and smiled. He leaned forward to speak to his sister but the words did not come. A scraping of chairs on the floor of the room above, the clumping of boots, and the sound of loud, good-natured voices interrupted him. There was a rush of heavy feet on the stairs, then the steady progress of some lone invisible figure. The door at the side of the judge's bench opened and Judge Morgan Lewis entered. A bailiff called on the audience to rise, but the black-robed justice, florid of face, serious and businesslike of tone, raised a hand for silence.

"Despite the well-arranged bill of indictment presented by District Attorney Howell," he said, "I have been obliged to instruct the members of the grand jury that by the laws and constitution of the State of New York blasphemy is not an indictable offense. Therefore the defendant in this case is herewith ordered released. There is no charge against her."

The crowd sat motionless, stunned by this unforseen development.

"Court is adjourned until tomorrow at ten," said Justice Morgan Lewis.

"No ye don't," shouted Elijah, rising from his front-row seat. "It stands to reason blasphemy's a crime agin God and man. I been planning to bring this daughter of Beelzebub to justice for two years and I'm not goin' to be done out of it."

"Sit down, Judge Parker," said Morgan Lewis calmly and agreeably. "If the defendant were unquestionably guilty of

319

blasphemy I could take no other action. The same is not true,
I warn you, of contempt of court."

As Elijah, muttering and stricken, sank to his seat there
was a sudden stir in the far corner of the room. The Publick
Universal Friend rose from a seat among her followers. She wore
the purple robe and white stock of her public appearances and
they stood out in bold and rich relief among the drab costumes
about her.

"Judge Lewis," she said quietly, "now that court is adjourned and I am no longer a prisoner, because the Lord hath
heard the voice of my supplications, may I speak to these
people?"

"You may not speak on the charge made against you or
the conduct of the court."

"I do not wish to. I ask for less than a minute to say what
is in my heart."

"I see no reason you should not do so."

At once The Friend moved forward to the dais on which
stood the judge's bench. Behind her in her simple gray dress
and neat white collar walked Rachel—head bent, hands folded.
The prophetess ascended the steps of the dais, moved forward
to its edge, and then knelt with arms outstretched. Rachel knelt
behind her.

"Many here are lawyers," said The Friend simply. "They
have pled for others, but have they pled for themselves before
the throne of God? Let me, then, plead for them and for all
here. This is a good country where the children of God can be
together. May we all live here peaceably what few remaining
days we may spend in Time, for all good souls long to dwell in
peace. May we dwell here and no one hold a possession any
longer or upon other terms than those of being true friends.
I say unto all of you—deal justly with all men and do unto all
men as you would be willing they should do unto you. Live as
you would be willing to die, for no one knows when God shall
call upon him to depart."

As Nathan heard the plain words rolling from her lips he
wondered if he had not at times misjudged The Friend. She
had fought him bitterly and unfairly when he had tried to take
Rachel from her and he had hated her. Now she seemed a
good and honest woman—except for something too fundamental

to change. Elijah called it blasphemy but Nathan knew there was a blasphemy greater than a silly pretense to divinity. It was assumption of power over the will of another human being. He did not hate her now. Much that she was saying was admirable and true, but her premises were wrong. She was merely stupid and pathetic. The voice of the judge broke in on his reflections.

"We have heard good counsel," he was saying in a surprised and moved way, "and if we live in harmony with what this woman has told us we shall be sure to be good people here and reach a final rest in Heaven."

Eleanor put a hand on Nathan's sleeve at the end of the judge's remark. He turned to her as the crowd rose to go.

"I don't see how you could ever have thought her pretty," she said.

"I don't believe I ever said she was pretty, but The Friend is sometimes beautiful."

"Not The Friend, silly. That fat, blowing little priestess behind her."

Thomas Morris insisted that Nathan and his two companions spend the night and the next day as his guests. He would ride with them to Geneva on the day of the launching, he said. There was no use trying to find room in Geneva now. Word had come that the town was so crowded that people were sleeping in rows on the sands beside the lake. Nathan was greatly amused when Morris hurried the party up the stairs on their arrival. He had seen through the window on his way up the walk that his portrait of his host was gone from above the fireplace. Trumbull's irascible remarks had done their work. But when Nathan came down to sit in the long pleasant room where he had painted the picture it was hanging in its old place— a little askew. He studied it carefully. It really was not so bad. Trumbull was a cantankerous old fool.

It was raining when they awoke in the morning. Canandaigua Lake was somewhere down below them, lost in low-hanging clouds. Nathan lay late in bed. He rose and dressed only when he heard Morris's voice calling again and again some word he could not understand. He found his host in the kitchen reading a note written on a greasy bit of paper.

"*Ich bin mit Berezy nach Toronto ausgegangen.*"

"It's Buckendahl," said Morris excitedly. "I let the rest of the servants go on to Geneva and now he's deserted me. Says he's gone to Toronto with Berezy, whatever that means. If you'll excuse me I'll ride to the square to find out. I'll try to find a servant to come and cook us breakfast."

"Don't take the trouble," said Nathan. "I'll have it ready when you get back."

Morris looked at him curiously:

"You're a strange fellow," he said.

Bowls of hominy steamed before Peregrine and Eleanor when he returned. The smell of coffee permeated the house.

"Come to breakfast," called Peregrine as Morris entered the dining room. "My sister couldn't have cooked it better. In fact she couldn't have cooked it at all."

"The Germans are gone," said Morris breathlessly. "They sneaked out during the night, Berezy in command. He left word he'd made arrangements with Simcoe to settle them in Toronto."

"Good riddance," said Peregrine.

"But they're needed for the harvest," said Morris irritably. "They hadn't worked out their fines yet and the farmers to whom they are bound out will be desperate."

"Good," said Peregrine placidly. "They can hire the free Negroes I brought from Maryland. I told Colonel Williamson I'd find work for them—and here it is already."

At once the talk centered on his scheme for the colony of manumitted slaves and Peregrine grew eloquent in his description of its future.

"You sound like Williamson," said Nathan.

Peregrine laughed.

"You should have seen his face when I told him of it. He didn't want to offend me for fear of spoiling his sales to other Southerners, but he didn't want to sell land to free blacks either. He kept pointing out that the sort of people to whom he expected to sell Genesee lands wouldn't want to live next to them. All the plots I suggested he said were already spoken for. When he saw I was getting angry he finally sold me a tract of wet marshland near Sodus. It's divided up into ten-, fifteen-, and twenty-acre sections; the Negroes will have a hard time filling them in and clearing them but it's the best I could do."

"I wouldn't have sold you a single acre for such a crazy dangerous undertaking," said Eleanor, and Thomas Morris turned his gaze gratefully upon her. Nathan had been enjoying his look of discomfort as Peregrine made fun of Williamson.

The four of them spent most of the rest of the day in a futile, wordy argument about Peregrine's project. It had ended when Nathan, stung by Eleanor's statement that slaves were only a step removed from animals and could not be treated as rational humans, rose and walked out into the drizzle. He returned, damp and nervously depressed, an hour later.

"Just in time to save us all from a dinner poisoned by my sister's cooking," said Peregrine. "Perhaps you don't know that her aristocratic hands have never touched a pot."

Eleanor directed a cold glance at him so packed with sudden hatred that it set Nathan to wondering if she would ever look at him like that and what he would do if she did.

"That joke isn't funny the second time," she said.

The next morning was sunny and rain-washed. Morris and the two Fitzhughs were gay as their horses danced down the road beside the lake. But Nathan's depression continued though he tried to rouse himself from it. He could not understand the reason for his nervousness and lack of anticipation. A clump of trees beside the road looked familiar and he remembered that it marked the trail from the lake to the encampment where Catherine O'Bail had lived at the time of the treaty. Sudden nostalgia swept into him. He had been happy with the Indian girl through the gold of that September. He remembered the racing ponies, the ballplayers, the babies hung with bells, and the happy sound of the tribe at evening when he brought Catherine home through the clean, deep-shadowed woods. He remembered her good-night kisses and he was miserable with longing.

"Come, come," said the voice of Peregrine. "This is a celebration—launching day on Lake Seneca—the beginning of our mad, gay fall—not a public hanging."

Nathan laughed. After all, the past was not to be recalled. What had happened then was unreal—an unreal man walking with an unreal girl in an unreal world. The present was entirely satisfactory to him. He was happy with these people. He loved Peregrine and he believed that he loved Eleanor too. He

could win her. There was no wall too high for climbing between her and him. He smiled at himself for thinking resentfully
of the Indian girl, as though she had chosen to be born of
another race in order to be unattainable. But with the smile
his desperate yearning returned with such intensity that he
knew at last, no matter what his future might be, he would
never be free of the thought of Catherine O'Bail.

The riders were amazed when they rode into Geneva. The
porches of the big hotel were black with people and there was
a roaring everywhere. Flying stores—a lean-to and a counter—
had been set up along the streets, and loud salesmen did their
best to get the passers-by to stop and see their wares. A crowd
of curious had gathered before a round bough house such as
the Indians inhabited in their forest encampments and kept a
grinning squaw busy selling beaded moccasins, grass baskets,
and toy tomahawks; while her husband solemnly beat upon his
water drum and sang weird songs in the tongue of the Senecas
to draw more patrons. A peddler pounded battered dippers together in intricate rhythms, shouting to all who would listen
to observe the luster of his wagon which, hung with tin utensils,
blazed in sunlight like a chariot of fire. Down by the lake the
crowd spread out like a massive, irregular thunderhead and the
white schooner seemed a glittering star striking through it. The
tall masts were two brown fingers pointing toward the sun. A
stiff wind blowing in irregular gusts from the east brought the
chatter of hundreds of voices up the slope.

The launching was scheduled for two o'clock in the afternoon, but already every available hummock and dune near the
boat was covered with people. Nathan helped Eleanor and
Morris and Peregrine hitch their horses to long rails just set up
for the purpose and the four of them walked down on the
beach. The wind was freshening and the gusts raced crazily
across the water. When within a hundred yards of the schooner
Morris saw Williamson standing on her stern and he was determined to greet him. He made way for the others, pushing
through the milling people, and at last the little group stood
looking upward where, above the stocks and the white encrusted
hull, like a tiny banner shaming lake and sky, whipped the
cloak of the Land Agent.

As Morris waved and yelled Nathan saw that Williamson

was talking to Whirl Gragg. The little man seemed excited and kept running to the windward rail, pointing down at the stocks and returning to continue his argument. Williamson was obviously disagreeing and wholly indifferent to Whirl's protests. At last his eye caught Morris's gesturing and he turned his back on his companion and walked to the stern, lifting his hat as he did so and smiling gaily down at Eleanor. At the same moment Whirl saw Nathan. With a leap he had outdistanced Williamson's measured progress and stood, bald head gleaming in the sunlight, at the rail.

"Nate," he shouted, and the wind seemed to increase the volume of his voice, "you long-legged, scrawny catawampus, the Colonel wants ye to git up here an' paint her name on 'er afore this wind scrooges 'er into the water. I says ye'd tell him to go to hell only more polite."

Nathan saw Eleanor's mouth twitch in a sudden involuntary sneer. He saw no reason why he should not paint the name, and her scorn of his partner angered him.

"Mr. Hart," called Williamson, "I would be grateful if you would paint the schooner's name on her prow at once."

Nathan cupped both hands and shouted into the wind.

"What name?"

Williamson seemed to hesitate for a moment, then sang out boldly.

"She's the *Alexander* to honor the great Hamilton."

"Tell him to paint it on his backside," screamed Whirl.

Nathan heard an exclamation beside him. Morris was taut with anger. Eleanor, standing beside him, had the same set, cold look in her eyes that she had directed at her brother the night before.

"You'll need a better painter," yelled Nathan. "Get Trumbull."

He saw Williamson's face flush and harden at his words and at the same moment he heard a crack. A quick gust had hit the schooner broadside and two of the stocks' supporting timbers had given way. The vessel rolled under the impact and returned to her upright position. Her momentum carried her strongly against the props on her windward side and there was a terrific sound of splintering wood. Another gust and she heeled far over, almost capsizing on the sands, righted herself, and began slowly to move down the ways. Careening wildly she gained speed as she approached the water. Nathan heard the crowd screaming, saw her prow meet the lake in a burst of white spray as she rocked far over to starboard. The impact hurled Williamson from his feet and his long body was describing a smooth parabola toward the water when Whirl, darting forward like an animated billiard ball on short legs, grabbed the edge of his long cape and snubbed it about the mast. Williamson came to a sudden, almost neck-breaking stop. Gracefully the vessel righted herself and floated on the sparkling whitecaps as the wind swung her about and beached her in shallow water. The wind had launched the *Alexander* ahead of schedule.

Nathan saw Williamson scramble to his feet and advance toward Whirl who sat hugging the mast. He grabbed the little man's shoulders, pulled him to his feet, and shook his hand fervently. The crowd cheered. They had come to see a launching. They had seen a melodrama in which a man had probably saved the life of another. They were satisfied.

Men had run into the water. They had ropes on the schooner and were towing her to her mooring. Whirl stood at the stern rail looking for Nathan, while Williamson waved his hat from the prow. As he finally drew to windward Whirl waved to the group in which his partner stood.

"Democrat wind," he yelled.

VI

Every road into Bath was a straggling route of jovial people.
It seemed to Nathan that the whole three or four thousand who
had watched the launching of the schooner had immediately
raced southward to encamp on the slope above his cabin. They
were mostly Yankees, he discovered, and they had come from
Maine and New Hampshire and Massachusetts and Vermont,
crowding through Albany and rattling along the whole length
of the Mohawk valley through Indian Castle and German Flats
to Fort Schuyler; thence through Deep Spring, Onondaga
Hollow, Nine Mile Creek, and Geneva. Fortunately they dis-
trusted the flat lands down by the river and set up their tents
and lean-tos on slopes like those they had come from.

The great south road was emptying itself of travelers long
on the way. The first cavalcade from Maryland and Virginia
jingled into Pultney Square at the end of the first week of
September. Though it stretched out along the river for over a
mile its leaders announced that it was merely the first and lesser
portion of the original party that had set out from Baltimore.
By the time that they had reached Harris's Ferry they had
realized that they could move northward in greater comfort if
the procession were divided into two parties, each with its own
officers. Their comrades, they said, would be arriving in about a
week. By that time they would themselves be settled and able
to aid those behind them. They hoped it was understood that the
great race between Silk Stocking and Virginia Nell was not to
be run until all Southerners on the way were present and had
made their bets.

Before mid-September every inn, house, and cabin was
crowded with strangers. Sleeping space under cover, even on
floors, was unattainable. The Senecas from Squawkie Hill each
morning set about building leafy bowers for travelers, but once

their wages had amounted to enough money to insure complete drunkenness for the whole tribe for the rest of the day they quit work, leaving many a late-comer no alternative but to sleep upon the ground under the open sky.

The second caravan from the South arrived with more of gentry and of slaves than the Yankees on the hills had imagined they would ever see. The next day the Pennsylvania raftsmen roared into town, a dozen at a time. Now came the followers of swift horses, the fast boys of New Jersey and the wise jockeys of Long Island, shrewd little men, spitting and talking the jargon of the fancy tracks around New York. Shell gamblers set up their rigs in the square, loudly advising one and all to wager on the whereabouts of an elusive pea. A juggler wandered about, stopping now and then to balance a row of three tobacco pipes on his chin. A little Indian boy followed wherever he went and set up a wild cry when he was about to perform. A hundred Indians would then appear as if by magic and watch his act solemnly. As soon as it was over and the entertainer began to pass the hat there was a wild scramble and no Indian left in sight.

Each night the fires reached higher toward the leaves of the maples and oaks lining Pultney Square. Each night within a level, fenced-off inclosure made light as day by the blaze there were wild doings. Sometimes a bear fought off four fierce dogs until he or they had died. Sometimes a wildcat, snarling and spitting, faced two dogs. The stout red bull that had been invincible at the Williamsburg Fair proved more than a match for the biggest black bear ever captured in the Laurel Mountains. There was talk of matching the red fellow against a black bull nearly twice his size that had been brought from Livingston's manor lands on the Hudson. Whenever there was a lull in the night's singing, drumming, and shooting, hammers sounded a steady beat from within the barnlike log rectangle at the corner of Morris and Steuben Streets. Colonel Williamson had been obliged to revise his plans for the theater hurriedly and now the carpenters were working night and day to complete it before the Fair's opening.

Already playbills nailed on the outer walls and on trees about the town announced exciting news:

On the evening of September 20, 1796,
will be performed by the distinguished

PHILADELPHIA COMPANY *of* JOHN BILL RICKETTS'

the comedy of

THE SULTAN, or

A PEEP INTO THE SERAGLIO:
(*with Elegant Dresses*)

to which will be added Molière's Comic Farce,

called THE MOCK DOCTOR,
or THE DUMB LADY CURED.

PIT 6 SHILLINGS, GALLERY 8 SHILLINGS.

Tickets to be had of Mr. Andrew Smith,
Capt. George McClure, *and*
James McDonald.

Doors to be opened at half-past five and the curtain rises precisely
at half-six.

All day and all night the betting went on. The Yankees and the Southerners were putting their money on Virginia Nell —the former because they thought the younger horse the faster, and the latter because they knew no Northern gelding could defeat a Virginia mare. Against their boastful parading of the money the smart boys from Jersey and the Susquehanna raftsmen set every shilling they could coax from their purses. Almost immediately the betting took on the bitterness of political difference, for the Virginia and New England men were almost solidly Federal while the Jerseyites and Pennsylvanians were predominantly Democrat-Republicans. Silk Stocking, his adherents shouted, was the "Poor Man's Choice," "Jubilee Gelding of the Republic," "The Whiskey Hero." They could not find money enough, however, to match the sums offered on Virginia Nell. Among the Yankees and Virginians the rumor ran that the President himself had sent a messenger from Mount Vernon with a tidy sum to lay on the fleet heels of Colonel Williamson's mare.

Nathan had never seen Eleanor so excited. She was happy, she said, that already Bath had become a theater town. Colonel Williamson was to be congratulated on bringing Mr. Ricketts's company all the way from Philadelphia. The program was calculated not only to entertain but to be very improving. Few of her friends in Maryland had had the opportunity to see a comedy by Molière or so smart and sophisticated a drama as *The Sultan*. As for the race, she had no doubt of the outcome and she hoped no one would think her immodest in her sureness that the mare named for her would win easily. Nathan and Peregrine had grinned at her on hearing that, and she had pretended anger and flounced out of the room only to return very demurely a few moments later and ask them anxiously which of her gowns she should wear to the theater.

Nathan dined at Springfield House that evening. The big rooms blazed with armies of candles. Thirty guests sat at two long tables in the dining room, all—with the exception of Williamson, Morris, Trumbull, and himself—new-come Southerners. There was much gay talk about Maryland and people left behind, and Nathan felt ill at ease until Eleanor, sitting at his left, reached a hand beneath the white tablecloth to touch his own. He clasped the hand fiercely and she smiled, looking deep into his eyes.

"Do you like my dress?" she said finally, looking mischievous.

Nathan looked at the heavy gown of pale-green silk, embroided with sprays of pink and white apple blossoms, and suddenly realized that her questions as to what she should wear had all been preparations for this surprise.

"It's new," he said confusedly.

She laughed.

"Father sent it by the Baltimore gentleman sitting at the foot of the other table. You haven't answered my question."

"You are very beautiful," he said, "too beautiful for a backwoods village and the life around here."

"I talked to Colonel Williamson this morning," she said. Nathan was wondering what relevance this remark could have, when, after a little pause, she continued.

"He says that his lands are selling at six dollars an acre now and still increasing in value. He has sold many thousands of acres."

"I know."

"He says that if Virginia Nell wins tomorrow he will give me a thousand acres of rich land a few miles from Williamsburg as a wedding present."

"A wedding present!"

The girl looked at him thoughtfully.

"It will look over the lake," she said, "and it will be fertile land. My father's slaves would build a fine house there for me and my husband."

"What husband?" he said roughly.

"I don't know," she said, looking straight into his eyes, "but life there would not be that of what you call a backwoods town. The fields would yield crops to sell, there would be fine cattle and finer horses, there would be many black servants, and visitors would come from the South, from New York, from Canada."

"Why does Williamson want to give you the land?" said Nathan bluntly.

"You are not very gallant," she said mockingly, "but I'll answer in as plain words. He believes that by establishing more big estates like this one he will increase the value of these lands. He thinks other people of family and means will find them desirable and pay high prices for them. He talked to me about Aaron Burr and the plans he has made with him to cut this western country off from the plebeian eastern part of the state. The Genesee Country will be richer than Virginia, more aristocratic than Maryland, more suitable as a residence for people of background and learning—"

She was interrupted by the scraping of chairs and a wave

of loud conversation. The dinner was over. Though it had begun
at four in the afternoon it was now well past six.

He did not get an opportunity to be alone with Eleanor
on the ride into town. She rode demurely, talking only occasionally to her bumbling, giggling uncle and leaving Nathan to
his thoughts. He was satisfied to have it so. He needed a chance
to think. There could be no doubt of the girl's meaning. Even
at those moments when she had showed greatest affection for
him he had never fully believed that Eleanor would be willing to
marry him. Yet here in the midst of her own kind, with the
memories of her life in Maryland all about her, she had given
him ample proof of her wish to become his wife. He was elated
and at the same time troubled. She would marry him if he
were willing to accept a fortune of her choosing—a pleasing
picture based on her own way of life. He must become one of
her kind. He saw himself riding about his lands, being generous
to tenants, speaking kindly to slaves. It would be gracious, easy
living. He would build a big home, like Springfield House, and
entertain Eleanor's friends in it. There would be riding up and
down the Conhocton Valley and the Genesee Valley to dinners
at Williamson's, to dinners at Springfield House, to dinners at
Trumbull's or Wadsworth's. He would enjoy all that, and yet
there was something that held him back from complete surrender to the idea.

VII

The whole party dismounted before Williamson's house on the square. Servants took their bridle reins and they strolled across the green toward the theater. It was nearly seven o'clock when they entered the big log house, waved generously past the ticket takers by Williamson. The widespread ground floor was jammed with people who gazed at them curiously as they passed through the murky lamplight to the stairs leading to the gallery. They had been waiting impatiently since half-past five for the curtain to rise. Many stood on the benches to make room for others standing in front of them on the earth floor. They glared angrily at the Southerners as the latter climbed upward.

Colonel Williamson saw to it that his guests were seated in the first and second rows of the gallery and then hastened down to the stage. Lightly he leaped upon it and stood facing the audience and smiling. There was silence:

"Welcome to the Genesee Country," he said.

The crowd in the pit roared response, their irritation magically disappearing before his genial grace.

"You will find the Genesee Country abounding with situations both valuable to the farmer and amusing to the gentleman and man of leisure. The gentleman fond of a rural life or the amusements of the field may here gratify himself. He may find a situation for a country seat that will please the most romantic fancy. It is in this country as Yorkshire is to England: it is near enough to the large cities to draw a revenue from their markets but too distant to be affected by their vices and follies."

A loud whoop of approval for vices and follies from some roisterer brought a surprised laugh from the speaker. The crowd in the pit had been silent and uncomfortable during his words, but at this they roared once more.

"Men of property anxious to secure to their families estates in America will experience great satisfaction in joining their countrymen, perhaps their former friends and neighbors." He looked up to the front rows of the gallery and smiled meaningfully. His gaze dropped to the pit. "Those who have been born to labor for their livelihood are rapidly settling the whole adjacent country with a most respectable yeomanry."

Out into the little open space just below the platform of the stage bounced Whirl, his round head agleam in the lamplight.

"I'm a yeoman," he shrieked in a feminine falsetto, switching his backside alluringly as he paraded about with ladylike gestures.

There was an ominous note in the sound that came from the crowd this time, a growl of rage that rose menacingly. Williamson held out a hand and it subsided.

"I have three announcements to make," he said quickly. "First, the management informed me this afternon that due to unexpected difficulties in staging their entertainment in a new theater they have been obliged to reverse the order of the plays. The Molière comedy will be produced first. Second, we have just received the new curtain before which I stand. Hence it is blank, the appropriate scene with which it should be adorned is not yet painted. Perhaps in the future our distinguished neighbor, Mr. Trumbull—"

"Hart," shouted Whirl suddenly. "Hart's the name."

"Hart," shouted the crowd. "Hart, Hart, Hart."

Again Williamson held up his hand. "Or Mr. Hart," he said smiling, but that gentleman, red and miserable, was not too embarrassed to observe a quick flicker of resentment pass over his face. Nathan cast a sidelong quick glance at the girl by his side. Her face was set and expressionless. He knew she was aware that he was looking at her but she would not respond.

"Third," said Williamson, "I am obliged to announce that the company has informed me that no more small tracts of ten and twenty acres may be sold along the Genesee and Conhocton. In the future the lands in these valleys will be sold only in estates of at least a hundred acres. Those seeking small parcels of land will find them available to the north of us in the region around Sodus. Let the evening's entertainment now begin."

He leaped down and strode swiftly through the crowd. He was in his seat in the gallery before the full purport of his last remarks reached the minds of the men and women in the pit. Slowly the growl of angry menace grew again. This time there was no speaker to wave it down. It swelled like the coming of a quick line storm on a lake. The building seemed fairly to shake with the sound. Men were staring up at the gallery and shaking their fists. Then the blank white curtain trembled suddenly and went up. At once there was silence. Curiosity had stilled the storm.

It was not until the middle section of the Molière comedy, when the husband discovers that the lovely wife whom he has cured of dumbness is the most annoying of rattle-brained chatterers, that Nathan heard below in the crowd a laugh that brought memories racing into his mind. Frantically his eyes moved over the mass below. The blaze of lamps on the stage cast only a dim mellow glow out over the audience, but he could see Catherine O'Bail standing in a far corner. She was clothed in homespun but her long braids still dangled down her back. Otsiquette stood beside her and both were intent upon the play. She looked taller, Nathan thought, and more dignified, perhaps because the light-brown skirt fell below her knees. Even so far away in the dimness he thought he could see the sparkle of her black eyes. Nathan's heart beat faster and he looked at Eleanor. The long lean face turned to him a moment and then toward the stage as if to urge him to concentrate on Molière. She was obviously receiving each line as it was spoken, considering it, analyzing it. He looked back to the eager face of the Indian girl.

When the performance was over Nathan asked Eleanor if she would walk outside the theater in the interval between the plays. She looked surprised and said there would be too great a crowd. He excused himself and hastened below. The square was lined with leaping fires and he saw Catherine almost immediately. She and Otsiquette stood in earnest conversation near the fence surrounding the bull pit. He had not made up his mind to approach them when she saw him and came directly toward him.

"Good evening, Mr. Hart," she said. "I am sorry there was

not time for you to paint the curtain. I know I would have liked it."

Otsiquette, following her and coming up just in time to hear her last words, said solemnly:

"It is far better in the original French."

Catherine laughed delightedly at the big Indian's misconstrual of her remark. Then she saw that Nathan had held out his hand and she raised her own to it. Nathan felt the smooth strength of her fingers but only in a formal pressure. He felt dissatisfied and uncertain.

"I have seen the next play in Philadelphia," she said, as if volunteering a subject for a languishing conversation. "It will be interesting to see another actress in the role of Roxalana. I saw Mrs. Melmoth act it at the Southwark Theater one night when I was supposed to be on my way back home from school. She was fat and stupid."

Nathan found himself listening to her chatter as if it were matter of great importance. His eyes sought to get one gleam of personal warmth from hers. She talked on easily but as if to a stranger. He stood dazedly beside her until he heard, "We must return to the theater earlier than you. We have no seats in the pit and might be crowded out." Then he was alone. He turned and walked back to his seat, mechanically climbing the stair, seeing no one. Eleanor greeted him with a smile. Peregrine looked at him for some time before he spoke.

"You are lucky to know so beautiful a woman as that Seneca girl," he said. "I asked Williamson who she was in the hope that he would present me."

Eleanor looked at her brother and Nathan in surprise. "A beautiful Indian girl? I must see her myself."

Peregrine laughed.

"Many of them are beautiful."

"In a wild way, of course," said his sister.

"She was telling me that the Molière is far better in the French," lied Nathan.

Eleanor flushed, looking at him incredulously.

"That seems impossible," she said sharply.

"She is a graduate of a fine Quaker school in Philadelphia."

"But Molière could mean little to a girl brought up a

savage. Indian blood does not lend itself easily to genteel pursuits."

"Some of our Virginia cousins would hardly thank you, sister," said Peregrine Fitzhugh drily. "Great Grandma Pocahontas is a favorite of theirs."

"But she was made a lady of the English Court," said Eleanor indignantly.

"And that changed her blood?"

"Egad," said Jonas Hogmire explosively, "handsomest woman I ever saw was the Indian wife of Captain Chew of the British Army. Sir William's Johnson sent Chew to Baltimore and she took the place by storm. They tell me Sir William married a chieftain's sister himself."

"Chew?" said Peregrine reflectively. "You don't suppose that girl I'm hoping to marry, the Chew girl from Ann Arundel, could be a cousin?"

"Don't be ridiculous," snapped Eleanor.

Nathan was uncomfortable. He hated their looking upon the women they mentioned as members of an alien race rather than as human beings. He wondered what they would say if he were to blurt out, "I am unhappy because that girl treated me casually."

A bugle blared and the curtain went up on the tarnished hangings of the Sultan's Court. The play was as tawdry as its setting and heavy with forced wit. The men of the pit shouted wild obscenities at the fat woman in veils who was acting the role of Elmira, A Circassian Slave, and the actor playing the great Sultan winked at them lewdly. The atmosphere seemed tense and nervous, heavy with foreboding. Then a slight, pale woman, obviously older than the part required, bounced gaily on stage as Roxalana, White American Slave. She had a pretty, birdlike voice, an impudent manner, and a snub nose, and these were enough to bring fascinated attention from the house. Though her lines were dull to the point of stupidity she spoke them as if they were barbs of lightning wit, and at every sally the crowd laughed and applauded.

Nathan felt the tension increase suddenly as the silly farce drew near its end. The men below had had time to mull over Williamson's astounding announcement that a poor man could no longer buy a few acres of the best land. They understood from it that they had been betrayed to the complacent rich who would buy large estates and follow "the amusements of the field." They looked up into the gallery and saw fat Jonas Hogmire, giggling like a jelly, Eleanor Fitzhugh in a gown no woman they knew could afford, the smug faces of the well-born Marylanders, and the dour features of John Trumbull, cross-hatched with little purple veins made prominent by luxurious living, and they began to give the lines of the play more meaning than Mr. Ricketts or his actors or Williamson could have fancied into them. Suddenly the Sultan had come to represent all pretensions to aristocracy, all assumptions of superiority which threatened their dream of democratic living.

The storm blew up innocently at first. It began with the loud, ugly laugh that followed Roxalana's quick answer to the Sultan's incredulous question:

"As far as I can perceive then, you would be very glad to get away from me?"

"You were never more right in your life."

The Sultan spoke sternly. "Come hither, Roxalana."

"No, I thank you: I am very well where I am: Now if you were an American—" She managed to intimate that the change in his nationality would bring about a complete reversal of her cool manner.

"Tell me, then, is it in this light manner women behave in America?"

"Pretty near it."

Her curt rejoinder brought shouts and a grumbling of resentment against the Sultan's insulting inquiries.

"And suppose I should for once forget and pardon your national vivacity?"

"So much the worse for you. I see my frankness is disagreeable but you must grow used to it. Think yourself happy to find a friend in a slave, a slave who will teach you how to love. For 'tis in America that love is in its element. It is there all life and tenderness—" the woman stopped a moment and then stepped quickly downstage, her arms outstretched to the audience—"because it is free."

Pandemonium greeted her. The raftsmen and the bully boys, the jockeys and the gamblers, the wild Canisteers, and the farmers and the keepers of the flying stores beat upon each other's backs and whooped; they leaped upon the benches and screamed. A deep bass voice began to sing:

"God save the rights of man!
God give us hearts to scan
Blessings so dear!"

Nathan's eyes seeking Catherine's saw that the Indian girl was looking steadily at him as if to convey to him the full meaning of the lines the actress had just spoken.

The actor playing the Sultan saw at once an opportunity to take advantage of the moment. He marched threateningly upon the frail defiant creature who had dared to cross him. The noise subsided in breathless anticipation as he shouted in thunderous menace:

"Consider who I am and who you are."

The actress stood up to him valiantly, turning her snub-nose profile to the audience and standing on tiptoe to deliver her reply.

"I am your slave, but I am also a free-born American woman—prouder of that title than all the pomp and splendor Eastern monarchs can bestow."

The bellow from the pit was deafening and dangerous. A knife whizzed by the head of the astonished Sultan, buried its point in the wall behind him, and stuck there quivering. He turned and ran for the exit. The actress stood astonished for a moment by the reaction she had caused—then raised a hand in a wild gesture of triumph, screaming at the same time:

"Liberty, Equality, and no King!"

Even as the roar of her admirers answered her there was again the sudden graceful flight of Colonel Williamson leaping to the stage. He stood beside the actress, smiling deprecatingly as though the noise were a tribute to himself. Calm, poised, he waited. But the roar did not die down. He raised a hand for silence and it grew louder. Fists lifted under his gaze.

"We want good land," shouted a deep voice, and a rumble of uncontrollable anger began deep in the throats of the men around it. "To hell with all aristocrats and Federalists!" screamed a woman in a hysterical soprano.

Nathan saw a look of puzzlement come into Williamson's eyes. He had never admired the Land Agent more, for there

was no hint of fear about him as he stood there meeting the
first situation of his life that he could not handle. Whirl Gragg
must have seen it, too, and realized the danger that a single
irresponsible action might cause, for he suddenly grabbed the
edge of the platform with both hands and scrambled awkwardly
but with incredible speed to stand beside the tall figure of
Williamson.

"Hart," he yelled in his piercing high voice, pointing at
Nathan in the gallery. "Hart."

The men below looked puzzled but one of them took up
the call, then another. The rest remembered they had been
shouting the same thing a few minutes ago, remembered that
the name had had some connection with opposition to the rich,
smooth fellows up there beside him. "Hart!" they boomed out.
"Hart, Hart, Hart," their eyes following the direction of Whirl's
forefinger.

Eleanor turned to Nathan.

"This is outrageous," she said intensely without raising her
voice above its usual level. "These peasants should be taught a
lesson." Jonas Hogmire took her left hand in his as if to silence
her, but no other indication came from any of Williamson's
party that they were hearing or seeing anything unusual. They
sat and stared at the stage as if the play were still being
performed.

As Nathan rose to his feet Eleanor put out her right arm
to bar him, but he moved relentlessly up until he stood, hands
on the gallery rail, looking at the crazed lot below. He felt that
no word would come from his mouth and he knew no word to
say. Panic possessed all of him. Then his glance wavering over
the crowd rested on the familiar figure of the girl in the corner,
and he saw her looking up at him and smiling gently and with
no trace of excitement or uncertainty in her face. She seemed
to be waiting for something she knew surely would come. He
tried to lift a hand for silence as he had seen others do and his
gesture stopped almost as soon as it began. He felt that this
was a bad start and looked down in embarrassment at the of-
fending arm. The crowd laughed and were silent. Then the
words came, words that surprised him because he was not
conscious of his brain's working as he spoke them.

"I guess that's a pretty good end for a show," he said.

"Let's go out to the square for some more fun. We can settle the rest of this business in a month or so when we make Tom Jefferson the next President."

Good humor returned to the crowd. Nathan's embarrassment, his slow, hesitating speech, and his obviously sincere agreement with their point of view pleased them. There was no threatening undertone in their applause now. The incident was over. They were facing the hastily opened doors. The fires in the square beckoned. Eagerly, stumbling over each other, they piled out of the theater.

Eleanor walked silently beside Nathan as they and their companions came out into the square. She did not seem displeased with him though he had expected that she would be very angry. She took his arm and as they stepped down from the theater entrance Williamson was beside them.

"Thank you, Mr. Hart," he said. "I fear I was at my wit's end when you came to the rescue."

"It was Gragg," said Nathan. "If he hadn't thought of it there might have been trouble."

"You are too modest."

"What was me?" said Whirl, appearing beside them. "Nate, ye shouldn't a called that show off. That purty piece o' mischief was just beginnin' to sort me out o' the crowd."

Nathan felt the pressure of Eleanor's hand on his arm, urging him forward, and saw Williamson starting forward with them, smiling pleasantly and impersonally at Whirl.

"Nate," said Whirl, and Nathan thought there was urgency in his tone. "Could I speak to ye jest a minute? Beggin' yer pardon, ma'am?"

"Will you excuse me?" said Nathan. "I will join you shortly." Gently he dislodged Eleanor's hand and, leaving her with Williamson, walked a few steps with Whirl.

"I got somethin' t'tell ye."

"What is it? You can see I can't talk right now."

"It's somethin' an' Injun said he got from some birds."

"What do you mean?"

" 'Voices o' birds' he said, but I couldn't see none around —'voices o' birds.' "

"Well, what did they say?"

"Said Silk Stockin' can't run good without a good rider. Some horses is thataway."

"See here," said Nathan impatiently, "what's this all about? What are you trying to tell me?"

"Silk Stockin's goin' t'have a good rider an' the Injuns have put up all they can lay hands on. Traded a lot o' the blankets an' stuff they got at the Canandaigua treaty fer money an' bet every last pistereen. Jest thought ye'd like to know." He turned away and walked a few steps, then turned quickly about.

"Ye'd be a fool not to put money on that nag. An' if I was you—as I ain't—I'd put all ye got on the rider." He darted away.

Nathan looked after him, understanding at last. The talk in Bath had been that both horses would be ridden by Negro jockeys. Now Sheriff Dunn had had the good sense to put the horse's old owner back in the saddle—the girl who had won with him at Williamsburg.

"Nathan," said Eleanor sharply, "answer Colonel Williamson. Your friend has bewitched you as usual." Her slight emphasis on the word friend implied her scorn.

Nathan started. He had not realized that while his mind was on Whirl's words he had rejoined his former companions.

"I was saying, Mr. Hart," said Williamson genially, "that despite our political differences I have great admiration for you and hope that you will become one of the important figures in this, our little western paradise. From some rather vague hint that Miss Fitzhugh has just let fall I am inclined to believe that this may be possible. If so I would like to be the first to congratulate you and wish you well."

Eleanor looked at the Colonel with level, unagitated gaze.

"You've probably ruined everything," she said calmly. "He never wants to do anything that anybody else wants him to."

Williamson laughed delightedly.

"My wager is on the lady," he said. "I'll be losing that thousand acres of my best land sooner than I anticipated—but there will be compensations."

Nathan looked at them.

"Eleanor is right," he said. "I have a natural distaste for being influenced by others—even toward acting for my own advantage. I am feeling both greatly honored and greatly puzzled at this moment. If you will forgive me I beg your permission to retire. I need to be alone."

"You see," said Eleanor to the Colonel. "I told you how it would be." But Nathan was already lost in shadow.

VIII

Eleanor stood on the platform built for the judges and the gentry. Sunlight played on the tan plumes of her hat and a gentle breeze ruffled them. She had spread the wide folds of her riding skirt, holding the brown fabric out with her hands so that it formed a deep bag, and gold coins were flashing into its depths. At her right stood Mrs. Williamson, her blonde hair gleaming, her full lips moving as she counted the metal disks she tossed from her full purse. At Eleanor's left, tall, scrawny Mrs. Dunn, a sharp-faced, thin-nosed woman, matched coin for coin, counting precisely with clipped accent. Before the three women engaged in this procedure stood a crowd widespread, hushed, and staring—hypnotized by the flickering lights that darted from the golden eagles as they fell.

"Seven hundred," said Abby Williamson, and she turned abruptly away as if she had just completed a distasteful bit of drudgery and walked to her chair.

A sigh went up from the multitude in front of her. Nathan, seated between Peregrine and Jonas Hogmire in the second row of dignitaries, saw Indians, raftsmen, carpenters, farmers—his neighbors—following with their eyes every movement of the curving figure of the Land Agent's wife.

To many of them he knew she was a surprise. They gazed at her avidly. She was the sort of woman they understood, the kind a healthy man enjoyed the sight of, and they had hardly credited rumors that she lived among them. He remembered the first time he had seen her and how she had angrily declared that her husband kept her from associating with the people of the settlement because of his ambitions. Now, Nathan thought, he is forcing her to play her part as his schemes begin to work.

Williamson stood at the front of the platform, lifting a hand above his head as the crowd began to cheer.

"You have just witnessed the wager between the wives of the owners of the two horses," he said. "Seven hundred dollars in gold eagles against an equal amount, the stakes held by the beautiful young woman for whom my horse was named. This money is in addition to the thousand pounds sterling offered by me as representative of the North American Land Company. You have seen our exhibits of cattle and grain—evidence of the incredible riches of the Genesee Country. You have raced your horses against each other on this fast track and in this invigorating climate, calculated to improve the quality and the spirit of any fine animal. You can see from this spot—the beauties of this land." His arm described a wide arc, and the eyes of the listeners, following its direction, saw the high bluff above the river and the level plains below. Some of these were covered with straight pines that made intricate patterns of shade and sunlight upon the clear, needle-covered ground. Others were cleared and flat and dotted with shocks of withered cornstalks. In the distance smoke was rising from a few cabin chimneys in the town.

"I hope that many of you will make this land your home," continued Williamson. "Demand for the better areas has brought about a gradual rise in the price to six dollars an acre. It is my honest belief that the land itself will cause a continuous rise in value to twice or thrice that sum. Those of you who have not yet purchased may approach me or Mr. Cameron or Sheriff Dunn or any of my appointed agents and we shall be glad to make most generous terms.

"Now," his voice rose and held a note of excitement, "comes the most exciting sporting event of recent years in this hemisphere—the mile race between my four-year-old mare, bred in the Old Dominion, Virginia Nell and Sheriff Dunn's famous six-year-old Jersey gelding, Silk Stocking."

The noise of the crowd broke over him like a great wave. Vainly he tried to stem it, holding up both hands, but it did not lessen. Finally, laughing good-naturedly, he turned and walked to his chair beside the grave, distinguished-looking sheriff. As he did so the notes of a bugle sounded above the wild whooping of the Indians, the husky cries of Negroes, the deep roaring of the Susquehanna bullyboys, and the shrill cries of the blackleg gamblers and sharpers from the cities down below. The crowd scattered, frantically racing for places of advantage along the wide, circular, one-mile track. Jonas Hogmire twisted about nervously.

"Mr. Hart," he said, "Eleanor tells me you have made no wager. Now I realize that you would not wish her to know that you had bet against a horse named for her, but I am a man who can keep a secret. I want to lay on the Southern mare one of those black boys I've lent you against a flattering portrait of myself—something recognizable as me but somewhat more lithe than I have been of late years."

Peregrine leaned forward quickly as if fearing that Nathan would resent the offer.

"Take it, Nathan," he said. "You can free the slave to join my colony if your horse wins. You'll be in line to paint your uncle-in-law anyway as a matter of family duty or I miss my guess. Not that I approve of your surrendering to my sister's campaign to make you her husband. I don't. You'll be a damned unhappy man if you marry her. Are you going to?"

"I don't know," said Nathan slowly and seriously. "I admire her. Sometimes I believe I love her."

"She is a fine woman," said Peregrine. "God deliver me from a fine woman. Just wait till you see the ridiculous Chew minx from Ann Arundel. She's no fine woman."

"Do I get my wager?" asked Jonas Hogmire testily. "Who cares about women at a moment like this?"

"I accept," said Nathan smiling.

"Where the hell are the horses?" said Hogmire.

In the space around the platform a tall man in buckskin was waving a packet of Williamson's land bonds.

"A hundred acres ag'in two hundred dollars, jest what I paid for 'em," he shouted. "You own an estate on the Genesee if I lose. Come on ye soft-talkin' macaroni."

"A strong black boy against your acres," said an immaculately dressed young Marylander quietly. "He's worth more than two hundred I promise you."

"Done," said the tall man.

The bugle sounded again and the betting grew more frenzied. A roar from the far side of the track gained all attention. Two horses were ambling gently along the course. Their riders were sharp splashes of color on their backs. Nathan felt the jump of his heart as he again saw autumn-leaf red above the gray gelding. He would know in a few moments if Whirl had been right in implying that Catherine O'Bail would ride Silk Stocking. As the horses rounded the turn he saw that the jockey on the chestnut mare was a black boy. He rode expertly with his head down close to the ears of his mount. His jacket and breeches were bright yellow and he had placed a yellow cap on his head backward so that the long visor ran down the back of his neck almost to his hunched shoulders. The other rider wore a red cap of similar shape but the visor was pulled far down over the forehead, hiding most of the face. A whispering went about among the crowd. Nathan heard a man's voice saying authoritatively:

"It's the sheriff's daughter. She raised him from a colt."

"It ain't no sech a thing," someone replied indignantly. "It's a Jersey City jockey. I seen him exercisin' the horse yistiddy."

"It's an Injun," said a man in a homespun coat, looking intently at the little figure on the gray. "Rides horse like an Injun. I been watchin' 'em all my life an' I know."

"I know damn' well who 'tis," shouted a huge fellow whom Nathan's memory suddenly identified as Eli Stephens, the wrestler, "an' I'm stakin' my last ha'penny on Silk Stocking."

The gray walked quietly, unperturbed by the crowd. His coat was clean and glistening. From hoof to knee on each of his long legs, close black hairs made the smooth silky casings that gave him his name. Nathan remembered his first sight of him—the unkempt, bur-knotted, scraggly nag which Colonel William Wadsworth had admitted over Williamson's protest to the race at the Williamsburg Fair. He looked about the platform until his gaze rested on the dark, eaglelike countenance of Wadsworth. The tall colonel's deep-set eyes were fixed upon Silk Stocking in so earnest a look of hope that Nathan nearly laughed aloud. Here was one owner of great lands at least who would not bet on a horse owned by Williamson. As Nathan's gaze returned to the track he saw Virginia Nell dancing skittishly about. The crowd gave her room as she approached the starting line. She was a beautiful animal, spirited and eager.

The drum tap came sooner than Nathan expected. One moment the horses and the crowd were leisurely preparing for an event that would eventually take place. And before the mind could grasp the sudden sequence a complete change had occurred. There was the single hollow clap on the drumhead and the two horses were away. Before he could focus his entire attention on them they were rounding the first turn, and he could see the mare taking a scampering lead while the rider of the gelding pulled him into an easy lope behind.

The rest of the race seemed to him as unreal as had its beginning. As the horses raced into the backstretch his eyes caught the full panorama that stretched out across the flat land. Williamson's workers had done their job well. The field inside the track was as green and level as the lawns of Philadelphia. Hundreds of spectators stood at its edge, cutting off his view of the legs of the horses, but he could see the two heads moving along as if suspended on wires. The crowd was roaring out its suspense-laden agony. He saw a man and woman drop to their knees, their faces uplifted and their lips moving in prayer. The figure in the red shirt was not performing in the bouncing, devil-may-care fashion of the gray's rider at the Williamsburg race. Nathan was sure that the face under the red visor was that of Catherine O'Bail, and yet, if it were, she was riding with care and with tense determination.

As the animals reached the curve that would lead them into the stretch their positions were the same as they had been after they had covered the first hundred yards. Virginia Nell was out in front by a length and a half—running strongly but with less zest than she displayed at the start. The gray was still galloping in long smooth bounds, automatic, unworried. Then through the bright air as the horses burst into the stretch Nathan heard the sound he had been expecting, a sound that made his identification of the Indian rider sure. It was the wild ululating cry of a Seneca warrior in battle, and though it was choked and husky and seemed farther away than he knew it to be Nathan recognized the distinct quality of its tone and he knew that Catherine was riding desperately. Standing on tiptoe he gazed down the track, but the crowd barred his line of vision. He jumped into the air trying to stay up as long as possible, and he saw in the instant of his beginning to return toward the earth the gray horse swing wide, at the same time seeming to stretch out along the ground. Nathan launched himself into the air again. The racers were neck and neck and the noise of the crowd was one long chaotic scream. Once more he jumped. This time he could see them plainly—less than fifty yards from the finish. The black boy was lashing the flanks of the chestnut furiously, and the horse, wild-eyed and exhausted, was responding gamely. Catherine, lying along the gray's outstretched neck, was still yelling, but the crowd was thundering so loudly that, though her mouth was wide open, no sound seemed to come from it. The gray's ears were back as if he were angry that any horse dared challenge his speed, and Nathan saw his dappled haunches gathering for a last effort. Now, as the straining beasts came in full view of the spectators on the platform, Silk Stocking flashed out in front as if he were a gray-feathered arrow just loosed from the bow. As he passed the finish line he was ahead by half a length.

A Virginian who sat in the front row turned around to Jonas Hogmire, his face working grotesquely as he strove to speak calmly.

"I am a pauper."

It seemed that the roar of the crowd would be interminable. Standing at the front of the platform Colonel Williamson and Sheriff Dunn shook hands formally, and Eleanor poured into the lap of the winning wife a skirtful of gold. Williamson faced the group on the platform, cupping his hands to make himself heard.

"I am expecting all of you to dine with me at my house within the hour. At Sheriff Dunn's generous suggestion we shall broach the pipe of wine I lost to him in this glorious event."

Nathan saw the face of the Land Agent's wife grow dark with anger and mortification. Though she was mistress of the luxurious, sprawling log house on the square her husband had not mentioned her in extending the invitation. She walked swiftly to the edge of the platform and leaped lightly to the ground. There the crowd closed about her, hiding her from his sight.

Eleanor Fitzhugh was trying to make her way to Nathan through the silent, disappointed group of her countrymen. He saw her and went to her. Her eyes were shining and there was no hint of bitterness in her face.

"It was a perfect race," she said, "and that Indian girl

rides better than any jockey I ever saw. I wonder what there is
about people of primitive origins that makes them so successful
with animals."

He looked angrily down into her eyes.

"Oh, I forgot about Mr. Jefferson," she said, playfully
putting a hand over her mouth as if she were a schoolgirl caught
in a prank. "I'm sorry but I just can't remember even for you
that all men are created equal."

He jumped from the platform and lifted a hand to help
her down. She put out both hands and, when he had taken
them in his, leaped close to him so that, to steady her, his arms
must go round her. She stood close against him, looking up.

"I hear you won a slave from Uncle Jonas," she said. "But
you'll have to paint his portrait anyway. He says he'll give you
a good horse for it so that you may get rid of the impossible
Lottie."

"I'll not do anything of the kind," said Nathan severely,
feeling both loyalty to his horse and resentment at her assuming
to influence his actions.

They made their way through the crowd to her carriage.
The black driver helped them in and drove off toward Bath.
Other carriages, scores of them, blocked the road, making their
progress slow. Beside the long procession frolicked men on foot
and on horseback, singing, shooting into the air, and blowing
horns.

At the dinner gaiety returned to the Southerners. Wine
loosed their tongues and there was good-natured repartee at
the long tables.

"I'm taking land on credit," shouted a young man in a red
velvet coat. "I have to stay here, can't pay my way back to
Baltimore."

"It's a scheme of our host's," said Hogmire, giggling. "His
horse loses and assures him new settlers."

Williamson laughed.

"If my horse had won," he said, "we might all have been
scalped. The Iroquois wagered more than they received at
Canandaigua on the outcome."

"They tell me the jockey was a girl, Colonel," said Hogmire. "Was it the same one who defeated my horse at
Williamsburg?"

The Land Agent's face was serious. Nathan saw in the burning blue eyes a look of weariness and sadness.

"Yes," he said simply. "It was the same one."

Abby Williamson did not appear at the tables. "She is exhausted by the excitement of the day," said her husband. "She will join us shortly," but when the guests rose from their chairs she was still absent. Soon after that Williamson disappeared into the recesses of the house. Returning after a quarter hour he said:

"Shall we walk out to watch the merrymaking? I regret that my wife is still unable to be with us."

Nathan and Eleanor walked arm in arm into the square. Piles of fallen autumn leaves and of dry underbrush were blazing fiercely all about the arena. The light was yellow and intense. The crowd that lined the fence on all four sides were roaring with laughter at the antics of two self-appointed masters of ceremony who were encouraging a snarling wildcat and a shambling, half-grown black bear to engage in combat. The animals struck out savagely, more than willing to fight their human tormentors, but terrified of each other. The men skipped about, dodging comically.

"Nate," screamed the high voice of Whirl Gragg, and turning Nathan saw the little man lurching toward them.

"Got another communication fer ye," he said thickly. "Allus got a communication fer ye. Hope the young lady'll excuse ye fer a time—excuse me, too, fer bein'—fer the time bein'—someat transmogrified."

Eleanor clutched Nathan's arm firmly.

"Go away," she said distinctly. "You are drunk and disgusting."

Whirl bowed low with elaborate courtesy.

"Drunk is true, miss," he said, "but disgusting depends on taste. They's things I calls disgusting what you might powerfully admire."

"Nathan," said Eleanor, "are you allowing this drunken companion of yours to insult me?"

"I'm sorry that Whirl seems a bit stimulated," said Nathan good-naturedly, "but you'll agree that it's understandable. Whirl, I can't talk to you now."

"But my communication," said Whirl doggedly.

"It can wait."

Whirl stood looking at Nathan incredulously. He swayed back and forth on his short stocky legs. Then he turned about and made off swiftly across the square.

After the bear and the wildcat had been chased into their cages to await a night when they would be in more aggressive moods toward each other there was a quick scattering of the crowd at one side of the arena. A giant wooden cage resting on a wooden sled had been dragged up to the gate by a yoke of oxen. Inside it bellowed and stamped the famous unconquered red bull. When the deerhide thongs binding one narrow wall of the cage had been loosed and the wall lowered the animal bounded out into the center of the square and stood tossing his short, viciously pointed horns up and down as if expecting his adversary.

He had not long to wait. The enormous black bull, brought west from the Hudson River hills, was already at the gate and being prodded out of his cage into the arena. The smaller beast did not wait for the new arrival to accustom himself to the situation. Lowering his head he tore across the intervening space and, catching the bewildered enemy on the left flank, ripped him open from belly to buttocks. The black bull bellowed in agony and, wheeling about, charged on his assailant. But the red enemy had been too quick for him. He had turned at the end of his murderous dash and was already in motion in a countercharge. This time the two thundering beasts met head on. There was a deep hollow thump of impact and the black bull sat down on his haunches, looking surprised and silly, obviously stunned. A moment later the horns of his enemy had caught him full in the chest and he lay dying on the reddening ground.

The enraged victor raced toward the side of the arena as if he would attack the entire crowd, and the men nearby tumbled over each other in their fear that the fence would not hold. He brought himself up short and stood with head stretched forward and moving slowly from side to side.

Suddenly a groan went up from the far side of the enclosure. A little Negro boy, no more than five years old, had been playing with his companions in and out among the crowd. Seeing a free space he had darted into it and then, startled by the light and the circle of faces, had begun to run toward the opposite fence. He reached the middle of the arena before the eyes of the red bull caught with a side glance the quick moving of his little body. The beast responded instantly. Once more the fierce head went down. Once more the sharp horns were moving over the ground at terrific speed. A man who had been sitting on the fence dropped bravely inside, waving his arms and shouting—but he was too late to divert the galloping bull's attention. Now the child saw the animal and stopped, motionless and terror-stricken.

Then, as Nathan and Eleanor and all the rest of the crowd stood helplessly watching, a figure not a great deal larger than that of the boy shot into action. It seemed to drop from nowhere. There was a moment when it was not in the arena. In the next split second it was there and racing with incredible speed for its short legs toward the child.

"No! Whirl! No!" shouted Nathan in an agony of anxiety for his friend.

The round bald head shone in the firelight and the sturdy feet raced surely on, no longer uncertain as they had been a few minutes before. Nathan remembered when he had seen Whirl run like this once before. It was when he had butted the fat Buckendahl on the night of the Geneva Ball. Once more the little man dove forward head first. The bald poll struck the youngster full in the backsides and rolled him a good twenty feet across the arena. But even as it struck the bull dashed in and with a sudden side flick and upward toss of his horns threw Whirl into the air. The whole crowd saw his grotesque wriggle in the air and heard the sickening crushing sound of his body as it dropped to the ground. Then all at once the enclosure was crowded with excited, cursing men. Great-bodied Elias Stephens had grabbed the bull by the murderous horns and was slowly forcing the big head toward the ground. An Indian hurled his body against the beast's back legs and he went down heavily. Ropes were quickly bound about him. Men were calling, "Bring a doctor."

Nathan knelt beside Whirl. The little man's chest had been pierced and blood welled from the wound beneath his shirt. Whirl smiled.

"It's the jumpin'-off place, Nate," he said. "Used to

wonder if I'd know it when it come. Wa-a-l, I do." He paused
for a moment, then reached a groping hand to his belt. It came
away stained with blood, bearing a fragment of brown paper.

"Here's that there communication," he said slowly.
"'Member what I said—put all ye got on—" His head dropped
suddenly back and he lay very still. Big Tim Hosmer came
running through the crowd and knelt beside Nathan.

"He's dead."

IX

Nathan did not look at the piece of brown paper for a long time. In the first agony of his grief he turned from the lifeless form and walked away. Eleanor put a hand on his arm but he shook it from him with a fierceness that frightened her and plodded on. When his thoughts finally returned to a consciousness of himself he was sitting on his own doorstep. He had walked home alone, leaving his mare tied before Williamson's house. The stars were very bright above him in the clear September night. He put his head on his knees and sobbed, then rolled off the step and lay beside it, face upward, looking into the light-spattered, deep blue of the sky. Though reason had forced him to try to control himself his sorrow kept forcing his mind back over the incidents that preceded Whirl's death. In the first wildness of his despair he had found himself hating Eleanor with deadly intensity. If she had not urged him to snub the drunken little man the timing of the whole episode would have been different and Whirl would be still alive. If she and her kind had not brought the Negro slaves to the Genesee Country the black child would not have run into the arena and Whirl would be still alive.

His hatred turned upon himself. It was not Eleanor's fault that he had told Whirl to go away. She had been brought up to act as she did. But he, Nathan Hart—partner and friend of Whirling Gragg—had let a woman influence him to act against his convictions and his natural self, and the result had been the death of Whirling Gragg. He groaned and clutched the grass about his head in a storm of self-reproach. His self-torture was so intolerable that he could conceive of no relief—ever. Frantically his mind sought comfort in some memory of a time when his soul had been wounded and he had found healing. Somewhere in life there must be a remedy, if only partial, for the

355

unbearable pain within him. As if forced by a psychic and irresistible power his thoughts went back to Whirl lying crumpled and helpless and yet talking to him as if this violence that now stopped the beating of his heart were a commonplace —a reasonable, acceptable portion of a larger pattern of living. "Here's that there communication." Nathan's hands went through his pockets in anguished searching. It was not there. Whirl had brought the paper from his belt. There it was— folded and hooked over his own belt. With trembling fingers Nathan lifted it, unfolded it, and held it close to his eyes. The starlight was not enough. He sat up and, reaching about him, made a tiny pyramid of leaves and dry grass. He plucked a long dry weed and rushed into the cabin. The banked fire glowed dully. Shielding the candlelike flame of the weed with his hand he ran back. In a moment the little pile was ablaze.

My dear Nathan:

I hoped to see you before I returned, but memories of the before and after of the Williamsburg race three years ago have sent me back to my work at once to find what peace I can. Perhaps you would like to know, now that you are about to begin a different kind of living, that I was entirely responsible for what happened to you and me. I could have avoided it. I am not sorry.

Knowing you, I am sure that you will be happier when I tell you that everything that I have done since our first meetings is explained by the fact that I loved you. I still love you.

I wish you happiness and I know it will be yours. I try hard to forgive the Maryland girl for wanting you. Mr. Kirkland has told me that I must, that it is the civilized way. In that I must remain the savage she thinks me. Good-bye. I hope, for my own content, that I will not see you again.

Catherine.

Nathan stood upright and stamped out the fire. There was something else that Whirl had said as he died, something he had said before and thought important enough to repeat with

his last breath—"Put all ye got on the rider." Again memory led
his mind back but not this time to torture. A woman followed
a fever-crazed derelict through the high-grass jungle beside the
Genesee and brought him safely to sanity and cool rest. After
the cure of his fever by the Jesuit root there was yet the diseased
mind, twisted and misshapen by disgrace and humiliation—and
there was a woman who gave her body to him and it became a
symbol of the enemy he fought. He conquered it and was
possessed of serenity and courage to go on. There was a woman
who saved his life and the lives of his companions when the
British planned their attack on Sodus and the capture of Williamson. She gave him not only life but love there on the warm
sands beneath the starry skyfields that lay above Ontario.

There was a woman who had been his happy companion
during the days of the treaty-making at Canandaigua. She had
read with him and talked with him and loved him. There was
a woman who had risked her life to save others, others whom
she did not know, from death of the awful plague at Geneva.
Risked her life to save others—and suddenly Nathan's mind
was back within the circle of fires about the arena and seeing
again the black child hurtled to safety, and the grotesque paw-
ing gestures of the little man wounded to death and tossed into
the air by the raging red bull. He heard again the little man's
last words—and Nathan strode toward the square.

A dim lamp burned in Williamson's house. The mare
whickered softly as Nathan untied her bridle. A latch clicked
and the Land Agent walked swiftly out to Nathan in the
starlight.

"No use saying how sorry I am."

"No!" said Nathan fiercely.

"I would have sent your horse to you in the morning."

"I'm riding her east tonight."

Williamson looked at him incredulously.

"How far east?"

"Kirkland's."

"You're going after her? To bring her back?"

"Yes."

There was a long silence. Williamson broke it. His manner
was stiff and his voice sounded tight and controlled.

"I have heard that in Buffalo and farther west in the Ohio

country alliances such as you evidently contemplate are not looked on with disfavor. A man could begin again there and neither he nor his children—"

"I've done all the beginning again I'm going to do," said Nathan. "The alliance as you call it will be a marriage and the children will have to take the same chances their parents take."

"You're going to live here?" Williamson spoke as if stunned.

"With my wife on my own land."

"But it will be impossible."

"I don't agree. At any rate you and I will find out eventually."

Again silence. Nathan put a foot in the stirrup and rose to the saddle. For a reason he could not have explained he felt sorry for the man who stood looking up into his face.

"I couldn't do it," said Williamson bitterly, "not even if I were free to. Something in me would not allow it—not even if I wanted it above everything else on earth. I began my career in America as a prisoner. I am still one—behind walls of my own building this time. You can act against authority and the wishes of the powerful majority. I cannot. My friend Burr can bring down upon his head the disapproval of a nation—of both his enemies and allies—and still be gay. He can deceive the men of his own party, commit crimes against the opposition, and betray the trust of . . . while I—" He stopped abruptly and turned as if to go back to his house, then turned again and took a step toward Nathan, holding out his hand.

"Mr. Hart," he said, "there are understandings between us we have never discussed and in all likelihood will never mention. We are in utter disagreement on the answers to questions that seem to us both to be fundamental to the future of this country. Whatever that time may bring between us I take this moment to tell you that I envy you and admire you and wish you personal happiness. I—" His voice broke in a quick catch of breath. He walked swiftly, almost running, into his house.

X

The cabins in Elijah's clearing were dark and lightless against the late moon. Nathan grinned, thinking of the sleeping judge who had once been an energetic prophet and who even now could find no time in which to sit for his much-heralded, often-ordered portrait. The house of The Publick Universal Friend lay white and quiet as Nathan passed—remembering the sunny morning when the voices of girls sounded within it like the clear chirping of birds. He was desperately tired when he rode into Geneva as the yellow noonday sun beat straight down on the long slant of the banks of Seneca Lake. At sight of the dock where the proud schooner *Alexander* rode under furled sails he remembered Whirl at her launching, and tears came to his eyes as he urged the tired Lottie on. He stopped at Sanborn's tavern, fed and watered the mare, and ate something—he did not know what was on his plate. Kind-hearted Mrs. Sanborn forced a package of food upon him and he thanked her and rode on. One by one he passed the long blue lakes—Cayuga, Owasco, and then Skaneateles rippling in the glow of another midnight of stars. He gave up then—too exhausted even to give the stable-boy at the log inn directions for the care of his horse. The proprietor, a big and kindly Irishman, took him by the arm, gently pushed him up the stairs, and removed his boots before letting him fall upon the bed.

It was nearly noon when he awoke.

He covered little distance that day, though he rode on doggedly until late at night. Always now he kept his eyes fixed on the road ahead in the hope that he might overtake the pursued one. He slept under a tree, tethering the mare nearby, and rose at sunrise. The sight of the broad, rolling Mohawk gave him encouragement and he knew now that before this day was over he would reach his goal. Early in the afternoon he saw the waters of Oriskany Creek tumbling into the river and he turned south to ride upstream along the path that crowned its western bank.

It was midafternoon when he came upon the wide and shaded red-shale path that led up Kirkland's hill. Ten minutes later his heart beat fast at sight of the neat white frame house of the missionary, standing in yellow sunlight just under the crest. Near it were three small log cabins and one much larger, obviously the schoolhouse. When he had ridden nearer he dismounted, tied Lottie at the long hitching rail in front of the school, and walked on. A tall Indian lay sleeping on his blanket a few yards from Kirkland's door—Otsiquette. While Nathan paused looking down upon the beautiful weak face of the redeemer-drunkard Catherine came out of the door of the school. She walked toward him swiftly. It seemed that she feared the afternoon light might be creating visions to deceive her.

"Nathan?" she said.

"Yes, I have come to fetch you."

"You—you want me?"

"Yes."

"Then I will get ready."

"Not before this," he said, putting his arms about her and his lips on hers.

"Now," he said, "you and I will find this teacher of yours and make him perform a ceremony."

While Kirkland was making his simple preparations for the wedding Nathan told her about Whirl's death. She wept bitterly, her head on his shoulder. "He was our friend," she said. "I will always love him."

They were married in the little white house at sundown. The grim-faced missionary looked small and weak beside Otsiquette and Nathan. He read the ceremony carefully and then preached them a sermon of dire foreboding, urging upon them faithfulness to each other, arguing that the wages of a sin against the marriage covenant are more awful than most punishments. When it was over Samuel Kirkland smiled a wan, world-weary smile and blessed them.

"It will be very difficult," he said.

"We know."